W9-CCH-023

# TSARINA

J. Nelle Patrick

An Imprint of Penguin Group (USA)

A division of Penguin Young Readers Group
Published by the Penguin Group
Penguin Group (USA) LLC
345 Hudson Street
New York, New York 10014

USA / Canada / UK / Ireland / Australia / New Zealand / India / South Africa / China
Penguin.com
A Penguin Random House Company



ISBN: 978-1-59514-693-9

Printed in the United States of America

1 3 5 7 9 10 8 6 4 2

*For Nelson,*
*who knows all the history*

# CHAPTER ONE

The rioters at the gates were loud, but no match for the music inside the Winter Palace.

The musicians played a mazurka, a bright, full number, while couples danced along in the grand ballroom. It wasn't my favorite dance—too much hopping—but at least a waltz would come next. I positioned myself by the wall in the meantime, spying on the dancers, taking note of who was paired with whom, who was wearing the most expensive dress, and who looked weary of her partner.

It was hard to be critical, truth be told—everyone looked beautiful here, especially since the room itself leant a refined elegance to even the most homely of courtiers. The ceiling stretched out high above us, painted ivory and accented in a rich, dark gold that extended down to arched porticos. A glittering railing lined the upper story, set at the same level as the chandeliers, which were intricate and heavy-looking, like the sheer power of the palace held them aloft. Surrounding the room were gilded pillars, broken apart by windows that revealed an inky black world outside, given the late hour.

I looked up as the mazurka ended, and tried to find *his* eyes in preparation for the waltz. He didn't need to ask—I knew we would dance it together. It wasn't appropriate, exactly, for us to gravitate to each other time and time again, but it was something our parents and the rest of court had long accepted. *Natalya and Alexei will dance together.* Which, we all knew, really meant: *Natalya and Alexei will end up together.*

*Where is he?* I smoothed my dress. It was a beautiful gown, dark violet and made by Madame Olga's studio, but it was immensely heavy. I suspected this was because of the thick embroidery that ran along the sleeves and skirts, a rocaille pattern of flowers and leaves. I was grateful to be going on seventeen, finally allowed to wear my hair up. When I was younger and wore it down my back, it combined with my velvet gowns to make me feel faint from heat.

My eyes wandered, waiting, wanting—*there he is.* Alexei's gaze found mine, a smile pulling at the corners of his mouth. The musicians started up—the waltz—but Alexei nodded his head at a corner of the room. I lifted an eyebrow, watched him nod curtly at a few men in military garb, then casually walk away from his family and into the crowd. I followed suit, heading to the corner he indicated. It took ages to get there—every few steps I was forced to stop, smile, curtsey, prattle on in French. All the nobles spoke it, though I personally saw nothing wrong with Russian. Finally, I dipped behind one of the massive pillars and began to move nonchalantly back toward the corner. A hand suddenly slid into mine; I jumped and spun around.

"You startled me," I scolded Alexei.

"You ran into me," he countered, grinning. He glanced down at our hands, then over his shoulder to be certain no one was watching us—namely, his guards, two sailors from the Imperial Navy. They had to at least put on the appearance of stopping Alexei from misbehaving, though they had a decent sense of humor where I was concerned. They knew I loved him and was ever-mindful of his condition. How he would bleed forever if he got the slightest nick, how a substantial bruise meant he'd be bedridden for weeks. For the past year, however, he'd done markedly better—though I still cringed when I saw him knock a table or miss the bottom stair.

"What are you doing?" I asked him suspiciously as he drew me farther into the corner of the ballroom.

"Oh, Natashenka. Don't you trust me?" he said, using my baby name. His eyes were gleaming, bright blue, and his bone structure was fine and delicate, almost like a girl's. His lips, however, were shaped like his father's, and the way he held his shoulders was decidedly masculine. There was something elegant about the contradiction, something that mesmerized me. Perhaps that's why I was so easily convinced to follow him along the edge of the room, toward the door servants were buzzing around. I cast a look back at the ballroom, at the jewel-lined skirts swirling around the dance floor before we slipped out into a hallway.

Alexei and I rushed along, past servants who regarded him with fond exasperation. At his request, they no longer bowed, and at his demand, they never tattled on his escapades. We cut through the rotunda and then out to the tsarina's garden. The palace soared above us, moonlight illuminating muted red walls and shining the way along the limestone path. Night air bit at my neck, my wrists, each bit of exposed skin in a way that felt delicious after the ballroom's monstrous heat.

When we arrived at the doors on the opposite corner, I thought for a moment we were headed toward Alexei's apartments, a prospect too scandalous even for me. But no, we wound down halls until we arrived at a door I'd never ventured behind—the door into the tsar's own salon. Alexei turned to me, his long lashes silhouetted on his cheeks in the dim light.

"You've seen some of the Easter presents my father commissions for my mother?" he asked, voice hushed to match the stillness of the hall.

"The eggs," I said, nodding. "The ones the House of Fabergé makes."

"Yes," Alexei said. "Well, there's a special one. One you haven't seen before." Alexei rarely dabbled in secrets, and yet his voice was full of them; it threw me, left me at a loss for words. Alexei was likewise silent for a long time, like he was waiting for something.

"Well, are you going to show me?" I relented, and he laughed—loud, so that the sound bounced up to the high ceiling.

"Of course," he said, and pushed open the salon door.

The tsar's salon had massive windows that faced the palace's side gates; without the music and revelry from the ball, the roar of the rioters easily reached our ears. This particular room was oddly cheery in comparison; the walls were papered in a buttery yellow damask pattern and the floors covered in garnet and emerald rugs. The ceiling was painted with sky blue murals, and chairs upholstered in silk lined the far wall.

I glared out the window at the rioters and followed Alexei to the far side of the room, where a set of bookshelves rose to the ceiling, their shelves thick with heavy ancient tomes. Alexei reached forward and placed his hand on the spine of Pushkin's verse novel, *Eugene Onegin*—not one of my favorites. I lifted an eyebrow, wondered how a Fabergé egg was going to fit into this escapade.

Alexei froze suddenly, glanced over his shoulder at me.

"Natalya," he said, voice gentle. "You and I . . . we're . . . it's *us*, isn't it?"

This was the game Alexei and I played, the dance we spun through almost every time we were together. Each of us prancing around the words "I love you," afraid to say them aloud, afraid to admit our future plans always involved each other. It wasn't appropriate—after all, there was always the possibility the tsar might want Alexei to marry some foreign princess. Tsar Nicholas, however, was more progressive than the Reds thought—his children would be allowed to marry whoever they wanted, and thus, one day Alexei would marry me.

"It's us," I whispered. "It's always us." This exchange was the closest we'd ever come to something involving the word "love."

Alexei smiled, inhaled, and pulled the Pushkin book toward him. It tilted slightly, but instead of falling off into his hands like an obedient book, it pulled back, more like a lever. I saw why almost immediately—it was a handle, a contraption that turned the entire bookcase into a door. It creaked out, opening for us, revealing a hidden room.

"Surprised?" Alexei teased, and I realized my jaw was hanging open. I snapped it shut, smiled at him, then followed him into the secret chamber.

It was small—barely larger than a closet. Tapestries bearing the Romanov double eagle hung on the walls, along with oil paintings of the royal family. The carpet was thick and burgundy, and on the far side—only a few steps from the secret door—was a dark credenza. Centered on its surface, on a white silk cloth, was a Fabergé egg. I inhaled, my breath slow and drawn.

It was not the tiny sort of Fabergé egg that the other nobles and I wore on necklaces; like the other Romanov eggs, it was the size of my hand. The egg itself was made of cobalt glass in a shade of blue that reminded me of Alexei's eyes. It rested atop a pillar of white stone, carved to look like a throne of clouds. Throughout the blue glass were diamonds, bright and shining, some with lines etched around them to make the gems look like stars and the egg itself a night sky.

"It's called the Constellation Egg," Alexei explained. "See these stars at the top? Fabergé etched a lion there, because of when I was born."

"It's beautiful. I've never been so close to one like this before," I said softly. Everything about the egg gleamed and made the rest of the already ornate room look bedraggled in comparison. "What's the surprise?" I asked. It was well known—each egg contained a surprise inside. A jade rabbit, a miniature screen with portraits of the Russian palaces, a gold statue of Peter the Great on a sapphire platform. . . .

"The egg *is* the surprise," Alexei said. I rose, looked at him curiously. He pressed his lips together, then met my eyes. Alexei's eyes were a thing of wonder—they were like his mother's, the color of skies and oceans, a color that seemed to go on and on forever. He trapped me in them easily, held my gaze, then walked to his father's desk and lifted a letter opener. "Don't be scared," he said gently, holding it firmly in one hand.

"Of what—"

Before I could finish my question, Alexei yanked the sharp end of the opener across his palm. I screamed, loud, shrill, dashed to him—he'd lost his mind, clearly. Alexei couldn't bleed; he would die—he would die right here in my arms. He stood still as I grappled for his hand, heart pounding, pressed the spot on his palm. I pulled on him, he had to get out, we had to find the doctor. I could stop the blood flow for a few minutes, but I didn't dare try to stitch him up myself—

"Natalya!" Alexei said, voice loud but calm. "Natalya, stop! Look." He pulled on my arm and the motion forced me to release his palm; when I grabbed for it again, he caught both of my wrists, held me—he was stronger than he appeared. "Look," he repeated. He slowly opened his hand, the one he cut, palm facing me.

There was nothing. A small line of blood, which was quickly fading. Beneath the red, his skin glowed like a thousand tiny stars were in his veins. The glow brightened, then burned out, leaving me blinking, unsure if it had really been there to begin with. I stared, furrowed my brow. Alexei's palm was fine, his skin unbroken. My lips parted.

"I saw you," I stammered, shaking my head. "I saw you cut yourself. There's blood—"

"I'm sorry," Alexei said, pulling a handkerchief from his pocket. He ran it over my fingers. I stared as he did it, watching blood stain the white fabric. "Natalya?" Alexei said my name again. I finally found his eyes. "I'm fine. I wanted to show you. You'd never have believed me otherwise."

"You wanted to *show me*?" I asked shrilly, pushing him backward.

"You nearly scared me to death." There were tears on my cheeks, the sort not from sorrow but too much emotion bubbling up, and my heart was still racing. It was only as it slowed, as I looked between Alexei's bloodied handkerchief to his unbroken skin and back again, that I realized what he meant—what he wanted to show me. "How did you do that?" I asked, voice rocky, doubtful.

Alexei smiled, reached down and took my hand, folding his fingers gently around mine. I could tell he had practiced this moment for a long time. "The egg, Natashenka. It wasn't me, it was the Constellation Egg." He inhaled, continued in a hushed way. "Before Father Grigori was killed, he made the egg for my mother. It contains his power. It contains his love. His protection."

As usual, Alexei spoke of Father Grigori with kindness in his eyes. I suppose it only made sense—the man did, after all, save Alexei's life dozens of times. When Alexei would bang into a table or nick his finger, he would bleed and bleed, fall to bed and knock on death's door—they even prepared his death certificate once, he told me. Father Grigori—Rasputin, as everyone else called him—changed that with his strange powers, a mysticism that came with old-world charms and words uttered in a whisper. Yet I still found him unsettling: his stare, his voice, the way he spoke in riddles and thought in circles. He strode around the palace and showed up at parties like we were all his dear friends, but . . . I was afraid of him, and privately did not mourn his death at all.

"I still don't understand what you mean," I said, pulling my hand from his. I placed my fingertips on the credenza and leaned down over the egg.

"Father Grigori was a powerful mystic," Alexei said. "He knew many at court were displeased with him and his friendship with my family. And he knew the Reds were growing louder, stronger. So he created the Constellation Egg, poured the power of the mystics into it. It keeps us safe, healthy, *alive*. It ties us to the land, the animals, the air, to Russia. It keeps the Reds at bay and our world safe and lifts my father's crown ever higher."

He exhaled, the breath shaky, like he was nervous and excited at once. I blinked, shook my head. "And . . . it heals you?"

Alexei nodded, grinning. He knew that for me, this was the most important bit of the egg's power.

"So . . . that's why you haven't been sick recently. It's why the tsar and tsarina have let you dance with me, it's why they've let you ride the horses—"

"Yes," he said. "It's why animals eat out of Tatiana's hand, why Anastasia can make a vase of dying flowers bloom again. It's why my father can wish for snow and it begins to fall. It's why Russia is ours, forever Romanov."

I swallowed, expected him to laugh, to smile, but his eyes were hushed just like his voice. "But . . ." A seed of doubt sprung up in my mind and grew quickly. "Father Grigori was murdered. How can his magic protect you if it couldn't even protect him?"

Now Alexei's face hardened. We rarely spoke of Father Grigori's murder, the details of which were still shady—specifically, who was responsible. Everyone knew it was noblemen who killed him, but no one was willing to point fingers because, save for the Romanovs themselves, everyone was happier with him gone. Alexei looked at the egg, swallowed.

"They poisoned him. Then they shot him, stabbed him, and

drowned him. He was very hard to kill. I suppose even the mystics' powers can't stop that level of intent."

"But," I said, eager to turn the conversation back now that I had my answer, "it's enough to keep you well. The bleeding—"

"I rarely bleed anymore," Alexei said.

"And your mother, your sisters—"

"It heals them too. The one the tsar loves and his heirs, inherited just like a crown," Alexei said. "No matter where we are, no matter what we're doing, it heals us, the same way Father Grigori healed me." He paused, blushed pale pink. "And one day you, it will work for you, Natalya. You'll be tsarina, and the egg will be ours. *Russia* will be ours."

Now it was my turn to blush, but I couldn't stop a grin from spreading across my face. I opened my mouth, but before I could speak, a bright crash rang out from outside the palace. Alexei frowned, and together we turned from the egg and hurried out through the bookcase door to the window. Across the lawn, an automobile passed through the palace's iron gates, inching into the mob that stood just beyond them. The mob jeered at the automobile and began a chant with the rhythm of a spell. *Land, peace, bread! Land, peace, bread!*

Anger rippled through me. *How dare they?* They disrespected their tsar, their capitol, but more importantly, their country. This was not the way Russians behaved. Like insolent children throwing tantrums, crying out and pointing fingers. It was shameful.

"They're saying we might need to return to Alexander Palace, permanently," Alexei said, looking drawn. "That our distance might calm the Reds down. Though the Octobrists are suggesting my father abdicate the throne—they say if he doesn't, the Reds won't stop till there's a fight."

"Does it matter?" I said, glowering out the window. "You have the Constellation Egg. You'll win."

"Father Grigori didn't win," Alexei said. "He was a powerful man, Natalya, but I'd rather not test the mystic's magic against a nation of Reds. If my father abdicates, I become the tsar. I'm too young to rule, especially when Russia is at war, I know that. But if *I* abdicate . . ."

I tried to hide the shock in my eyes—it was lunacy for Alexei to talk this way. He was the tsarevich; the crown was his birthright. He couldn't simply give it away. I swallowed as Alexei turned to face me.

"If I abdicate," he began again, "then the monarchy is over. We lose the egg's power entirely. I go back to being . . . like before."

"Sick."

"Yes. I worry there's no way for my family to win, even with the egg. We keep the throne; the Reds test the egg's limits. We give the throne away and . . ." Alexei shifted, lost in the memories of how he was before, when his life revolved around blood and doctors and being treated like a porcelain doll.

But was moving to the Alexander Palace the solution? It wasn't far, but it hurt my pride to see Russia run and hide from the Reds, especially since my father led one of the strongest divisions of the tsar's White Army. *Can't he stop this nonsense?* Alexei must have seen the hurt on my face—hiding my thoughts from him was nearly impossible. He saw every blink, every fidget, every half-sigh. I suspect it was because, given his condition, he spent much of his life being watched and worried about; he learned to be equally aware of others' pain, be it of the body or the heart.

"You think we should stay," he said. I nodded, but Alexei sighed and shook his head. "Perhaps if we're gone, the Reds will disband. They can't keep this up forever. I wish they knew how hard we're trying. We don't *want* them to be hungry . . ." Alexei's heart was often heavy when mine was lit with frustration. I was certain that if the rioters outside the palace knew Alexei, really *knew* the boy who would one day rule them, they'd put down their sticks and cries for revolution. If only they understood that Alexei would be the greatest thing to ever happen to Russia.

"Do you have a hiding place for the egg in the Alexander Palace?" I asked.

"We leave it here," Alexei said. "It's not safe to travel with it and risk getting intercepted by Reds or thieves. No one knows about this room, Natalya. No one—except you, now."

This made me smile—I couldn't help it. I looked at his reflection in the window, saw he was returning the expression. My hand crept out, my fingers brushing along his palm gently.

The automobile honked its horn. I jumped at the sound, then scowled. "Can't the soldiers fire a warning shot, at least?" I asked as the automobile finally cleared the bulk of the mob and hurried down the street. "Just to scatter them? Or perhaps we could lock the worst of them up in the Fortress. They're ruining the party."

"I don't think they care much about the party," Alexei said, reaching out and intertwining his fingers with mine. "Come on. We shouldn't stand here—they'll see us."

"I'm not afraid," I said. "Look at them. Some are barely older than us—how can their parents allow them to take part in this? They're not even old enough to fight *for* Russia, much less against it."

"In that case, am I not old enough to lead Russia?" Alexei said. I whirled around, and his eyes were sparkling, clever.

"*You're* different," I said.

"Why?"

"Because," I said, trying not to laugh as he ran his fingers from my hand, up my forearm, against the skin where my dress sleeve split. I stepped forward so that his hand on my elbow became his hand on my waist. "You're the tsarevich. You were born to lead Russia." I could barely feel his fingertips through the thick velvet, but knowing they were there made my heart feel too small for my body.

"I suppose," he said, though the sound barely made it from his throat. He hesitated. "My family would be so angry if they knew I showed you the egg already."

"Do you regret it?"

"Not for a second," he said. "I've wanted to show you since Father Grigori made it. My secrets are yours. And besides, I don't want you to be afraid of the Reds, Natalya. The egg protects me. And it means I can protect you." Alexei pressed his palm harder against my waist, let it slide to the small of my back. He lifted his other hand; I jumped, smiled when he ran the back of his fingers down my cheek and stepped so close I could now feel his breath on my face. Air refused to let itself out of my lungs as he urged me forward, till I was inches from his chest. He'd grown so tall over the last year, more and more like his father every day.

I lifted a hand, wished it would stop shaking as I let it wander up to and around his neck. His skin was hot, his pulse racing, which was a relief—it meant mine wasn't the only fluttering heart in the room. He inhaled, dipped his head, and the sounds of the rioters outside faded. Indeed, everything faded except the warmth that was pulling us closer together.

*It's us*, I thought, and I could tell he was thinking the same. *In the end, it's always us.* His lips found mine, and it felt like stars were swimming through me. It was our first kiss, and it was brief, so brief, but so perfect. Even after our lips parted, we held each other close, afraid to step away and sever the tiny heartstrings binding us together.

"Forgive me," Alexei said through a smile, eyes locking on mine in a way that told me he wasn't really sorry. He slowly released my waist, inhaled like he was coming up for air. I reluctantly pulled away from his neck, brought my fingers to my lips—I could still feel his mouth on mine. Alexei smiled at me like I was doing something wondrous, then motioned to the door. "Come on. They'll miss us. I suspect Emilia's uncle came all the way up from Moscow just to steal you for a dance."

"Oh . . . him . . . He won't stop telling me about his new post. Something to do with patrolling the Kremlin in Moscow. It sounds terribly boring," I said, rolling my eyes a bit—Emilia's uncle knew about Alexei and I as much as the next person, but he persisted in quietly attempting to win my heart at every opportunity, which was rather exhausting. It never bothered Alexei quite as much as it bothered me, though I wasn't certain if that was because the tsarevich had no need to feel threatened, or because he was simply that confident in our relationship. Alexei moved back to the bookcase and pushed the Tolstoy book into its spot. The door to the secret room closed, and I found myself wishing I'd gotten to see the egg a moment longer.

"I can hardly blame the man," Alexei said of Emilia's uncle, smiling as he walked up beside me. He held the door to the salon open, and we retreated back into the hallway. The space felt massive, having been in the egg's secret room. My heels clicked against the ground loudly as we made our way back through the tsarina's garden, me clutching my arms against the now potent cold. Just as we were about to go back inside, Alexei stopped, took my hands in his.

"You won't—I know you won't, but just in case—you won't tell anyone?" He looked sheepish, like he was embarrassed to even ask me.

"Of course not," I said, squeezing his fingertips lightly. I wanted to draw his hands to my lips so badly. "You know I won't."

"I do," he admitted. "But I had to ask. After all, you told your friends about me crying over Anastasia's dog dying." He tried to fight a smile, but it didn't work; I blushed hard nonetheless, laughed a little.

"That was different," I said. "It made you seem especially sweet. And besides, the dog wasn't *really* a secret . . . a magical Fabergé egg is different. I promise—"

I froze, looked over Alexei's shoulder. He turned around to follow my gaze to the place where the walkway met a garden bed. A waiter was standing there, basket of unfolded napkins in his arms. His eyes were hard on mine, pale gray in the moonlight. He was enormously tall and broad shouldered; when Alexei turned, he dropped the basket, spilling napkins everywhere, and sunk down in a bow.

"Your highness," he said swiftly.

"Relax," Alexei said, motioning with his hand and sounding somewhat irritated. "You know you don't have to bow to me unless it's an official event."

The boy slowly rose, dwarfing the both of us. "My apologies. Old habits die hard I suspect, sir." He hurried ahead of Alexei and me, letting his eyes flit to mine a few more times than was entirely appropriate. The boy opened the door for us, now staring at the ground.

"Come on, Natalya," Alexei said, brushing past the boy without a second thought. I followed him, glancing back over my shoulder as we made our way down the hall. The waiter was closing the door behind us, shutting out the moonlight. He turned, met my eyes for a flicker of a moment, but then Alexei and I were around the corner. Back through the kitchen, into the ballroom and into the glitter and laughter and scent of champagne that rose from every surface.

Back where I belonged—at least, so I thought.

# CHAPTER TWO

Saint Petersburg was a city of illusions.

There were the little ones, the sorts of illusions that most would simply call lies: The couples dressed in finery, invited into fancy shops only to quietly slip jewelry and silver spoons into their pockets. The groups of boys who acted like wealthy students in order to sneak into parties. The women who dressed as messengers to enter their lovers' homes without suspicion. These were the illusions—the lies—the newspapers talked about, sensationalized, splashed on their front covers. These were the tales turned into cheap books that workers read on the streetcars every morning, hummed about in marketplaces, whispered over wrestling matches at the circus.

Then there were the bigger illusions, the ones so dangerous we never uttered them aloud. The illusion that the sparkling, flashing, gold and cream and burgundy version of the city was all that existed. The illusion that the war with Germany wasn't going poorly. The illusion the war with Japan hadn't gone worse. The illusion that the tsar would prevail, that Russia would go on being a place of fine wines and ballets, and we would never fall, never gray, never be anything but glittering. These were the sorts of illusions that most would call fantasies.

Perhaps the biggest of these sorts of illusions was also the simplest—the illusion that we were a single city. Saint Petersburg was naturally divided, a series of islands and canals laced together into a capital by Peter the Great centuries ago. There were bridges from one to the next, and the canals were deep, maintained with stone walls that held the Neva River at bay. But we divided ourselves with harsher lines than the land did: the rich and the poor, the merchants and the nobles, the Whites and the Reds. When the river would occasionally flood the canals and blur the lines between islands and districts, we would hastily fix it, tighten things, firm up the boundaries and make sure the illusion, the lie, the fantasy held.

Lately, upholding the fantasy was harder and harder. It was a cold October, though we'd had little snow, which seemed particularly cruel—what was the point of the low temperatures without a blanket of white to coat the rooftops like sugar icing?

Mornings were the worst. I creaked my eyes open, stared at my bedroom's crosshatched gold stripes that covered the lavender ceiling. Alexei's eyes were still in the forefront of my mind, bright blue like sapphires, like the sky, like the Constellation Egg he showed me the last time we were together. It had been months now since he and his family moved to the Alexander Palace, but I could still hear the sound of his voice, could still feel his hands, his gaze, his lips . . . I closed my eyes, kept Alexei's face in my mind and tried to lull myself back to sleep, to dictate a dream of Alexei and I married, living in the palace, with parties and jewels and laughter and happiness and all the things we planned.

But no. I was in my bed, alone, and my mind refused to drift off to any place happier. I sighed and crept from under the layers of fur and velvet blankets, cold snapping at my skin. The hardwoods creaked under my feet as I stepped out of bed and pulled a pale dressing gown over my silk chemise. The chemise was probably a little more mature an article than my father would have wanted me wearing—namely, the lace and black ribbon detailing. He didn't know I had it, however—as he was a military man with little fashion sense and my mother was in heaven, I was largely left to my own devices when it came to clothing.

There was a gold clock on my mantel wedged between enormous vases and candlesticks with flowers carved into their bodies. It was nine o'clock. *So late, and no one woke me?* That was never a good sign; it meant the staff was busy, and when the staff was busy, it often meant . . .

I cringed, hurried to the arched window, and peeled one of the curtains back. It was difficult to see much of anything through the layer of frost; I put my lips close to the glass and exhaled, warming it just enough that I could spy onto the street below. I prepared myself for the worst—soldiers on horseback, men carrying banners, the sound of guns firing and clubs cracking against bodies. I'd slept through riots before—they were so common, now. Worse than waking to a riot, however, was waking to the aftermath of such an event: loose articles of clothing, bloodstains like roses in the fresh snow, the empty, quiet feeling in the streets . . .

I exhaled in relief. Sadovaya Street was normal—not quiet, as we lived at the center of Saint Petersburg, after all—but normal, full of citizens bundled up, hurrying about on errands or visits, to and from appointments and—given the neighborhood I was in—teas and shopping trips. I sighed in relief, let the heavy curtain fall shut. Today marked three weeks without a riot . . . were the Reds giving up? The idea burned inside me, warmed me—though not so much that I could wait to ring for Kache to come start the fireplace.

"And what will you do today, Miss Natalya?" Kache asked absently as she poked at the flames, coaxed them until they grew strong. The room gradually thawed, though my toes continued to feel like blocks of ice stuck to my feet. I walked to my closet, retrieved a dark blue dress that I draped over one of the chairs by the fire. Kache was slightly older than me, my compromise with my father—I didn't want a governess, but I wasn't yet old enough to justify a lady's maid. Kache was the in-between, a slight girl with a big nose from an unlanded noble family.

"I suppose I'll visit Emilia," I answered, sighing and slipping off my nightclothes. "Again." Kache nodded, tugged a little step stool over to stand on so she could help me slip my dress over my head.

"Shall I have them ready a carriage for you? It's bitter out today. October is certainly here." Kache laced the back of my dress, pulling silvery ribbon through what felt like a million little eyelets. Her fingers were quick, practiced; I pinned my hair up as she finished, then sat down so she could tame the stray bits. It hardly seemed worth it to go through the trouble of looking pretty. There were no parties, no balls—no one to throw them, really, as most of the other nobles had gone to France on account of the riots. Those of us who remained were orphaned, wandering about, waiting for the world we'd always known to spin back around and claim us. It was lonely now, our houses islands amid broken seas of our old lives.

Sometimes I darkly envied my father, off with his troops—at least he had a purpose. He wasn't just shipwrecked, stranded.

"I'll walk," I said, fiddling with the bustline of my dress.

"Shall I join you? Or call for the driver?" Kache asked. Her voice always hinged carefully between hopeful and bored; I found it difficult to tell, at times like this, if she was asking my permission to come or permission to stay home. I couldn't imagine wanting to go sit at Emilia's all day, so I assumed the latter, shook my head to both questions.

"I'll be fine. It's not far." Like most of my social group, Emilia also lived in Upper Nevsky. For ages, we'd been little more than formal acquaintances, but as more and more nobles left Saint Petersburg, we became friends, despite the fact that she was of a higher ranking than me—a countess, the youngest in the Russian court. Now that most of the houses in Upper Nevsky were closed up and our neighborhood felt ghostly, we clung to each other, like together we could fight off the Reds. They made walking to Emilia's alone uncomfortable, and yet, I did it often. The Reds needed to see we were not afraid. That we were not all rushing to Paris to hide in the countryside.

Kache stepped back, having finished my hair. I rose, smoothed the front of my dress; my nails pricked along the paisley brocade. Kache glanced at me, made sure everything was in order, and I smiled at her. She and I rarely talked politics but I suspected our opinions were similar. For a noble girl, I thought myself quite liberal; after all, I wanted many things the Reds wanted. I wanted the people to have food, money. I wanted people to be happy. But the Reds thought their happiness meant tearing down the nobility, destroying people like me. Like the other Whites, this notion left me far more angry than piteous. I didn't make them poor, nor did I make my family wealthy. If we handed over our wealth, who would employ them? Who would give them work? Were there not the wealthy and the poor in France, in England, in America?

The tsar always said to pity the Reds, that they simply did not understand. I found it increasingly more difficult to feel anything but hate.

Kache made my bed as I left the room, wound my way through the halls and downstairs, to the dining room. It was painted aqua blue, with yellow-gold banister railings and oil paintings along the walls. Only a year ago, we'd acquired a table that sat fifteen, but I couldn't begin to remember the last time it was full. Typically, it was just my father and me eating here, and rarely the two of us at once now that he was gone to fight the war with Germany. I took a seat and waited, staring at the chandelier until my bread and sugared pomegranate seeds arrived via the kitchen maid.

"Is there a newspaper?" I interrupted her as she walked toward the kitchen door.

She gave me a halted look. "There was."

I groaned. "And Father asked you to keep it from me?" The maid nodded, and I groaned. My father was concerned I'd read the war news and be frightened.

"At least tell me," I asked the maid, before she could go. "What's the front story today?"

The maid sighed. "Germany is progressing slowly, but the army is having difficulties with wolves prowling around the forests outside of Minsk. The armies have called a temporary truce to fight off the packs."

"Wolves?" I asked, eyes widening. "My God." The maid gave me a pointed look, and I tossed my hand at her. "I find it far more frightening to not know the details. My mind creates monsters more impressive than wolves."

"Yes, ma'am," the maid said. She curtsied and left the room. I said a silent prayer for my father and country, for the men my father commanded.

This was the weight of being a soldier's daughter—the constant concern that my father wouldn't come home. That he'd be taken by a bullet, a bomb, or, now, a wolf. Alexei, on the other hand . . . he couldn't be a soldier himself—or rather, could be technically, but because of his bleeding disease, he would never be able to ride into battle. This was something Alexei was keenly aware of, and to make up for it, he strategized. He planned, he read, he moved toy soldiers around on maps and memorized attack methods.

And he did so safely. From a room where there were no blades, no guns, no explosions. Alexei considered this his greatest weakness—that he could only protect his country, his crown, and his people from afar. I considered this the happily ever after. At least, I did before the Constellation Egg. Now I couldn't work out where I stood; was I glad the Constellation Egg kept him alive and well, or upset to know it meant he might one day ride into battle?

It was a hateful thing, to be upset about something that made him well, but I couldn't stop the thought from curling up into my mind like candle smoke. I wanted Alexei in the Winter Palace, safely surrounded by guards. I wanted him to be a hero, but a hero from afar. A hero who wouldn't die young, who wouldn't be wounded, who wouldn't be in pain. A hero with a happily ever after.

I abandoned my breakfast half eaten, and then went to fetch my coat from the closet. It was heavy, lined in fur and with what felt like a thousand silver buttons down the front. I had a matching hat, kid leather gloves, a fur stole—it seemed ridiculous for a short walk down the block, but the street looked mean and cold, largely due to the misty rain hanging over the city. I remembered what Alexei said, about the Constellation Egg allowing his father to make it snow on a whim; the clouds and cold were the norm, but this drizzly rain worried me. Did it mean the tsar was unhappy? Or merely that he had priorities greater than wishing for sunshine? I stepped outside and the wind whipped at me, tried to knock me back through my front door.

I'd been to other countries during the summer, and truth be told, they weren't all that different from Russia. Moscow, for example, felt like Paris in July. Saint Petersburg felt like London. In the warm weather, it might have been easy to mistake one city for the other. But there was no mistaking a Russian winter. It was a unique thing, a creature born and bred for Russian soil, one that sometimes brutalized the natives but often served as our secret weapon. Napoleon's army was defeated not only by the Russian people, but by Russia herself—a story my father told me before bed as a child, one I was still particularly proud to recall. The Russians burned the city to the ground, destroyed the food, the shelter, even the water; the invading army froze to death. Not that I wanted to see Saint Petersburg burn, but I occasionally wondered if that would be the shortest route to both ending the war *and* quieting the Reds. Freeze them out, rebuild our country properly—a country that both respects its tsar *and* cares for its poor, supports its workers, loves its heritage. Though I suspected even *fire* wouldn't quiet the Reds.

Sometimes I questioned if they really wanted to make Russia better, or simply wanted to shout the loudest.

I pulled my coat tighter, bowed my head into the wind. The people of the city were clever; their hats and scarves were tucked safely into their coats, their gloved hands lifted to shield their eyes from the sting of the air. It was a particularly enjoyable pastime, spotting the visitors—the people who didn't know just how to bow into the wind, who hadn't learned the slippery bits of the streets. I paused on a corner to allow a carriage to jangle past, the driver so bundled up he looked like a lump of darkened wool rather than a human being. Breath smoked from the twin black horses' nostrils, and I found myself sorry for them—why shouldn't they have coats as well? I passed the bakery and inhaled the scent of vanilla and cardamom.

It didn't take me long to reach Emilia's house, a grand place they were borrowing from another family that left for Paris ages ago. It was enormous, nearly a palace, painted bright yellow with white pillars and filigrees along the roof. I approached the front door, twice as tall as me, and rapped on it gently. The middle-aged butler answered almost immediately.

"Lady Kutepova," he said warmly. "Here to visit the countess?"

"I am—let her know I've arrived?" I said, gratefully brushing in, melting in the warmth of the foyer. My heels tapped across wooden floors, the sound bouncing back up the wide staircase before me. Every surface was touched with a fancy molding, an accent, like the entire room was carved rather than built. A maid hurried from a door behind the staircase to help me remove my coat, while the butler laid a hand gently on the stair railing and walked up to fetch my friend. I was shown to the nearby parlor and sat down, wondering if

Emilia would have the forethought to bring a pack of bezique cards down so we had something to do.

"Ten o'clock this time. You're getting earlier and earlier, Natalya," Emilia's voice called out from the second-floor landing. I heard her heels on the stairs, clicking closer, closer, until finally she whirred around the corner.

Emilia—her real name was Ludmila, but she refused to answer to it—hated wearing her hair up. As a result, it was always too puffy and needed to be smoothed. Her hair, however, was the only thing that needed assistance of any sort; everything else about Emilia Boldyreva radiated class, power, and money. She was smooth lines and shiny fabrics, and carried herself unapologetically. She was not proud to be wealthy; rather, she simply didn't notice it, I suppose because it had been a part of her family's legacy for so long. Today Emilia was wearing a chartreuse dress with a deep purple ribbon around the waist—shades I suspected would make me look pale as a corpse and colors I knew would be out of fashion soon, but were the pinnacle of style at the moment. They made her look like some sort of elaborate European flower, or a character from a play come to life.

"Shall I start stalling till noon then?" I responded, grinning when she shook her head so quickly it loosened a few bits of hair.

"Never. Bezique is even duller alone," she said, holding up the pale blue deck of cards. "Like my dress?"

"It's lovely," I said.

"Don't lie. It's the most garish thing I own. Isn't it delightful?" She twirled around to make her point, and I laughed. "Though what's the point of wearing something like this if there's no one to see you in it?"

"Am I no one?" I asked teasingly, and Emilia rolled her eyes. She moved to my side, hugged me quickly, and we settled across from each other at the card table. I raked my fingers across the table's pearl inlay while she dealt. She flipped the last card up—the six of hearts, the card we had to beat.

"Is your newspaper still here?" I asked as Emilia trumped the six of hearts with an eight.

"No—oh, Natalya, you've got to stop reading the stories. They're the stuff of nightmares."

"My maid said the armies are having trouble with wolf attacks—"

"See! Exactly what I mean," Emilia said, cringing at the idea. "You've enough to dwell on without adding wolves. For example—how many days has it been now?"

"Hm?"

"How many *days*?" Emilia asked again, now meeting my eyes. I sighed, put down the queen of diamonds. Emilia was quick when it came to matters of love; she was the sort of girl who, while the rest of us were learning to draw our letters, perfected drawing hearts.

"Four months, two weeks, three days since I've seen Alexei," I answered, a little embarrassed at how easily she saw through me. "We've never been apart for so long, not in all our lives."

"But he's still writing you most weeks, isn't he?" She stopped playing, gave me a sincere look.

"Most *days*," I said, smiling a little. "It's hard, knowing he's nearby yet I can't see him—a thirty-minute train ride, but between the war and the Reds, the Alexander Palace might as well be on the other side of the world. I see his eyes all the time, in my dreams. I'm afraid one day, I won't remember what they look like."

"Now you're just being dramatic," Emilia said playfully. "No one can forget Alexei Romanov's eyes. That shade of blue? If you wanted them painted on a piece of jewelry, the artist wouldn't be able to. That shade doesn't come in paints."

I laughed a little, though the sound died quickly as I remembered those sorts of charms were for ladies whose husbands or lovers were away. Alexei was neither of those things, not officially. He was merely . . . mine. And I his, and—

"Come on," Emilia said, slapping her cards down on the table. She rose, extended a hand to me. "We should do something different today."

"Such as?"

"Go out. Go . . . somewhere."

"To lunch? We did that on Thursday," I said.

"No," Emilia answered. "On an adventure. We'll go . . ." Her eyes lit up as the idea took shape. "We'll go to the bookstore in Lower Nevsky."

"A bookstore?" I asked, surprised. "Why?"

"There's a mystic there," Emilia said. "And I think it's time we check in on our fates."

# CHAPTER THREE

We rumbled through the cobblestone streets of Saint Petersburg in the back of the Boldyrev family's Type SMT, a cream-colored automobile that looked boring compared to the buildings around us. As usual, gray clouds were flocking to Saint Petersburg; they tended to roll in across the Baltic Sea and loom over our heads for months at a time. We fought back with buildings painted sunshine yellow, cathedrals of red, pale pink, gold, and orange. The automobile passed the Church on Spilt Blood, built where Tsar Nicholas's grandfather was assassinated by a crazed Red—it boasted fat onion domes of checkered green, blue, and white that dominated the skyline above murals of Biblical scenes painted right onto the brick. Paris had blue skies and green meadows, perhaps, but our city glowed, invited you in out of the cold.

Still, as we moved away from our side of town and into Lower Nevsky, things did become rather monotone—tall houses of plain brown that looked like they sagged under the weight of their residents. People were thick in the streets, on balconies, in windows, in long food lines that stretched around entire buildings. They all had a single-mindedness in their eyes that made them seem less like people and more like parts in some great machine. This section of the city often felt foreign to me—like the people were from a different country entirely. The people I saw outside the car didn't care about who was courting whom, or the intrigues of foreign courts, or even the tsar's plans for Germany. I wasn't so self-centered to be surprised such people existed, of course, but it left me feeling adrift, uncertain what the people in Lower Nevsky *did* care about.

Emilia and I huddled together in the backseat under a blanket; it felt like the driver's body did more to block the wind than the pop-up roof. People turned their heads as we rolled by—perhaps they thought we were royals, as the tsar had an automobile identical to this one. Or perhaps they were Reds—Reds were everywhere in this neighborhood, hidden among the merchants. The driver glanced back at us worriedly as we took another turn, crossed over one of the canals, and rumbled ever farther from our neighborhood.

"Relax," Emilia told him, sounding annoyed. "You worry too much." She often acted like this—like she was invincible, like the Reds were merely a prolonged nuisance. She was confident they could never hurt her, I suspect because she merely ignored anything that might warn her otherwise. It was ignorant, but a sort of easy ignorance that I envied from time to time. Perhaps she was right—my life was better without wolves.

"It's not just you I'm worried about, Miss Emilia," the driver called back, voice low and rumbling like the car's motor. He flashed a smile in our direction, one almost entirely obscured by the scarf wrapped high on his neck and the fur cap pulled down over his ears. "I'm the one who has to sit outside for the next hour."

"You don't have to wait on us," I said. "Go have some tea to warm up."

"Thank you, Miss Natalya, but if I leave you two alone in Lower Nevsky, General Kutepov will have me sent to Siberia." He said so kindly enough, but it was probably true. My father tended to be black or white in his handling of staff, and no amount of telling him that usually *I* was the one to blame in any given catastrophe—getting lost in London, fattening his new dog, tipping sleds over more times than one could count—eased his anger, and more than once I'd borne the guilt of getting a member of our household staff fired. I certainly didn't want to start offing Emilia's employees as well.

"All right then, here we are," the driver said, easing the automobile to a stop at a storefront. The windows were fogged up, turning stacks and stacks of books into lumps of blue, yellow, and tan rectangles. There were no lines for this store—the people's dire need for bread, after all, outweighed their need for books. The driver jumped from the front seat, nearly slipped on a bit of ice by the curb, then swung around to open the door for us. He helped us down and I linked my arm through Emilia's. Together, we crunched through the snow and pressed open the bookstore door. A bell rattled, announcing our arrival.

"Hello—oh! Hello," the owner said, looking at us in mild surprise. I saw his eyes travel up our coats to our hair, the gemstones that hung from Emilia's ears, the rings on my fingers. I smiled at him then spoke.

"We've heard there's a mystic who works here some days—is she in and available for readings?"

"Ah. Yes—in the back. Right down that stack and on the left," he said, motioning to an aisle of books. Emilia and I walked single file through them, our boots clacking on the floor, to the back of the shop. The smell of pages, cinnamon, and age mingled with the scent of incense here. There were thick worn-velvet curtains hanging down in a doorway; behind them, someone was quietly humming a song I could almost remember, but not quite. Emilia looked at me, brown eyes twinkling like this was a great game, and I grinned in response. Secretly, however, my heart was pounding, and had been ever since we left Emilia's—this would be the first time I'd see a mystic since I learned about the Constellation Egg. Since I learned that a mystic had created a charm so powerful it could heal Alexei and save the country.

I'd kept the Constellation Egg a secret, and of course Alexei and I never mentioned it in our letters, so I often felt like perhaps that entire night had been a dream. Could I possibly have watched starlight from a blessed egg heal Alexei's hand, *and* kissed him for the first time all in the same half hour? It felt like a fable, and I was convinced that seeing a mystic, seeing a bit of old magic, would reassure me it wasn't.

Still, I wasn't sure what to expect. Rasputin was, after all, a very different sort of mystic than the type who told fortunes from the back rooms of shops. I reached out tentatively, took a breath, then brushed the curtain aside.

"It's you!" Emilia cried.

The mystic looked up at us from a wooden chair on the far side of the table. She was old and squat, with deep-set eyes and heavy lips that reminded me of my childhood governess. She wore a thick brown skirt and billowy white top that made her look even larger than she was, and wrapped around her head was a floral shawl. Her eyes brightened upon seeing us, though there was something of a character in her expression—like she was interrupted while being herself and had to drum up the fortune-teller we expected.

"Lady Kutepova, Countess Boldyreva!" she said warmly, smiling. Her teeth were crooked, yellowed. "I haven't seen you in ages!"

"Indeed not, Babushka," I answered, taking her hand and squeezing it familiarly. "Emilia suggested we visit the bookshop today for a reading. I'm so glad she did—we've missed you!"

We'd seen the Babushka many times before—she often set up shop outside our favorite movie theater, offering fortunes to finish off an evening of wine and American films. Occasionally, she was even invited to birthday celebrations, anniversaries, and engagement parties. That said, she always existed to me as a sort of ghost rather than a person—she came with the celebration and disappeared afterward, just like the decorations and fancy foods. It was strange seeing her here, a place clearly more permanent. The candles were burned so low they were little more than piles of wax. There were boxes and boxes of incense, of crystals, of tiny figurines and smooth rocks. The room was full, well used, and the table had a worn patch across the center, evidence of years of laying tarot cards across it.

"Of course, of course," the Babushka said, rising; she barely came up to our chests. We shrugged off our coats and stoles, which the Babushka took to a crooked coat rack, trying—and failing—to keep them from dragging on the floor by holding them high above her head. She shuffled back around us, still humming under her breath, and motioned for us to sit like we were old friends—despite the fact that we didn't know her real name.

"Now, what can I do for you? Cards? Runes? Leaves?" she said, motioning toward the shelves behind her. "There's a much better selection here than outside the Mariinsky, isn't there?" she chuckled as we tried to make sense of the clutter.

"Indeed," Emilia said. "I'd like to do leaves. What about you, Natalya?" I nodded in agreement. Typically, I preferred tarot cards—the art was stunning, and it was something of a riddle to me, trying to guess what one might mean before the mystic said it aloud. But now that I knew the mystics' powers were real, and that therefore it was very probable my fortune would come to pass, I wagered leaves were the more palatable option. Somehow soggy leaves were less ominous than, say, drawing the Death card.

"Excellent," the Babushka said. "Let me see . . ." She ran her fingers along the canisters of tea leaves and settled on one labeled "Caravan." She moved quickly, tugging it down along with mismatched teacups and saucers with lilies around the edges, which she placed before us. She poured us two cups of hot water from a dented kettle and dropped a scoop of leaves in. We wrapped our fingers around the cups while it brewed, warming our fingers. It was something we'd never have done at a formal service but it seemed perfectly acceptable here.

"You're not the only nobles to seek me out here, you know," the Babushka said. "Seems everyone misses hearing their fortunes."

"Missing more than that," I said. "Saint Petersburg feels practically dead."

"I do miss the parties," the Babushka said. "No one makes

borscht like the cooks at the Winter Palace. I couldn't attend the last ball—the river rose and flooded my house that night, I'm afraid. I spent hours bailing the Neva out of my bed. But was the party lovely?"

"It was," I said. "Though now that you mention it, I realize I missed out on the borscht!"

The Babushka opened her mouth to say something, but Emilia giggled, cut her off. "Was that when you snuck away with Alexei to the tsar's salon?"

"Emilia!" I said, flushing. "Who told you about that?"

"Oh, relax," she teased, sparkling. "Alexei himself did, once you two returned to the hall. I was afraid you'd gone off to *his* room and—"

I buried my face in my palm, causing Emilia to erupt in bright, candied laughter. The Babushka chuckled along with her. "No need to be ashamed, Lady Kutepova. Young love is a beautiful thing."

"And apparently not a private thing," I said, lifting my head.

"Oh, please, it's *me*," Emilia answered. "You'd have told me either way. And if you didn't, I'd hear the gossip soon enough. I have my ways."

It was true—if Emilia didn't hear about it, it didn't happen. Her trades were gemstones and gossip, and she was a master of both, collecting rumors the way scholars collected books. Her inability to keep secrets didn't make her the most popular girl in Saint Petersburg—though now that we were friends, she was careful with my secrets. Emilia Boldyreva was nothing if not loyal.

"All right, all right, you two. Quick. Drink," the Babushka said, waggling her eyebrows at us. The action cast her eyes in and out of shadow; at the darkest moments, it looked rather like she had no eyes at all.

The tea was bitter, unsweetened, but I tilted the cup back and gulped it down, leaving only a teaspoon or so of liquid; Emilia did the same. She slammed her cup down on the table hard enough that the tea leaves sloshed up the sides. She then looked at the Babushka so eagerly that the three of us had to pause and laugh for a moment. Emilia had always been particularly delighted by the mystics—she insisted a whole group of them serve as entertainers for her sixteenth birthday party, even though so many in one room was a little less stylish and more tacky than her father would have preferred.

"Swirl what's left a bit," the Babushka said, motioning to us with her hands. We swirled the dregs of leaves and tea around in our cups, waiting until the Babushka held her palms flat, signaling for us to stop. "All right. Whose shall I read first?"

"If Emilia doesn't go first, I fear she'll faint," I said, snickering. Emilia grinned, and I found myself relieved—perhaps I wasn't as ready to hear my future as I thought. I glanced in my cup, trying to sneak a look at what it held, but I couldn't make anything out.

"All right—give it here, Countess Boldyreva," the Babushka said. She reached across the table and slid Emilia's teacup toward her. The Babushka frowned, concentrating, and tilted the cup side to side. "Let's see . . . you'll soon be taking a trip, yes?"

"To Paris," Emilia said, grinning. Her father had decided Saint Petersburg was too unpredictable for his daughter—she would be sent to live with her grandmother in Paris, in a house I suspected was the size of the Winter Palace. The prediction rather dampened my mood—without Emilia, what would I do here?

"By train," the Babushka continued. "Though the train is a bit unclear in these leaves, which leads me to suspect it will not be an easy journey."

"The train never is," Emilia grumbled.

"Though you shouldn't worry too much," the Babushka went on. "I see several friends with you on the trip."

"Several? Does that mean Natalya is coming with me?" Emilia said, eyes lighting up again.

"I can't tell if Natalya will be there or not," the Babushka answered, rotating the cup. "But there's a second fortune here. A skill, something you can do that few can. It will save someone's life."

"One of Emilia's skills? She'll save someone's life by dressing them fashionably?" I teased.

"Sometimes I feel the need to remind you that even a crown is merely a fancy piece of jewelry," she said, poking me. I laughed with her for a moment as the Babushka set Emilia's cup back down.

"All right, and Lady Kutepova—your cup?" the Babushka said warmly, hand extended.

I looked down, realized both my hands were holding tight to my teacup. I smiled falsely, looked down at the lumps of leaves. Did I really want to know my future, now that I was certain the mystics weren't all for show? The candles on the shelves were still, so still, tendrils of smoke curling up to the ceiling. The Babushka's palm waited, but . . .

"Natalya?" Emilia said. "Are you all right?"

"I'm . . ." I swallowed, tried to sound bored, faint, *anything*. "Perhaps I don't want to know my future, come to think of it."

"What?" Emilia asked, shaking her head. "Come on, now. Let's see." She reached forward, bolder than the Babushka, and, before I could stop her, plucked the cup from my hands. I grimaced, fought the urge to dive for it. The Babushka took the cup from Emilia, but kept her eyes trained on me.

"I don't have to look, Lady Kutepova," she said to me, voice kind.

"Nonsense! We drove all the way here!" Emilia said. My strangeness was starting to bother her; she nudged my elbow, but I kept my gaze on the Babushka.

"Or perhaps I can tell you only the happier signs I see?" the Babushka offered.

"No," I whispered, then found a bit more of my voice. "No, unless—can it be changed? If there's something horrible in the cup, will I be able to change it, or am I doomed?"

"Ah, well," the Babushka said, frowning. "I'll admit that fates can't be changed. They can be twisted, perhaps, but destiny is destiny."

"Then perhaps I shouldn't hear—"

"But what if it's a good fortune, Natalya!" Emilia whined, stamping her feet a little for effect. I gave her a tired look. "Come on," she answered. "Where's your sense of adventure?"

I hesitated. Emilia had a point—what if it was, in fact, a grand fortune? Something that would relieve me of my worries for Alexei, my father, the eternal gray that slumped over my city. If I knew there was a bright light at the end, perhaps it wouldn't be so bad. And besides, with the Constellation Egg, surely there couldn't be any bad news for Alexei or his family. I bit my lip and finally relented.

The old lady grinned, and I saw she was missing a few side teeth. She tipped the cup toward her, frowned as she studied it carefully.

"*Well*," the Babushka said brightly, like a grandmother doting on my future. "Speaking of crowns—I see a heart atop a crown. I suspect the heart is yours; the crown is the tsarevich's. Their positioning means your lives are forever intertwined."

I exhaled, releasing a breath; my lips curled into a smile. Weight I didn't know I was carrying lifted off me—I'd hoped for this, of course, but hearing it from a mystic was an astonishing relief. Alexei's exile, our separation was only temporary. Something to be endured, but not a punishment. I felt light and airy with happiness.

"And . . . I see . . . an egg. A pregnancy, maybe?" the Babushka continued.

My eyes widened a little, and I saw Emilia bounce happily. "Can you see if it's a boy?" Emilia asked. This sort of thing was her treat, sweet and silly and delicious.

"Hush," I scolded her. "Maybe by the time Alexei and I have children, a little girl will satisfy the country just fine. His great-grandmother is Queen Victoria, you'll remember. Her husband was her consort, not the king."

"Oh, calm down," Emilia said, rolling her eyes at me. "I'm just curious. Let me see?" She leaned forward to look at the egg in my cup, ringlets of dark hair falling from behind her ears as she did so. I leaned in to look along with her.

It wasn't the leaves that made the egg shape—it was the void, a place outlined by leaves. A few dotted the interior, and the leaves bunched together strangely at the bottom. Emilia brushed her hair back for a better look, then frowned. It was as she did this that I realized something—something that couldn't be true.

"Is it bad that it's spotted? It looks sick—you don't suppose the baby gets Alexei's bleeding disease . . ." Emilia said.

"Those aren't spots," I answered before I could help myself, voice breathless. "Those are diamonds. It's a Fabergé egg." It wasn't just any Fabergé egg. It was the Constellation Egg tilted on its side. The memory of seeing it in the secret room was still vibrant, loud in my head. I'd know its shape anywhere, even after seeing it only a single time.

"A Fabergé egg? Oh, I see! And that's the base?" Emilia said brightly. She looked from me to the Babushka and back again. "Is Natalya going to get a Fabergé egg from Alexei?" she said, voice so high-pitched I suspected only certain varieties of birds would be able to hear her soon.

The Babushka tsked under her breath, shook her head. "I've never seen a Fabergé egg in leaves before. Maybe we're meant to see it upside down; it looks a bit like a rabbit—"

"*If* it's an egg," I interrupted, "a Fabergé one, I mean, what does it symbolize being on its side?"

"Typically that means something disrupted," the Babushka said; I felt a drop inside me, heavy with worry. The Babushka didn't see this and continued, "But I really feel like this rabbit—"

"Disrupted how?" I couldn't stop myself, couldn't stop the fear from forcing itself past my lips. I thought of the Church on Spilt Blood, of Alexei's great-grandfather; the Reds had already killed one tsar. If the egg was disrupted, they'd likely love to kill another. Surely Alexei was fine, as the leaves said we were fated to be together, but what about his father, Tsar Nicholas? I bit my lips, sat back in my chair nervously.

"Perhaps it would help," the Babushka said slowly, "if I knew what you're really asking."

I didn't speak, didn't dare. The egg wasn't my secret to give away, but . . .

"Because," the Babushka said, "this looks rather like a Fabergé egg I heard of once. A special one. Blue with diamond stars in the shape of a lion."

There was no doubt in my mind—as there was likely no doubt in the Babushka's—that we both knew of the Constellation Egg, that we both knew what I was really seeing in my teacup. Yet we were each unwilling to relent, and so we stared at each other, my knees shaking, until finally Emilia spoke up.

"Will one of you tell me what's going on? I've never heard of an egg with diamond stars," she said, frowning as much over our game of wills as the fact that she didn't know something that went on in the palace.

"That's because it's a secret," the Babushka said, and I let a breath out. She was giving up first.

"A secret?" Emilia asked, finally noticing my face and lowering her voice, immediately serious when she saw my expression. "Natalya? Was it a secret?"

"It . . ." I hesitate. "It was. Alexei shouldn't have shown me—"

"Indeed he shouldn't have," the Babushka said. "Rasputin's egg was made for the Romanov family and them alone. But I suppose he knew you'd be joining the family soon enough." Her voice was warm, inviting, and her eyes crinkled into a smile. "Calm yourself, Lady Kutepova. I know all about the Constellation Egg. I'm a mystic, after all. One of Rasputin's people."

"Will someone please tell me what this secret Constellation Egg is?" Emilia said, pouting and folding her arms, like we were ruining her fun.

The Babushka looked at me, offering me the chance to spill Alexei's secret. When I stuttered, didn't know where to begin, she spoke instead. "The Constellation Egg is a piece Mr. Fabergé was working on as a gift for the tsarina. An egg with diamond stars set in blue glass to form the tsarevich's birth sign. Just before he was murdered, Rasputin imbued the egg with his powers. With its protection, the Romanov family will always rule Russia."

Emilia grew quiet, frowned. "How does it work?"

"It keeps them healthy, safe, for one," I said, inhaling. "That's why Alexei has been allowed to dance, to ride horses, to travel with his father. But it also . . . it ties them to the land. Russia is *theirs*: the animals, the plants. *Everything*. It keeps them in power."

"So one day it will keep *you* in power. You and Alexei, anyway," Emilia said, eyes now glowing. There wasn't a scrap of doubt, of hesitation now. I don't know why I expected anything different—Emilia was the sort eager to find wonder, the sort who preferred to pretend all that glittered truly was gold.

"He said the egg protected the tsar and the one he loves," I said, nodding, blushing at once. "But Babushka—you said the egg would be disrupted. Can you see how? Or what that even means?"

The Babushka sighed, gave me a weighty look. "Unfortunately, that is difficult to tell. Perhaps it symbolizes it passing from Tsar Nicholas to the tsarevich. Perhaps something more sinister—like the Romanovs losing their claim to it. Tell me—is the egg in a safe place?"

"Yes," I said. "It's in a secret room at the Winter Palace—where no one can find it."

"Given the size of the Winter Palace, I doubt anyone could find it anyhow," the Babushka said kindly, nodding. "This is good to hear. Such a powerful thing must be well protected. After all—even strong magic can't compete with a perfectly aimed bullet."

"Oh, don't say things like that!" Emilia scolded the Babushka, her voice serious. "Besides, you just told Natalya that she and Alexei are *intertwined*. Don't start making her second-guess her happily ever after."

"Apologies," the Babushka said. I could tell she was rather bothered at being reprimanded like this, but Emilia didn't notice. "I'm just glad the Constellation Egg is safe."

"It is," I repeated warmly, trying to take the edge off Emilia's words. "And as long as it is, as long as the Romanovs are on the throne, we all are."

# SAINT PETERSBURG

*The Babushka, as a rule, did not believe in luck.*

*She believed in good fortunes; she believed in happiness and sorrow and destiny. But luck implied something that certain people had and others did not, like red hair or pretty eyes. Luck was something that supposedly swept in and changed a person's fortunes. And fortunes, the Babushka was certain, could not be changed. She'd seen too many clients try and fail, over the years, to change their fates. It might work for a while, perhaps, but eventually, what she saw in cards or runes or teacups always came to pass.*

*Which was why the Babushka was somewhat disappointed in herself. How had she not seen this in her own future? Why had this particular fortune eluded her, when she read her own leaves? Because it certainly wasn't luck that brought Natalya Kutepova to her door. It was fate.*

*Rasputin's Fabergé egg. The mystics' curse, put in place by the most powerful of them all. The Babushka's already weak powers were growing ever more so—she could no longer cause the earth to crack, steer the floodwaters from her home, cast a simple charm. She could barely even see auras, some days. This was all the egg's fault—all*

*Rasputin's fault. He hadn't just given the Romanovs his powers—he'd given them the powers of every mystic in Russia, slowly draining them of their birthright.*

*The Babushka arrived at her tiny house. Most of the neighbors were women like the Babushka, who traded fortunes for rubles in markets or at parties. Plenty of the mystics in the Moscow camp thought poorly of women like the Babushka—thought it was demeaning, silly to use power to entertain the populace. The high priestess, Maria, was particularly cruel about it—but as their powers waned, the Babushka felt she had little choice in the matter. The nobles paid well, and how else was she to survive?*

See who's silly now, *she thought as she pushed open her front door.* I—an old lady who read cards for rich little girls—might be the route to save us all. *She stepped inside and dropped her bag of cards and young potatoes on the floor, hurrying to pull candles from her stores in the kitchen. There was no time to waste.*

*Rasputin stole the mystics' magic, threatening everything they had. He was more loyal to Alexandra and her sick son than to his own people, a fact that the Babushka loathed him for with a white-hot, heavy sort of hate.*

*She drew this hate up in her as she lit candles and incense. The emotion fueled her, made what little bits of her magic were left spin in her head. What she was preparing to do might, in fact, kill her, but it was something that had to be done.*

*She knew now that the egg was in the Winter Palace—in a secret room somewhere within the tsar's suites, if she had to guess. Why else would the tsarevich take Natalya Kutepova there? It was possible, of course, that the egg had been moved to the Alexander Palace with the royal family, but Nicholas—for all his doltishness—was surely too smart to keep the key to their rule under their noses now that things had become even more tumultuous. It was safer in the Winter Palace, guarded, in rooms never frequented by staff.*

*And if it wasn't there? Well. It was at least better to know for certain than to sit here and watch her powers fade away, until she was just another useless peasant beggar.*

*The Babushka opened her kitchen window so the sound of the Neva filled her house; she lit candle after candle until the entire room glowed. The Babushka could no longer create an entire idea in a person's mind—that sort of magic was but a memory now that the egg had stolen her powers. There was, however, enough power sparkling and swirling around her heart to allow her to whisper into the minds of a few. The Babushka began to chant: secret words, words to inspire, words to call to action, words to encourage.*

*The city was so close to breaking. It wouldn't take much to change a protest into a riot. That was the only way she'd be able to slip into the palace and the tsar's suites. That was the only way she'd be able to get the egg—under the cover of Red and White. Maria would be so pleased . . . The reward would surely be handsome.*

*It wasn't that she wanted a war. It was simply fate.*

# CHAPTER FOUR

There were people in the streets.

They were walking toward the Winter Palace. I could hear them, the slap of feet on cobblestones, the murmur of conversation. It was dark outside, the wind cruel and stars bright. I should have been asleep—it was nearing ten o'clock. Yet I couldn't close my eyes, not with what was happening outside. I'd opened my curtains, let my room bathe in gray starlight. If things got very, very bad out there, I wanted to be able to see.

*Relax*, I commanded myself, turning my back, staring at the cherubs carved atop the bedposts. *It's just another protest. There have been dozens before now, and there will be dozens to come before the Reds are stomped out.*

A knock on the door made me jump. I cursed under my breath, then, "Yes?"

"Miss Natalya?" The door cracked open. It was the new laundress, a woman in her thirties or so. Her uniform was a little lopsided, put on in a rush—the help typically retired after eight o'clock, so I supposed she'd had to dress again. She held a lantern in one hand, its light low and warm, turning my room from ghostly blues to gentle purples. "Count Pahlen sent word that the crowd outside the Winter Palace is particularly large tonight. He advises we gather downstairs in case they should come this way."

"Come this way?" I said, trying to scoff, but my voice betrayed my concern.

Her words were cut off by a bright sound, something sharp and cutting—a gunshot. No, not a gunshot—something louder. A cannon? My mind struggled with the possibility. I knew the sound of cannon fire; I heard it often when the navy tested their weaponry in Odessa. But cannons were meant for war, not for an angry mob. I looked down, ran my fingers along the hem of the silk bedsheets.

"Are we at war with the mob, then?" I wondered under my breath. "Is it that bad?" I rose, took several tentative steps toward the window.

"Miss Natalya, please," the laundress begged. "We're hiding in the pantry—come join us."

I swallowed, yanked the thick curtains shut. "Give me a moment," I said. "Let me get dressed."

"Miss Natalya, I don't think—"

"If they come for me, they're not taking me in my nightclothes." I tried to say this firmly, like my father would have, but my voice shook. I kept my chin up and walked to the closet, pulled down the green and gold dress I'd worn that day. The laundress helped me put it on, her hands sloppy and unpracticed. I pulled on my boots at the same time, struggling to steady myself long enough to slide my feet in.

As I laced them, I said, "They won't make it here. If they're at the palace, the army will destroy them. All the cadets are there—young, strong soldiers. You'll see." I exhaled, pinned my hair up neatly, then turned to the laundress, who looked on the verge of tears. She exhaled in relief as I finally linked my arm with hers, and together we hurried down the steps.

"I'm sure you're right, but it's better to be safe, Miss Natalya," the laundress said. "The cook next door says there are so many Reds that they're starting to attack nobles in their homes. They're stretched out along Nevsky Prospekt, but they've completely filled Voznesensky Avenue—"

"Wait, Voznesensky Avenue?" I asked, stepping away from the laundress, my eyes wide—how had this night become even more frightening? "That's where Emilia is! Is she safe? Have you heard?"

"I haven't heard anything," the laundress admitted. "But there's nothing that could be done for her at the moment anyhow."

"No, no, she should come here. She could go out her back door, take the side road here. She could get out. But she won't know to do that, she'll only hide . . ." Emilia was many things, but I knew her well—she was not a fighter. She was shaking in a pantry somewhere, praying the door wouldn't be flung open, that the Reds wouldn't find her. She was one of the highest-ranking nobles in the city—if they were on her street, they'd certainly come for her. She was all I had left, my last friend, my last connection to my life before the Reds . . . and now they were going to take her from me.

*They've taken enough.*

"I have to go get her," I said quickly, abandoning the laundress's hand.

"Miss Natalya, your father would never forgive us," the laundress said, voice grave but firm, like she was talking to a crazy person. "Come now. To the pantry."

"I'm not asking your permission," I answered. "I'll be fine. I can cut along the canal. They'll never see me." Now even *I* could hear the lunacy in my voice, but I forced myself to ignore it—I didn't have time for others to doubt me, much less any time for me to doubt myself.

"You are not a soldier, Miss Natalya. You're a lady. Someone bring Kache to talk some sense into her!" This was from a different maid, the head of our household. She was standing at the bottom of the staircase, framed by the jade-green Oriental rug.

"I'll need to borrow your coat, just in case someone sees me. So they won't realize I'm a noble." I reached out a hand to the laundress. She looked frozen, unsure if she should try to force me to stay or let me go—I suspect there wasn't protocol for the lady of the house barging out in the middle of a riot. I tapped my foot impatiently, wondering if I should have to yank it off her.

"Oh, Miss Natalya," the laundress said, shaking her head Her voice was wispy, her eyes broken. She looked to the head of household for support, but the woman was gone—disappeared into the pantry with the others.

"Come on, now. The longer you hold me up, the more dangerous this will be. It'll only take a moment to get her. It's nothing." This was a lie, and we both knew it.

The laundress sighed and shrugged off her coat, handed it to me. I flung it around my shoulders; it was wooly and smelled like lemons and vinegar, though not in an unpleasant way—in a way that reminded me of the house on Sundays. The scent comforted me as

I dashed away from the laundress, through the kitchen and to the front door.

I heard the butler call after me, but I ignored him, bursting out into the back garden. *Don't stop. Don't stop now or you'll never start again.* Night air snapped at me, instantly freezing my ears and hands as I cut around the rosebushes. Smoke was heavy in the air, hanging like a weight over me, and the noise, the awful noise of the mob was growing louder and louder still up on Nevsky Prospekt. I longed to hear another cannon shot, another sign that the army was destroying the Reds before they destroyed Saint Petersburg, but it didn't come. I hurried through our garden and knocked my shoulder into the back gate to open it, releasing me onto the little road behind us. I instantly turned my head toward the Winter Palace.

I could see it gleaming in the distance, pale red, and the angel atop the Alexander column that stood in the courtyard. But I could also see torches, heads, raised hands, banners, and signs. There were so many people they didn't look like people at all; they looked like a monster, even from this distance, something writhing and angry and big as the sea.

*They're so close to the Constellation Egg.* I watched the crowd, thought of the egg in its secret room. Thought of the disruption the Babushka predicted.

*No one knows it's there. It's hidden. Emilia isn't.*

I sprinted along the street, toward the canal that loomed ahead, black and still. The slight wind shifted, and the mob's words reached my ears. Chants against the royal family, against Alexei's mother, Alexandra, as if she were some beast instead of the tsarina. I pulled the hood of the laundress's coat over my head as I ran along, my boots sliding on the streets that were damp from the mist floating over the city. Between the houses to my right, I caught glimpses of Voznesensky Avenue. It was, as promised, packed with people. I couldn't see Nevsky Prospekt from here, but if it was anywhere near as full, I was trapped in Upper Nevsky. Perhaps Emilia would be no safer at my home after all.

I could see the shapes of torches and streetlamps reflected in the water as I approached the canal and turned left to start toward Voznesensky, toward the chaos. I bowed my head down, tried to stare at my feet, at my reflection in the canal water. The rioters were so fixated on the Winter Palace, surely they wouldn't look over and see me approaching from the west? I only needed to be in their line of sight for a moment, just till I reached the road that cut behind Emilia's house.

There was a crash, loud, glass breaking, followed by a resounding cheer from the mob that spread from the Winter Palace outward, a wave of fury. There was no telling what had happened, of course, but my heart sank anyhow at what I saw now that I was growing closer. Soldiers. Soldiers in uniform, not fighting back the mob but encouraging it, part of it. Traitors with red fabric tied to the end of their bayonets. Who would protect us, if Russia's soldiers were lost?

I swallowed the question, jogged the last few steps to the street behind Emilia's house. Whatever the first crash was, there were now answers to it—things breaking, streetlamps being pulled down, people falling into the canal. Smoke was growing ever heavier in the air; a house was on fire. I reached Emilia's back gate and hurried into the garden, ran past fountains and fruit trees to the kitchen door. I knocked furiously.

"Emilia!" I shouted—it's not as if anyone would hear me over the mob. Still nothing—maybe she'd gone. Maybe she got out.

"Natalya?" Emilia said; a curtain parted, her face appeared. Her hair was down, her face pale and lined with pillow marks and fear. She vanished from the window. I heard the door click.

"Come inside," she said. "Hurry." A few household servants were behind her, all looking equally tousled. Emilia grabbed my wrist—I could feel her hands shaking.

"No, we have to leave," I said, instead pulling her toward me. "All of you have to leave. They're burning houses, and my maid said they were hunting down nobles—"

"We're well hidden," someone—the butler? I didn't recognize him in his nightclothes—said. "Come on, quickly now, Lady Kutepova—"

"They will find you," I said, voice sharp now, furious at the delay. "Emilia, trust me. Come on."

Emilia looked from me to her butler, back again. She wasn't going to come—I could feel it. I couldn't blame her. Me and her, at night with a mob, versus the comfort of her home? But then we heard the sound of wood splintering, of voices echoing through the house—of the mob breaking down her front door.

"Now, Emilia. Come on!" I shouted.

Emilia caved, jumped outside with me—she was barefoot, wearing a flouncy summer dress that I'm sure was the first thing she could pull on quickly, though she was so scared I don't think she noticed the cold. The butler shut the door behind her to cover our escape—surely they wouldn't hurt him? He wasn't a noble, after all, but he wasn't a Red either . . . I swept the laundress's coat off, wrapped it around Emilia's fine shoulders. "Let's go," I said. The Reds were already flooding the route I'd come on—we had to run in the opposite direction, toward a different canal. We reached it just as another crash rang across the city.

We ran along the edge of the canal, Emilia slipping often, her bare feet slick against the cobblestones. Finally, we reached a tiny road that would lead us back to Sadovaya, back to my house, to shelter . . .

*No, no, no.*

The Reds had already filled Sadovaya, women with hard faces and men with angry scowls. They chanted up at the houses—at *my* house—like they expected the buildings to apologize, to surrender. There were more soldiers now, ever more soldiers. The world had gone mad. It felt as if all of Saint Petersburg might fall apart like bits of paper lit on fire.

"We can't go toward the palace," I said, nodding toward it but unable to really *look* at it again. "And we can't go home. So we have to . . ."

*Run away.* That's what I was trying to say. *We have to run away.*

# CHAPTER FIVE

The thought of fleeing made my stomach twist, made me want to scream or fight or cry—did running mean I was abandoning my home, my city, my country to the Reds? I swallowed hard, tried to keep my heart from swelling up through my throat.

"Calm down," I told Emilia, though my voice shook with fear and anger. I rubbed my hands on her sides to warm her, looked down at her feet. They were already purple and cut, though the blood looked black from cold. I beat down the grimace that almost crossed my face—that wouldn't help her right now. "We'll find a place to hide. Can you imagine the punishment for this, Emilia? They'll be hung. Every last one of them."

"I don't care," Emilia said, voice fragile. "I don't care about any of it, Natalya. I'm just scared. I just want to go home—"

"Hush. Saint Petersburg *is* our home, and we'll take it back. But for now we need to find a place to hide. Who do we know in Lower Nevsky? We're right on the edge."

"We don't know anyone in Lower Nevsky!" Emilia said shrilly. "They're all merchants! Everyone we know is gone! I should have gone to Paris when I had the chance . . . I didn't think they'd really rise up. I thought they'd learn . . ."

I looked away, ashamed to admit I agreed—the Reds had fooled me, convinced me they were merely angry students with sticks. "It'll be all right. Come on, I've got an idea. We'll go to the tailor's house, that one who lives in Lower Nevsky. He'll shelter us." I wasn't nearly as certain as I sounded, but he was our best shot. He wasn't a noble, but he was wealthy so he surely didn't sympathize with the Reds; fitting suits for the nobility made up his entire business. I'd only been to his house once before, when my father sent me to deliver a payment and his gratitude—was it a gray house? I thought it was gray, but would I know it in the dark . . .

Emilia and I hurried along, afraid to draw attention to ourselves by running, yet too scared to walk. We finally reached Lower Nevsky, where the streets had numbers instead of names. The houses here were small but pretty, with no gardens out back and dirty windows. We were the only living things in sight, though the roar of the mob still reached our ears, like a ghost howling after us. I stared at house after house, desperate to find the one I recognized as the tailor's.

"That's it, Emilia. We're here." I sighed in relief, pointing to a little gray house with a gate hanging on its hinges. It was made of stone and wood, and even from the street it was clear the curtains were a finer fabric than such a house would typically have. I opened the front gate, ran to the door, and rapped gently; my hands were so cold that my knuckles seared with pain each time they struck the wood. Nothing. The fear that I'd managed to keep from spilling out of me was growing more impossible to crush down. I pounded on the door again, again, harder, until finally a candle appeared at the downstairs window beside the door. A middle-aged woman brushed the curtain aside, her face cross and eyes squinty. I left Emilia huddled on the front stoop, climbing through the bushes toward the window.

"Is this the tailor's home?" I asked through the glass, voice frantic. "The one who fits General Kutepov?"

"It's the middle of the night. He's sleeping," the woman said, looking appalled. "I'm his wife. What do you need?"

"Of course, we don't mean to wake him—but the Reds, they're rioting. They've burned Upper Nevsky—"

"We're not interested!" she barked at us. "Keep your revolution away from us." She moved to yank the curtains shut.

"We're not Reds!" Emilia shouted, voice echoing down the street. She was breaking, the line between fear and fury dissolving. "I am Countess Emilia Boldyreva and this is Lady Natalya Kutepova. We need shelter. We barely escaped Upper Nevsky with our lives. Let. Us. In."

The woman went silent, and I could tell she recognized our last names. She wasn't interested in helping the Reds, and it was clear she also wasn't much interested in helping us either—but turning away two noble girls with military fathers wasn't a wise idea. She vanished from the window; a moment later, I heard her unlocking the front door. Emilia limped ahead of me, nearly collapsing through the door when it creaked open, like she'd used the last of her strength to yell.

The tailor's home smelled like bread and soup, and it was warm, so warm that it almost hurt. I slung an arm under Emilia's shoulders and helped her limp to a sitting area. There was a thick rug on the floor and chairs that were oversized and comfortable. Emilia sank into one, closed her eyes, began to mumble prayers. I lowered myself to the floor, panting, fighting the urge to scream. I wasn't sure why the scream had taken till now to rise up, but there it was, demanding to be let out, demanding that I break down. I closed my eyes, tried to slow my breathing, tried to stop shaking. Emilia's hand grasped mine; I peeked to see her slumped across the chair, sweaty and pale like a sick patient.

The tailor's wife moved to the hearth, threw several logs in, and coaxed up a small fire. "I'd make it larger," she said, nodding to the unpromising flames, "but I worry the Reds will see the smoke. Are they coming this way?"

"No," I said, shaking my head. "They're in Upper Nevsky mostly, everything around the Winter Palace. Though I suppose they could spread—I don't know. I don't think they themselves know, honestly. It was just . . . they were breaking things, burning things, they were everywhere . . ."

"Damn," the woman said, wringing her hands together. "They know we fit the officers sometimes . . . Still, surely they won't spread here. Surely . . ." She didn't sound convinced.

"Thank you for giving us shelter," I said quickly, worried she was having second thoughts now that she knew how bad it was. "I'll be sure to personally tell the tsarevich about your generosity, Madame . . ."

The woman frowned, realizing I didn't know her name, though she didn't look especially surprised. "Ashund," she said. "Our name is Ashund." She walked to the kitchen to pull the curtains shut. I rested my head on the side of Emilia's chair, dared to look at her bare feet. They were in the early stages of frostbite.

"Do you have some warm towels?" I asked Madame Ashund. "Her feet—"

"Lady Kutepova?" a man's voice said, sounding wonderstruck. "What's going on? And oh—oh, Countess Boldyreva!"

The tailor's face was the opposite of his wife's: warm and concerned, worried for us. He had a limp and a cane to match it, but still he hurried to my side, extended his hands to guide me to standing. I repeated our story for him, watched as his eyes grew wider, his breath shorter.

"My God," the tailor said when I'd finished, shaking his head. He had kind eyes, dark brown and deep. He turned to his wife. "Where are they now? If they're spreading this way . . ."

"I'll go find out," she said immediately. There was something softer, gentler about her when she spoke to him; all her edges melted down. "You stay and watch them."

"No, it's dangerous—"

"Everyone knows you work with the military. They won't care that you're an Octobrist," Madame Ashund said, casting me a wary look as she said the last bit. I tried to hide my surprise that someone so close to the nobility wasn't a White—this was no time to be judgmental. "The Reds are against everyone who wants to negotiate with the tsar. No one knows me. I'll be able to slip in." She didn't mention his limp, the fact that he wouldn't be able to run from them, but I knew that was the real reason she wanted to go in his stead. I thought of Alexei, how he loathed it when I brought up his sickness, and felt a pang of pity for the tailor. He wanted to argue—I could see it in his face—but his wife had already vanished upstairs. She reappeared a few moments later wearing a day dress and older boots. Madame Ashund walked to her husband, took his hand. Emilia and I looked toward the fire as they embraced.

"I'll be back in an hour," she promised him, voice gentle. "If I'm gone longer, come find me."

"Don't be gone longer," he said gravely. I heard her kiss his cheek, and then her heavy boots on the floor. The door opened, slammed shut.

"All right, all right. Let's see what we can do about this," the tailor said, motioning toward Emilia's ripped feet. He wobbled around, loading several dish towels into a cooking pot, which he then placed over the hot coals in the fire. A few moments later, he removed it; the towels were warmed, and when we wrapped them around Emilia's feet, she cried out.

"No, no, leave them," she said when I nearly pulled them away, worried we moved too fast—perhaps we should have given her toes more time to reach the temperature of the room. "They'll be fine. I'll be fine," she assured me, voice wobbly but proud.

"You're being terribly brave," the tailor said, nodding at her. He sat back. "I'm going to go change into clothes more appropriate for the company of young ladies," he said, motioning to his dressing robe. "If you'd like something to eat, please help yourself. By the time I'm back down and have made us all a cup of tea, I wager this whole ordeal will be over."

The tailor vanished upstairs; I climbed next to Emilia in the chair. She leaned against me, closed her eyes.

"This can't really be happening, can it?" she asked. "I was supposed to be fitting for a Christmas dress tomorrow, and now . . .

the house. The city . . . the war is supposed to be with Germany, not with us."

"It's only for the night," I said, sounding more confident than I felt. "Can you imagine what our fathers will do to the Reds? What Tsar Nicholas will do? This is it. The entire movement will be finished."

Emilia looked down, spoke quietly. "Do you suppose the Romanovs are safe in the Alexander Palace?"

"Of course," I said immediately, shrilly. I dropped my voice. "Besides. They have the Constellation Egg. They're safe no matter where they are." This sounded practiced, careful on my tongue. The truth was, all I could think of was what the Babushka said—that the egg would be disrupted. How even strong magic couldn't stop a perfectly aimed bullet. My stomach lurched and I had to close my eyes. *You don't need to worry. You and Alexei will be together—it's fate, and fate can't be changed. He can't die.*

The tailor came back downstairs, offered Emilia one of his wife's coats so she wasn't sitting around in a summer dress. We discussed a myriad of silly things—when the next party might be, whether or not my father would need a new jacket soon, if the nobles who had gone to Paris would find the tailors there to be insufficient compared to Mr. Ashund. We filled time desperately, waiting to hear the sound of chanting, of singing growing closer, finding it impossible to relax even after three cups of hot tea. It had only been forty minutes, but I could tell the tailor was growing anxious about his wife.

Finally, footsteps—the door swung open, crashed into the back wall. I leapt up, Emilia screamed, but it was just Madame Ashund. Her face was pale, her hair soaked with sweat, and she was panting.

The tailor rushed to her, shut the door, and pulled her coat off as she shivered her way to the fire.

"What's happened?" he asked her frantically. "Is it over? Have the Whites stopped them?"

"No," Madame Ashund said, and I realized she was shivering from far more than the cold. "No one can stop them. There are so many, Gustav. They've filled the streets in Upper Nevsky and have spread down to the Tsarskoye Selo station."

"What of the White Army?" I asked.

"They've been driven back," she said. "I'm not sure where. But listen. The family—the Romanovs. They've been captured by the Reds and taken someplace secret—no one seems to know where."

"What?"

"The Romanovs—"

She repeated herself, but it didn't matter. I knew what she said. I knew, and I was falling, falling, and falling.

*They've been captured by the Reds.*

# CHAPTER SIX

"Did I want it too badly?" I sniffed to Emilia. We were in the tailor's guest bedroom, which seemed to be mostly a storage area for thick bolts of fabric. I spotted a navy blue material among them that I recognized from military jackets, which only sharpened the edges of my heart. I lay at the end of a bed, curled into a ball, hair sticking to my face.

"Want what too badly?" Emilia asked. She looked pale, her eyes sunken, though her feet were finally normal again save a few burns from the cold. She sat at the top of the bed, back against the headboard and legs folded beneath her. Her refinement was back—her posture, her carefully held lips. I, on the other hand, felt like I'd been crumpled up and tossed into this room. I played with a loose thread on the quilt absently.

"To be tsarina," I finally whispered. Saying it aloud felt so wrong, like I was betraying a secret.

Emilia answered my question now, her voice gentle. "Who wouldn't want to be tsarina, Natalya? But we all know you love Alexei, not just his crown."

"It's Alexei who loves his crown. His country," I said quietly. If the Reds had the Romanovs, did it mean the Whites were through? The Constellation Egg was supposed to keep them in power, but I didn't see how that was possible if the Romanovs were imprisoned. And even if the egg kept them alive, saw them released . . . while I would love Alexei without his crown, I wasn't sure he'd love himself without it.

And admittedly, I would miss it. I'd miss the jewels and parties and dances. I'd never imagined my life without those things; it felt impossible to do so. I hated myself—how petty, how vain was I, to think such things at a time like this? The thoughts lodged in my brain, thick and black and evil, seeping into my sorrow.

I exhaled, trying to breathe the darkness out of me, and tilted my head to look out the window. The idea of dawn was on the horizon, pale blue light silhouetting the tops of buildings. I could see the domes of the Smolny Convent bell towers in the distance, bright white, though their edges were blurred by the smoke that lingered over Saint Petersburg. Usually, on a cold morning like this, you could see for miles; right now, the world seemed to end just beyond the bell towers.

Emilia moved and lay down beside me. I could smell her perfume, like it was so deeply lodged in her skin that even tonight's chaos couldn't uproot it. The oil lamp burning on the nightstand was nearly spent, though I didn't see how the dark could be any worse than the light.

Emilia said, "Perhaps this will all just blow over. But either way, I say we get on a train bound for Paris and leave this bog behind. Alexei and his family can meet us there, and your father, and everyone from court, and it'll be just like it was before only, well, in France, not Russia."

"Not Russia," I repeated.

"Exactly," Emilia said warmly, assuming I was agreeing with her. I wasn't—not at all. *Not Russia.* Not my country, my home. "Let's go to sleep and stop thinking about it," she continued. "There's no use dwelling. There's nothing we can do now but save ourselves."

We didn't sleep, of course. We stared at the ceiling, listened to the tailor and his wife talking under their breath in the next room, taking some small comfort in the fact that we weren't the only ones lying awake. As dawn broke, I finally hovered in the space between awake and my dreams, my thoughts circling what Emilia had said—that there was nothing we could do but save ourselves.

How could a city so full of people feel so void of souls? Emilia and I didn't dare go out while the mob had dispersed, packs of Reds roamed the streets like wolves. They broke into stores, destroyed everything in their path, tipped carriages and stole horses. They were a swarm of locusts with a never-ending hunger for destruction and the tireless chant for *land, peace, bread. Land, peace, bread. Land, peace, bread.* The words were beaten into my brain so hard that they hardly sounded like words at all anymore.

But we had a plan: for the two of us to take the train to Paris immediately. Emilia was excited, and talked quickly about her grandmother's estate, about the dressage horses and pastry chef that lived on the premises. She spoke of warm days and fine wines, comfortable beds and silk robes.

*Not Russia.*

"You'll love it, Natalya. You'll wonder why you stayed here so long," Emilia said. I could tell she was working thoughts of Paris into a daydream large enough to blot out what happened last night. I could hardly blame her.

I wanted to go, and hated myself for that. How could I leave Russia, my home, especially at a time like this? When Alexei needed me, when my tsar needed me, when my *country* needed . . . well.

My country needed saving, though I wasn't entirely convinced it needed *me*. Like Emilia said last night—there was little we could do but save ourselves. Being dead, I knew, didn't do me, Alexei, or Russia any good. Still, as I nodded along to Emilia babbling about French cheeses, I couldn't escape the shame of feeling treasonous.

"I'm sending for my nephew to drive you to the train station," Mr. Ashund said near lunchtime. He'd spent the morning out, trying to gather information but finding few people who knew anything for certain; the city was a web of stories. "Though I fear you might not be able to catch the four o'clock train . . ."

"Why is that?" Emilia asked, folding her hands in her lap as if this were a perfectly normal teatime discussion. She was still wearing her summer dress, a pretty white-and-blue smock with butterfly brocade along the edges. After last night, it was rather ripped and torn, and she clung to the fire to keep warm, and yet she somehow managed to look polished regardless. She continued, "If the tickets are sold out, I'm sure we can pay for a private carriage to Germany, then go to Paris from there, given the circumstances." Madame Ashund looked a little affronted by this—I suspected private carriages were a luxury she could not afford. Emilia didn't seem to notice.

"It's not that," Mr. Ashund said, perhaps more accustomed to being around nobility than his wife was. "They're saying the transit workers have left their posts—that many were in the riot. There may not be anyone to operate the train."

"Well," Emilia said firmly, though I saw her eyes waver. "We'll just hire a carriage then."

"Let's hope for the train," Mr. Ashund answered. I wondered if Emilia knew what the tailor and I so clearly did—that she and I would make for excellent ransoms: a countess and the tsarevich's girl. Finding a driver who could be trusted when such a thing was on the line was unlikely, as was making it all the way from Saint Petersburg to Germany in the middle of both a revolution *and* a worldwide war. I prayed for a working train as Emilia and I went downstairs to help Madame Ashund prepare afternoon tea.

"Can we assist?" I asked pleasantly, ducking the low beam at the end of the staircase. I took the kettle from Madame Ashund's hands and filled it with water while Emilia prepared the cream and sugar containers. Madame Ashund watched us warily, namely Emilia, who had probably never prepared tea before—the Boldyrev household staff was too large to warrant that. She sloshed quite a bit of water out onto the table and overfilled the cups. Madame Ashund sat between Emilia and I, and the three of us struggled to make conversation. Despite years of training on polite tea discussion, it simply seemed ridiculous to discuss the weather when our lives were being upended. I was relieved when an hour later there was a swift knock at the door. It opened before Madame Ashund could answer.

Emilia and I waited cautiously in the parlor until we heard Madame Ashund's voice go cheerful—her nephew. We rose as she escorted her nephew back to greet us.

"Lady Kutpova, Countess Boldyreva, this is my nephew, Leo Uspensky," Madame Ashund said fondly, turning to gesture to him.

Leo Uspensky was young, broad shouldered with a thick jaw and square face. He looked strong, though I'm not sure how I could tell, as he was still bundled up in a dark coat spotted with snowflakes. He nodded his head at Emilia and me; we curtseyed in response. Something in the gray of his eyes, the curve of his brows was familiar, but I couldn't place him. He pulled off his coat, draped it across his arm.

"I already know them, actually," he said kindly as he unwound his scarf, though he didn't smile. He didn't seem unfriendly, but rather like his face simply didn't make cheerful expressions. It was all hard lines, carved and smooth, like anyone who hit him would walk away with a shattered fist.

"Oh? I'm so sorry, I'm rather clumsy with names," Emilia said swiftly, practiced. "Though you do look familiar."

"I wrestle down at the theater, occasionally," he said thoughtfully, "but you might know me from the Winter Palace? I worked there as a waiter, sometimes a page, sometimes everything in between. Regardless, we would never have been formally introduced." His voice had a thick accent, unapologetically Russian—it was strange to hear, as most everyone I knew affected a French one.

"Well, it's a pleasure now, Mr. Uspensky," I said. "Thank you very much for offering to take us to the station."

"Certainly. Though I suggest we don't leave until the last possible minute. No need to be out in those crowds longer than necessary."

"So you think they can make the four o'clock train for Paris, then?" Madame Ashund asked.

Leo nodded. "Likely. Most of the trains are still running—it's really the streetcar drivers who have walked out." Emilia and I exhaled together in relief, and he continued, "Don't worry, ladies. You'll be on your way to Paris today, I'm sure."

Emilia grinned broadly, reached over to squeeze my hand. "That's wonderful to hear, Mr. Uspensky. In the meantime, will you join us for the end of tea?"

"Call me Leo, please—I'm not so fancy as to go by my last name," he said.

"Well, *Leo*—tea?"

"Of course," he said, though he sounded uneasy about the invitation, like we might be playing a trick on him—it wasn't normal for girls of our station to invite someone of his to tea. But then, these were not normal times. I smoothed my hair, checked the pins were still tight.

"I'll fetch some more water," Madame Ashund said as the three of us turned and walked toward the parlor. Once there, Leo dropped into the chair Madame Ashund had been sitting in. It looked comfortable when she occupied it, but with Leo it looked too soft, like he was sinking into it. He slouched back, wiped his brow with a hand; his eyes were reddened, I suspected from the smoky air outside.

"How did you fare in the madness last night?" I asked, lowering myself back onto the edge of my chair and folding my hands in my lap. Emilia took her seat as well, crossing her feet at the ankles and tucking them back behind the chair to hide the fact that she was still barefoot.

"Well enough," Leo answered. "Your home is fine. Very few houses burned, and none on Sadovaya Street."

"You know where I live?" I ask.

Leo smiled. "Everyone knows where the noble families live, Lady Kutepova. Perhaps you forget your own fame," he said, then paused. "It's interesting—when my uncle told me two noble girls were staying with him, that they'd run here in the night, I didn't realize it was you and Countess Boldyrev."

"You were expecting someone in particular?" I asked, confused.

"No, not at all," he said. "It's just that out of all the nobility I should finally have the opportunity to sit down with, it's strange it would be you."

"And why is that?" I meant to add his name to the end of the question, but it still felt dreadfully inappropriate to speak to him so familiarly.

"Several reasons," Leo said, inhaling deeply, frowning. "But mainly because you're the only one in Saint Petersburg who can tell me more about the Romanovs' magical Fabergé egg."

# CHAPTER SEVEN

"I'm sorry?" Emilia said, as if it were at all possible she'd misheard. I was relieved she spoke first—my heart was pounding too hard to allow me to form words. My stomach clenched, and my neck began to heat up.

"A magical Fabergé egg. One that's somewhere in the Winter Palace. One that, I wager, the Reds are desperate to find," Leo explained plainly, like we were discussing the best way to get to a butcher shop from this part of town.

I stared. A few halfhearted syllables danced off my tongue before I finally feigned coughing, smiled broadly. "I'm afraid I haven't heard this legend, Mr. Uspensky." *Did my voice shake? Please say it didn't shake.*

"Leo," he corrected me again; his name sounded different on his tongue than it did in my head, like he was speaking a foreign language. "And are you sure? Because the last time I saw you, you were discussing it with the tsarevich."

"Last time? When—"

*Oh. Yes, yes.* That's where I knew him from. *He's the boy Alexei and I ran into when we were leaving the tsar's chambers, just after seeing the egg*. My mind danced in a thousand different directions—what did he know?

"Perhaps I should start again," Leo said. "There was *always* a rumor around the palace, among the staff—people forget we have ears too." Emilia stifled a bright laugh meant to imply, "Don't be silly," but it didn't work. Leo gave her a rather pointed look, then continued. "A rumor about an egg that keeps the Romanovs in power. It seems wild, perhaps, but given the tsarevich's health recently, given how Tsar Nicholas was able to delay the revolution for so long . . . and given what I heard the tsarevich say to you, Lady Kutepova, I can't help but suspect the rumors are true."

"Well, you know how rumors are," I answered, resting back in my chair. I was keenly aware of every tuft in the fabric, every lump in the cushion, my nerves were so on edge. "Truth and lies knotted together, easily misheard by a waiter spying on his employer."

Leo didn't look offended, which unsettled me. Instead, he said, "It's quite a mystery. No one knows which of the Fabergé eggs it is, or even where it is, but they say Rasputin himself blessed it. It contains his power."

"Do they say that?" I asked, trying to sound dismissive.

"They do," Leo said. "That Rasputin poured his love for the tsarina into it. That it's more powerful in his death than he was in his life."

"And do you believe that?" I said.

Leo then nodded. "I've been in the palace for some time now. I saw Rasputin and the tsarina together often. He stared at her, watched her—"

"If you're going to suggest an affair, Mr. Uspensky, I assure you I've heard *those* rumors. I've seen the silly little cartoons passed around the markets, the tsarina and Rasputin, her *daughters* and Rasputin. They're both disgusting and ludicrous. The tsar and tsarina are very much in love." I wasn't saying this merely to protect them—it was simply true. I'd seen dozens of noble marriages, a handful of royal ones, and never saw a pair whose love matched Nicholas and Alexandra's. I glared at Leo, and was pleased to see Emilia wearing an expression similar to mine.

Leo's eyes widened a bit, though not apologetically—almost wearily. "I wasn't going to suggest an affair."

"Oh. I . . . I'm sorry?" I stuttered.

"I wasn't going to suggest an affair," he repeated. "But I say with complete confidence, Lady Kutepova, that Rasputin was in love with the tsarina. Oh, come on—don't look like that. Tell me you didn't know that to be true."

"I don't know that to be true," I said shortly, but now Emilia, master of rumors, gave me a weighty sort of look—we both knew *that* was, in fact, true. *Everyone* knew it was true—it was part of the reason noblemen orchestrated Rasputin's murder. It was unacceptable, a man so clearly infatuated with the tsarina calling on her at home, visiting when her husband was out, making state decisions with her. Rasputin even predicted that Russia wouldn't beat Germany until the tsar went to the front, a prediction I suspected was more an attempt to get the tsarina alone than prophecy. I'd always pretended to like the man for Alexei's sake, but everything about Grigori Rasputin unnerved me, *especially* the way he watched the tsarina, the softness in his voice when he spoke to her, the way he took her hand.

Leo exhaled—I noticed his shoulders barely moved when he breathed, like he was part statue. "We've digressed anyhow. My point is merely that I never saw Rasputin lie to the tsarina. In my opinion, if he said he endowed one of the Fabergé eggs with his powers, I'm inclined to believe him. She may not have loved him back, Lady Kutepova, but I know a man in love when I see one." He leaned forward in the chair, propped his elbows on his knees, and looked at me. "The tsarevich, for example, is wildly in love with you."

I was now stunned to total silence—in part because it was incredibly forward of Leo to comment on something like that, but also because hearing it said aloud drowned me in relief. *So people did know.* People did understand, even people I hardly knew. I wasn't alone in this after all—or not entirely, anyway. My lips parted; I had to look down. When I spoke, my voice was a whisper. Leo knew. He knew everything. There was no use denying the egg—it would be as pointless as denying my relationship with Alexei.

"Thank you, Mr. Uspensky. I should hope it was obvious that I'm in love with him as well."

"I'm less skilled at reading the emotions of ladies," he said. "But assuming you do love him, Lady Kutepova—you know how important it is that Rasputin's Fabergé egg doesn't fall into the hands of the Reds."

I held my breath, looked down. "The egg was made for the Romanov family and them alone. Alexei told me—it's inherited, like a crown. Just possessing it doesn't mean you possess its powers, so what use would the Reds have for it?" I tried to say this disdainfully, but I was too caught up in admitting the egg's existence to Leo, a stranger, to tame my voice.

Leo looked at me as if I were a child. "A mystic created the egg—surely a mystic could repurpose it for the Reds' use. Can you think of anything the Reds would want more than a charm that secured their revolution?"

"I somehow doubt an ordinary mystic could undo power as great as Rasputin's. But regardless, it's well hidden in the Winter Palace. It's safer there than out on the streets of Saint Petersburg," I said. Truthfully, I'd never considered that a mystic might be a Red. They were *mystics*, and other than Rasputin, they seemed largely uninterested in politics.

Leo looked down, ran a thick finger along the rim of his teacup, then spoke. "The Reds have taken the Winter Palace, Lady Kutepova."

My lips parted, but words froze on my tongue. "I'm sorry?" I asked, sure I'd misheard.

"The Reds," Leo repeated. "Last night, they stormed the Winter Palace. My understanding is it wasn't especially difficult—most of our trained men are off fighting the war with Germany. The palace was guarded by a handful of barely trained cadets and the new Women's Battalion. The Reds . . . well. You saw how many there were. They had the entire place by dawn. They even took the Peter and Paul Fortress, released all the prisoners inside. Rumor has it they're using it to lock up Whites now."

"The Winter Palace?" Emilia said, blinking, unable to get beyond that part of Leo's claim. "You can't be serious. It's . . . it's . . ."

*It's too big for them to take.* It was Russia's, it was the tsar's, it wasn't a store window or a picket sign. If the Reds were in the Winter Palace, they'd certainly find the Constellation Egg's secret room eventually. Even if it took months or years, eventually they'd have the egg, and if a mystic really could change its blessing, Alexei would go back to being a sickly boy, and Russia would become . . . Red.

*So this is the Babushka's foretold disruption.* I sniffed, tried to keep my fear from showing. "So what do you propose?"

Leo met my eyes, a long, weighty look that refused to release me. When he spoke, his voice was serious, firm. "I propose you tell me where it is, so that I can sneak into the Winter Palace and get it before the Reds stumble across its hiding spot—unless it's already too late."

"I'm afraid I don't know you that well, Leo," I said. "What's to stop you from finding a mystic, claiming the egg for yourself?"

Leo pressed his tongue against his bottom teeth and looked away, clearly frustrated. He opened his mouth as if he had an answer, but his aunt brushed back into the room. She refilled our teacups, sprinkled a few additional tea leaves in them.

"Would you be so kind, Madame Ashund? Emilia and I are feeling rather tired. We might nap a bit before we need to catch our train," I said, casting Leo a wary look.

"Of course," Madame Ashund said, though she looked annoyed to have just wasted tea leaves on us. Emilia rose, nodded politely to Leo, and together we retreated upstairs. She waited until the door was shut to speak.

"For starters, he's wildly inappropriate, isn't he?"

"Indeed," I said tartly. I went to the window, drew one of the shades back a tiny bit and stared at the street. Smoke still hung low over the city, thick and mean.

"Are you considering telling Leo where the egg is?" Emilia asked. I turned around, lifted my eyebrows.

"No," I answered. "Not at all. I was thinking about our tea leaf reading with the Babushka, actually. When she said the egg would be disrupted."

"You think the Reds getting it is the disruption, then?" she said.

"Yes . . ." I turned back to look out the window. The skies were gray, as usual, but in the daylight, I could see the bright blue panels on the Smolny Convent, as well as a bit of the Church on Spilt Blood's highest dome, green and blue and white stripes. That's where they killed Alexei's great-grandfather. That's where the Reds gained another foothold in the destruction of Russia.

"But I wonder," I said. "I wonder if *I* could be the disruption?"

"I'm sorry?" Emilia said. I looked back at her.

"Remember what the Babushka said? Fortunes can't be changed, but they can be twisted. So right now, if the Reds are the disruption, the Romanovs lose Russia. It belongs to the Reds, we go to Paris, we live in exile for the rest of our lives."

"Exile on a country estate," Emilia reminded me.

"But what if I was the disruption, Emilia? What if I got the egg out of the palace, kept it from the Reds? It would still be disrupted, Alexei and I would still be together, just like the Babushka predicted, but he'd still be the tsar someday."

"Natalya . . ." Emilia said, looking at me gravely. "Isn't being with Alexei in Paris just as good as being with Alexei in Russia?"

I gave her a hurt look. "Russia is *his.* It's mine, it's yours. And if the Reds get it, Emilia, then not only do the Whites lose Russia, but Alexei goes back to being a sick boy who bleeds too much.

How will I ever tell Alexei I could have saved our way of life, the Romanov dynasty, *and* his happiness, but handed all three over to the Reds?"

"I surely don't know," Emilia said. "But you'll have plenty of time to tell him that. In Paris. Where we're going on the four o'clock train, before we get burnt to crisps by a band of lunatic factory workers."

"Emilia . . ." I reached to my neck, ran my fingers along the top of my dress. "Emilia, when Alexei showed me the egg, he said that with it, he'd always be able to protect me. But he's the one who needs protecting now, and I'm the only one who can do it. I know exactly how to get to the Constellation Egg. I could slip in, get it, then keep it safe in Paris. No one would even know I had it."

"The Reds have the Winter Palace. They'll recognize us. They'll . . . Natalya, I never want to see them again. Not after last night," Emilia said, and her mask fell away, her face became lined in worry and shadows. She was angry, but moreover, she was scared.

"You could wait here," I said. "Or you could go ahead to Paris. I'd understand—"

"I can't leave you," Emilia said so ferociously I nearly stepped back. "No. You saved me last night. I can't just leave." She inhaled, taking the breath with the same sort of final resolve as a man gulping his final shot of liquor. "Promise me, Natalya. Promise me you'll go and look, and then we can get on the train."

I pressed my lips together. "I promise. It'll be fast. And then we'll be on our way to Paris, and one day, when the Reds are through, we'll come back to Russia, Emilia. Alexei will be the tsar, I'll be tsarina. It'll be perfect."

"You had better give me a *very* high position in court that day," Emilia half teased, sighing.

"It's just that it seems safer for us to go in relative disguise," Emilia said brightly to Madame Ashund. "Who knows who will be at the train station? If we look like nobles, we'll certainly be spotted. Surely you have something else we can wear? Anything? We'll reimburse you as soon as we get to Paris, threefold."

"I'll go see," Ms. Ashund said drily. I supposed it was a bit insulting—asking to borrow her clothes because the dresses we were wearing, even after running through the streets, were so nice that we'd be too easily recognized as nobles in them. But what choice did we have? Madame Ashund returned after only a few moments with three dresses, each slightly uglier than the one before it.

"Oh, perfect!" Emilia said, giving me a smug *we're in this together* look. "We'll mail these straight back to you."

"Oh, don't bother," Ms. Ashund said. "They aren't actually mine."

"Oh?" I asked, confused.

"No," she said, and smiled at us—though there was something sneaky lurking in the expression. "They belonged to our last house girl. She fell to her death on the tracks and her family never came for her things. I think I might have a pair of her shoes as well, Countess Boldyreva."

"Ah. How . . . convenient," Emilia said tensely. She gave me a horrified look when Madame Ashund left the room.

"I really need different shoes," I said, looking at our reflection in the bedroom mirror ten minutes later. The dresses were dull brown and spattered with old stains—the two we selected from the stack were the most presentable, but not by much. The material was soft, though, and admittedly more comfortable than my normal clothing. They were little more than jumpers with once-white shirts underneath. Emilia was too tall for hers, but was so delighted that she had shoes—even old, nearly worn-through maid's shoes—that I don't think she cared. I, on the other hand, was still wearing my nicer boots, and they gleamed in a way that showed off the dress's shabbiness.

"I don't know," she eventually said, tilting her head at our reflection. "I think we look rather convincing, even with your boots." Emilia seemed to have cheered, like she was pretending this entire thing was a costume ball instead of a rescue mission. It was rather dramatic—the sort of thing we'd read about in a book, not the sort of thing people actually *did*.

We pulled up the bed linens like our maids at home did—it seemed polite, though neither of us could get the blankets smooth—and tidied the room a bit, then descended downstairs. Leo was waiting for us near the doorway, arms folded across his chest.

"The carriage is ready," he said, then looked at Emilia and me, frowned. "I see you're dressed as . . . not yourselves."

Emilia smiled. "You like it? We thought it clever to go in disguise."

"And this passes for a disguise?" Leo asked doubtfully.

"What's wrong with it?" I said, spinning around. "Aside from my boots, I mean."

"The boots are one thing," Leo said. "But mostly, it's just that a dress isn't enough to erase your nobility. You still look like . . . nobles."

"Well, it's the best we can do," I huffed. "We'll keep our heads down."

"Of course," Leo said. He turned to his aunt. "Do you have some red fabric, so they can have armbands?"

My eyes widened. "Absolutely not."

Leo gave me a dismissive look. "You'll blend in better with them—"

"I'm not wearing one," I said, voice hard, uncompromising. "I'd rather get discovered." Emilia shifted and didn't look like she entirely agreed with me, but kept silent. Leo folded his arms.

"Fine. Then at least take your hair down. Only the nobility wears it up like that."

My jaw tightened. It was just hair, I knew, but the Reds already had so much. I wasn't giving them this too. I couldn't find the words to say this aloud without sounding every bit as mad as the rioters; luckily, Emilia spoke up.

"I think we're as disguised as we can be, Leo," she said authoritatively.

Leo made a grim face, but shook his head and walked out the front door. We followed him out to the waiting carriage. As we each took Leo's rough hand and climbed into the back, Emilia gave me a serious look, one that asked: *Are we really doing this?*

I nodded at her. She looked sick for a moment, then swallowed, forced a smile across her lips.

"Leo?" I asked as we started away from the house. Madame Ashund was waving at the gate.

"Yes, Lady Kutepova?" he called back. I inhaled, leaned forward.

"Would you be so kind as to take us to the Winter Palace before we go to the station?"

Leo sat up straighter, looked over his shoulder; the wind tousled his hair into his eyes, but I could still see the surprise there. "The Winter Palace?"

"There's something I need to get."

# CHAPTER EIGHT

Leo took us west, past the Tsarskoye Selo station, then toward the Fontanka River. Emilia and I moved closer together—we could see the Winter Palace in the distance, where the road ended. The pale red color of the palace looked less inviting and more like blood than I cared to reflect on. I tried to look only at the road just ahead, tried to think that each cobblestone passed, each rotation of the wheels got me closer to the moment this would all be over.

The Fontanka was hemmed in with stone walls, just like the canals. People were in the streets all around us, many of them wearing red armbands, others surveying the damage with slack jaws and watery eyes. Even among the Reds we passed, there seemed to be a sort of sorrow, like they couldn't quite pinpoint how things had gone so wrong.

We started across the river, over a stone bridge with iron railings. At each of the bridge's four corners were statues of bare-chested men taming horses: great frozen beasts rearing, prancing, and thrashing their tails, their bronze nostrils flared and angry. Three of the statues looked promising—like the bronze man was moments from breaking the horse, but there was one where the man had fallen, and the horse looked a heartbeat away from stomping on him. I stared at this man, the black canal water behind him, gray skies beyond that even the brightest of Saint Petersburg's buildings couldn't combat, and I questioned the taming of wild things.

"Natalya?" Emilia whispered. "They're looking at you."

I jumped, turned away from the statue. Emilia was right—people were looking. Not *staring*, but looking in a way far too intense for my comfort. I sunk into the back of the carriage, pressed against Emilia and bowed my head, staring at the nearly stripped fur blanket instead. Emilia rested her head against my shoulder, but I could feel her trembling.

"Don't worry," I whispered.

"We'll be all right. The Reds destroy buildings because they know it's impossible to destroy a Russian's heart."

"I fear you overestimate my heart," Emilia said. I exhaled just as Leo glanced over his shoulder and caught my eye.

"Are you all right?" he asked.

"We'll be fine," I answered. "Eventually, anyhow."

He nodded and turned back to driving the horses. We drew closer to the palace, the road lined in tall, connected buildings witn shattered windows and broken doors. The bakery I often went to boasted the worst damage. Everything inside that could be shattered was. The shelves were picked bare, the tables overturned. The windows and door weren't merely broken, but gone entirely, like a missing tooth in the smile of the street. Suddenly, Emilia lifted her chin, sucked in a hard breath—I looked over to see what she was staring at: the Winter Palace.

I smiled. I didn't mean to, but it happened, because the palace was still beautiful. Still strong, still standing, still the crown of Saint Petersburg, the place I knew. I found myself questioning Leo's sources—it certainly didn't *look* like the Reds had taken the building. It was still dusty red, the white columns gleaming, windows glinting when bits of sunlight broke through the clouds and smoke and hit the glass just right. Somewhere in the recesses of my mind I could even hear the music and see the lights. I tried very hard to pretend Emilia and I were merely off for lunch with the grand duchesses, after which I'd sneak away to meet Alexei in the tsarina's garden.

My game of pretend didn't last long. Emilia choked down a sob beside me.

"Oh, Natalya. It looks awful," she whispered.

"What? I don't think it looks so—"

And then I realized that hope was blinding me to the truth. While the palace was still red, the pillars still gleaming, I now saw that there were bits of windowsills missing. Holes in the stonework, great chunks of the columns gone. The courtyard was filled with torn clothing, fallen signs, spent liquor bottles, and bits and pieces from all the buildings the Reds had torn apart on their way here. Every now and then, in a place where the cobblestones dipped low, I could see blood pooling in the cracks.

I grimaced, looked to the palace gates—thick iron gates that always seemed strong, seemed heavy, seemed *enough*. They still stood, hung between a series of solid white columns, though the gates were flung open and unguarded. Worse, the golden double-eagle, the symbol of the Romanov family that had perched atop the gates for three hundred years, was missing. I couldn't bear to look at the vacant spot, so I turned my head to the side and unintentionally laid my eyes on something more frightening.

"What's the *Aurora* doing here?"

My voice was dead as I asked because truthfully, I knew. I knew exactly what the *Aurora*, one of our grandest battleships, was doing in the Neva. I eyed its three great smokestacks, the guns that lined its side. I remembered seeing her fire those guns in Bangkok when we went to celebrate the King of Siam's coronation. We drank champagne and ate spicy foods, wore pearls and beaded dresses at a party that lasted for days. A party that seemed so far away from this world. The *Aurora* now floated perfectly still on the Neva River, silent, a pawn in a game heavier than the ship could ever hope to be.

I knew why the *Aurora* was here—this was just like the mutiny in Odessa, years ago. The *Aurora* had surely been seized by the Reds, used to fire on the palace. My eyes ran between the shell marks on the Winter Palace's walls and then to the the guns on the *Aurora* accusingly. The ships were supposed to protect us, were supposed to keep Russia safe. We weren't supposed to fear them. They were *ours.*

"They used it to signal the attack," Leo said. "They took it long before they took the palace."

"What time?" I asked.

"I'm not sure—around nine, I think. That's when things got hectic."

I closed my eyes, collected myself. Nine o'clock. I heard the cannon fire. I thought it was the Whites firing into the crowd, protecting us. I thought it was the sound of our success. I rubbed my eyes, tried to force the memories away, but it was difficult as Leo drove the carriage straight for the palace gates. There were no guards, no soldiers, nothing but the eyes of the statues that stood at the edge of the palace's roof—Athena, Demeter, Zeus, muses and lions watched us silently, useless guardians that they were. Thick white columns lined the entryway and arched over our heads. The entrance used to glow, used to beckon me closer. Now it felt like we were willingly descending into a monster's throat.

"Where is everyone?" I asked quietly.

"I'm not sure," Leo said, stopping the carriage. He jumped out wiftly. "I suspect the Reds raided the palace before realizing there sn't much they can do until Lenin gets here."

"Lenin is returning?" I said, shaking my head. The Reds' leader, he man the tsar exiled rather than executed. What a way to show hanks for Tsar Nicholas's mercy.

"That's the rumor," Leo said as he looped the horse's reins around a pillar. I reached for his hand so he could help me out—how many times had I descended from a carriage on this very spot? remembered the music, the smell of perfume, the way new shoes pinched my feet and the polished feeling of fine clothing. I turned, looked up at the soaring facade, the gold lion heads above the windows. When Leo released my hand to help Emilia, I felt adrift, horribly dreamlike for a moment.

"Ready?" Emilia asked quietly once she was on the ground beside me.

"I have to be," I said, breathing slow, even.

"Paris," she said, looking up at the palace. "We'll be in Paris soon."

There was an entrance to the family's apartments to the right; those doors, I was relieved to find, were locked. Instead we went through the state entrance—no guards, no eyes, no sentries, no

signs of life at all, the wrongness made chill-bumps rise and stay o
my arms. The familiar foyer was massive, with a soaring ceiling an
deep red rugs running along a grand staircase that went up a doze
steps, then turned off to both right and left. A Romanov crest onc
hung on the staircase landing; it was torn down, crushed, lying like
carcass on the floor. Everything was trimmed in bright yellow gold
but despite this and the wide windows, the room was darker than
remembered. I realized after a moment that it was because no on
was here to turn on the massive chandelier above me—

"I hear someone," I snapped, grabbing Emilia's hand. I pulle
her behind a pillar; Leo jumped to join us. Voices, several of them
grew louder and echoed up to the gilded ceiling. I couldn't mak
out the words, but they were becoming louder, faster, nearer.

Movement on the far side of the foyer as a door burst open
A group of men—seven, maybe eight—spilled out. They were i
peasant clothes, dirty and wearing heavily patched coats with telltal
red armbands. They looked wrong in the palace, in the grandeu
dull browns and grays against silvers and golds and creams. Emili
and I pressed tighter against the pillar as they started toward us—fo
a moment, I was certain we'd been spotted, but I quickly realized th
men were far too drunk to see much of anything. One tripped ove
the edge of the grand staircase and tumbled, his face slapping again
the inlaid wood floors. The others laughed; one spit on the floo
held a bottle of red wine above his head, toasting his clumsy friend

"Is that—" Emilia whispered.

"Yes," I answered, rolling my eyes at the men. It was a bott
of Chateau de Calme, one of the tsar's favorites and more expensi
than all my jewelry combined.

"Fancy wine?" Leo asked, raising an eyebrow at us.

"Incredibly," Emilia said. "It was made before my father was born."

"I suspect that's a fact looters don't appreciate," Leo answered, hunching down lower as the group stumbled toward us. They clapped one another on the back, staggered forward, then vanished through a door on the far side of the grand staircase, singing some manner of Red song horribly off-key. I grimaced as I heard one retch just as the door slammed shut.

"Well," Leo said, stepping out from the column. "Where to, Lady Kutepova?"

"I . . ." I took a deep breath, trying to shake off the image of Reds—*drunk* Reds—in the Winter Palace. "I think we need to go back to the Nicholas Hall," I said. "I can find the room fastest from there."

"All right," Leo said grimly, "Let's just hope everyone we encounter is drunk on old wine."

The only route to the Nicholas Hall I knew was through the doors the Reds had just used; luckily, Leo knew another way. He led us through several closets, pantries, coatrooms that still smelled like perfume and cigars, until we appeared in a kitchen. I froze—I recognized it. This was the kitchen Alexei led me through at the last ball: our hearts pounding, cooks giving looks both kind and disapproving, the music from the party loud in our ears. Before I saw the Constellation Egg, before he went away, when our love was a thing we held and touched instead of something we locked up and observed.

Leo didn't notice my hesitation. He walked to the opposite side of the kitchen, his shoulders knocking into some pans on the way. He cringed at the noise, then, hearing no reaction, inched the far door open. He poked his head out cautiously.

"Come on," he called back to us. "There's no one in here."

I didn't need to see the Nicholas Hall to retrace my steps—now that we were in the kitchen, I was fairly sure I knew the way. But I couldn't stop myself, couldn't surface from the memories that swirled around my head and threatened to drown me. I walked forward, brushed past Leo; he jumped back, allowed me to lean out the door and suck in a deep breath.

The room hadn't been touched by the riots, but it was still nearly unrecognizable. The chandeliers were there, the grand staircase, the golden columns and elegant balcony level. But there were hospital beds—dozens and dozens of them—lining the walls. I knew that the Romanov family allowed the palace to be used as a hospital for fallen soldiers, but had never seen it in person. Crisp white sheets on metal frames, neatly folded blankets, and stiff-looking pillows.

"Look at this," Emilia said, sounding awestruck as she peered around me.

I meant to say something, but all that escaped my lips was a sigh. Something about the contrast of the hospital beds and the gold was right in all the ways that the contrast of the drunks in the other hall was wrong—it was beautiful. I found myself wishing photos of *this* had made it into the newspapers, that people knew what the tsar was doing for his men. I stepped out into the hall, turning, looking at the ceiling as the scent of antiseptic mingled with the oils used on the wooden floors. *How has this place changed so much, and I feel like I've been trapped, frozen since the moment I was here last?*

"Can you find your way now?" Leo asked, sounding bothered and interrupting my thoughts. I lowered my eyes to him.

"I . . . yes," I said, letting my hand trail along the nearest bed. I wanted to be left alone with my memories, but memories wouldn't help Alexei now. I pivoted, for a minute pretending I was merely mid-waltz, and walked back through the doorway. Emilia and Leo followed me.

I paused in the hallways, Alexei's voice in my head, laughing, calling me Natashenka, his fingers on mine. I was certain Leo, Emilia and I would be stopped—by a guard, by a Red, by *someone*. But we rushed through the palace, across the garden without seeing another soul, as if everyone had vanished in the night. When we reached the doors to the royal family's apartments, I glanced back at the others.

"Through here," I said as I pushed open the door that, if memory served, led to the breakfast room.

My heart fell so steeply I thought I might faint.

The tapestries on the wall were shredded, threads hanging and piled on the floors. The mahogany table still gleamed, freshly polished, but there were now deep knife gouges in the wood. Shattered china was everywhere, chairs were tipped over and broken, and the room smelled like wine and urine. I gingerly stepped into the room and a plate with eagles painted around the edges cracked under my boot. Tears slipped down my cheeks.

"Fools," Leo said, shaking his head as he looked around. "These people weren't Reds. They were just rioters and drunks."

Emilia and I picked our way through the room, delicately as if we were stepping over bodies. Leo had more trouble, looking like a draft horse as he balanced and wobbled around, trying not to crush things under his heavy feet. He gave us an apologetic look as he knocked a chair with his foot.

"I think . . . I can't remember exactly," I whispered, now opening the door that led to the tsar's salon. It was equally as horrifying: the dozens of photographs along the walls were sliced through, everything upturned, even the carpets bunched up and charred. I couldn't look at the photos, knowing I'd see Alexei's face on them, his eyes. If I saw his eyes, I would stop, be forced to stare, and if I stopped, I feared I might never move again. Furniture painted a rich silver color was cracked, revealing its pale wooden bones. The blue velvet curtains were at an angle, torn from the wall so that bits of the plaster were in chunks on the floor. Still, I exhaled in relief when I saw the bookshelf. Many of the books were tossed off, shredded, but the secret door was sealed shut. I walked over to it.

"What are you doing?" Leo asked.

"This is the way," I said simply, and grabbed for the Pushkin book. I tugged it forward; the secret door opened up obediently, easily as it had when Alexei did it. Emilia gasped behind me; Leo chuckled under his breath at the ingenuity. I shook out my arms and curved my body around the bookcase to step inside.

"Oh."

Such a stupid word—hardly a word even, but it was all I could get out. All my mouth remembered how to form, because after everything that had happened, I couldn't possibly articulate anything more elegant. The room, the secret room—it was perfect. It was completely untouched. The carpets were still pristine, the framed photos still lined up perfectly, the furniture righted and polished.

But the Constellation Egg was gone.

"Natalya?" Emilia whispered urgently. "Is this . . . where is it?"

I couldn't answer; I merely lifted a finger, pointed to the empty pedestal, to the spot where it was before. Blue glass and quartz and crystal, Alexei's egg, Alexei's saving grace—and it was gone, along with the cloth it had rested upon.

"Lady Kutepova?" Leo asked, his voice now sounding frantic. "Is this the place? You're sure?"

I nodded. Was I crying? I couldn't tell—crying didn't seem enough. I had never felt so ornamental: a useless noble, the very thing the Reds accused people like Emilia and me of being, the thing I never believed I was. This was my chance, the one thing I could do to save my country, and it was lost.

"It's gone?" Leo asked. I didn't say anything, which I suppose was answer enough for him. "But the room is fine—it isn't torn apart."

"Perhaps the family had someone move it for them," Emilia said encouragingly, though I didn't believe it. Alexei told me himself—no one knew about this room. No one except me.

"Perhaps," Leo answered Emilia, his voice dropping. It was a strange reaction—more disappointed than hopeful. I turned to him, thinking perhaps I'd misinterpreted his tone. He was in the doorway, shaking his head, jaw gritted. "Come on. Let's get out of here."

Leo easily found his way back through the hallways—I wasn't entirely certain what route we took out of the palace, as I dragged my eyes along the soiled carpets. We emerged through a side door in the courtyard, close to where we entered. I glanced up—there were drunks on the roof, performing lewd acts with a few of the statues. I rolled my eyes at them, looked to our carriage.

I froze. Standing around it was a group of boys, our age, all with red bands around their arms. They had furrowed eyebrows and smudgy cheeks, and they constantly moved their hands—cracking their knuckles, adjusting their shirts, wiping their noses—like their bodies contained too much energy for total stillness.

Emilia made a noise like a small animal behind me, then grabbed my forearm with both hands. I looked to Leo desperately, though I didn't know what to say. He couldn't fight them all on our behalf, nor did I think the Reds capable of reason at the moment. Leo met my eyes, then turned back to the boys; I tugged Emilia back behind him.

"Any luck?" one of the boys said, walking toward us.

"Nothing," Leo answered. He reached forward and took something from the nearest boy's hand—a red band. "They're the best bet, though."

"Leo?" I asked, certain I was misunderstanding. He wasn't—this wasn't . . . no. "You're a Red," I said incredulously.

"Grab them," Leo said, nodding his head toward us as he fumbled to loop the red band around his bicep. "And let's go."

# CHAPTER NINE

Emilia didn't speak, though I couldn't tell if it was because she was angry with me or because she was simply too scared to form words. Or perhaps it was that after everything, she didn't have the energy. She sat up straight in the carriage, eyes vacant, staring at the boys who sat silently across from us. I tried to focus my thoughts, come up with a plan, but my mind kept reverting to fantasies where the Whites came sweeping in, double-eagle flags waving, kicking up the ash of our fallen world as they pulled us to safety.

*It's not going to happen. Focus*, I thought. We could try to leap from the carriage, but I didn't think we could outrun Leo and his thugs. Besides, we were crossing the Neva onto Vasilevsky Ostrov, an island across from the Winter Palace that was populated mostly by immigrants and students. I certainly didn't know it well enough to survive the streets.

Something, I had to do something. I turned to one of the men across from us, caught his attention. "So Uspensky is your leader, then?" I asked, dropping my voice so Leo couldn't hear.

The boy, who was wearing a ripped and stained palace uniform, snorted, but didn't answer. The others looked exasperated, but likewise stayed silent. I inhaled, tried harder. "The irony of it all. You don't want a tsar leading you, but you'll let a waiter do the job—" I began.

I flinched when the boy raised a hand like he meant to slap me. Emilia dropped her head, covered her ears; the boy's hand hovered in the air, steady, strong, terrifying.

"I'd watch what you say, Miss Kutepova," he snarled, his voice mocking my name. "That waiter is the only reason you weren't in handcuffs from the moment you left his uncle's—he's kinder than I am. This is the new world. We're done starving and freezing and dying while you go to little dances. Done bowing and pretending that you're better than us."

"I never said I was better than you," I told him.

"No," he said, lowering his hand slowly, fire in his eyes. "You never said anything to us at all. We weren't worth the effort."

I opened my mouth again, but Emilia jabbed me in the side, silencing me.

The carriage came to a hard stop, nearly flinging me from one side to the other. Leo jumped down, motioned for us to step out first. To my surprise, he offered Emilia his hand. She was too frozen to take it.

"Move," one of the men in the carriage snapped.

"Give her a minute," I answered, though I was too afraid to meet his eye.

"Come on," Leo told her. His voice was far from gentle, but it didn't come with the threat the other boy's did. Finally, I nudged Emilia; she inhaled deeply, like she was waking from deep sleep, and slunk out of the carriage. She didn't want to take Leo's hand, I could tell, but the sun was setting, a layer of ice was forming across the road, and it didn't take kindly to her heels.

"Now you," one of the others said to me. Leo's hand stayed extended, ready to take mine.

"Come on," he said. "Let's move."

"Whatever you say, Mr. Uspensky," I muttered, and stepped out of the carriage. I refused his hand—I'd rather fall on the ice than touch him. When my foot was about to hit the ground, however, one of the men still in the carriage brought his hand down hard on my backside. I jumped away, tried to spin around in outrage and not fall at the same time. Emilia grabbed to steady me, but missed; my right foot twisted under me and I tilted, crashing into Leo.

He moved fast, grabbed my arm, and pulled me up easily; I was already standing by the time I sorted out what just happened. The indignity of it all faded away, was replaced by rage, especially when I saw the men in the carriage were guffawing loudly. I lunged forward, uttering every curse I'd learned from undiscerning soldiers. My hand made contact with the nearest man's wrist; I dug my nails in deep, raked them across his skin until blood sprouted. He shouted, leapt from the carriage.

"Stop! Both of you!" A deep voice. It was Leo—and he had his arms around me, was shoving me behind him. "You had it coming, Yuri. Stop showing off." I stepped back to free myself from Leo's hands. I wanted to be protected, but not by *him*.

"I had it coming?" the boy, Yuri, the same one who threatened to hit me earlier said, snorting. "Her kind have had it coming for three hundred years. Ought to treat her like they treated the Women's Battalion in the palace last night—"

"That won't get us any closer to the Fabergé egg," Leo said sternly while my stomach flipped at the thought of the Women's Battalion, at any woman unlucky enough to be in the way of the Reds last night.

"Take the carriage back to my uncle's, will you?"

"Fine," Yuri said, rolling his eyes as he jumped into the driver's seat. Leo stepped forward, turned to face me—

I slapped my hand across his face, a bright, cracking sound that reverberated in the air. He flinched to the side, grabbed the side of his face. Emilia looked pleased as he opened his mouth, popped his jaw. I heard Yuri howl with laughter as the carriage jolted away. Leo glared, rubbing his cheek.

"Come on," he hissed. "I just saved your life. Or at the very least, your virtue."

"After kidnapping us," I said. "So you'll forgive me if I'm not especially grateful."

Leo opened his mouth, looked like he might say something, but then shook his head, dropped his hand. There was a bright red handprint rising on his skin, which I hoped would take a long time to fade.

"Go on," he said, motioning behind me. For the first time, I was able to focus on where we'd stopped—a small house that had been converted into a theater. It was tall, made of stone and plaster, the exterior walls painted shades of turquoise and pink that were faded with age. A sign hung out front, naming it the Emerald Theater and advertising cheap vodka and singers with stage names like Heidi Holliday and Wink Dubois. The curtains were mismatched print fabrics, the door nearly falling off its hinges, but there were people streaming in, men and women alike huddled in coats and with their heads down.

Emilia and I trundled forward, trying to keep our eyes on both the building and its patrons at once. The other boys from the carriage moved ahead of us like a pack. By the time we got to the doors, people were staring—they recognized us, I could tell. I heard the ends of our names in whispers as we walked through the front door.

The theater's lobby was something like a repurposed parlor. People hunched over on high-back chairs and settees that lined the edges of several frayed Oriental rugs. The room, like the people in it, was tired-looking, worn—the wallpaper was torn, the ceiling chipped, the rugs threadbare in places. The only thing in the room that had the faintest hint of shine was a far corner with walls covered in tin icons—pictures that displayed the Virgin Mary and various saints. There were curtains straight ahead, thick and dusty, hanging over a wide doorframe. I could hear voices beyond the curtains, just loud enough that if I listened carefully, I could likely have picked out the words. Leo stopped in front of them, turned to us.

"Wait here," he said. "I need to warn them."

"That they're all dead as soon as my father discovers what you've done?" I muttered.

"That two noble girls are about to walk in, and they shouldn't shoot," Leo answered. "Don't run. They'll stop you," he said, nodding to the others in the lobby. I didn't need to look to know their eyes were on us, hard and angry. Leo brushed the curtains aside, stepped into the other room.

I leaned in close to listen; the sound of Leo's shuffling footsteps was soon absorbed by murmurs, greetings. Then, a booming voice, thick and strong, a voice that reminded me a little of my father's.

"Comrade Lenin will arrive in the next few days, courtesy of the Germans. He should have no real opposition, at least not here. The Cheka report the tsar's new home is in Ekaterinberg—though that information doesn't leave this building, are we clear? Comrade Lenin and his friends will depend on the Cheka to keep the family away, but on *us* to help run Saint Petersburg."

I gritted my teeth. The royal family—in Ekaterinberg? I knew the town, though only by name—it was days away by train, a tiny, tiny village in the freezing east. I swallowed angrily and dared to peel the corner of the curtain back with my finger so I could get a view of the room.

There was a stage—short but deep, raked at a slight angle so that the back was a few inches higher than the front. There were tables and seats scattered throughout the auditorium, most occupied by faceless, shadowy people. The lights running across the front of the stage were on, glowing pale orange and shining through the half-emptied decanters of wine till they looked like jewels.

"Ha, yes," a voice called, this one close to the curtain; it made me jump. "Let the royal family enjoy Siberia for a while. See if that changes their perspective. If they still think their rule is God's will."

Leo cleared his throat. I flinched and released the curtain as heads turned toward him, eyes glinting in the scant light.

"Mr. Uspensky," the loud man said. "Did you retrieve your prize?"

"It . . ." Leo paused. "It was already gone." There was a strange hum in his voice—nervousness. The room erupted into curse words that carried out into the lobby. I started when I realized the people in the lobby were now leaning toward the auditorium as well, listening closely while they sucked on cigarettes.

"Calm, calm, everyone," the loud voice said again. "Remember that our revolution doesn't depend entirely on a Fabergé egg. The people of Russia will have their voice, one way or another." This did little to quiet the room; their grumbles turned to exasperated sighs and clipped insults.

"Wait, wait," Leo said, shouting at first. "I don't have it, but I've brought someone with me who can help me find it."

This quieted the room. The loud voice asked, "Who?"

"Two . . . girls," Leo said, an awkward hesitation in his voice. The hesitation, the concern, it gave me a hint of strength—Leo was not as powerful as he wanted us to believe. He wasn't supposed to take prisoners. He had a single job: get the Constellation Egg—and he'd failed.

This might be the only time Emilia and I had the upper hand—they were disorganized. Thanks to my father I knew military strategy well enough to know an army was weakest in a moment like this. I closed my eyes, took a breath.

"Come on," I told Emilia, then took a breath and brushed through the curtains.

Leo's eyes locked on me, confused, panicked, perhaps—exactly what I wanted. I clasped my hands at my waist, felt Emilia walk up beside me. The room hushed, first the tables around us, then the quiet spreading out like a wave. The element of surprise, my father always told me, was priceless in a battle. I hoped he was right.

"Two *ladies*," I corrected politely. Finally I turned to the room, keeping my eyes just above their heads instead of meeting any one person's—an old finishing school trick. "I'm Lady Natalya Kutepova, and this is Countess Emilia Boldyreva."

To my dismay, most of the crowd were wearing battered palace uniforms, household servant attire, army uniforms. Their voices were hushed and concerned—which is exactly what I'd hoped for. Leo mashed his lips together, tried to stammer an explanation to the crowd, but they weren't listening. Revolution or no, it was risky to kidnap girls like me and Emilia. Even if the government fell and was unable to seek retribution, our fathers certainly would. I glanced at Emilia, who didn't seem to understand my intentions; despite the calm, collected expression on her face, her hands were shaking.

The man on the stage was so tall and broad shouldered that he reminded me of the statue of Peter the Great that stood in town. His eyes were coal black, as was his expression.

I knew him.

"Lieutenant Lukirsky. You're a long way from the war," I said coolly.

"Please, Miss Kutepova," he answered, voice matching mine. "There are no lieutenants or tsars or ladies or countesses here. I am merely 'Viktor' now. Leading an army for a tsar who doesn't care for me didn't suit me in the end. But I welcome you to my new army—the Palace Soviets." He walked to the edge of the stage, leaning out so that his face fell into shadow. There was no mistaking, however, that he was glaring directly at Leo. "Quiet down, everyone. Leo, please tell us why you've brought two noble girls to our meeting?"

Leo turned, glared at me; I smiled kindly at him, knowing it infuriated him and unsettled the room. "They're not just nobles,"

Leo said quickly. "This one," he jabbed a thumb toward me, "is the tsarevich's girl." Those at the table nearest me lit cigarettes, blowing the smoke at me and Emilia; I tried not to breathe so I could avoid coughing.

"Nobles *and* a personal friend of the former royal family," Viktor said, laughing coldly. "And yet, no Fabergé egg. Excellent, Uspensky."

"Come on, Viktor!" Leo finally said, exasperated. "As best I can tell, Natalya Kutepova is the only one outside the family who knew where the egg was kept. If she didn't take it, she's our best route to whoever did."

"Is this true, Miss Kutepova?" Viktor asked. He hopped off the stage and edged closer, dragging his fingers across the backs of chairs as he moved. "It would be much easier if you were honest with me."

"I don't know who took it," I said. "I don't even know who else knew about it."

"I don't believe you, Lady," Viktor said, voice firm.

I shook my head. "Alexei said they'd never told anyone else—he wasn't even supposed to tell me. You've kidnapped us for no reason whatsoever, sir."

"Uspensky kidnapped you," Viktor said, grunting at Leo. "And while I'll confess it was foolish, what's done is done. So either you are useful to us, Miss Kutepova . . ." He paused, ran his fingers across the knife at his belt lovingly. "Or you are not."

Emilia's eyes widened. She looked at me, desperate, begging me to give them *something*, some lie, some bit of information, something, anything to keep us safe. I tried to look reassuring as I shook my head. My body was drunk on fear; another shot of it hardly touched me. "Of course. That does seem to be in line with what the Reds are about. Burning stores. Destroying property. Killing innocent girls."

"You," Viktor said tartly, "are many things, Miss Kutepova. But you are not innocent." He paused, looked around the room. "No noble is, if only by way of willing ignorance." Viktor eased himself down on the closest table; it creaked under his weight. "So what will motivate you to tell us where the egg is, if not your own death?"

"Her father," a voice called out. "The Whites are coming back to try to take the city, but half of the soldiers here are with us now. We'll be able to capture her father easily."

I squinted—the voice was female, from a corner by the stage, but I couldn't see who in the light.

"Her father, you say?" Viktor said, looking smug. The speaker stood, continued.

"We can draw him in with her," she said, weaving through the tables carefully, gracefully—in silhouette, she moved like someone from society, floating, never looking down. "Tell us what we need to know, Natalya, or it'll be your fault that he dies."

I recognized my name on her tongue before she stepped into the light. "Kache?" I asked, feeling as if I'd been punched.

"Miss Kutepova," she said curtly. She looked as she always did: put together, hair pinned nicely, skin clean and pale as any noble girl's. But there was a bitterness in her eyes I didn't recognize, and yet it came so naturally that I was keenly aware: the anger was the truth, and the kindness she'd shown me the lie.

"Her father, you say?" Viktor said, nodding. The Reds around Kache gave her approving nods. She glowed, proud of her contribution, and I saw her and Leo meet eyes for a beat, a gentle smile flitting between them.

"I was always kind to you," I whispered before I could stop myself.

"You were," she said. "But you never forgot that I was merely the help."

"Did you not *want* a job—"

"Quiet," Viktor snapped. "There's your deal, Miss Kutepova. The information, or your father's blood on your hands."

Emilia took my hand, gave me a mournful look. Everyone was staring, dozens and dozens of eyes on me. I looked first to Viktor, then to Leo. I narrowed my eyes. We were losing the upper hand.

"Fine," I said firmly. "By all means, draw my father to you. It will be a fascinating endeavor indeed, to watch a group of mismatched militia up against the Preobrazhensky Regiment, especially when his daughter is on the line."

The room exploded in jeering, tossing crude insults. Leo put a palm to his forehead. Viktor shook his head and held back a man who lunged for me. Kache was shouting, Emilia was huddling closer and closer. I did my best to look strong.

Leo yelled something. I turned to him, my lips parted—surely I misheard him.

"What, Uspensky?" Viktor said, his booming voice gradually quieting the room. A few of the lights on the stage flickered out, further darkening the space; it felt like we were in a cave, dangers ever multiplying.

"Paris! The countess wants to go to Paris; it's all she's talked about. You'll help us, Miss Kutepova, or we'll lock . . ." He paused, looked from me to Emilia. "We'll lock Miss Boldyreva up in the Fortress until you do. She'll never get to Paris. She'll never leave Russia."

Emilia fainted.

It happened so quickly that I hardly had a chance to realize what was happening before her body slumped to the floor. The Reds laughed—actually laughed, like this was all a game. It felt like my body was falling away, leaving nothing but fury, a skeleton of myself engulfed in the emotion.

"I don't know where the egg is! I told you, I don't know who took it!" I shouted as I slumped to the ground beside her, put a hand on her back. Emilia would never survive in the Peter and Paul Fortress—even if they let me go, if I could warn my father . . . she'd never make it that long. She was built for parties, not prisons.

Emilia curled into a ball on the floor as she came to, while Kache looked at the two of us unfeelingly. Leo knelt down, spoke just loud enough that we could hear him over the roar of the audience.

"Think," he said. "Think. Who else knew about it? I promise you—no one in the household knew about that room. It had to be someone the tsar trusted."

"No one." I choked on tears, but then it came flooding back. "The mystics. A few days before you tore Saint Petersburg apart, we had our leaves read by a mystic who knew all about it. Perhaps she has it, or knows about another mystic who does."

The room went quiet; whatever I'd said, I could tell it was serious, more serious than they expected. Leo looked at Viktor, eyes wide.

"A mystic would know how to do the claiming ceremony for

a new owner," Viktor muttered. "She could claim it for anyone, anyone she wanted."

"Or keep it from being claimed for Lenin," Leo said.

Viktor nodded. "Indeed. Rasputin led the mystics—they're mostly Whites, like him, I'd think. I can't imagine they'll betray him by handing the egg to us. But if this mystic knows Miss Kutepova . . . if she trusts her . . ." He looked to me. "Do you know where to find this woman?"

"I know the bookshop she works in, in Lower Nevsky," I said, looking over at Emilia, who had barely moved. "We had our leaves read there a week ago."

"Excellent. Go find the bookshop owner and convince this woman to give you the egg."

"Not a wise idea," Leo said quickly, shaking his head at Viktor. "Lower Nevsky is mostly Factory Soviets. They're with us, but plenty of White soldiers are still there, or at least, were when I cut through to visit my uncle this afternoon. I think we'd have better luck avoiding problems with a daytime crowd."

The room didn't like this; they mumbled and whispered. Viktor folded his arms. Finally, he nodded.

"Fine, tomorrow. First light. But hurry, Uspensky. We must present the egg to Lenin when he arrives in Saint Petersburg. We'll be heroes," he said, nodding warmly at his fellows. "Let the Cheka handle the Romanovs, Russia's past. The Palace Soviets will hand Lenin Russia's future."

# CHAPTER TEN

We were led back through the lobby and to the second floor. There, what were once bedrooms had been converted into dressing rooms and prop storage; there were rows and rows of dulled party dresses alongside wooden suns, moons, painted backdrops, glittery curtains, and furniture with wheels on the legs. We made our way down the hall slowly, Leo ahead of us, another Red behind. Emilia was gripping my arm so tightly I could feel her fingernails through my dress sleeve.

Finally, Leo stepped aside, motioned into a room with a lit vanity on one wall and a drab loveseat on the other. "Countess Boldyreva," he said, nodding toward it. It didn't escape me, or, judging from the grunt, the Red behind me, that he used her title. From his tone, I suspected he felt guilty and meant it to comfort her, but Emilia was too deadened to notice. She stepped into the room, shivered, and I moved to walk in after her. Leo stood in front of me, so thick he completely blocked my view of Emilia.

"You're staying down the hall."

Emilia spun around. Her eyes were full of pleading, full of misery.

"Why can't we be together?" I asked, my voice quavering. "I agreed to help you so we could stay—"

"Because I don't want you plotting together," Leo answered. "You might be nobles, but I know you aren't stupid."

"We won't—" Emilia began, but she didn't get any farther—the other Red stepped forward, grabbed her door, and slammed it shut. He jammed a key into the lock despite my protests. Emilia screamed, pounded on the door uselessly, and then thudded to the ground. I called back to her, tried to duck around Leo and race back to her room.

"Stop it. You're lucky we're not holding you both in the Fortress overnight, with the other Whites," Leo growled at me, grabbing hold of my shoulders and spinning me around so I faced away from Emilia's cries. His face was impatient now; he folded his arms, nodded toward the room behind me. "That's yours. We can throw you in or you can walk in, but either way, you're going in."

He held all the cards, and he knew it. My tongue felt swollen in my throat, the sound of Emilia weeping was strangling me, but I marched into the room, spun on my heel to face Leo. The room was full of broken rhinestone crowns and comically fake jewelry that glittered in the dim light.

"You're a monster," I whispered as the Red behind him laughed at me.

Leo ignored my words, pointing to the window. "Don't try to jump," he said seriously, motioning toward the window. "You're on the second floor."

"I noticed," I said.

"Enough, Miss Kutepova," Leo said, rolling his eyes at me.

"We're not interested in prisoners, not really. Do what we've asked, and you can go on to Paris or London or wherever you like."

"What *are* you interested in, exactly?" I asked, waving a hand to the window sarcastically. "Burning down a bank? Homes? Stealing wine from the palace cellars?"

"No," Leo said. "We're interested in the people of Russia ruling Russia, instead of a few wealthy nobles. Nothing more."

"Ah, I see. So lighting Emilia's home was just for fun then?"

"A casualty of war," Leo said drily. "Good night, Miss Kutepova." He backed out of the room, moved to shut the door. Seeing the sliver of hallway disappearing made the anger in me grow taut again. I grabbed an empty inkwell off the nightstand and lobbed it at Leo's head. It found the doorframe instead, shattered into a thousand pieces. Leo growled, flung the door open; it crashed against the back wall, bounced back toward him.

"You entitled brat," he snapped, stomping toward me.

"Brat? Fine," I yelled as he stopped a few feet from me. "But I'm also the daughter of a war hero. A man who protected Russia from the Germans, who is fighting for this country. What are you, Leo? A thug who kidnaps girls? You're pathetic." I raised a hand to slap him again, but he grabbed my wrist before I could strike.

"Don't try that again. You won't like the result," Leo snarled, throwing my hand down. "And don't stand here and pretend you're better than me. The only reason you're still in Russia is because you're afraid you'll lose your chance to be tsarina if you run away. I've seen you at dances for ages, Miss Kutepova. I know what you're all about. You love parties and fancy foods and owning jewelry that would feed my family in Samara for a year. You love yourself, not this country. That's all people like you are capable of loving."

My wrist was still in Leo's hand, so I did the next best thing—I drove my knee up as hard as I could into his crotch. He yelled, fell back, clutching his groin. I meant to kick him again, to run, to do *something*, but I was shaking. I could feel tears brewing, and suddenly they were falling down my cheeks, my lungs were filled with stones, my knees weak. *He's wrong, why can't he understand that he's wrong?* I loved Russia—I loved her parties, I loved the beauty and the splendor, yes, but I loved my country like any soldier or king. *I love Alexei, for more than just his promise to make me tsarina.*

I did not understand how both Leo and I could be Russian. I did not understand how both Leo and I could be human.

I took two rocky steps backward and sat down on the edge of the bed, buried my face in my palms as Leo hauled himself up via a dresser by the door.

"I love Alexei Romanov more than you'll ever love anything, Mr. Uspensky. I love my *country* more than you'll ever love anything," I whispered. Leo strung my name into a series of curses, glowered at me from where he stood doubled over. I found I wanted him to rush at me, to hit me—better yet, to render me unconscious. It would be a brief respite from this, from the thousands of emotions flooding me, the hurt, the fury, the sorrow. I closed my eyes.

Leo exhaled; I jumped, anticipating him to lash out in anger, but was surprised to see him still standing by the door. A little hunched over, his face still a little twisted in pain.

"Just help us get the egg, Miss Kutepova, and soon this will all be a bad memory." He firmed his jaw, stood up straight, and slipped out of the room, shutting the door behind him. I was about to fall back on the bed to cry again when the door clicked open and Emilia stepped in, her face as swollen and tearstained as mine surely was. Leo met my eyes for a moment from the hallway, then pulled the door shut and locked us inside.

"I was jealous, once," Emilia said. Her nose was still red, her eyes bloodshot, but she smiled a little at me as we lay side by side on two settees we'd pushed together. The act badly scratched the floor and caused a rack of men's costumes to slide off the rack, both of which offered some small satisfaction.

"Jealous? Of me?" I answered.

"No, not of you," she said, elbowing me in the ribs. I sniffed, tried to swallow, but found my throat still too swollen from tears. "Of you and Alexei."

"What do you mean?" I asked, surprised. I turned onto my side, wiped the stray hairs from my face. Shouting rose up from the streets; it sounded like a few drunks fighting. We listened for a moment before I continued. "You were jealous that I might be the tsarina?"

"Perhaps a little," Emilia said thoughtfully. "But mostly I was jealous of how easy it was for you and Alexei. It was like you didn't even mean to be in love, you just were. I grew taller, my hair grew longer, my French grew better—well, a little better, anyhow—and you and Alexei grew more and more in love."

"I wonder if it's like that for everyone," I mused, reaching down to strum my fingers across the strings of a broken balalaika. "It should be."

"I admit," Emilia added, "it was quite the example to live up to. I worried I'd forever compare all of my own romances to yours."

"I'm sure the great love of your life will be just as easy and just as beautiful. It'll be perfect."

"If there is a love of my life. If we get out of here," Emilia said, face falling.

"We'll get out of here," I said. "You, me, Alexei, his parents, his sisters. We'll all get out of here."

"But you and me," Emilia said tensely. "To Paris, Natalya. Like you promised. Right? You and Alexei will be terribly happy there."

It was a strange thing, picturing a life with Alexei where he wasn't wearing a crown. Where he wasn't in a suite at the palace, wasn't being bowed to. I closed my eyes, pictured him in common clothes instead of a military uniform, standing in a field of green. His hand in mine as we stood under the summer sun and stared across fields and fields of lavender to where the violet blended into the sky. Who would he be, without a country to rule? Without a populace to think of? Without politics to follow and people to lead?

It was a strange thought, though not an unpleasant one.

"Of course. We'll go to Paris. As soon as we can," I said, nodding vaguely.

"Good. Leave Russia to the Reds and their stupid egg. They'll run it into the ground soon enough anyhow," Emilia said.

I should have agreed with her. It should have been easy, even. A life in Paris with Alexei, a life that would be happy and beautiful and as lovely as anything. And yet . . .

*Not Russia*. It was not Russia.

# CHAPTER ELEVEN

Leo came for us just after dawn, when the sky was still half navy with night. The city was quiet and cold, and we could hear the sounds of the Neva from our room. Emilia and I hadn't slept an hour combined—if the fights in the streets hadn't woken us, the wars in our heads had. I was pleased to see Leo looked equally exhausted, his shoulders sagging as he stood in the doorframe.

"Are you ready?" Leo asked. Emilia tensed beside me on the mattress that smelled faintly of mildew.

"Not quite," I said. "Is a lady's maid coming to dress us?"

Leo's eyes widened; when he realized I was being sarcastic, he narrowed his eyes, shook his head. "Let's move." He vanished down the hall, walking fast.

We laced our boots back up; we hadn't changed out of our clothes, which felt wrinkled and twisted wrong against my body. I pinned my hair up carefully then helped Emilia with hers, hating myself at how much better Kache was at this.

"Maybe," she said as I jammed the final hairpin in, "a soldier will ride by. One who's still loyal. He'll see us and rescue us."

"If they recognize us," I said with dismay, lifting my arms and letting them flop back down. "I look worse than any maid we ever hired, that's for certain." Emilia's face instantly fell. "But they'll surely recognize us anyhow—a jewel with a little dirt on it is still a jewel," I said, which made her smile again.

Leo reappeared moments later, tapping his foot as he wrapped a gray scarf around his throat. I found Emilia's eyes; we silently agreed to take our time smoothing our dresses, untangling our eyelashes, turning back and forth in front of the tiny mirror until Leo cleared his throat loudly.

"I believe we're ready now, Mr. Uspensky," I said sweetly, turning toward him.

"How excellent, Miss Kutepova," he answered, bowing obnoxiously and motioning out the door. We walked to the end of the hallway, back down the stairs and to the front door, which hung wide open. Reds were asleep in the lobby, draped across furniture, curled into balls with blankets and snoring softly. At the front door, Leo stopped and spoke, voice a whisper.

"Let me make myself clear," he said testily. "Viktor has me checking in with the other Reds every two hours. If the two of you even *look* like you might give me trouble, I send word back to him, and your life gets even less comfortable. Are we clear?"

"You're taking us alone?" I asked, trying to hide my genuine surprise. "No gang of boys to glare at us while you drive the carriage?"

Leo countered with a stony look. "I'm quite confident I can handle the two of you. Besides, the rest of the Palace Soviets have their own responsibilities."

"Like burning houses?"

"Like preparing for Lenin's arrival," Leo said.

"They don't all actually *believe* in the egg, do they?" I said accusingly. "Not the way you do, at least."

Leo didn't answer, firmed his lips together. "It's hard for some to believe, Miss Kutepova, that a pretty egg made from jewels means all our hopes and goals and revolutions are useless. Perhaps everyone here doesn't believe with my conviction, but trust me when I say every Red in this house—every Red in this country—believes that something wrong, something unnatural, something *unfair* is keeping us at the bottom of the heap and you at the top. So while they handle Lenin, and the marches, and the remaining soldiers, I'll handle the egg. We all do our part."

He said the last bit like I couldn't possibly understand what he meant, then spun around and began to walk, stomping along like the ground insulted him. The entire thing made me even more annoyed with him, but I followed along with Emilia behind me.

The sun crested over the horizon, painting the sky gold and orange, colors that would soon give way to the usual watercolor of gray clouds. It was freezing; my breath formed smoke as I exhaled, and my fingers turned red. I thought of the fur muffs I had at home, the leather gloves, warmer coats than this borrowed wool one. Leo took us the long way around Upper Nevsky, crossing from Vasilevsky Ostrov to another island, Petrogradsky Ostrov, where we could see the Fortress they'd threatened to lock Emilia up in. I looked back at her, saw her face had gone pale.

"Don't worry," I whispered. "You're never setting foot in there."

Emilia nodded, but her color remained ghostly white. "I'm a

countess," she said. "How can this be happening? Two days ago, I woke up at home, in my bed, *clean*, and now . . ."

I didn't have an answer for her.

We took a long bridge across the Neva. It was lined with elegant iron streetlamps, covered in curled filigree, almost like oversized candlesticks. I could see the Church on Spilt Blood ahead, and was doing my best not to dwell on it and the prospect of murdered tsars. People were starting to fill the streets now, filtering around Emilia and me. I couldn't help but wonder where they had to be, exactly, in the middle of all this.

"How far from the bookshop are we?" I asked. Leo turned around. "I thought you'd been to the bookshop before."

"I have," I said as we reached the end of the bridge and crossed into the mainland. "But you can understand, I don't frequently arrive on foot."

Leo gave me a terse look. "Well, Miss—" he stopped short, realizing using my last name in the middle of an ever-busier street wasn't wise. I folded my arms, daring him to call me by only my first name. He ignored my stance and continued. "The streetcar drivers are on strike, so unless you want to spring for a private carriage, we can't afford anything but walking."

"Alas," I said. "I left my purse behind when I was fleeing for my life."

"Can't we take your aunt's carriage?" Emilia interrupted. I gave her a pitying look—she was wearing my shoes, which I suspected were too large for her. She used me for balance and rubbed her ankle.

"No," Leo answered shortly. "Yuri returned it yesterday for me, remember?"

"And you can't borrow it again?" I said as Emilia put her foot back down, winced.

"Not . . . now," Leo said, brandishing a hand in our direction.

I stopped. "Your aunt and uncle don't know you're a Red, do they?"

Leo spun around. "I don't see why it matters, but no. Not everyone is in a position to stand up for what's right, I suppose."

"So tell me this," I said, ignoring his answer. "Were you ever going to drive us to the train station? Or did you always want to kidnap us?"

"Did I *want* to? Does this look like something I *want* to do?" Leo said, bowing his head as a particularly cruel streak of wind whipped at us, rattling the doors of houses. People leaned into the wind, shivered, then returned to their work as soon as it passed. Leo continued, "I *wanted* you to tell me where the stupid egg was, so I could go get it while you two went off to Switzerland or Paris or England. And *then* I wanted the egg to be in the palace, so the others and I could drop you at the train station and be done with you." He began to walk fast, forging ahead angrily.

Telegraph lines had been torn down, their posts lying on their sides like fallen trees. At first I thought this was more destruction by the Reds, but then I saw a Romanov flag tied around one. This was the Whites' doing—they'd destroyed the telegraph lines rather than let the Reds use them. I thought of Russians burning Moscow to the ground once, rather than allowing Napoleon to take it. *We aren't backing down*, I thought, *not to foreign enemies or monsters from within*. I could see down the street that the lines were down all over the city; Leo glanced at me, scowled at my smile.

"The bookshop is just ahead, I think," Leo said twenty minutes later, and indeed, the street looked vaguely familiar. There were shops below apartments here, groceries and butchers and similar. Just like Upper Nevsky, most of the stores bore the signs of the riots, with broken windows or torn-down signs.

"So this claiming ceremony that the mystics perform on the egg," I asked Leo as we took a right turn. "What is it?"

Leo shrugged. "Exactly what it sounds like. The egg belongs to the Romanovs until it's claimed for someone else."

"And how does that work? The claiming?"

Leo gave me a rocky look. "I don't see how that matters."

"Call me curious," I answered, smiling sarcastically at him.

He rolled his eyes at me. "I don't know, actually. We'll hire a mystic who does when we claim it for Lenin."

"And if they won't help you? You'll threaten to imprison the ones they love too?" Leo ignored me. "Forgive me," I said in a simpering voice. "Just trying to understand what the Reds are all about."

Leo answered darkly, "The Reds are about equality. About the people ruling themselves. About having votes and voice. Meanwhile, the Whites kill peasants, trample on factory workers—they even murdered Rasputin."

I opened my mouth to protest, but Emilia cut me off. "I'm glad they killed him. He was a horrible drunk," she said, shivering. We turned to her, seemingly both surprised she was no longer frightened to silence. She looked at us, blinked. "What? He was a drunk and a lunatic and he smelled terrible. He was a completely inappropriate fixture at court. I can't believe the tsarina kept him around as long as she did."

"It was for Alexei," I said, dropping my eyes to the ground for a moment. "It was all for him." The tsarina would have done anything for her son, traded her crown and title for his well-being, if that's what it took. Alexei's condition made her desperate. While the world saw a shy woman falling victim to a wild mystic, I knew she was a mother going to any length.

"Do you suppose he told her?" I wondered aloud as we arrived at the street the bookshop was on. Leo and Emilia turned to me, waited for me to clarify. "You say you know for certain Father Grigori was in love with Alexandra," I said. "Do you think she knew?"

"No," Leo said simply. "I think she was too in love with her husband to notice the way his eyes went different when he spoke with her. Despite your own experience, Miss Kutepova, love doesn't always require two people."

"That's tragic. He died and she never knew," I said, glancing up at the sky. There were hundreds, thousands of lies about the tsarina and Rasputin that all of Russia heard one way or another, and the singular truth never found its way to Alexandra's ears. "He should have told her."

Leo and Emilia seemed united in their confusion over my pity for Rasputin—and their distaste for him. We were silent as we approached the bookshop. The red and yellow blocks of books came into view through the windows, the place where Emilia's driver stopped the automobile now occupied by a truck of beets being unloaded for the grocery next door. It seemed astonishingly normal except—

"It's closed," Emilia sighed, pointing to the door that only came into view once we passed the truck. "Until further notice."

"Damn it," Leo said, looking deflated. He knelt down, looked nto the shop; it was nearly impossible to see inside due to the frost on the windows. He rubbed at it as I walked up beside him, cupped my hands to either side of my mouth, and blew against the glass.

The bit of glass cleared, creating a palm-sized spot to peer hrough. The shop looked fine from where I stood—nothing out of place, nothing ransacked. But there was no one inside and the bookcases faded into darkness as they stretched farther away from he front windows.

"That was strange," Emilia said. I turned to see what she was alking about only to find her pointing at the bookshop window. I stepped back and saw it had defrosted entirely in the brief moment I was looking inside, droplets of water running down the glass like rain. frowned and ran my finger along a pane.

"Perhaps they left a stove on?" I said.

Leo seemed unimpressed with a thawing window; he cracked his knuckles, looking very wrestler-like. "Do you know where the Babushka lives?"

"No," I answered. He gave me a pointed look, like I might be lying. "Why would I know where a fortune-teller lives?"

Leo looked like he desperately wanted to argue with me—though was beginning to think that was merely his standard expression—but turned back to the shop. "You have to know something. Did he mention having children?" Leo asked. "A husband? If she lives alone, I suspect she's on the east side. Plenty of spinsters in that neighborhood."

"I'm not sure," I said, shaking my head. "Did she ever mention hildren, Emilia?"

“I don’t know,” she said. “It never came up.” She stepped to peer into the bookshop herself, grimacing as her boots sunk into the mud by the bricks.

“What about . . . I don’t know, did she ever mention how far she had to walk to get here?” Leo continued.

“No,” I said, my voice firmer this time. “She said—she said once that the Neva flooded her house. But that could be anywhere—”

“When did it flood?”

“During the last ball. The one where you listened in on me discussing the egg with Alexei,” I answered, folding my arms.

“That has to be to the south then, below the convent . . .” Leo began to pace, bouncing one hand in the other as he thought. “Tell me anything else she said about where she lived.”

“She has sunflowers growing in her garden?” Emilia offered.

“They’re probably dead this time of year,” Leo said. “They usually die in the first frost. Though that would mean her garden is in full sun . . .”

“You’re a connoisseur of sunflowers?” I asked, hovering between impressed and sarcastic.

“My family grew them in Samara,” he said, waving me off. “What else?”

The beet truck pulled away, pumping smoke in our direction. I sighed, looked from the bookstore to the street and back again. “Why don’t we go south of Smolny Convent then? It’s a start,” said.

“Is it far?” Emilia asked miserably. I could tell she was even more turned around than I was. She looked at the sky, as if the clouds might offer some direction.

"Not terribly far," Leo answered, and I heard something almost like sympathy in his voice—though his face, as usual, remained stony. "A half hour or so. First, I need to check in with the Factory Soviets, so they can send word to Viktor . . ."

Emilia swallowed. "All right. And if we start now, Natalya and I can still make the four o'clock train," she muttered, and began walking.

"Emilia," Leo called out. She gave him a horrified look, like she expected to hear him say he planned to send her straight to the Fortress.

"What?" she asked, voice shaking.

"You're going the wrong direction," he said.

"Of course I am," she muttered, and rejoined us.

The sky settled on shades of gray. I stared at the black canal water as we trudged along. I couldn't stop myself—I pictured Rasputin's body floating there. They threw him in the water, after his murderers—nobles, people like me—were done shooting, poisoning, stabbing him. The freezing water, in the end, was what killed him.

*He should have told her.*

# CHAPTER TWELVE

Leo stopped by an old apartment building with red banners limply hanging out the windows like great streaks of blood. Emilia and I stood nearly on top of each other in the dingy entry hall as Leo sprang up the first flight of stairs and knocked loudly on a door. A wiry-looking man, the total opposite of Viktor, appeared, leering at us through wire-rimmed glasses, nodding as Leo explained what he was doing there. The entire conversation took mere moments, like this sort of thing were totally normal—perhaps among the Reds, it was. Then a young boy with a smudgy face raced off toward the theater on Vasilevsky Ostrov to deliver the news of our continued submission.

With that settled, we cut beneath the convent and into the southern marketplace. It was crowded, full of feet and hooves and wooden wheels. Emilia and I clustered nearer to each other to avoid having our toes run over, dodging the eyes of men with hard glares and crooked teeth. There were carts, tents, and makeshift storefronts set up in the streets that at first made it look like a single fat line of humanity. To my surprise, there were few Rec banners and armbands—indeed, it looked as if the marketplace was blissfully unaware of the war going on just a few streets over. It was heartwarming to see that not *all* of Saint Petersburg was against us, and yet frustrating to see they weren't with us either. Surely they could choose a side?

Leo ducked and wove into the crowd easily, leaving Emilia and me struggling to keep up. He reached back once, grabbed my wrist to help me around an apple vendor, but I yanked my hand away, glowering at him.

"Fine. But don't look so nervous. You're drawing attention to us," Leo hissed. I fought the urge to slap him again, focused instead on firming my jaw and moving through the crowd. Strangely enough, if I closed my eyes for a moment, it felt like I was at a ball—swirling, moving people all around me. But it didn't *sound* like a ball—there was no laughter. It certainly didn't smell like a ball either.

"All right, one block over is the Neva. Her house has to be in this stretch," Leo said. He pointed with his hand down the strip we were on, but my eyes landed on a cluster of children selling matchboxes. They were bundled up tightly, but their shoes were too small—the ends had been cut off to allow their stocking-clad toes to poke through. The oldest girl was seven, maybe eight, big eyes and quick fingers, flipping matchsticks along her knuckles with practiced skill. I jumped when Emilia suddenly touched my arm, trying to gather my attention. I glanced back at the little girl. Emilia, then Leo, followed my line of sight.

"Come on, we need to move," he said, though I heard a note of pity in his voice.

"Their toes," I said. "They must be cold."

"You can't help them," Leo said, shaking his head. "Come on."

I didn't move. Leo sighed, then walked toward the oldest girl. He reached into his pocket and removed a coin, thrust it at her.

"This for a box of matches and a little information. Do you know where the mystics live in this part of town?"

The girl smiled. "Easy—three more blocks down then to the right. The houses with all the curtains drawn."

"Thank you," Leo said, and she plucked the coin from his fingers. Leo shoved the box of matches into his pocket, lifted his eyebrows at me.

"There you go. Let's *move*, Miss Kutepova. I have to check in again in thirty minutes. I don't want to report that you're giving me trouble."

I sighed, not entirely convinced that the proceeds from a single pack of matches would do the girl any good. Still, I followed Leo farther down the road to where the lanes grew wide and the wall of people was less intrusive. There were fewer carts out here, fewer vendors hocking liquors, dried fruits, fish. I peered down the street, frowned—there were dozens of houses here, many of which looked abandoned and all of which had roofs patched so many times they looked like quilts. People hurried in and out of them, mostly dirty children and their world-weary mothers chasing after them.

We limped along—my feet were blistered and bruised now just as Emilia's were—until the road split, with one branch leading to slightly nicer houses away from the river and another leading to ever tinier cottages that sat right along the riverbanks. Stray cats wandered back and forth between the buildings, and as the matchgirl promised, most of the curtains were drawn—mystics, I supposed, made most of their money after sunset. It was no surprise, really, that the Babushka's house flooded: the river lapped at its banks just a few strides away from the nearest homes. Stone walls held the worst of the water back, but I'd seen enough floods to know how easily the water could overcome man's obstacles.

Leo craned his neck to look around houses for signs of sunflowers. "They'd have to be in the back," he said. "There's not enough morning light here for sunflowers . . ."

"Surely the Babushka isn't the only person around here growing sunflowers, though," I complained as he slunk away from a house when a cranky-looking woman appeared in the window. "I see sunflower arrangements everywhere. I bet a hundred houses on this road have sunflower gardens."

"No," Leo said. He didn't meet my eyes as he spoke, like he couldn't be bothered to. "Hundreds of people don't grow them. Most of those flowers you saw came from my family's farm, or one like it. Every week a man came to pick up batches and batches of them for corsages and bouquets."

I blinked. "I suppose it is the tsarina's favorite flower," I said. "She's called Sunny, you know. By her family."

"Believe me, I know," Leo said. "I know everything there is to know about the damn things. Three years running, we couldn't afford to keep oxen, so my father and brothers and I pulled the plow ourselves, all so the tsarina could have her sunflowers."

"No one *made* you grow them," I said. Leo laughed, though it hardly sounded like a laugh, and peered around another house as he answered.

"That's like saying no one *made* you borrow a maid's dress, Miss

Kutepova. You did what you had to in order to survive. There—there are a few behind this one. And it looks like there are a couple in the place next door as well." I poked my head around the side of the house, looked at the wilted, frostbitten sunflowers—keeled over and mostly brown, just the base of their stems still green and clinging to life. The flowers themselves looked uncomfortably like the backs of heads from this angle.

"It's the one next door," Emilia said behind me.

"How do you know?" Leo asked.

"She's short," Emilia answered, and pointed to the side of the house next door. I frowned, looked back to Emilia; I was pleased to see Leo was equally confused. "The climbing roses," Emilia said. "She only pruned the bottom."

"Clever," I said, smiling. She was right—there were climbing roses creeping out of the soil right in front of the house. There was no garden here, so they were planted right beside the foundation. The rose vines were bare this time of year, but it was clear the bottom halves were carefully pruned, the thorns there thick and proud. At the top, the vines became leggy and skinny. There was a distinct line where the change occurred—the highest the Babushka could reach.

"How did you figure that out?" Leo asked, clearly impressed.

"Our gardener is short," Emilia said a little wistfully. "He always had to get a stepladder. He was so proud of his roses, though—the Yusupovs planted these gorgeous burgundy roses in the back garden ages ago. Did you ever come over in the summer and see them, Natalya?"

"I never got the chance," I said.

"That's a shame. Especially since they're ash now," Emilia said, voice dropping to a dark tone; she glared at Leo.

Leo pressed his tongue against his teeth rather than respond, then walked to the front door. He rapped on it, the sound abrasive against the flickering rhythm of the Neva behind the house. Nothing happened. He tried again, louder, rubbing his knuckles as he waited for a response.

"Perhaps she left Saint Petersburg," I said. "It's dangerous these days, you know."

"That wouldn't be good," Leo said, "seeing as how you have to help me find her before you can go to Paris."

I sighed, marched forward, knocked for myself; the wood scraped my knuckles but I refused to wince in front of Leo. "Babushka?" I called. "Are you there?" I leaned in close. "It's Lady Natalya Kutepova and Countess Emilia Boldyreva."

Still nothing.

"She could be telling fortunes somewhere else, since the bookshop is closed," Emilia suggested. "She's often at the Mariinsky Theater."

"Which is on the opposite end of Saint Petersburg," Leo said.

"Pity the streetcars aren't working," I said pointedly.

"If the drivers were treated like humans instead of cattle, they would be," Leo bit back, but I could tell he, too, recognized how much easier this all would have been with a streetcar to help us.

"Wait," Emilia said from where she stood in the tiny strip of grass out front. She was peering in one of the windows, angled so she could see past the drawn curtains. "What if she is home, and someone beat us here?"

"Who could have?" Leo asked, spinning to give me *that* look, the one where he appeared to be trying to turn me to stone.

"Glaring at me like that doesn't mean I know more," I answered. "Haven't you worked that out yet?"

"Stop it, both of you," Emilia snapped, brushing past me to the front door. She began to rap hard, then push on the handle. "I think I see a shadow. What if one of the other Reds came over here last night?"

"The Palace Soviets are the only Reds who know about the egg," Leo said.

I shrugged. "Then maybe one of *them* came and got it last night."

"Are you suggesting one of my friends is a traitor?"

"I'm suggesting they're all traitors to their country—"

"Enough! Help me open the door," Emilia said, voice harsh. Her tone made Leo and me jump in near unison; we dropped the argument and knocked louder, jiggled the handle, hoping the ancient lock would give. It held tight. After a few moments, Leo stepped back, cracked his knuckles.

"I can break it down," he said. "Step back—"

"Oh, don't be stupid, Leo. Just because you're the size of an ox doesn't mean you have to act like one," Emilia muttered. She pushed him aside, reached up, and yanked the pins out of her hair. It tumbled down her back, still curled, still lovely, but more unwashed than I'd ever seen it before—it looked like a maid's hair, now. I watched as Emilia jammed both pins into the keyhole and pressed her shoulder to the door, feeling for something with the pins.

"I used to do this all the time as a little girl," she muttered to us, grimacing as one pin temporarily jammed. "When Mother locked the kitchens up, afraid I was getting fat."

"You?" I said, laughing.

"Trust me, Natalya," she said. "If I had things my way, I'd be delightfully fat. Fat and full of cakes and in Paris."

"Soon—" I began, but didn't have time to finish. The lock suddenly clicked; Emilia nearly fell into the house as the door gave. Leo and I were behind her, eyes skirting for any sign of the Babushka.

The house was similar to her space at the bookshop—dusty, old, but warm-looking. There were a few small rugs lined up together to make one large one in the center of the floor, and a fireplace full of ash with a single rocking chair in front of it. There was a wooden bed, tiny and squat just like the Babushka, tucked away in a corner and partially obscured by a curtain. Leo dashed to it, upset the blankets, but there was no one. He ducked into the bathroom, then the kitchen.

"The shadow I saw was just the icon, I think," Emilia said, looking dismayed. She pointed to an icon of Saint John hanging in the small kitchen window. The window allowed a square of light into the kitchen—which was little more than a cast-iron stove and a basin—and the icon disrupted that, creating a shadow across the floor that looked like a person looming. Emilia slumped into the rocking chair and pulled her boots off like she was a welcome guest.

"Come on," Leo said, staring at her like she'd lost her mind. "We can't stay here."

"I can't walk any farther," Emilia said, voice breaking. She was moments from crying or screaming, perhaps both. "Grant me a moment, at the least. And shut the door—it's freezing out there."

Leo looked unsettled, like he was suddenly aware of the fact that we'd just broken into a house, but moved forward and clicked the door shut anyway. He paced back and forth in front of it for a moment, boots heavy on the wood floors. "We could wait here," he finally said. "Maybe she really is just out reading fortunes."

"She's not," I said, rising. My voice felt far off, broken, as I picked my way over to the bed. Among the blankets that Leo had thrown back searching for the old woman was a piece of fabric, silk while the rest were wool. It gleamed dark blue, a royal blue, and I saw the head of a golden eagle spying at me among the folds. I stooped, lifted the scrap of material. It was sleek and gentle in my hand.

"What is that?" Emilia called from the rocking chair.

"It's from the Winter Palace," I said, cradling it against my chest. "It's from the room the egg was in. She must have taken it herself. I assume one doesn't take a magical Fabergé then go to work as per usual." Leo marched over, held out his hand; I shot him a disgusted look, displayed the scrap but kept it out of his reach. His lips parted, half angry, half confused.

"Where would she have gone?" he murmured, more to himself than Emilia or me. "If she's taken it for the Reds, she's still in Saint Petersburg, surely. The revolution's home is here." He walked to a wooden dresser with a faded filigree pattern across the sides and flung one of the drawers open. It clunked open easily—the drawer was completely empty. Leo growled, slammed the drawer shut; I couldn't stop myself from smiling.

"Maybe she's protecting it," I said. "Honoring Rasputin's wishes. Taken it out of Saint Petersburg to keep it away from your revolution."

"Again, I will remind you that you two don't go to Paris until we have the egg. I wouldn't look so pleased with yourself, Miss Kutepova."

Leo tugged the hair at the back of his head for a moment, thinking. I ran the fabric from the palace through my fingers, watching it curve around my knuckles.

"I've got an idea," I said. "Come on."

"Wait, what—" Leo began, looking uncertain as I walked toward the door. I left the Babushka's home and went down the street toward another house, Emilia limping along, Leo following behind her reluctantly. "Miss Kutepova. Miss Kutepova! If you say anything—the mystics are Whites, and if—"

"I know," I snapped. "Stop shouting. Though I suppose it's probably not too lovely, to look around and discover you're surrounded by the enemy, is it?"

"No different from the last eighteen years of my life," Leo said darkly.

I rolled my eyes and approached the door. This house was almost identical to the Babushka's, save for the lack of roses out front. A cat hustled out of the windowsill as I walked up, sending a salmon-colored curtain swinging. I lifted a hand, rapped hard on the door.

"You're just going to call on a neighbor and ask where the Babushka went with a Fabergé egg?" Leo asked. I ignored him, leaning forward to listen. I knocked again as Leo continued, "If she took a train, maybe someone at the station remembers her . . ."

The door swung open so fast it caused all three of us to jump. The woman before us had thick silver hair and deep wrinkles, but she was tall and bony, like a stretched-out version of the Babushka. Her eyes were small and tired-looking, and the memory of last night's lipstick and kohl eyeliner hung on her face.

"I'm sleeping," she said. "What do you want?"

I exhaled. "My name is Lady Natalya Kutepova," I said, lifting my chin and straightening my spine. "My friend—Countess Emilia Boldyreva."

I could tell the woman was torn—I spoke like nobility and yet my clothes didn't make any sense. She rubbed her eyes, made a face. "And who is he?" she asked, pointing to Leo. "King George?"

"No, he's a footman," I said pleasantly. Leo sighed behind me as I continued. "I apologize for our appearance—we had to disguise ourselves to escape Upper Nevsky with our lives. A group of us are on our way to Paris, but thought it prudent to consult with the Babushka before we leave—the old woman who lived in the house with the roses? She doesn't appear to be home. Do you know when she'll return?"

The woman leaned in her doorway, folded her arms. The ends of her elbows stuck out, knobby and red, and she chewed her tongue for a moment. "Afraid I don't know." It was impossible to tell if this was a lie or not. Still, I carried on.

"Oh no!" I said, affixing my best dismayed face. I looked at Emilia, who mirrored my extreme disappointment. "Our families will be so upset. We've consulted her for ages now—"

"Yes, she always was popular among the nobility," the woman said drily. "Sorry for your poor luck."

"Indeed," I said, turning away from the door. I walked away, linking my arm with Emilia's as I did. "Her poor luck too," I said to Emilia. "Father would have paid any price to find out if Paris is the right decision."

We made it a few more steps, Leo at our heels, when the woman called out. "Wait!" She wrapped a shawl around her shoulders, walked toward us. "Perhaps I can help. I'm as experienced a mystic as your Babushka."

I smiled. "Oh, thank you, but no. We'll just hope she comes home before our train leaves—perhaps she's just in the market. We have a bit of time."

"She's gone," the woman said, shaking her head. There was a hunger in her voice now, a powerful sales pitch. "She's out of town. She won't be back anytime soon."

Emilia and I glanced at each other. I frowned, rocked on my heels. "I'm not sure. We have a relationship with her, you see. I'd hate for her to come back from someplace nearby and find we've asked someone else—"

"Lady Kutepova, she's in Moscow," the woman said, shaking her head. "She's gone to the mystic colony there to visit with our high priestess. She won't be back anytime soon, I'm afraid. Perhaps it was fate that brought you to my door instead. Let me help you know your future."

I bit my lip, sighed, then nodded. "All right. All right, I suppose that would work. Could you meet us at the Tsarskoye Selo station tomorrow afternoon? Three-thirty? Our train leaves at five."

"That sounds fine," the woman said, looking pleased. "Cards?"

"Perfect," I said, and reached down, took the woman's hand. She looked perplexed, but allowed me to squeeze it gently. "Thank you so much," I said. "It's such a frightening time."

"Indeed," she said. "I can expect payment there?"

"Naturally," I answered, and we parted ways, wishing each other a fine evening despite the city's chaos. It wasn't until we were nearly back to the Babushka's that Leo spoke.

"Well done," he said, the compliment awkward in his mouth. He held open the door as we walked back inside the Babushka's home. Emilia dropped into the rocking chair again and began unlacing her boots while I leaned in the kitchen doorway.

"There's a group of Reds not far from here—I have to check in and let them know we're going to Moscow," Leo said, looking from me to Emilia meaningfully. "I won't be gone long." The last bit wasn't a promise, but rather a threat—that he wasn't walking so far he wouldn't be able to keep an eye on us.

"Moscow?" Emilia sighed. "I hate Moscow."

"It's a fast trip," Leo said, then walked toward the kitchen. He grabbed a broom, then stalked toward the front door; after pulling it shut behind him, he wedged the broom between the knob and the frame, so that it locked the door shut from the outside. He gave Emilia and me a stern look through the window, then hurried down the street.

"Emilia," I said firmly, keeping my eyes trained on Leo's back.

"Hm?"

"Put your boots back on. We're leaving."

# MOSCOW

*Saint Petersburg was a cup tipped over, its contents splattered across the floor. Moscow, however, was a cup balanced on the edge of a table. The people in this city walked carefully, spoke carefully, breathed carefully, keenly aware that any wrong movement could leave them spilled across the Russian landscape as in Saint Petersburg.*

*It was the price, the Babushka supposed, of getting the Constellation Egg. Though it didn't really matter to her what the Reds or the Whites did, who stormed whom, who won the fight. The affairs of common Russians were, to her and the other mystics, beneath their meddling. The mystics' identities were precious, their traditions handed down, their secrets locked up tightly.*

*Still, it was making the journey through Moscow rather irritating. Reds and Whites glowered at one another across the square, each daring the other to snap first. She stopped to complete a few card readings so she could afford to take a carriage through town, all with the egg tucked away in a satchel made of rags. When her carriage rounded the big brown train station, she saw the monastery, finally. She was home. And soon, she'd be a hero.*

*She walked across the bridge to the island in the Moskva, one of a handful that dotted the river at its widest point. The monastery on the island was older than the Romanovs, so old that no one remembered exactly who built it or why they left it behind. It was no matter; it was the perfect place for the mystics, and the rumors they spread of ghosts in the buildings meant they were largely left alone.*

*Mystics greeted her, ran out of their tents, and patted her back. She smiled, nodded, hugged, but kept the egg tight against her body. This was something for the priestess to see first. The Babushka wound her way through the monastery, stepping over fallen bricks and broken glass, cringing as bats dove from the empty bell tower, flying far too close to her face for comfort. She walked to the former sanctuary, where the priestess's rooms were.*

*She knocked on the door once, waited to hear a call to enter, and then pushed it open. The sanctuary was an enormous round room. The pews were gone, replaced by tables, a bed, dressers lined with tarot cards and crystals and tools for séances. Rays from the setting sun streaked into the sanctuary from the open door, falling across a girl sitting at a desk. She had thick black hair and a long, oval-shaped face that was pretty at first glance, and rather frightening at the second—something to do with the angle of her cheekbones, the Babushka always thought.*

*"Sister," the girl said. She was eighteen, but she was well aware of the power she held as the high priestess. "A vision last night predicted you would arrive with news of our curse."*

*"I've done far better than news, Maria," the Babushka said, stepping into the sanctuary.*

*The door slammed behind her, taking with it most of the room's sunlight. The room was now lit mostly by candles that were lined up on every flat surface, their flames still and tall. Maria rose, tall and elegant—she'd once nearly been a full-fledged member of the Russian court, but in the end she embraced this life instead. It was probably for the best—the aristocracy likely couldn't have come to accept the far-off, haunted look in her eyes.*

*"You don't mean . . ." Maria began, biting her lip, like a child speaking of Christmastime.*

*"I do," the Babushka answered, grinning at her own cleverness. "I have the Constellation Egg. Alexei Romanov's girl stumbled into my studio and told me exactly where."*

*"Show me," Maria demanded, clapping her hands together. She looked almost frightened as the Babushka walked to the table in the center of the room and set her satchel among the spilled tarot cards. She unwrapped it slowly, piece by piece. Finally, the last bit of fabric fell away and the Constellation Egg was revealed.*

*Here in the dim of the sanctuary, it looked more inky black than royal blue. The diamond-stars gleamed in the candlelight, the quartz base looked so cloud-like it was hard to believe it to be a solid thing. Maria seemed to have stopped breathing. She extended trembling fingertips toward the egg; when they finally made contact, she exhaled, melted in relief.*

*"My God. This is it," she whispered. She now looked on the verge of tears; when she spoke again, her voice was raspy. "Do the Whites know it's gone?"*

*"No," the Babushka said. "I took it from the Winter Palace myself. I was able to sneak in through a back door during the riots—it was guarded by a wounded soldier. It hurt my heart to kill him."*

*Maria lifted the egg in her slender fingers. She held it closer to a* candle to allow light to bounce through the blue glass, then rapped on it with a well-manicured nail; her time with the nobility meant she was perhaps the most polished of all mystics.

"Shall we claim it for the mystics then?" the Babushka asked. "I imagine the Reds will want it. If we take it, we rule Russia as we always did—in silence. The Reds will overpower the Romanovs, they'll think they've won, and we can go about—"

"That won't work," Maria said sharply, like she was being woken from a dream. "It can't be claimed for all of us—it must be claimed for one. For a new tsar—or, I suppose, in our case, tsarina."

"One?" the Babushka asked. Her heart fell to her feet—all this, and her powers wouldn't be returned?

Maria smiled brightly, in a carefree way that reminded the old woman of fashionable ladies in Saint Petersburg. "Don't worry, Babushka. That is merely the limitation of an object—it follows the rules Rasputin set. I will claim the egg, then return the power to the mystics. I'm not Grigori Rasputin—you can trust me."

Maria walked across the sanctuary and lifted an athame from an end table. She quickly, easily slid the blade across her palm—it wasn't a pretty thing, this sort of magic, but blood was necessary. Maria watched her blood rise like it pleased her, tilted her hand, and watched a few drops fall to the floor. When Maria looked over and saw the Babushka staring at the wound, she narrowed her eyes. The Babushka dropped her gaze to the floor, muttered an apology under her breath—it was a well-known fact that Maria hated to be stared at.

Maria sniffed; the apology was nice, but didn't erase the hot feeling that was bubbling up in her chest. She'd spent far too long being stared at, being the odd, dirty, strange girl in the Russian court. The little pet to the real nobles, something to play with until a better toy came along or her father returned from a romp in the bedroom. Eyes, eyes that told her she wasn't good enough, wasn't pretty enough, wasn't powerful enough.

She hated to be stared at.

Maria shook off the heat of her memories and tried to focus. Her lips slowly parted, though it wasn't clear if she was smiling or baring her teeth.

"I claim this," she said to the egg, like she were speaking to a lover. "I claim you."

Maria expected a thunderclap. A storm, lightning. Something grand and frightening, something worthy of the act. Instead, there was nothing, save the cry of a few ravens in the rafters. The Babushka looked up at them warily. Maria cursed, pulled her hand away. The excitement that had been building in her, waiting, eagerly gnawing at the corners of her heart, fell away so sharply that she sucked an angry breath in and slammed her hands down on the table.

The Constellation Egg's secrets were locked up tighter than she anticipated. But she would break in. She would find a way. No matter the cost.

# CHAPTER THIRTEEN

"We're leaving?" Emilia asked, eyes widening like she was certain she'd misheard me. "But Leo's—"

"The window in the kitchen," I said swiftly. "We can fit through it."

"And then what?" she said, though she spoke with little doubt—and she was already lacing her boots. "I don't know the way back to Upper Nevsky. It hardly feels like we're in Saint Petersburg, to be honest."

"Look," I said, pointing out the front window. "The Smolny Convent towers. If we follow the towers, we'll eventually reach Nevsky Prospekt. We can take it straight to the Moscow train station."

"Wait—what are you talking about?"

I wrung my hands together—we didn't have long. "Your uncle is in Moscow—he can keep us safe once we get there. So we'll board the train, go to Moscow, find the Babushka, get the Constellation Egg ourselves and take it to Paris. We can keep it safe there for the Romanovs—we can still save Russia, Emilia." The plan didn't ꞌeel real until I said it aloud; suddenly it wasn't just a plan, it was a nission, something that wasn't an option or up for debate.

"They'll put me in the Fortress," Emilia said, eyes wide. "Natalya, ıo. They'll lock me up, I can't—they'll just telegraph ahead, have ꞏeds waiting for us at the station."

"The telegraph lines are down. They can't contact anyone. Think of it, Emilia, we'll be heroes—"

"I don't want to be a hero," she snapped. "I want to be alive vhen this is over! All I wanted to do from the start was go to Paris!"

"I know, please, Emilia—Leo's gone," I said, motioning to the vindow. "We're not far from the station. We can make it. We can lo this."

"And if we can't?"

I stopped, looked down. "What if they don't let us go to Paris vhen they're done either way, Emilia?"

Emilia blanched, trembled. "But they said—"

"They said they were Russians too, but look at them."

Emilia's face crunched up. She folded her arms across her chest ınd looked like she might be sick. Seconds were ticking by—

"We have to go. Now." My words were sharp, so sharp that ꞏmilia almost looked hurt. Still, to my relief, she ran after me as I ›olted for the kitchen window. I yanked the Saint John icon down ıs I wrenched the window open—one of the peddlers outside the tation would surely give us a little money for it, enough to get on he train.

One of the windowpanes shattered as it slammed against the op of its sash. I helped Emilia through first; I glanced over my houlder, certain I'd see Leo barging through the door as I placed a boot firmly in the basin and heaved myself into the frame. It was a farther drop than I anticipated; I crushed dying sunflowers as I fell into the garden.

My feet were burning with blisters, and Emilia was limping, but we sprinted along the Neva, behind the house's gardens. The road twisted ahead, curving up and into the marketplace; I grabbed Emilia's hand as we entered it. Everything was a blur—faces, hands, livestock, children flitting around by our feet. I wanted to move faster, run faster, but every few feet there was another body, another wall of humanity that slowed us down, and my heels kept slipping between the cobblestones. I glanced back—I didn't see Leo anywhere. Emilia met my eyes and gave me an encouraging look.

I couldn't see the Smolny towers for a moment, my view blocked by a massive apartment building with boarded-up windows. We broke through the other side of the marketplace, panting, sweating so hard I desperately wanted to shed my coat. *Yes*, there they were, the towers ahead of us again, slightly to our left. When we took a third turn, I dared to slow to a walk, panting, gasping for breath. The roads here were thin, uneven, and busy; it felt like the buildings on either side might crumble on top of me from the flow of the people rushing by them. I jumped at the dull sound of a whistle blowing, then turned to Emilia, perplexed. I realized the answer to my question before I could ask it.

"The factory whistles," I said, and she nodded. I'd never heard them so loud before—but then, the factories were far from any part of Saint Petersburg I frequented.

"Do you think Leo's realized yet?" Emilia asked, bumping into at least a half-dozen people as she looked behind us warily.

"Surely," I said, eyes darting to the skyline as I hugged the Saint John icon closer to my chest. The sun seemed to be against us, descending ever faster. When it set, we wouldn't be able to see the towers at all. We took another sharp turn; music from a bar across the street danced in our direction, as did the eyes of several men standing outside smoking cigarettes.

Now that workers were released by the factory whistle, the already-busy streets were beginning to truly fill with men walking home, roaming in packs and covered in grease, sweat, or both. I realized Emilia and I didn't look entirely unlike the other women walking about—maids and housekeepers heading home for the evening, still in uniforms similar to the borrowed ones we were wearing.

The horizon glowed red; the Smolny towers were silhouettes now and the streets grew shadowy and frightening—all strange lights, strange leers, strange signs advertising female impersonators and nude dancing. It was a section of Saint Petersburg I knew existed but never would have ventured to. There were plenty of boys my age in the streets, students from the mining college and sons of merchants eager to spend their parents' money. Most seemed harmless, but plenty looked like they had dark evenings ahead. I swallowed hard as one such man crossed in front of us, his eyes wandering up and down our bodies in a way that made me shiver with disgust.

"How far away are we from the station?" Emilia asked, voice filled with dread. The streetlamps flickered on. The ones in this part of town were rather plain, and instead of bathing us in comforting light, they merely made the shadows even more spiky and threatening. To our right was a police wagon lying on its side by an alleyway, like an animal's corpse. Someone had painted *Down with the German woman!*, a reference to the tsarina, across its undercarriage in bright red.

"We can't be far," I said. "I remember I could always see the convent towers from the left windows of the station. We should reach Nevsky Prospekt any minute now. We're almost there, Emilia."

There was a circus ahead. Two women stood out front in clothes so small I knew they had to be freezing; corsets that pushed their breasts up, tiny sleeves that barely covered their arms, hair down and tangled seductively. They called out to groups of men, lured them in with promises of a French movie followed by a wrestling match. After the circus, the crowds on the street got thinner. There were stores here, but groceries, pharmacies, places that were closed and locked up for the night. I was relieved for a moment—there were fewer lecherous eyes, fewer people who might recognize Emilia or me as nobles. This section of town, after all, was surely crawling with Reds who meant us harm. I looked up at the horizon.

The towers were gone.

"Natalya," Emilia said suddenly, voice a grave whisper. "I think we're being followed."

"By who?" I asked, not daring to turn around. "Leo?"

"No," she said, voice now breaking. "A group of men—I'm not sure."

I waited a few beats then pretended to fix my hair, turning just enough to look behind us. My stomach dropped, turned in on itself. Three men, our age, perhaps, but with shadows under their eyes and tension in their shoulders. They were staring, staring so hard I could feel it as I turned back around.

"Do we run?" Emilia asked.

"No," I said. "Not yet. See the corner ahead? If we turn there, it should take us back around the block, near the theater. There are more people there."

"Natalya," Emilia said tensely. We were walking faster, but I could see their reflection in store windows—they were keeping pace with us, glancing at one another. Worse yet, I could see the man in the middle was smiling, smiling in a way that made me feel sick. *I should turn around*, I thought. *Turn around and face them. See if they can advance while looking me in the eye.* It was, after all, easier to shoot someone in the back than meet face-to-face. Yet I couldn't. I felt hypnotized, afraid to turn around, look at them, confirm this was real. It made me feel weak, feel stupid, but I pulled Emilia around the corner.

I opened my mouth to tell her to run, but there was no need—our feet pounded on the dirt. We leapt over mops and buckets and empty milk crates that were stacked outside the back doors of storefronts; I finally felt free from the paralyzing fear and looked over my shoulder.

They were behind us. Behind us, laughing, walking fast—but not running. Why weren't they running? I turned back to the path ahead, stumbled over a broom handle.

*That's why they aren't running.*

Ahead, where the alley should have let out by the theater, was the overturned police wagon. The back section was tilted toward us, blocking the alley entirely. I heard Emilia cry out, but she didn't stop, so neither did I—we kept going, ran up to it. I grabbed hold of one of the wooden benches, tried to climb up, feet scraping against the wagon bed. I could hear the music from the theater on the other side, hear people milling around—but it was so crowded, so humming with nightlife that I don't think they heard me as I screamed out for help. The men were running now, they were getting closer, closer.

I turned to face the boys, then swung the Saint John icon back.

"Oh, we're going to fight, are we?" the boy in the middle said, rocking back on his heels. "I like fighting."

I charged forward, swung hard; the icon made contact with a loud *clank*, and the boy bent over, clutching his cheek. The icon was crumpled now, cheap and bent. The boy rose again, came back toward me.

The plank hissed past my face. Emilia. She'd grabbed one of the planks from the wooden benches, and cracked the boy so hard that he fell into a heap. The boys cursed at her, ducked to help their friend up as I looked over at Emilia's panicked but furious form. She had the plank lifted, her nails digging into the wood and jaw clenched.

"Whore," the one we hit growled as he clambered to his feet. "I thought we could do this the easy way." His face was badly bleeding where his sparse beard met his cheekbones, his eyes glowing dangerously. He and the others looked at one another, had some sort of silent conversation, then advanced again, this time all three at once. I steeled my jaw, waited until they were close to lash out with the remains of the icon.

This time they were ready. The nearest one knocked the icon away so easily I was ashamed of myself. Emilia managed to strike one other with the plank, but there were too many; she screamed as they grabbed her by the wrists. She kicked the closest boy hard, but he grunted, fought back; one of her borrowed shoes went flying. Another one of the boys grabbed hold of my arms, pinned them behind my back. The one we hit was suddenly on me, grabbing my face with his hands, snarling.

"Shut up," he hissed at me, and I heard the clattering sound of him frantically undoing his belt with one hand. I closed my eyes, screamed again, again, but nothing—

A thick sound, feet hitting the earth. Then a scuffle, and suddenly I was free. I opened my eyes, disoriented with fear, and fell backward. Emilia was there, caught me by the shoulders. I turned to her, grasped her dress, and suddenly realized what was happening.

It was Leo, hands curled into tight fists. He moved fast, swinging first at the boy who threatened me. Leo socked him hard in the eye then barreled into him, pulling him to the ground and getting in two more punches before the other two boys hauled Leo off. One tried to hold him so the other could punch; Leo twisted away easily, shoved one boy into the other so they both toppled backward into a store's back door. They were quick to recover, along with the first boy; all three approached Leo slowly, methodically. Leo looked from side to side; the plank Emilia fought them with was near my feet. I ducked down, slid it through the dirt to him.

Leo grabbed it, swung out. He cracked one boy on the side of the head. Another dove for Leo, knocked him backward and into the dirt. Leo struggled, tried to claw his way out, but they were on him; one boy held him flat to the ground while the other ran up, kicked Leo so hard in the chest that I heard his ribs crack. The pain seemed to give Leo new life; he flipped over, kicked the boy holding him away. He grabbed the one who kicked him, yanked him to the ground, and pushed his face into the dirt. Leo then shoved the boy toward Emilia and me; we pounced, taking advantage of the dirt and dust in the boy's eyes, kicking him hard in the shins. I knotted my hand into a fist, punched him hard; it felt like my hand was exploding, though I was pleased when he collapsed to the ground, rubbing his face dizzily.

The last boy—the one who threatened me—was approaching Leo when he realized that both his friends were down. Leo grinned; his lip was busted and his eye blackened, and I could tell by the way his arm was twisted that at least one bone was broken. Still, he looked strong, looked ready—looked happy, even, to be fighting. The boy lunged forward, Leo ducked, wheeled back around, and cracked the boy hard in the throat with his elbow.

The boy coughed, sputtered. He nearly dropped to his knees, but seemed to think twice about it; instead, he turned and ran. His conscious comrade—the one I punched—stumbled after him. Leo glanced toward the unconscious one, and, seeing that he wasn't waking anytime soon, exhaled. He turned toward us, face now fallen. He grabbed his broken arm, limped to the doorway of the nearest store, and silently sank to the ground. I could hear him wheezing, his eyebrows knitting together in pain with each breath.

Emilia looked at me, sweating, still reeling from what had just happened. I pressed my lips together, then walked to Leo's side. In the distance, I heard the whistle—the train. We'd missed it. Emilia closed her eyes and exhaled, defeated.

"Let me see your arm," I told Leo flatly. He glanced up at me, trying to hide the pain in his eyes. It didn't work, especially when he tried to lift his arm for my inspection.

"Stop, stop," I said, kneeling down beside him. I squinted—the light was dim here, the sounds of the revelry on the other side of the toppled wagon picking up. "It's broken."

"Clearly," he said through gritted teeth.

I ignored him. "I can set it."

"You can what?" he said, eyes widened. He pulled his arm away from me, crying out in pain as he did so. "You're not setting anything."

"I worked in a hospital ward with Olga Romanov for months," I said. "I can set it. Trust me. It's easy."

"Natalya," Emilia finally said. Her voice was shaking, but not weak. "Perhaps we should get out of the horrible alley before we set anything?"

"Of course," I said. "It's just . . ." I rose, looked down at Leo. "Can you walk?"

Leo nodded, went to stand, but doubled over clutching his ribs. Before I thought about it, I swooped in, relieved to see Emilia was doing the same. We each looped an arm under his shoulders, steadied him. He gave me a concerned look, like he was certain I was moments from breaking his good arm. I couldn't exactly blame him—I considered doing so. Perhaps I would have if I weren't becoming keenly aware of the scrapes on my own palms, the cuts and bruises swelling up across my body.

"Where are we going?" Emilia asked me. I wondered that she assumed I had a plan.

"How far are we from the Babushka's house?" I asked Leo.

"Not far," he muttered. "You two doubled back on yourselves."

I exhaled. "All right. Come on."

# CHAPTER FOURTEEN

"Ready?" I asked, grimacing as I looked at the blue, swollen spot near Leo's elbow. He was down to a thin undershirt, the sleeve of which we'd rolled up as high as possible in order to see the break better. Despite the fire we'd built in the hearth, he was shivering from the combined cold and pain.

"There's no vodka," Emilia called from the kitchen, letting a cabinet slam shut. "Sorry. I looked everywhere." She didn't sound terribly sorry, which seemed quite reasonable.

"Figures," Leo muttered. He gave me a hard look. "How bad is this going to hurt?"

"More than stubbing your toe, less than getting shot. You're a wrestler, I thought you'd be better with pain."

"I'm terrible with pain," Leo admitted. "That's why I just *win* at wrestling before I get hurt. Are you sure you know what you're doing?"

I didn't answer; instead, I grabbed Leo's forearm and pressed hard against it with my thumbs. He jerked in pain, howled loudly, then fell backward as I pulled my hands away. He heaved himself to sitting, beads of sweat rolling down his face.

"I always had a knack for setting breaks," I said, smiling at my andiwork. Emilia walked to my side, handed me a kitchen towel, nd helped me fashion it into a sling. Leo watched us, at first ıspiciously, but then as if he suddenly could think of nothing at all ) say. I rose, aware of how I was now unnecessarily close to him, ıd sat in one of the rocking chairs. Leo remained by the fireplace, ack pressed against the wall as Emilia stoked the fire. She and I ere barefoot, our heels wrapped in cold compresses to help the velling go down.

We were silent for a long time, during which Emilia brought ver hot water with lemon in it for me, though the lemon was old ıd hardly flavorful enough to make it taste like anything. She sat ɔwn on the edge of the Babushka's bed, held her cup tightly in her ınds to warm her palms.

"So," Leo said, slumping down even more against the hearth. You ran."

Emilia and I stayed silent; I sat up straight in the rocking chair. he three of us were at an impasse, one I knew we all recognized. milia and I couldn't allow Leo to tell the Reds about our escape. ɛt we clearly weren't built for this end of Saint Petersburg. Yes, caping again would be easy enough—especially with Leo's arm ırt—but making it far with our virtue intact felt impossible.

Leo adjusted the sling, fidgeted for a few moments like he wasn't ıite sure what to say. "I can't believe you fit through the window. akes me look like a complete fool." He paused, met my eyes as he lded, "I wouldn't want anyone to find out, in fact, what an idiot vas."

"That would be embarrassing, indeed," I answered, the tiniest

bit relieved. That was settled, at least—he wasn't planning to tell th
Reds about our escape. There was no need to worry about Emil
being sent to the Fortress.

"So," Leo said cautiously. "We'll need to leave early, tomorro
to catch the morning train to Moscow." He said this in a stilted wa
an unspoken threat in his voice—that while he wouldn't tell tl
other Reds this time, if we refused to go, he'd have no choice bu
to report us.

But our plan could still work, perhaps. We could find Emilia
uncle when we arrived, hand Leo over, go get the Constellatic
Egg from the Babushka. It was even better than before, actually;
meant Leo would pay for kidnapping us instead of running free
Saint Petersburg. I nodded, then glanced at Emilia meaningfull
she quickly looked away, but it was clear she understood that v
weren't going along as placidly as it might look.

"Just don't run again," Leo said, interrupting my though
"This area isn't safe for anyone, but especially people like you.
can't protect you if you don't stay with me."

"And what if I don't want your protection?" I asked, raising
eyebrow.

"Maybe you don't want it, Miss Kutepova, but right nc
you need it. Perhaps one day you won't and we'll reevaluate t
arrangement."

"I look forward to it," I said briskly, and Leo almost smiled, b
stopped just short.

"What's this?" Emilia asked. She motioned to an assortment
bags at the foot of the bed, partially hidden by blankets. In a n
created by the folds was a kerchief with a half-dozen vegetables

carrots, beets, potatoes, all of which were small and scraggly-looking. Still, I couldn't remember when I'd been so happy to see a carrot. My stomach rumbled—we hadn't eaten since the tailor's.

"Food," Leo said, sounding strangely embarrassed. "I got it while I was out."

"We can make soup!" Emilia said. "I saw a pot."

The glee in her voice broke me a bit; to be so happy over making a meager meal, while kidnapped, after nearly being assaulted . . . it seemed especially sad. Leo gave me a grim look, and for a moment I felt a certain strange solidarity with him in our shared pity for Emilia. I rose, followed her to the kitchen where she fumbled with a pot of water. Neither of us knew much about cooking—we'd never needed to, before—but we managed to break the vegetables into pieces and throw them in boiling water.

"You should add some spices," Leo suggested. He was still sitting by the fireplace, but had moved to face us. He shrugged—wincing, since it pulled at his broken ribs—then added, "Pepper, salt, maybe some basil. Whatever's there." Emilia paused, then began opening the dozens of tiny ceramic containers that lined one side of the kitchen. She dashed them into the pot with a manic vigor, brown hair falling from its pins. I couldn't tell if she was moments from laughing or crying as she stirred the pot slowly.

"There," she said after fifteen minutes. "It's done."

"How do you know?" I asked.

"I have no idea," she said. "But it's something, at least, isn't it?"

There was only one soup bowl in the house, which Emilia gave to me, offering to eat out of some sort of wide-mouthed mug herself. I glanced at Leo, who was studying his sling again; Emilia inhaled, dropped a serving—a small serving, but a serving—of soup into some sort of gravy boat, and walked it over to Leo. Emilia avoided his eyes, handed the gravy boat over, then joined me in the rocking chairs. I sipped at a spoonful of my soup.

"This tastes like tea," I said, frowning.

"I think some of the spices *were* teas," Emilia answered. "The Babushka really should label things better."

"I reason she didn't anticipate strangers making soup in her house," I said.

"That makes two of us," Leo answered, sipping his. It wasn't good—not by a long shot—but it was something: it was food, it was warm, and it suddenly felt like all I needed in the world. I felt myself relax.

*No. You don't get to relax until the egg is found. Until you and Alexei are together, forever, and the crown is safe in Romanov hands.*

*Which will happen. Once you get to Moscow.*

Emilia fell asleep quickly. I wanted to follow suit, but my mind was too crowded despite the burning exhaustion in my eyes. I sat in the rocking chair, flipping through one of the Babushka's cheap serial novels, the sweet sort with obsessive lovers and fearless heroines. I kept turning the pages even though it was hard to hold the thin book aloft; my arms were tired, my feet were still wrapped in now room-temperature rags, and my hand ached from punching the bo in the alley.

Leo was trying to get comfortable leaning against the hearth—if anyone could find a wall of stones cozy, it'd be him, and yet h appeared to be struggling. He twisted to one side, which apparentl tweaked his arm. He winced, clutched it, uttered curses as the pain subsided.

"It'll get worse before it gets better," I said. "Especially your ribs. The bruises really come out the second day."

"Perfect," Leo said, gritting his teeth as he shifted positions again. "What about the third day?"

I frowned. "Most patients said it became a dull ache after the third day. Except the ones who had their arms amputated."

"You know how to amputate an arm?" Leo said. He was doing his best not to look concerned, but I could see fear in his eyes. Part of me wanted to relish it—after all, he'd caused us plenty of fear, but I'd seen fear like it before, dozens of times in soldiers at the hospital, and Leo's was just as disconcerting as theirs. Scared young men, younger than they looked, someone's lover, someone's brother, someone's son . . .

"Tell me you're not considering cutting my arm off," Leo said seriously.

"No," I answered, blinking. "I don't know how to cut your arm off. We were nurses, not surgeons."

"You and the grand duchesses?" Leo said. He studied his arm as he said this, like there was something interesting to be found in the makeshift sling.

"Just Olga and Tatiana," I said. "Olga asked all the young women at court to join her. I suspect it was her idea, in fact, to use the Winter Palace as a hospital."

"What about Emilia?"

I shook my head. "Emilia can't stand the sight of blood. Or the idea of bathing a man, or the idea of . . . dirt."

"I suppose that's not unexpected." He looked over at Emilia. "She has always seemed rather . . . delicate."

"Right," I said, though I couldn't decide if I was offended or not at being called indelicate by comparison.

"So that's where you learned to set broken arms," he continued, looking back to me.

"Set broken arms. Sew stitches. Patch burns. A handful of things," I answered.

"Did you like it?"

I inhaled, considered the question for a moment before answering. "I liked helping soldiers," I admitted quietly. "But so many came in with bullet wounds. Horrible, bleeding things." I cringed, looked at the fire. "There was this one, my first week there. He was shot in the stomach, and the blood came through the bandages. There was just so much, I kept putting more on and more on and he was fading in and out."

"What happened to him?" Leo asked.

"The doctors told me to move on," I said. "That it was hopeless and there were men who could be saved coming in. The other nurses—most of them were experienced, not nobles—they listened. But I kept putting towels on his stomach, and he kept waking up and looking at me." I stopped, looked down at the rocking chair, dragging my now-chipped and broken nails across its arm. "And then he died. Just like that, while my back was turned so I could get more towels. And then the man in the bed next to him died, and the man in the bed next to that."

"Sometimes," Leo said, voice strangely rocky. He took a breath. "Sometimes it's just too late."

I shook my head. "It was too late from the start. They never had a chance, not any of them."

"A bold thing for a general's daughter to say."

"A thing *only* a general's daughter could say," I corrected. "I may be a lady, but I know the difference between a Gewehr and a Karabiner. I can tell you about every major battle Russia has fought for the last hundred years. I was in Odessa, lived through the rebellion there. And I can tell you, without question, that it's too late for any man who goes to war. Even if he lives, he'll never come back the same."

I was always so darkly happy to know Alexei would never go to war—would never change, would never bleed, would never hurt. Yet still, every patient I saw in the Red Cross Hospital made me think of him. Every time I failed to heal those soldiers, I saw him in their eyes. Alexei had always existed to me as a boy who needed to be fixed. The boy I was prepared to spend a lifetime fixing. Perhaps the Constellation Egg changed my future every bit as much as the Reds did—because even if I did get the egg before the Reds, if the Romanovs stayed in power and I became Alexei's tsarina, the life I always anticipated would never happen. It would never be the same—because with the Constellation Egg, Alexei was no longer broken.

Leo exhaled loud enough that it jarred me from my thoughts, then spoke. "The story is that the egg is what healed the tsarevich. That it's the reason he's been so healthy lately." I didn't answer, but my silence confirmed Leo's suspicions. He looked down. "Lucky for him, I suppose, to have that power at his disposal. Unlucky for your soldier shot in the stomach that he wasn't born the tsar's son."

"I did everything I could for that soldier," I snapped.

"Perhaps you did," Leo answered. "But you've never wondered, Natalya, how fair it is that by virtue of being born lucky, you get to rule a country? To never get sick? To be blessed with something like the egg—"

"Fair?" I asked, shaking my head. "What makes you think the world is interested in fair, Mr. Uspensky? The world is the world, and we're cast in whatever roles we fall into. It's not my fault I was born wealthy any more than it's your fault you were born poor."

"So we should just accept our lot and move on?"

"That's not what I said," I answered. "You want to destroy a world of mountains and valleys to create a plain flat field."

"This isn't about mountains or valleys or whatever you're talking about. It's about the fact that we're expected to follow the laws, but have no role in making them. Pay taxes, but have no say in how they're spent. We're supposed to trust that a man who happened to be born luckier than the rest of us will do what's best."

"He's the *tsar,*" I said, my voice rising on the last word. I glanced at Emilia, waited to make certain I hadn't woken her. She was still, breath slow and even. I turned back to Leo, continued. "He was educated by the greatest minds of Russia. He's studied military strategy, agriculture, economics. Who would you trust more than him?"

"The soldiers," Leo said. "The farmers. The peasants."

"You mean people like Yuri?" I asked. "People like those drunks in the Winter Palace?"

"And people like me," he said.

"Not your soundest argument, as you're my kidnapper," I reminded him.

"People like *you*," he added, interrupting me. "Not you as Alexei's fiancée. You as a person."

"I, as a person, trust my tsar," I said. Leo sighed, drummed the fingers of his good hand on the hearth.

"Perhaps we're too different to ever agree," he said. "I used to think anyone could be convinced. That people like you just needed to have it explained. That people like you didn't understand, but could." He looked up at me; the flames made his eyes look more orange than gray. "But I suppose you thought that about the Reds as well."

"I thought the Reds loved Russia," I said coldly. "I see I'm wrong."

Leo firmed his jaw, somehow making it even more square. He inhaled deeply and looked over at Emilia, like he wanted to yell but was torn over waking her. Finally, he shifted, laid down in front of the hearth, his back to me. He bent his good arm up under his head as a makeshift pillow.

"Good night, Miss Kutepova," he said swiftly.

I rose, was about to turn when a strange shadow caught my eye. Something just outside the kitchen window, bouncing in the breeze, almost like a lantern. I frowned, walked closer—was it a person? An animal? It cast strange shapes along the kitchen floor in the moonlight. I reached the kitchen, pressed my palms against the freezing window to look out.

The back garden was frosted over, everything coated with tiny threadlike icicles. Except for the thing creating the shadow: a single sunflower. Tall, its stem bright green, thick leaves and a dark brown face curved up toward the moon, like the flower was watching it move across the sky. Rows and rows of fat yellow petals that faded to orange as they neared the flower's center rustled in the wind, velvety and warm-looking.

I frowned, stepped back from the window. *They were all dead earlier, weren't they?* I was sure of it. Yet here it was, alive.

Alive despite the cold.

# CHAPTER FIFTEEN

Emilia and I woke to the sound of the Neva lapping at its banks, angry with the light rainstorm that had descended upon Saint Petersburg. I blinked, searched for Leo—he wasn't by the fire, where I'd last seen him. Had he decided to go tell Viktor about our escape after all?

"We'll need to leave soon," Leo said, voice low. I snapped my head around, realized he was peering out the window we climbed through yesterday. I felt my heart jump—did he see the sunflower? How could he possibly miss it? It had been right in the window last night. I hadn't told him about it, hadn't even woken Emilia to tell her. What made it bloom in the cold? Maybe it was because the Constellation Egg had been in this house; maybe it was the mystic herself, I had no idea. Either way, I didn't understand it enough to inform Leo or to frighten Emilia. Leo stepped away from the kitchen looking bored.

"What were you looking at?" I asked, so quickly that Leo tried to lift an eyebrow. He was met with little success, as that eye was still a bit swollen. I was impressed, though, that it hadn't blackened entirely.

"The Neva," he said. "It looks miserable."

I exhaled—so the sunflower was gone. I found myself suddenly wondering if it had really been there to begin with. Did I imagine it? I frowned, put a hand to my temple. My movement woke Emilia. She yawned, tossed a bit, and sat up beside me, hair a knotted mess. She sighed, as if she had been dreaming of someplace else, and straightened her dress.

"When we get to Paris, Natalya, the first thing I'm doing is getting a silk robe and wearing it for a month and a half," she said. "No, wait—the first thing I'm doing is taking a bath. The sort where they fill the bathtub with milk."

I reached under my own dress and tugged at the corset I was still wearing. The boning was forgiving, much better than the stiff sorts some of the older women wore, but it was still uncomfortable, especially after several days straight of wearing it. From the wiggling Emilia was doing, I suspected hers had spun around her body during the night. She stopped, scowled, then looked at Leo.

"Turn around," she barked, and he obeyed so quickly that I'm not sure who—Leo or me—was more surprised. Emilia turned, motioned for me to unbutton the back of her dress. I did—one of the plain black buttons fell off in my hand—and she then reached underneath it, began twisting and turning and, before I knew it, pulled the corset through the skirt.

"Oh, thank God," she said, inhaling deeply and flopping back on the bed. She stretched her arms above her head till they struck the stone wall that served as a headboard. "Want me to do yours?" she asked when I buttoned her back up.

"I . . ." Did I want to be parading about in a dead maid's dress without underwear? No, not at all. But I wanted to breathe, and to release the pressure on my ribs. I sighed, looked at Leo, whose back was still turned. "All right."

It was a tremendous relief, I had to admit. When Leo finally turned around, he frowned as he surveyed us.

"What changed?" he asked.

"This is why men wear the same suit over and over," Emilia muttered.

It was perhaps more difficult to fold up the corsets and leave them behind than it should have been—it felt like we were stripping away one of our last bits of home, of our real lives. But we did, tucking them in one of the Babushka's drawers while Leo watched like he was experiencing some strange ritual.

"Right," he said when we were done. "Come on. We've got to leave if we want to catch the nine o'clock train."

"Should we wash the soup pot?" Emilia asked, looking in the kitchen. I could tell she was hungry again—I certainly was. In a way, it would have been easier to just keep on with the hollow, starved feeling, as now the soup felt like a taunting memory.

"I think she'll forgive us for leaving things a bit messy," Leo said. I thought the words were sarcastic, but when I looked at him, his face carried none of the mockery I expected. I frowned, walked to the glass by the front windows, and used the reflection to pin my hair neatly.

"You're doing that?" Emilia asked, frowning at me. "Should I?"

"Not much point," Leo said. "No one's going to see us on the train."

"Someone's always watching, especially when you're at your least attractive," Emilia said, which was something she used to tout as an excuse to wear ball gowns to tea. She sounded halfhearted now, though, not like she didn't believe it to be true, but like she believed it to be more true than ever. Emilia yanked her hair up, pulling it into a twist so halfhearted that she looked like one of the ladies who always drank too much at state dinners.

"So we're ready then?" Leo asked shortly, walking to the door. He was still wheezing a bit, though it sounded better than yesterday. He opened the door, looked outside, then turned back to us.

"Don't run," he said testily, though it was as much a question as a statement.

"We won't," I answered. And it was true—what would be the point? Like it or not, we needed Leo's help to get through Saint Petersburg; we'd likely need him in Moscow as well. At least, up until the point where we turned him over to Emilia's uncle.

We began to walk, the mist of early morning sweeping across the streets before us. The rain had left the roads glistening and the canals fuller than normal. We were headed back into the main stretch of Saint Petersburg, toward Nevsky Prospekt, the road Emilia and I were searching for during our failed escape attempt. It was a road we were familiar with—that everyone was familiar with, as it cut straight through Saint Petersburg, through Upper Nevsky, ending at the Winter Palace. It was always busy, and today was no exception; in fact, it was disconcerting how quickly people seemed to be returning to errands and trips and work. The red and yellow streetcars were stalled on their tracks, but people were merely walking around them, like they were new monuments instead of victims of the revolution.

Then there were the Reds. There were dozens—most Leo's age, some shabbily dressed and others, I suspected, not much worse off than the nobility. They chanted about victory, about the end of tsar oppression, about the new order that would fall into place as soon as Lenin arrived in Saint Petersburg. Emilia and I immediately ducked our heads as we approached them, and I noticed Leo tried to cross the street whenever one was ahead of us. They didn't seem angry, like they did the night of the riot, but excited, cheeks flushed and eyes shining.

"Don't say anything," Leo said under his breath suddenly, as we approached the side of a closed leather shop.

"To who?"

"Finally," a new voice said. "You're late, Uspensky. You were supposed to check in ten minutes ago." It took me a moment to find the speaker in the sea of bodies, and a moment longer to place the man—it was Yuri, perhaps the only Red I currently hated more than Viktor. Emilia sunk a little, looked at me warily.

"Yuri," Leo said firmly. "You can tell Viktor all is well."

"I will," Yuri said with a sort of sneer. "And I'm here to take the spare."

"What?" Leo asked, blinking. People were looking our way now, mild curiosity threatening to become real interest.

"The countess," Yuri said, voice brimming with disdain for Emilia's title. "You don't need to worry about two girls on a train. What did you do to your arm?"

Emilia took a sharp breath in, but held her ground, looking firmly ahead—it impressed me and seemed to shock Leo, who looked back at her like he anticipated more fainting. He turned back to Yuri, who looked irritated to have been assigned girl-prisoner duty.

Leo cleared his throat as I linked my arm tightly around Emilia's.

"It's fine, Yuri. I can control these two. Obviously," he said, motioning to the fact that we were standing so near him. "They're noble girls, not escape artists."

Yuri frowned, looked from Emilia, to me, to Leo. "Then how'd you hurt your arm?"

"I didn't," Leo said swiftly, reaching up and yanking the sling off. His arm dropped easily, and I knew the pain had to be intense. He didn't grimace. "I heard the trains are packed. Figured an injury and two girls might get me a free seat, since we don't exactly have the money for tickets."

"Oh!" Yuri said, nodding like this was obvious. "Still, though—Viktor wants the countess back."

Leo shook his head, stepped between Emilia and Yuri. "Trust me on this. They're easier to handle together—as long as I've got one, the other stays. You take the countess and I'll have a harder time controlling Miss Kutepova."

"What am I supposed to tell Viktor?"

"Tell him I'll be back tomorrow," Leo said brightly, then reached forward and clapped Yuri on the shoulder. Yuri looked unconvinced, but extended an arm and grabbed Leo's shoulder tightly, familiarly. I saw the faintest idea of a grimace on Leo's face; then Yuri dropped his hand and uneasily retreated. Leo watched him go for a moment, then winced and backed up to the leather shop, clutching his bad arm with the other hand. I snatched the sling from him and roughly reassembled it, ignoring the curious looks of passersby.

"Thank you," Emilia told him, though she seemed conflicted about saying it. Leo looked equally conflicted about answering, and opted to hold his tongue.

The train station was ahead, across from a massive church with domed towers. The Nicholaevsky Station was certainly one of the busiest in the city, and likely the most beautiful. It was two stories tall and painted pale peach. Enormous Venetian windows with white panes lined the upper level, and in the center of the station was a clock tower that stretched high into the cloudy sky. The lower story had a half-dozen or so doorways with crisp white arches above them, each capped with a little circular window, like a porthole no one could reach. People were filing in and out, mostly workers and merchants. Leo gave Emilia and me a harried look as we grew closer.

"We're going to sneak on the passenger train. Just get on, take a seat, and we're on our way. They key is to look like you know what you're doing. Think you can handle it?"

"My dear Mr. Uspensky," I muttered, "we're from the Russian court. We're excellent at looking like we know what we're doing."

We made our way into the station, Emilia and I pushing together to avoid the elbows and bodies of men who smelled like sweat and vodka, young women with smudges on their faces and kerchiefs holding their hair back. Everyone seemed to want out of the city, something that I could tell discouraged Leo—perhaps his revolution wasn't as popular as he hoped. I looked up at the ceiling, arced high above, a space that looked strange and empty compared to the sea of humanity around us. There was a roaring sound, screeching, the thrumming of a train pulling in. People milled about, rushed toward it—Leo grabbed my hand, met my eyes, and quickly switched to my wrist; I took Emilia's hand, and we hurried with the crowd. The train came to a stop; its whistle blew deafeningly.

"Back! Back!" someone shouted as soon as the whistle subsided.

The crowd stopped; disapproving mumbles rushed across us. I stood on my toes to see what the problem was. The conductor stood in a smart blue uniform, holding a gun above his head so the crowd could see it. "Ticketed patrons only," he shouted. "Ticketed patrons only! We will be checking! Ticketed patrons only!" My eyes ran along the various cherry-red cars I could see—there were railway employees at the door to each, all with guns drawn, hands extended for the precious tickets that so few in the crowd had to offer.

Leo cursed, released my wrist, and put his hands on his head. Emilia gave me a worried look.

"Lady Kutepova?" a quiet voice said, an old voice—one with the lilt of aristocracy. "Lady Natalya Kutepova? Is that you?"

I spun around, eyes wide; my gaze fell on an older man with practiced posture and a lifted chin. A woman was on his arm, dressed not unlike me—in a maid's dress that was slightly small, with skin and nails far too flawless to belong to any *real* maid. Leo shifted but was unwilling to make a scene by pulling us away.

"Count Demidov," I said, alarmed. He looked side to side nervously when I said his name, pulled the gray-haired countess closer. "I'm sorry," I continued. "I'm just so surprised to see you here."

"It's understandable," the count said. "We are, indeed, alarmed to be in such a state. We should have gone to England months ago. Poor Russia. Poor Nicholas—"

"I'm sure Russia will prevail," I said. Leo caught my eyes and gave me an exasperated look. I added, "She always does."

"Of course, of course," the countess said, though she looked at me worriedly. "Darling . . . you have heard, haven't you? The rumor?"

"There are so many," I answered. "One loses track."

"They're saying . . ." The countess caught the count's eye for a long moment, one in which I felt my heartbeat quickening. "They're saying that Nicholas abdicated the throne to try to please the Reds. That Alexei is the tsar now."

"Oh, I . . ."

These were the only sounds that made it from my lips. The only words my mind could form. It couldn't be real, it couldn't be true. Nicholas would never abdicate, he'd said so a thousand times—what sort of sovereign walks away from his throne? But of course, he could never have known his family would be kidnapped. Be put in so much danger. Held hostage. How did the Reds break him? I whirled around to look at Leo, hoping for some sort of confirmation that this rumor wasn't true, but I found him avoiding my eyes, which answered my fears.

"Alexei is the tsar?" Emilia murmured, shaking her head. I closed my eyes, tried to slow the swiftly tilting world beneath me. This wasn't how it was supposed to happen—wasn't how he was to become the leader of Russia.

*It doesn't matter. You and Alexei will be together, in the end. That's what the fortune said. And if you get the Constellation Egg for him, he'll rule for a long, long time. It's a tsar's legacy that matters, not his coronation.*

Or lack thereof.

"Is that you . . . Emilia Boldyreva?" the countess said while I tried—and largely failed—to reason with myself.

"Yes ma'am," Emilia said. "Where are you traveling?" I opened my eyes again, looked down at my hands; my mind felt too muddled. *God help him.*

"We hoped to go toward Paris," the count said somberly. "But it appears few trains are running, so we thought we might be able to at least get to Moscow. The rail workers are still striking; only a few companies have working trains. They don't seem to care if you're Red or White, thankfully, but they don't even care if you've got four times their ticket price—"

"Hush," the countess said swiftly. "We'll be mugged."

"Of course, darling," the count said. He finally realized Leo was not merely another passerby, but was standing resolutely behind Emilia and I. "Do I know you from court, sir?" he asked, clearly trying to place Leo among the many young nobles. It was a silly endeavor—Leo was twice the size of the noble boys. Even the noble boys in the military were mostly cavalry officers, lanky things whose entire bodies could fit in the space of Leo's shoulders.

"I suspect not," Leo said politely. I thought it kind he didn't laugh at the prospect of being at court.

"Leo is not from . . . *our neighborhood*," Emilia said carefully, nearly bumping into the count as a woman with a baby wrapped in a coat brushed past. "But he's helping us to Moscow."

"Oh, quite good of him," the count said. "How pleasing to see there are still royalists among the . . . well. You know. I don't suppose you have a cigarette I might borrow, do you, boy? I didn't think to grab my rolling papers before we left the house."

"I'm afraid I'm fresh out," Leo said tartly, though he patted his coat pocket as if genuinely looking.

"Ah, well then. Good luck to you," the count said, patting me on the shoulder. "Perhaps we'll have tea in Paris sometime? I've a summer home there."

I blinked. "Perhaps," I said. The word was difficult to say, as my mind was preoccupied repeating the impossible over and over: *Nicholas has given up his throne. Alexei is the tsar. The tsar. The tsar.*

The count and countess gave me a meek look, then vanished, headed back to the ticket counter. The farther they got, the less I noticed their gait, their raised chins, their trimmed hair. The harder it was to tell they were any different from anyone else in the station.

"Natalya?" Emilia whispered. "Are you all right?"

"He can't be the tsar," I said, voice hoarse. I looked up at Leo, narrowed my eyes. "Why didn't you tell me?"

"I only heard it last night, while I was getting food," he said, holding his palms up. "I thought it might be a rumor."

"This isn't . . . this isn't how it was supposed to happen," I said, shaking my head. I'd pictured the day Alexei would become tsar plenty of times. I thought we'd be married, when it happened, and I'd be well practiced in the art of being a royal. I wagered Nicholas would die an old man, and Alexei would be strong, loved, respected, a powerful military leader, a cunning strategist. He'd be crowned amid pomp and circumstance, a day of parties and parades and dinners and dances. I'd be at his side, of course, the tsarina, wearing the old-style Russian gowns and walking hand in hand with him to the throne in the Winter Palace. Soldiers would march outside, precise, perfect, marvelous, and we'd set off fireworks over the Neva.

I didn't think it would happen while I stood in a crowded train station and he suffered at the hands of kidnappers.

Leo looked at the train. "We can't sneak on. Not with the security they've got today." He looked around the room anxiously, like a solution might be painted on the walls or the back of someone's coat. I ran my eyes again over all the cars. Passengers were now seated, watching with dismay as the crowd grew ever angrier that the trip was sold out. The conductor was still shouting, brandishing the gun, calling out, "Passenger cars one through ten, two hundred seats only!"

"Wait," Emilia said, her eyes lighting. She spun to me. "Passenger cars."

"What?" I asked, dazed.

"Passenger cars," she said, nearly shaking me to snap me back to life. It worked, reminded me that standing here in a train station feeling overwhelmed did nothing for Alexei. He was the tsar now—keeping the egg safe for him was more important than ever.

"Passenger cars . . . I . . . oh!" I said, blinking as I realized what Emilia meant. We glanced at Leo, then hurried away, leaving him no choice but to follow. We ran down to the first floor, where the noise dropped off considerably and people were wandering about, like they'd given up. We walked outside, into the gray, and started around the side of the building. Leo was pleasantly silent as we guided him down the side of the building, to a smaller street and—

"I don't think the tsar's private car is attached this time around," Leo said witheringly as he saw where we were headed. It was the tsar's personal platform, a house-sized building that looked like a miniature version of the station. On the awning there was a bent, torn bit of metal where the rioters tore down the Romanov crest. The doors were smashed and open, but the interior was surprisingly untouched—I suppose the Reds had the Winter Palace's wine cellars to raid, after all. The space was simple, with inlaid wood floors and a high cupola in the center of the ceiling, where arched windows let in the scant daylight. On the far end was a portrait of Peter the Great; on the other, an oil painting of Nicholas, each with slim claw-foot tables underneath them. How did I never notice, before, just how much Alexei looked like his father?

"Now what?" Leo asked.

"Now we get on the train," I said, walked out onto the platform. The cars here were freight cars, and there weren't many at that. Up the tracks, where the main station was, we could still hear the dull sound of the angry crowd. But back here? It was strangely silent. I turned to Emilia, who looked less enthusiastic when she saw the empty freight car before her.

"We should get in that one," Leo said, nodding to the second-to-last car. "People will be trying to hop on the last one, if the station's any indication." He walked forward and heaved the rolling metal door open.

There were several chained up wooden crates inside labeled *Thirteen-Inch Gaslight Mantles*; I hesitated in the doorway until Leo walked around to the far side and confirmed no one was lurking behind them. Other than that, the boxcar was exactly what one would expect a metal box to be—loud, cold, and smelling slightly of fish. Far ahead, the train whistle blew—we'd be moving soon. The floor rumbled as the engines fired up. Leo moved to slide the door shut.

"Wait!" I shouted; my voice echoed a thousand times over, startling all three of us.

"It'll only be dark for a minute," he said impatiently. "We'll open it back up once we're out of Saint Petersburg."

"No, we won't," I said. "These things don't open from the inside."

"How would you know?"

"When I was seven, my father had a pony shipped to me when we lived in Odessa," I explained. "This little white horse. I ran into the car to see it while he signed the papers and the train lurched—the car slid shut with me in it. I had to wait for someone to come let me out."

Leo raised his eyebrows. "Oh." Emilia clutched her chest, horrified at coming so close to being locked inside.

The train began to ease forward. The tsar's platform disappeared, we passed by rocks and stray patches of grass, then the main platform in a whirl of gold and shouting. I saw surprised eyes catch the cracked boxcar door as we rolled past, but none were fast enough to do anything more than look alarmed. Leo was right—people screamed behind us, rushed for the final car. It was impossible to tell if anyone made it over the roar of the track under our feet, rising up through the crack in the door. And then we were suddenly out of the city. Buildings turned to trees, streets to smooth snow, shouts to the whistle of air.

I sat down beside Emilia across from the crates. "Don't worry," I whispered in her ear, confident Leo couldn't hear me over the noise. "It's a one-day trip. One day until we're in Moscow. Does your uncle still patrol the square, by the Kremlin? He talked my ear off about it at the last ball." I tried to make the last bit sound playful, the gossipy sort of tone Emilia usually loved.

"He does," Emilia said faintly. I could tell the realization that we were about to traverse the Russian countryside in a boxcar was just hitting her. Her eyes were wide, her face pale, and every time the car jolted, she cringed.

"We'll lead Leo straight to the square then. We'll find your uncle—he'll arrest Leo, we'll go get the Constellation Egg from the Babushka, and the Romanovs will have Russia forever."

"And Paris," Emilia said dreamily, and I got the impression that this, this idea, this place to go, was the only thing keeping her from tears. "Paris."

I nodded, but truthfully, I was more focused on Russia.

## CHAPTER SIXTEEN

The longest train ride I'd ever taken was to visit a cousin who lived on the edge of Siberia. I was in a luxury car, one with its own butler, and there was tea and coffee and the perfect, beautiful Ural countryside to take in, all rocky crests and trees and snowdrifts. The sun would break across the horizon in the morning and light the land up, and we would see wolf packs running among the trees, in a dance with one another and the cedar forests. It was a nine-day trip, but when I got off the train, it felt like it had been a single day at the most.

It had only been a day and a half on this train, however, and it already felt like a month. My body was numb, like all my corners had been filed down by the constant vibrations, and it felt like I had a permanent layer of silt and dust caked on top of my skin. We were moving slower than expected, creeping along at times, to the point that every so often, we debated the merits of getting out and walking alongside the train. So far, fear that the train would suddenly pick up speed and leave us stranded in the wilderness outweighed our desire to escape, but by the second day, I wasn't sure how much longer we could go without breaking—my head ached, and I was starving, hollow with the feeling of nothing but freezing air in my torso.

The sky was blue, crisp, and clear; we could see leafless trees that stretched out like wooden skeletons for miles. When the afternoon sun was just setting, we pulled the door open far as it would go to let a beam of golden sunlight in. If we sat three abreast on the wall opposite the door, each of us could sit in the light and warm up, if only the tiniest bit. Even in the sun, I felt cold to my core, like my bones had been turned to metal rods in my skin. Every jolt, every bump sent pain rippling up through my body, and my teeth ached from being rattled together for so long.

"Remember that time . . ." Emilia began as she slumped down on the wall between me and Leo. She stopped speaking, closed her eyes, and the sun made her lashes sparkle, like the memory of warmth. I got the impression that as cold and miserable as I was, she was colder—it worried me, to say the least. After a deep breath, one that reemerged as a puff of cold air from her lips, she continued, "That we traveled to Moscow in a boxcar, Natalya? And we were stranded in the country for weeks and weeks?"

"I seem to recall it," I answered, tilting my head down to rest it on her shoulder even though it made my neck stiff. My throat was raspy, protested conversation, and my lips were so chapped that speaking made them crack and bleed.

"They must be checking the tracks," Leo said hoarsely, staring straight ahead. There were dark circles under his eyes. "Making sure no one tore them up to slow down the Reds. Or the Whites. Or whomever. I don't even know anymore."

"I'm hungry, Natalya," Emilia said. Her voice sounded almost feverish.

"Me too," Leo said. "If we'd stop, I could get off, maybe find . . . something."

"Like what? Ice?" I asked disparagingly.

"Roots. Plants. I'd eat a rabbit raw at this point, if I could catch one," he said, and I hated to nod in agreement.

"When we get out of all this," Emilia said, "we're going to have an incredible story. Can you imagine sharing this with Paris society? We'll sound like . . . like Amazons."

"Amazons in a train car," I said, though her words worried me. After all—the Babushka foretold Alexei and I would be together. All she foretold for Emilia was a train ride, *this* train ride. From the faint blue of Emilia's lips, I worried it was because she had little future after this.

I scraped my fingers on the rough side of the boxcar as I rose, then walked to the train door and peered at the ground racing by below. It became a blur of rocks, with thick icicles hanging down underneath our car. There was a lake ahead, and a bridge to carry us over it, pale green steel that crisscrossed itself a thousand times like a card tower being stacked in the sky. The train began to squeal, slow down again. I grabbed hold of the doorframe to steady myself as we rolled to a crawl.

Leo cursed. "Enough." He rose, pausing to steady Emilia, who was looking faint, then walked to the chained up crates of gaslight mantles. He bounced back and forth on his toes a few times then ran forward, kicked one solidly right by its edge.

The crate rocked gently, but other than that hardly moved. Leo, however, fell back, grabbed his leg in pain. His voice ricocheted off the walls of the boxcar, and his writhing upset the injury to his ribs, which made him howl even louder. Emilia clamped her hands over her ears.

"Are you trying to fight a piece of timber?" I snapped. "Sit down! I'm not setting any more bones."

"I'm not trying to fight anything," Leo said through gritted teeth. He winced and used the back wall to climb to his feet. "I'm breaking apart the wood to burn for a fire. Maybe they even pack the oil with the gaslight pieces . . ."

"We're building a fire in a train car?"

"I'll starve to death or freeze to death, but not both," Leo said. "I've got a few matches from that girl in the market. This stuff would burn easily."

"Someone will see the smoke," I said, shaking my head. "We're going to get caught."

"*Freeze or starve*, Miss Kutepova," he said, grimacing, and ran at the crate again.

"Or I could help," Emilia said gently. Leo skidded to a stop at her words, this time crashing into the side of the crate with his bad arm. He winced, clutched the arm, and hobbled back to the patch of sunlight in defeat. Emilia's shadow stretched over the car as she walked up to the crate and drew the pins from her messily done hair. She slid them into the lock; it took her longer this time, I suspected because her fingers were so numb. Eventually, the lock fell, a loud *clunk* that reverberated across the floor. The chain unraveled, clinking along like heavy coins falling, then crashed to the floor as well. Leo rose, gave Emilia a grateful, somewhat embarrassed look, then easily pulled the front panel of wood down.

"Oh my God," Emilia whispered, voice barely audible above the rackling sound of the train. "Am I hallucinating?"

"The crate says it's gaslight mantles," Leo said, shaking his head like he too thought he might be seeing things. He hoisted up the wood panel he was holding, read the label, then dropped it back down. "But . . . am I crazy, or is that—"

"Food!" Emilia exclaimed.

"Well, sort of," I said, walking forward and running my fingers over the hundreds of shiny turquoise tins, stacked evenly to the very top of the crate. It was a logo I recognized: a fish leaping over yellow block letters that read *Fine Beluga Caviar.* I'd had it hundreds of times at parties, luncheons, fancy dinners, though it was something that usually garnished platters of sugared fruits and fancy cheeses. I looked over at Leo. "I guess we'll be freezing to death, rather than starving."

Leo reached forward, grabbed a tin from the top, and pulled it down. It was the size of his palm, and he stared down at it like it was something wondrous. "In the middle of a revolution, they're trying to smuggle caviar into Moscow?"

"What would a revolution be without a party?" I muttered. Emilia joined us, pulled one down for herself, and immediately wedged her thumbs underneath the lid to pry it off, shivering violently from excitement and cold.

"It's frozen on," she said, frowning. "That, or my hands are frozen off."

Leo tried to pry his open, though with his bad arm, I suspect Emilia came closer to actually breaking in. They turned to me in unison; Emilia held her tin out first. She dropped it into my hand, cold and heavy. I ran my thumb across the top, then clamped it between my palms, squeezed the sides, and—

“It won’t budge,” I said. “It hardly even feels like two separate pieces.”

I sighed, drummed my fingers on the tin, fought the urge to pry at it with my teeth. If we couldn’t twist them open, perhaps we could break the metal itself . . . I walked to the edge of the train, by the doors, and smashed the tin against the frame. Pain rocketed from my palm to my shoulder, a bright, stinging feeling. I shouted and dropped the tin, glared at it as I held my palm to my mouth and tried to warm my fingers. I turned back at Emilia; she looked like she would cry, if she had the energy, and Leo, who stared at the tin of caviar like it’d betrayed him. He gritted his teeth, stormed to the door, and slung the tin into the wilderness. It bounced off the ground then exploded open into the dirt. Leo and I groaned in unison.

I dropped down, letting my feet dangle off the edge of the train—something I never would have done the day before yesterday, but now seemed no more life-threatening than our current situation. I winced as my legs swung a little too far back, struck the icicles that coated the underside.

I frowned, looked at Leo, who was leaning against the doorframe beside me. He looked confused, especially when I suddenly swung my legs inside, spun around to my stomach, and grabbed underneath the train. I grabbed hold of the first icicle my hand slid across; it burned from cold, but I squeezed my eyes shut and pulled until it cracked from the metal undercarriage. I rose, kneeled by the door.

“Emilia,” I shouted—she was back in the sun, staring down at the tin of caviar in her hand. “Give me one.”

Emilia's brown eyes found me wearily. She looked at the icicle in my hand and slid the tin across the floor to me. I caught it, centered it just in front of my knees, then brought the icicle down hard in the center of the tin.

The icicle slipped from my hands as soon as it hit the metal. Worse yet, it didn't break through the tin, but rather dented it lightly. I sighed, lifted the tin, prepared to whisper words of concession. Instead, I blinked.

The edges—the edges had lifted. Like the point where the icicle struck was the center of a flower, the edged tilted up around it, breaking the seal. I grabbed it tightly and turned.

It opened.

The lid fell away so easily that for a moment, I couldn't process what had happened. But then I saw it, an even plane of tiny blue-black pearls, glossy and perfect. I stared, unable to move, unable to do anything until Leo began to laugh.

I looked up, alarmed. I didn't think he was actually capable of genuine amusement. But there he was, laughing loudly, cheeks flushing as he grabbed his broken ribs in pain, unable to stop. The car was moving so slow now that his voice overpowered the train, bounced around us, out and over the lake outside. It was bright, airy—it was a boy's laugh, not a Red's, and it shifted something in me that made it impossible for me to hold in the smile pulling at my lips. He wiped his eyes, shook his head and reached down. He took the caviar from my hands, then handed it to Emilia.

"Mr. Uspensky," she said, now grinning. "I'm so ashamed to admit I left my silver caviar spoon at home. Forgive my indelicacies?" She reached in with her fingers and scooped the caviar from the tin

It clung to her fingers like wet sand, the whole scene as unappetizing as I'd ever seen caviar and as unattractive as I'd ever seen Emilia. Leo didn't notice, however, as he was handing me another tin, then another. While Emilia ate with her hands, social graces be damned, I opened eight more tins. Leo rejoined Emilia in the patch of sunlight, the tins laid out before them like a feast. I ran my index finger through a tin, slumped down between them.

"This part," I said as I licked the caviar from my finger. I closed my eyes, relished the prospect of food for a moment before continuing, "we should leave this part out, when we tell it in Paris."

"I, on the other hand, will tell everyone about this. But no one's ever going to believe me," Leo said, finishing a tin. His hands were dotted in stray pearls, which clung stubbornly to his skin as he chucked the tin out the door and into the lake.

"I don't know, Leo," Emilia said. "Compared to the story about a magical Fabergé egg, this one might sound flatly sane."

## CHAPTER SEVENTEEN

Caviar, unfortunately, was not meant to be eaten by the tir It was a garnish, perhaps an appetizer at best. But an hou later, we'd eaten two dozen tins worth, washing it down with sno melted to water in our hands. Our fingers were stained gray and w were lying out across the boxcar floor, clutching suddenly swolle stomachs. Emilia, somehow, fell asleep, lying atop the remains c the crates to give her some small distance from the frozen floo Leo and I were awake, studying the fading light as the sun set o the far side of the lake. The train was clicking along slowly, at walking pace, but there was no getting out now—we were in th center of the bridge, with a respectable drop to the pale blue wat below.

"We should be there by now," Leo said, sighing.

"Believe me," I said, "I'm well aware. One time I was on a trai that made the trip to Moscow in fifteen hours."

"You go to Moscow that often?" Leo asked.

I frowned. "Not terribly often. Often enough to have assume we'd only be temporarily uncomfortable in a boxcar." I tried reposition my hand under my cheek to cut down on the train's vibrations, which were giving me a tremendous headache.

"This is the second time I've been on a train," Leo said after ausing for a moment. He shifted, sat up, rubbing his cheek. "First ime was when I came to Saint Petersburg from my farm. It's the nly city I've ever seen."

I lifted my eyebrows, tried not to let too much of the surprise egister on my face. "The sunflower farm?" I asked. I gave up trying o lie down, situating my dress under me to keep the cold steel from ouching my skin.

"We grew more than sunflowers," Leo said, sounding mildly lefensive. "We grew potatoes and wheat and raised sheep. But the unflowers were easiest, usually."

"Did you really pull the plow yourself?" I asked.

Leo looked at me hesitantly, then out the train door. "I have the cars to prove it."

I wanted to see them, but the idea of asking him to show me eemed lewd. Leo didn't speak for a long time, long enough for the rain to come to a complete, easy stop. We looked at each other, then ut across the lake. Everything was silent, quiet, still. We seemed to e surrounded by brown and gray fields, sandwiched between the lues of the sky and the lake; the only movement was the breeze unning across the grasses and dotted birch groves. I could still feel ie vibrations of the tracks in my feet and palms. Leo brushed a andful of stray hair from his face, then rose. He walked to the edge f the car, held onto the side, and leaned out.

"I can't even see the passenger cars," he said. "They're across ie bridge, around the bend."

"Can you see why we're stopped? Is there smoke?" I asked wondering if the train was broken.

"No," he said, looking back in at me. I had to squint to see him, as the sun was growing heavy in the sky just behind his head "There's nothing. Except . . . hmm." He leaned far out of the car and then, before I realized what he was doing, swung out and to the left, vanishing. I rushed to the door, looked over to see Leo clinging to a ladder that led to the top of the train.

"If there's ice on that, you're going to fall and die," I said.

"How lucky for you that would be," Leo answered, and began to climb, using his sling-arm for balance rather than support. There was, in fact, ice toward the top of the car; I saw him struggle with it for a moment, and held my breath until he regained his footing He vanished over the side, but I could hear his footsteps above my head on the roof.

I looked at Emilia, who was still sleeping, then up at the ceiling The view from there must be spectacular—and it seemed a shame to let only the Red see it. I walked back to the door, poked my head around the side to see the ladder. I extended my fingers—I could reach. I could easily reach, which was perhaps more disconcerting as it meant I had no excuse but cowardice—though that excuse was incredibly persuasive, especially when I looked down at the lake below. The fall might not kill me, but the freezing water certain would. My stomach twisted, nearly made me lose my balance.

"You can make it. Just don't swing too hard." Leo's voice w suddenly directly over me. He was crouched at the edge of the ca looking down. "I almost did. It's not as big a jump as you're afra it is."

“I’m not worried about the jump,” I grumbled. “I’m worried about the fall.” I held my breath, kept my eyes trained on the ladder, then swung out.

Leo was right—I hit the ladder easily, wrapped my other hand around the rungs. My fingers burned with cold, but I held fast, then began to climb. It took only moments to reach the top, which turned out to be the most frightening part. I grasped at the roof, crawled my legs up the final few rungs. My right boot heel suddenly slid out from under me, squealing along the ladder. I grabbed tightly to the roof, crooked my other foot to keep from sliding farther.

Leo dashed forward and grabbed my arms tightly. He didn’t need to—my foot found the support fast enough—but he hauled me up before I could tell him, sat me down atop the train as if I weighed nothing at all. There was a strange moment where I was in his arms, balancing myself. Leo made an apologetic sound in his throat, then stepped back, slinging his uninjured hand into his pocket. I stood with my feet apart, knees bent, arms out, afraid to budge.

Leo, irritatingly enough, didn’t seem fazed by the height at all, walking casually toward the center. I hobbled behind him, keeping my eyes locked on the metal ground to avoid tripping. It was warmer up here, at least, with the sun directly on us.

“You came all the way up here to stare at a boxcar?” Leo said. I sighed, looked up.

And immediately regretted having spent even a half-second looking at a boxcar instead of this view.

The sky stretched out forever, like a bowl of blue placed on top of us. The sun was setting in the gently sloping mountains on the horizon. Orange, gold, yellow, flickers of purple that glinted off a brush of snow in the fields that stretched for miles and miles. To the east, the fields faded into darkness, making it impossible to tell where the earth ended and the night sky began. This was not like the city, a place measured in blocks and buildings; it went on forever, went on longer than forever, and suddenly I felt very arrogant, to think myself anything grand compared to a place like Russia.

"A Fabergé egg to rule all this," I whispered under my breath.

"To rule, maybe, but not to tame," Leo answered, tilting his head back. We could see the ideas of stars in the sky, tiny flickers of light that were impossible to find on a second glance. "Being in Saint Petersburg, seeing *this* . . . it makes me miss Samara," he said.

"Why not go back there?" I asked.

"And leave this lovely train ride with you?"

I rolled my eyes at him. "You hate the tsar. You had a terrible job in the city. Why not go grow sunflowers again?"

At this point, something in Leo's face shifted. He let his eyes fall from the skyline, pried at a bit of the roof with his foot. "I left Samara because of my brother. I haven't gone back for the same reason."

"You don't . . . get along?"

"We get along fine—in some ways, better than ever," Leo said, hooking his fingers in his pockets and chuckling in an unamused way. "He's dead. He died at Tannenberg. You know of it?"

"Of course," I said, torn between being horrified at his joke and overwhelmed with pity. Everyone knew about Tannenberg. The Germans tore the Russian army apart so badly one of the generals killed himself rather than tell the tsar what happened. I suspected the horror stories of that battle were what made Olga insist on noble girls helping the Red Cross nurses.

"He should never have been there anyhow," Leo said. "He was older than me, but probably half my weight. And he was the sort always taking in dogs and birds and . . . God, even a snake once. He wrapped a bandage around its head and everything."

I smiled despite myself. "Why did he enlist then?"

"He didn't," Leo said. He took a deep breath, lifted his eyes to the horizon once more, like what he wanted to say was written in the trees. "He went to Saint Petersburg to try to find a better job—sunflowers didn't pay enough once nobles started leaving Russia. He got there, got a job—a good one, making guns for the war—but there wasn't any food. He'd go to work, and by the time the factories let out, all the shops were closed because there was nothing left to sell."

Leo now turned to me, though his eyes danced on and off mine. He licked his lips. "So he joined a group of Reds who wanted things to change. Who wanted the tsar to abdicate, wanted to create a government the people of Russia could trust. A few months later, the tsar's secret police showed up at his apartment, hauled him out, and stuck him on a train headed to the front with a car full of other prisoners. They threw him into Tannenberg without a gun. Told him to find a dead soldier and just take his."

Leo's jaw was stiff, his shoulders locked as he said this. I could tell he'd related this story dozens of times before, but also that the end never got any easier. Suddenly, I was the one with eyes dancing, unsure where to look.

"We didn't know any of that until I came to Saint Petersburg looking for him," Leo continued. "Another soldier remembered him and told me. I had to write my mother and let her know. I suppose the government didn't have time. We never even got his body back. He's just lying in a field somewhere, I suppose."

He wasn't in a field—as a general's daughter, I knew this. Leo's brother had been pushed into a mass grave, covered up, and abandoned without so much as a marker. I looked away, scared Leo might read this in my eyes.

"They opened new factories," I said meekly. "They made more guns. No one could have predicted the war would go like that—"

"You aren't going to convince me," Leo said, though his voice wasn't as cruel as I expected. "I know it's not Alexei's fault. Maybe it's not even the tsar's, deep down—maybe he didn't know how bad things were. But why would he? How could you know what suffering is, when you're sitting in a palace, graced by a powerful Fabergé egg? How can you know a soldier's suffering when your wounds always heal?"

"That's why you want the egg for the Reds so badly," I realized.

Leo shrugged, looked like he'd said too much. "You said it wasn't your fault for being born rich any more than it was my fault for being born poor. And you're right. But if we don't do anything to fix the world, if we just shrug and let children starve and soldiers die and people be treated like cattle . . . if we don't fix the world, Miss Kutepova, I believe it becomes our fault."

I opened my mouth—I could have argued. I could have argued for another day, another week, another month, such was my conviction that the tsar was Russia's rightful ruler, his reign inhibited rather than helped by the Reds. All my arguments, however, seemed very small, and I instead looked at my hands and said, "I'm very sorry about your brother."

"As am I, Miss Kutepova," Leo said. He nodded toward the horizon. "But, say I did leave Saint Petersburg eventually. I'd want a house right on that spot by the lake, near those trees. I'd be able to see the sun rise and set."

"It'd be lovely," I admitted. "It's the sort of place Alexei would like to live too. He and his father, they've always loved the country—" I stopped when I realized Leo was now looking away, his shoulders suddenly appearing to hang lower on his frame. "Sorry," I said quickly, though I wasn't entirely certain what I was apologizing for.

"It's fine," Leo said, but in a way that made me think it wasn't. "Maybe you and Alexei will live there together, someday."

"Perhaps."

"Tell me this, though," Leo said, turning to look at me. "You're afraid for Russia, but not for Alexei. Not at all. Why not?"

"Simple," I said. "The Babushka told me Alexei and I would be together when she read my tea leaves."

"And you believe her?"

"I watched a mystic's powers heal Alexei's hand, right in front of my eyes. If they can do that, they can read the future."

"What if that's not the future you want? Can you change it?"

I gave him a confused look. "Why wouldn't I want to be with Alexei?"

Leo shrugged. "I don't know. But there was a time when I thought my fate was to grow old and die on a sunflower farm—and I loved the idea of it. Now I think it's to help Russia become the country she's always been meant to be. The future I want has changed."

I considered this—it was so difficult to imagine Leo as a farmer.

"The Babushka said you can't change your fate. That no matter what, in the end, what will come will come," I finally said.

"Ah," Leo answered, looking at me. His face was a map of shadows and light, with darkness in the hollows of his cheeks and by his nose, but his eyes bright, sparkling in the sun. He said, softly, "I'm rather sad to hear that, Miss Kutepova."

I turned back toward the view, tried to quell the awkwardness spinning around us—miles and miles of unspoiled landscape, and still it felt like we were locked in a tiny room. "You know, if the Reds get their way and divide up everyone's money, you'll never be able to afford a house there."

Leo exhaled, smiled—really smiled, which was perhaps as alarming as his laugh. "Fair, Miss Kutepova. But what I want because of selfishness and what I want because I know it's right are two very different things. For example, if we're being entirely honest, there've been several times when I've wanted to throw you off this train." I folded my arms, dared him; he continued. "But I won't, because I know it isn't right."

"How generous of you," I said, releasing the smallest of laughs, relieved that the banter was back to normal. "I hope I have the moral fortitude not to roll you out the door in the middle of the night. But you know us nobles. Corrupt to the core." Leo grinned in response.

"Natalya?" Emilia's voice rose from beneath us. "Where are you?"

"On the roof," I said.

"Are you . . . coming down?" she asked warily. "Because I'm certainly not going up there."

"Yes," I said, though I immediately regretted it. I never wanted to come down, because up here, there was no revolution. There were no fires, no protestors, no divide between Russians. There was just space, space that looked plenty big enough for Reds and Whites.

Space that looked big enough for a hundred different fates.

I glanced at Leo, then started down the ladder.

# CHAPTER EIGHTEEN

Emilia and I huddled together that night, but the following evening, as we rolled along through darkened countryside, she was too cold for me to warm her. Leo and I exchanged worried glances as she struggled to uncurl her purple fingers.

"That's it," he said, shaking his head. He rose, walked to the opposite side of the car, near the broken caviar crates.

"What are you doing?" Emilia asked faintly.

"I misspoke earlier," Leo answered as he hauled wood from the broken crates into a pile by the door. The train was easing to a stop again, as it tended to do every few hours.

"About what?" Emilia asked him. Her nose was permanently red now, her cheeks sallow in the moonlight that filled the doorway where the sun once had. I imagined I looked similar, which was too unpleasant to think about for long.

"When I said I'd freeze *or* starve," he said, his voice coming from the pitch darkness on the far side of the car. "As it turns out, I don't much want to do either. We're building a fire." He emerged from the black, took the matchbox from his coat pocket, and opened it.

He looked up, face in shadow. "There are only three."

"Better than zero," I said. Leo nodded in agreement, then knelt down beside the pyre. He struck the match, keeping a hand over it to protect the flame from the wind.

It didn't take hold—there was no kindling, nothing to grab the flame. Leo frowned, then reached up and untied the sling on his shoulder. He winced as his arm relaxed, then opened and shut his fist. I could tell it still hurt—and he had no business taking a sling off so soon—but I kept my mouth shut. Leo balled the sling up and shoved it under a board, then struck the second match. Leo sighed, shook his head.

"It's the wood," he said. "They've coated it to keep it from burning. We need something else."

The three of us simultaneously looked out the boxcar door as the train fully stopped. It was quiet now, unsettlingly so, and the moon was so bright the forest looked gilded in silver. The field directly outside the boxcar was frosted—anything from the ground would be too wet to burn, I was sure, but within the trees, certainly there was *something* . . .

"No," Emilia said, folding her arms and turning to Leo. "Absolutely not. You'll get left behind, Leo, and even if you're a Red, I don't want you to freeze to death in the middle of nowhere."

"I wasn't going to suggest I go get firewood," Leo said. "I couldn't possibly carry enough on my own to even make it worthwhile."

"But . . . if all three of us went," I said.

Leo nodded. "Exactly."

"So we're *all* going to freeze to death?" Emilia moaned. She heaved herself to standing, walked to join Leo in the doorway; I was fast behind her. The three of us leaned out, looked down the line at the rest of the train, then to the trees. They were only a minute or two away if we ran, but it took far less time than that for the train to start up again.

"We stopped for hours yesterday," Leo said, though it sounded like he was trying to convince himself as much as Emilia and me.

"And minutes this morning," I said. We looked at one another.

"Freeze or starve, Miss Kutepova?" he asked.

"Neither," I replied. I walked to the edge of the car, sat down, and eased myself off.

The feel of real earth beneath my feet was astonishing. The ground was hard from cold, yet my heels felt wobbly and unstable, like I might sink into the soil at any moment. I took a step away from the train, trying to quell the panic that immediately rose within me—it was like swimming away from shore into dangerous waters. I turned back just as Leo jumped down beside me, making a guttural *welch* sound and clutching his ribs as he hit the dirt.

"Fine, fine," Emilia said, looking almost wistfully back at our miserable boxcar before slinking to the ground. It took her several deep breaths before she dared step away from it.

"All right," Leo said. "Let's just . . . walk fast."

No one moved.

"We'll be fine," I said, and to my surprise, I almost believed it. I exhaled, my breath a plume of fog at my lips, and started forward. Leo and Emilia followed. The train was silent behind us, strange black boxes against a silvery landscape. Frost crunched underneath our feet as we moved across the field, all of us waiting to hear the train's engines fire up, to turn and sprint back. We reached the edge of the forest and stopped, turned to look back at the train.

"You wait here," Leo told Emilia. "You can call for us if it looks like it's moving."

"Alone?" Emilia said, looking at the trees fearfully. The forest seemed like a simple thing from the train—a wall of bright white birch trees, something flat and unimposing. Up close, it was more like a cave that stretched forever, the remaining leaves waving in the breeze in a way that made it look like we were underwater. Everything felt *alive*, in a way that made my skin prickle.

"It'll be fine," I told Emilia, trying to mask the fear in my voice. "We'll be fine."

"Natalya . . ." Emilia said, shaking her head and looking from the forest to the train. "Be careful."

"We need to hurry," Leo said, then turned and walked into the forest. I smiled at Emilia, though I suspected the expression was lost to the dark, and went in after him.

The forest was quiet and cold, so much colder than the boxcar, like it was holding in the chill of the day. We navigated by patches of moonlight that broke through the trees, holding our arms out ahead of us like sleepwalkers through the dark bits. Leo ducked down every few yards and felt around at the base of the largest trees, searching for wood protected from the rain.

"Let me show you what to look for," he said, placing a warm hand between my shoulders to lead me into a patch of light. It was a broken branch, fallen but not rotted. "The outside's wet, but I can break this and get to the dry wood inside. So long as it's not rotted, it'll work."

"How many do we need?" I asked. In the moonlight, his eyes looked the same silver color as the frosted field.

"As many as we can carry," he said, giving me a dire look.

"All right," I said, jumping as something rattled in the trees behind me.

"And let's not go that way," Leo muttered. We stepped out of the light in the opposite direction of the noise.

We worked in silence, listening carefully for the sound of the train or Emilia's voice. The world was mostly still, and after a while, we began to stray farther and farther from each other, so focused on the task at hand that the eeriness of the forest faded away. My arm grew sore and tired from carrying the wood I'd collected—surely between Leo and I, we had enough by now to build a decent-sized fire? I looked back at him. He was a shadow in the darkness, his silhouette ruined by the branches poking out of it.

There was a fallen tree ahead. I could see its roots, pulled up from the ground when it fell, and found myself wondering if they were the same shade of ghostly white that the bark was. I stepped closer to see. I felt like a voyeur, staring at parts of the tree people weren't meant to see, cringing at the hairlike bits of root that hung amid clumps of dirt. I inhaled, and the scent of earth flooded my lungs.

The roots weren't white—they were brown, just like any other tree. I sighed, turned around, stepped toward the fallen limbs to salvage what I could for the fire.

My boot slid under an exposed root and I hinged forward. I tried to balance, but the armful of firewood was awkward in my arms. I tilted forward, everything I'd collected sliding from my hands. There was just enough time to turn my body and take the brunt of my fall on my side instead of my face.

"Are you all right?" Leo called, his voice far away.

"I'm fine," I shouted back, coughing to regain the breath that'd been knocked out of me. I sighed, glared at the fallen tree accusingly, and began to gather the wood I'd dropped, shaking stray hairs out of my eyes. I finally rounded it up into a pile, then went to lift it.

Something breathed.

Something breathed behind me, a snorted, rattled sort of breath, like a horse's. A crack, a shuffling sound.

I froze. My eyes were on the ground, my face turned the opposite direction. I needed to look, to see, to run, but I couldn't move, afraid even the slightest motion would spur whatever lurked behind me to attack. It took another breath. My stomach knotted, everything tensed so hard my knees began to shake. I opened my mouth, intended to scream, to shout for Leo, but no sound came out.

Another rustle of animal feet on the ground. It was getting closer, closer, and then a plume of fog floated by my face, the creature's breath. I wrapped my fingers tightly around the closest piece of firewood. I closed my eyes, summoned my courage . . . *If you can outrun the Reds in Saint Petersburg, you can outrun a monster in the forest.*

I flipped around, rising to my feet at the same time and stumbling backward. My arm was extended, ready to strike, prepared for teeth and fangs and blood, the cry of a wolf or the growl of a boar. My heart raced, my lungs tightened.

It was not a wolf. It was not a boar. It was certainly not a monster. Though it was terrifying.

It was an elk. Enormous, twice the size of any horse, larger than any animal I'd seen up close. A bright white hide, whiter than the birch bark—it looked like a phantom looming before me. Its head was lowered, gray nostrils flared as it snuffed at the ground. The elk took a small, uneasy step toward me, the hump on its back swaying as it did so. It wasn't until it moved that I truly saw its antlers—they were covered in brown velvet that blended in with the forest, wider than I was tall, so wide I couldn't see them in their entirety without turning my head.

I lowered my arm, let the stick fall. My heart was still beating fast, my feet frozen in place, but I no longer felt the horrible stillness, the utter fear that I was moments from dying. The elk lifted its head a bit—I flinched at how close the massive antlers were to my face—and looked at me through watery, soft black eyes. It stretched out its neck, inhaled, sniffing the air around me, then whined, a single, bright note that made my ears ring.

It edged closer, closer, till it was a wall of white in front of me, its sides rising and falling as it took deep, long breaths. Without thinking, I lifted a hand.

The elk jerked its head up; I yanked my hand back to my chest and cringed, certain it was going to trample me. But no—it bobbed its head before me, lips quivering, nose growing closer, closer, closer to my withdrawn hand until we finally touched.

A feeling raced through me, one I couldn't place at first—it was hot, liquid lightning rushing around my veins. It washed away my shaking, my fear, the frozen feeling in my feet. It washed away everything frightening about the forest. It wasn't a strange place. It was a place I knew, a place I knew well, despite never having been here before. The elk rubbed at my fingertips until I flattened out my palm against its wide muzzle, ran my hand up to the spot between its eyes where the hair splayed out in different directions. It stepped in closer, forcing its head over my shoulder. My hand moved, ran along the elk's thick neck, its antlers looming above my head like fleeced tree limbs.

My mind felt still, waiting, waiting for the moment I would understand. When it happened, I wanted to cry and smile at once; instead I turned toward the animal, let my forehead rest against it.

Alexei was the tsar.

Alexei loved me.

The Constellation Egg was working. *The tsar and those he loves.*

I healed fast, I wasn't as cold as I should have been, I wasn't *nearly* as hungry as I should have been. Frost melted, a dead sunflower sprung to life, and now the animals . . .

I had been a noble my entire life. I'd had fine dresses, furs, shoes, jewelry—most of what I owned was just as lovely as anything the grand duchesses had. I went on trips and lived in beautiful houses and ate expensive food. And yet, until this moment, I had never truly felt royal. I had never truly felt rich. And I had never truly felt unworthy.

The elk snapped its head up, snorted loudly at a sound in the trees. It jarred me back to reality. With the creature's head raised, I could easily see under its neck—Leo. His eyes were wide in the moonlight, his mouth open in fear. In his right hand, a stick broken off to a point, which he held aloft like a spear.

"Come to me," he murmured. It took me a moment to realize he was talking to me.

I shook my head, tried to find the words to explain—and yet, discovered I didn't want to. I didn't want anyone to know, anyone to realize that I was now a part of something so much larger than myself. Instead, I lifted my own hands, placed one on the elk's shoulder.

"He'll kill you if you don't move," Leo whispered. His voice was shaking—he was afraid, more afraid than I'd ever seen him. "Run. I'll distract him while you run . . ."

I ran my hand along the elk's shoulders, letting my fingers drag through the thick hair under its chin, then stepped away. Leo kept his eyes on the animal as I walked toward him. He flinched when the elk suddenly bugled, a high, haunting sound that echoed through the forest like a wail. I saw Leo's grip on the stick tighten.

I reached up, put my hand over his holding the makeshift weapon. Leo turned to me, furrowed his brow in confusion. I pulled his hand down gently, my eyes on his the entire time.

"It's all right," I said. "I don't need you to protect me, Leo." I wasn't sure I needed anyone to protect me ever again, though I was afraid to say so aloud. Leo seemed unconvinced, and put his other hand on my shoulder, guiding me toward him.

"What just happened?" Leo asked breathlessly, looking from me to the elk. It was slowly tromping away now, its massive antlers cracking against the lower branches of trees. It faded into the trees, swallowed by the black.

"Nothing," I said swiftly. I realized my hand was still on Leo's, that we were inches from each other. Leo seemed to notice this at the same moment and froze, giving me a chance to step away. I began to hurriedly gather the wood I dropped, avoiding his eyes. "I think it was blind. It didn't know what I was."

"It didn't look blind," Leo said, voice steady, disbelieving.

"I don't know," I said. I stood up, branches gathered like a bouquet and tucked in the crook of my right arm. "Maybe it was sick."

Leo exhaled, looked at the place where the elk disappeared. "Maybe," he said. He turned back to me; several long moments passed before he spoke again. "I'm glad it didn't hurt you."

I swallowed, looked down. "Right. We should get back to Emilia."

"Of course."

Leo wound his way back to where he'd dropped his firewood—it was thrown about, and I suspected he'd merely let it drop to run for me when he heard the elk whine. When we reached the edge of the forest, Emilia was wringing her hands nervously.

"What was that noise?" she asked immediately. She stepped forward to take some of the firewood from my arms, and the three of us started back to the train.

"It was an elk," Leo answered. "An enormous one."

"You saw it?" Emilia asked, eyes widening.

"It was old," I said swiftly. "It didn't bother us."

Leo made a quiet noise, something in his throat that told me he still didn't believe me. Emilia didn't miss it; she gave me a curious look that I answered with a shrug, something I knew wouldn't fully satisfy her. She kept quiet, though—we walked back in near silence, then tossed the firewood into the car. Leo gave Emilia a leg up to climb in, then went to help me. He leaned in, threaded his fingers together to give me a place to step and leaned in.

"Strange place," he muttered, looking up and meeting my eyes.

"Friendly elk and . . . that." He turned his head, looked out over the field.

When we walked toward the forest, the field was silver, gilded with frost. Hard, the memory of growing crops in its distant past. But now the field was rich, dark brown, almost black. It made the white birch forest look like a castle in a still ocean, and when the wind blew, the heavy scent of fresh soil spiraled around my head.

"Strange," I said, but I was shaking. Leo met my eyes longer than I would have liked, then nodded toward his hands. I placed my boot firmly in his palms, and heaved myself back into the train car.

The fire warmed the car quickly, its heat traveling through the metal floor to the point that I slid my boots off, warmed my feet on the ground. Leo and Emilia huddled so close to the flames I suspected they'd fall in were the train to jerk suddenly. I wasn't as cold as them, but the realization that the Constellation Egg was healing me made me huddle closer to the fire to cure a very different sort of chill.

We didn't speak for a long time, listening to the crackling of the flames combining with the wheels of the train and the rush of wind. I played with Emilia's hair absently. I considered taking my own down for the rest of the trip—what did I care how I looked?—but it felt wrong to do so, a betrayal. After all, I looked so little like a noble now, felt so little like a noble. A hairstyle was my last tie to my old life. Leo watched me braid and unbraid Emilia's hair for a few moments, then spoke.

"How do you do that trick, Emilia?" he asked. "With the hairpins and the locks?"

"Oh, it's easy," she said, beaming—I could tell she was pleased to brag about her skill. "Give me that padlock."

Leo lunged across the floor and grabbed hold of the lock from the crate as Emilia rose and went to sit down beside him. He clicked it shut and handed it to her. Emilia laid it on the floor, took the hairpins from her dress pocket, and jammed them into the lock.

"You just have to feel for the bits that turn," she said. "Don't try to look." The lock opened easily; Emilia grinned, closed it again, and handed it to Leo along with her hairpins.

It took Leo the better part of the evening to figure it out, but I was grateful for the distraction—it gave me something to watch, something to occupy my racing mind. I slowed my rambling thoughts and simply stared into the fire while they worked, talking as if we weren't Leo's prisoners, as if Emilia wasn't planning to help me get him arrested as soon as we reached Moscow.

Hours later, when the stars were bright white in the sky and Emilia rested her head in my lap, Leo continued to pick the lock. It seemed more an exercise to busy his hands than to actually practice.

"What do you suppose your wedding dress will look like, now?" Emilia asked, startling me—I thought she'd fallen asleep.

"What do you mean?"

"Well, if you leave Russia," she said, "you and Alexei, I mean, then it isn't a royal wedding anymore. You can wear whatever you like instead of those traditional Russian ones." There was a strange lilt to Emilia's voice—like she was reminding me that I would one day marry Alexei. Did she think my spirits had fallen to the point that I doubted it?

I smiled a little and answered. "I don't mind the traditional ones.

Besides, Alexei's mother didn't wear a traditional dress. Remember the pictures?"

"True," Emilia said. "I suppose Alexei won't wear a military uniform either, will he?"

"Not if the Reds have their way about it," I said, looking up at Leo. I meant for my words to cut a bit, but he was staring at the flames, like he wasn't listening to our conversation at all. With his head at this angle, I could see the bags under his eyes. I hesitated, then spoke. "You can sleep."

He looked up at me. *So he is listening.* "What?"

"I said that you can sleep. I'm assuming you didn't sleep last night?"

"If memory serves, Miss Kutepova, yesterday you said you might roll me out of the car and into the lake."

Emilia gave me a horrified look. "I was only joking," I said, though neither she nor Leo looked convinced. "Anyhow, you can sleep. If you like, I mean."

"Thank you for your concern, but I'll be all right."

"Fine," I said shortly. "Stay up. Stay up for your entire revolution for all I care."

Leo gave me a steady look, one that made me even angrier—I would sleep, if this were reversed. I trusted him at least that much, after all we'd been through. Why couldn't he trust me at all? I looked back down at Emilia's hair, braided another strand. She kept her eyes bouncing between Leo and me, as if expecting one of us to say something else. Leo was the one to finally break the silence, his voice angry but steady, quiet.

"I'm sure it'll be a lovely wedding, Miss Kutepova. No matter where it is or what you wear."

I opened my mouth, found myself at a loss for words. Emilia, however, smiled, turned over so she could see Leo better.

"It will be. You can keep Russia, Leo. It's cold and you burnt half of it to the ground anyhow. We'll get married in Paris, right, Natalya?"

"Of course," I said, though the words felt stilted in my mouth. "You'll meet some outstanding Parisian man, I'm sure."

"And he won't care that I wear my hair down," she added. Across the fire, Leo chuckled, stirred the wood a bit with a spare board. He finally lay back, removing his coat—it was, unbelievably, warm enough in the car to do so—and using it as a pillow. He glanced at me, swallowed, then closed his eyes, like doing so answered questions I wasn't asking aloud. It didn't take long for his breathing to become rhythmic, his body to curl up like a child's. Emilia was next, still mumbling about her wedding party as she went.

I stayed awake. I tended to the fire, put new wood on, kept an ear out for footsteps on the roof, in case one of the train employees saw the glow and came for us.

But mostly, I thought about Alexei. I thought about the wedding we'd never have—and the wedding we might have yet. I thought about Paris and Saint Petersburg and castles and cottages. I thought about how the thing we never said to each other, the thing we never said aloud—*I love you*—Alexei was able to say with the Constellation Egg. I blinked, realized I was watching the rise and fall of Leo's chest as my mind wandered.

*Alexei got to say he loved me. When would I be able to say it back?*

# THE SACRISTY

*Maria stood across from the Babushka in the monastery's sacristy. The Constellation Egg mocked them; it sat silently on a polished table, like nothing more than a trinket. Around them, dozens of other once-powerful mystics gathered, watching, waiting, longing for the moment when the egg's spell would be broken and their power would return to the high priestess.*

*The moment had not come. The moment, in fact, seemed farther away than ever. The mystics were silent. Maria could feel the nervousness in the room increasing with each version of the claiming ceremony she tried. She'd cut her palms to ribbons, used her blood as a conduit so many times she knew there would be scars. She'd prayed to every star in the sky, and still . . .*

*Maria worried the others doubted her. Most were older than her, after all, more experienced. But she was the most powerful, by birth and by practice. They knew that—Maria herself knew that—but still. She wanted to prove herself, show them how strong she was. She wanted to save them by undoing the evil Rasputin had committed.*

*"Why, why, why?" she muttered under her breath, grabbing fistfuls of hair on either side of her head. She lowered her eyes so she didn't have*

*to see theirs. "Why? There has to be a way. If he can create the magic, I can surely uncreate it . . ." She paced back and forth in front of the egg, licking her lips furiously. "Yes. Yes—perhaps we're trying to separate the egg from the Romanovs, when what we really must do is separate the Romanovs from the egg."*

*"What do you mean?" the Babushka asked.*

*"The egg is theirs," Maria said, shaking her head as her thoughts swelled. "It's like a crown—it belongs to the tsar and the one he loves, their children. What if there were no more? Of either?"*

*"You're suggesting we kill the Romanovs?" one of the younger mystics asked, eyes wide. She look frightened, like this was more than she was prepared for. She was twelve, perhaps thirteen, and likely still remembered life before her powers manifested, Maria thought. She didn't know what a horrible thing it was to lose them. How shedding the blood of one family seemed a small price.*

*Especially* that *family.*

*Maria smiled, tugged at the little satchel of herbs around her neck absently, staring at the egg again. She reached forward, ran her fingers across the blue glass, closed her eyes, and felt the thrum of power from its core.*

*"Not exactly," Maria answered as she pulled her hand away. "It would take more than a handful of mystics to break through the protection the egg affords the Romanovs. But . . . the Babushka here has already pushed the Reds and the Whites to the edge. If they were to go over . . ." Maria gave a meaningful look, an even more meaningful smile.*

*"People act foolishly," the Babushka whispered, nodding, "when they grow desperate."*

*They'll tear the country apart," the younger mystic said, appalled. "Grigori Rasputin wouldn't want—"*

*A little gasp circled the room, like a current. Maria lifted an eyebrow and walked toward the girl. The young mystic shrank back against the wall—Maria was tall anyhow, but her presence made her a giant. She glowered down at the girl, piercing blue eyes brighter than anything else in the room—save the Constellation Egg.*

*"Following what Grigori Rasputin wanted is what got us here to begin with," Maria hissed. "If you'd rather follow the will of a corpse than the will of your priestess, perhaps there's no place for you in the sisterhood, dear." Her voice took a strange tone, like a song, as she said this. The girl blinked, suddenly stood up straight. Her teeth gritted, her hands clenched to fists as she walked out of the room.*

*The others cast their eyes down as the young mystic broke into tears just outside the door, once Maria's gaze was off her. Tonight, the girl would pack her belongings and leave the monastery. It wasn't the first time Maria had hypnotized one of her own, nor was it the first time she'd expelled one from her camp. But it was the first time Maria felt out of control. The others could see her cracking, she was sure. Rasputin never cracked. Rasputin was always in control.*

*Hated by them though he was, Rasputin still commanded respect among the mystics, Maria included.*

*Rasputin was a better leader than her.*

*Maria flung her arms down to her side, uttered a string of curse words. No, no, he wasn't a better leader. He gave their powers away. He stole from his own people. He ignored his own family, his own kind, for Alexandra and her palace full of royal children. That woman led him on, tricked him into thinking she might, someday, leave the tsar for him. She used Rasputin for his healing powers, made him a broken shell of a man . . .*

*Maria scowled at the thought of the tsarina.* Remember how you looked at me, Alexandra? Like I frightened you? Perhaps you were right to be frightened of me.

*"Whisper to them," Maria said aloud, first quietly, then louder as she turned to the remaining women in the room. "Whisper to the people of Russia with what power you have left."*

*"And tell them what, Maria?" a middle-aged woman asked.*

*"Tell them they must act," she said simply. "Tell them there's no time for mercy, no time to waste. Drive the Whites to frenzy, drive the Reds to fear. Create a storm, sisters. A storm even the Romanovs with their protection cannot survive."*

# CHAPTER NINETEEN

We rolled into Moscow that morning. I almost missed it—I'd fallen asleep, but I was jarred awake before the others as the train slowed. I blinked—realized that I was looking at farmland. Fields recently harvested, houses in the distance with laundry on the lines, horses and cattle and *life*. I rose, went to the door, and looked ahead.

Saint Basil's. The cathedral poked out through the spruce trees, the bright gold onion dome the highest, then the red-and-green striped one just below it. I never grew tired of seeing it when I visited Moscow, but today it was especially inviting—it meant we were almost done. This horrible affair was nearly over.

"We're here." Leo's voice startled me. He walked to the train door, leaned against the side opposite me. I didn't answer, so he continued. "Not long now, Miss Kutepova. You'll be rid of me for good."

"I will be," I said faintly. I felt like I should say more—I *wanted* to say more, but couldn't work out what. Leo watched me for a moment, then turned to face outside the train.

"Are you going to tell Emilia what happened in the woods?" he asked, his voice suddenly harder than it was a moment before. "Was it what I think?"

"What happened?" Emilia said. I scowled at Leo, then turned to her.

"Just the elk," I said. "It actually did run at us, but we were fine. We didn't want to scare you."

Emilia lifted her eyebrows. "You're a terrible liar, Natalya."

I opened my mouth, shut it again. Leo snickered.

"No, don't tell me," Emilia said, sighing. "I don't care. Just as long as we get off this train. And then get on another train, to Paris. A train with a dining car." Her words were short—she was angry with me—but also defeated. She really *didn't* care at the moment.

The boxcar now smelled like soot, and I suspected the heat caused some of the caviar to spoil. Leo kicked a few empty tins out the door, then grabbed the ladder, climbed a few rungs up to see better.

"Do you both have your boots on?" he called down to us.

"Yes," Emilia said. "Why?"

Leo swung back into the car, looked at us with wide eyes. "Because we're going to have to jump off this train."

"Wait, why?" I asked, shaking my head as Leo grabbed Emilia's coat and thrust it toward her.

"The tsar doesn't have a private platform here," he said.

Emilia shook her head. "I don't—"

"There's a cargo platform," I said, heart speeding up. "Where the tsar's platform is in Saint Petersburg, there's a cargo platform where they unload everything."

*Now* Emilia understood. We wouldn't be able to wait for the train to stop and jump, because there would be rail line employees standing on the platform, prepared to offload the now-ruined crates of smuggled caviar. Even if Emilia and I were able to convince them that we were kidnapped nobility—which I doubted we could—it was likely they weren't on our side of the revolution.

Emilia shoved her coat on as Leo stood in the door, keeping an eye on the quickly approaching city. We were on the outskirts now, rushing through pastures and tilled fields. The station platform was located on the edge of Moscow; the city stretched out to its right. The platform itself was an exact match to the one in Saint Petersburg, clock tower and all. I could see people bustling about at the passenger platform, but the cargo platform was full of still figures, people waiting, waiting to unload—

"Ready?" Leo asked needlessly. "Wait for it . . . and . . ."

I thought he was going to count to three, but instead Leo reached down, grabbed our hands, and pulled us out in one swift motion. There was a split second where we were flying, when the wind was rushing through my hair, but then we hit the ground tumbled forward. I was yanked away from the others, flipped over grass mashed into my eyes, the ground was everywhere at once My lip burst, blood seeped into my mouth, but finally, finally, stopped.

My head ached for a moment, but the pain faded quickly. sprang to my feet, looked frantically for Leo and Emilia. Without Fabergé egg to help them recover, they were slower to rise, limping wincing. Leo clutched his already wounded arm and Emilia sat up rubbing the side of her head. I went to her first, eased my arm beneath her and pulled—

"Natalya!" she said, pushing me away and pointing over my shoulder.

Rail workers. They were sprinting toward us from the station—they had seen us jump. They were big, brutish men with stained faces and dirty shirts, and they would be here in seconds. My eyes widened.

"Leo!" I shouted.

"I see them," he wheezed, then stopped, stared at me.

Leo gave me a weighty look, lifted a finger and tapped the side of his lip. I narrowed my eyes, then realized what he meant. I touched the same spot on my own lip, realized that the place where I burst t after jumping was growing smaller, smaller. I drew my hand away, stared at Leo as it vanished entirely.

"Come on," he said, and we began to run.

The rail workers were fast, but we had a sizable head start. Goats hustled out of our way as we shoved through their fences, Leo taking he time to tip over troughs to try to slow the workers down. The center of the city was ahead, where the houses grew close together nd carts jostled down the street. The workers were cursing at us, voices gruff and furious.

We hurried around the corner of the nearest house, took another turn, another, another, till we were just a block from the passenger platform and the city's main street. The streetcars were still running here, people darting out of the way as they rolled along beside carriages. I could hear the rail workers behind us shouting to one nother, trying to get an eye on us again. We needed to hide—now. grabbed hold of Emilia's hand and the collar of Leo's coat and dove for the nearest store. We crashed inside, nearly slamming the door behind us.

Everything was still.

We were panting, sweating, choking on cold air and bruised lungs, but everything around us was beautiful. It was a silversmith's, with large display cases of cutlery and fine cups, jewelry and christening rattles, all of which gleamed like mirrors under electric lights. We stood in the center on floors that were covered in thick Persian rugs. There were photographs on the walls of various nobles—one, even, of Alexei's sister Maria, all holding pieces of silver I assumed came from this particular shop. The smell of sandalwood and cedar filtered around me; I breathed in deeply, let the scents take me back to my house in Saint Petersburg. For a beautiful, shining moment, I was able to pretend my hair wasn't sticking to my face, that I wasn't exhausted and thirsty and being chased.

"This isn't good," Leo muttered.

"What? We'll just wait—" I said.

"Out, all of you," a new voice interrupted, deep and heavy. I snapped back to reality, realized the voice came with a man—and the man came with a gun: the silversmith, wearing a tarnished apron, glasses, and, most frighteningly, wielding a long rifle he had trained on the three of us.

"Forgive us," I said sweetly. "We ran to catch our train, but missed it. We thought we might do a bit of shopping while we wait for the next—"

The man's eyes widened—I could tell he was trying to sort out the contradiction of my upper-class dialect with my clothing. "Who are you?" he asked, voice quieter, but not softer.

"I'm Natalya Demidova," I said, offering the count and countess's last name. "Perhaps you know my aunt and uncle?"

The man laughed, a horrible squelching sound. "I'll count to five before I begin shooting—"

"We haven't taken anything! We haven't even touched anything!"

"You expect me to believe *you*"—he motioned to me with the muzzle of the gun—"are related to Count Demidov? I'm far too old to fall for cons like this."

A flash of blue outside—the rail workers, just by the door. They were pausing at the corner of the street, looking for us in the crowd. We couldn't go out just now, we'd be done for.

"We renounced his wealth," Emilia said swiftly. "In favor of the revolution."

"In which case, you don't have money to buy any of my goods. Now. Get. Out," he said, and closed one eye to aim. I looked back over my shoulder—the rail workers were moving away. Still, I backed up very, very slowly, running into Leo before we both turned and cautiously stepped out of the shop. The silversmith shut the door hard behind us, kept the gun in his hand as we walked away. Emilia was jumpy, prepared to run, especially when we realized we weren't far behind the rail workers.

"Walk," Leo said under his breath, throwing an arm out in front of her. "Relax."

"They're going to turn around," Emilia hissed. "They'll see us."

"Trust me, Emilia. Walk. That's how I found you in Saint Petersburg," Leo said. "Running attracts attention. Walking doesn't."

The three of us locked eyes for a moment, then stepped forward as one. Leo shoved his hands into his coat pockets, while Emilia and I tried to affect bored, blank looks—forgettable looks. The train station soared above us, the clock tower indicating it was eight o'clock in the morning. There were signs of the revolution here—buzz about Lenin was around us—but other than that, Moscow seemed . . . normal.

So normal that it reminded me of Saint Petersburg several days before the true chaos had begun. I found myself growing angry that there wasn't running, wasn't panic. If they weren't going to bemoan the tsar's imprisonment, surely they could celebrate their foolish revolution's success? But apathy, going about as if nothing was happening when I was kidnapped and hurt and Alexei was the tsar in Ekaterinburg . . . I felt like I was in another world entirely, a universe where there was no Constellation Egg, no Babushka to find, no ransacked palaces. Didn't they know? Weren't they frightened?

"We didn't even touch anything!" Emilia said, and I realized she and Leo were arguing ahead of me.

"But we couldn't afford it," Leo said, shrugging. The incident hadn't shaken him at all. I wondered if he was accustomed to being threatened with a gun. It seemed something of an occupational hazard of being a Red.

"Well, I know, and I know we look poor, but still. We just went in a store. There was no need for a gun."

"He didn't care what we were, did he?" I asked, turning to Leo. I shook my head in disbelief. "Red or White. It didn't matter."

"It doesn't matter to most of Russia," Leo said, his voice oddly gentle. "You and I may be black and white, Miss Kutepova, but there are plenty of shades of gray in between."

"You can't be in between on something like this," I said, voice shrill. I forced it to quiet as I looked around at the open stores, th women in fur muffs, the streetcars rolling by. "It's our future. It's our country, our tsar. They have to pick a side eventually."

Leo rocked back on his heels for a moment, scratched his cheek with his shoulder. "They will. Everyone will, eventually."

The three of us walked the length of the train station, then turned and paused outside a butcher shop. A couple passed by us, surely members of the nobility—out in the open, wearing furs, fine shoes, unashamed. I reached up, smoothed my hair into its pins in response, smiled politely at the woman as her eyes found me. She didn't return the expression, letting her eyes glance off me like I was a lamppost or empty carriage. I tried to settle the gaping feeling in my stomach, turned to Leo as he spoke.

"All right," Leo said, apparently satisfied once the workers turned right and vanished. "Where would mystics be, in this city? The sooner we find the Babushka, the sooner you're on your way to Paris."

"Excellent," Emilia said. I gave her a short but weighty look. She nodded at me, though I think I saw a flicker of pity in her eyes. Mercy wasn't a virtue her uncle was very familiar with, nor was forgiveness.

"Near the square," she said firmly. "If I'm remembering my last visit correctly, that's where most of the mystics make their money."

*And where your uncle will be. Soon this will be over*, I thought. I meant to exhale, but found my breath was lodged hard in my throat.

Leo nodded curtly. "Lead the way then, Emilia."

# CHAPTER TWENTY

Emilia knew Moscow well—she'd visited her uncle and various other society girls here plenty of times—but it was still difficult for me to leave this aspect of our plan to her entirely. I'd clearly underestimated her, though—she walked along, surefooted, I suppose driven by the idea of soon leaving Russia forever. By nine o'clock, we'd reached the square. We entered through the Iberian Gate: twin arches made of dark red bricks with bright white windows and cone-shaped copper towers. There was a tiny green chapel between them with a vividly sky-blue roof splattered with golden stars. We were supposed to stop and pray—everyone visiting the square was—but I wagered I should actually *get* the Constellation Egg rather than pray about getting it.

"Leo?" Emilia said, turning back when she realized he'd fallen behind. He was staring at Saint Basil's with wonder. I had to admit that as beautiful as it had been on the horizon, it was glorious up close. Were it not for the fact that I was preoccupied with our plot, I suspect I would also have wanted to stay and gaze at the striped onion domes, the turquoise and soft red arches that decorated the building like icing on a cake. The detail grew more impressive with each higher dome—the tower that held the highest dome, the gold one, had stars inside the arches, gold ribbons that rippled up to the dome and the cross on top of it.

"It's incredible," Leo said, now turning his head to the cream-colored towers of the Kremlin. "I've seen pictures, but I didn't realize it was all these . . . colors."

"You can come back and look another day," I lied quietly.

"Right. Of course," Leo said, shaking his head as if he suddenly felt silly. "Maybe you should be thinking, Miss Kutepova, of what you're going to say to the Babushka to convince her to give you the egg."

"I've had the entire train ride," I reminded him.

Leo shrugged. "Are you going to tell her it's for me?"

"No," I said. "You're still a Red."

"You know, you don't sound as angry when you say that now," Leo said, giving me a wry sort of smile.

"Just used to it, I'm sure," I answered, though I wasn't certain he heard me—he was staring at the history museum, whose brick facade was so red it looked like a hot iron cooling. We paused by the patina statue of Minin and Pozharsky while Emilia frowned, looked across the square. Leo hardly noticed we'd stopped, but I looked to Emilia, worry in my eyes—we couldn't keep this up forever.

Emilia swallowed. She then looked across the square meaningfully.

It took me a moment to see it—the uniform, crisp navy with gold buttons running down the sides. He was on horseback, which helped, a great beautiful gray horse that walked delicately around the crowd. Emilia's uncle. Here was our salvation, only a few hundred yards away.

Here was our salvation, only a few seconds away.

My eyes widened as I watched her uncle, his eyes trained on the Reds, their eyes on him. Neither looked eager to engage the other, so they simply kept their distance, each wary but ever aware of the other's movements. I supposed it would only take a single shot, or a single brick through a window, for Moscow to fall apart like Saint Petersburg.

I turned back to Emilia. She would need to go to her uncle first. He wouldn't be able to take Leo in alone—he'd need a moment to gather a few men. I inhaled as she turned toward Leo, frowned.

"I think I should ask someone," Emilia said carefully. "I don't see many mystics here. Perhaps they congregate elsewhere now."

"Ask who?" he answered.

"One of the few mystics who *are* here." Emilia pointed to a group of women in violet and blue dresses, hair long and loose. They scurried throughout the crowd, flirting with men and shuffling cards in the faces of women, daring them to come learn their futures.

"All right," Leo said, and started for them. Emilia grabbed his arm, shook her head.

"I'm going to say I'm the Babushka's granddaughter," she said, fluffing her already chaotic hair so that it looked more like the mystics'. "They'll never believe me if I'm with the two of you. We look like hooligans." As she said this, she stepped off. Leo suddenly moved as if to grab her; Emilia spun around, gave him an offended look.

"I—I'm sorry," he said swiftly, sincerely. "It's just . . ."

"What?" I said, shaking my head. "I'll stay with you. Like you said back in Saint Petersburg, Leo—Emilia isn't going to run without me."

"After this morning, I'm not running anywhere for a long while," she said, and started away again. Leo seemed at a loss—like he knew he should stop her, but was ashamed that he wanted to. He watched her disappear into the crowd, and I worried he'd see her veer off from the mystics and approach her uncle. I pressed my lips together, turned around, and put my hand on the base of the Minin and Pozharsky statue.

"Do you know the story?" I asked, drawing his attention from her. It worked—Leo met my eyes, then looked up at the statue. It was of two men: Minin, the one standing, and Pozharsky sitting by his side and holding a shield.

"You think they teach that on farms in Samara?" Leo said, and smiled at me. I swallowed.

"You'll like it," I said, tilting my head at the statue. "It's one of my father's favorites. During the Time of Troubles, when the entire country was fighting about who would ascend the Russian throne, Polish soldiers invaded, hoping to capture the throne for themselves. Pozharsky was from the nobility, a Rurikid prince and a war hero. He rallied his troops against the Poles, but was injured and lost—the Poles nearly burnt Moscow to the ground. Minin, meanwhile, was a butcher, from the lower class. But he convinced everyone in the city—from nobles to peasants—to rise up together, to form a militia. Rumor is that he kidnapped the city's girls and held them hostage till the men agreed to fight," I said. I smiled at him. "I figured you'd like that part, being a kidnapper and all."

Leo half laughed, shook his head at me. He looked over his shoulder, and I hurriedly continued. "So Minin and Pozharsky combined their troops, the nobility and the peasants. They marched into Moscow together and took back the city from the Poles."

Leo stared at the statue for a long time. He let his eyes fall to the inscription on the statue's base: *To Minin and Prince Pozharsky, from a thankful Russia.* Leo ran his fingers across the words. He grew still, like he was admiring something far more beautiful than carved letters.

"What happened afterward?" Leo said. His voice was lower now. Flatter. He didn't need to say it aloud for me to understand—he'd figured it out. He knew what we were doing. I closed my eyes, tried to breathe. My stomach felt heavy, like this was a mistake, like I should tell Leo to run. But no, no, it couldn't be a mistake. This was the plan. Leo kidnapped us. He had to be caught. I had to get the egg. I had to. *I have to.*

"They put the Romanovs on the throne a year after," I continued quietly. "And then they made Minin a noble." I saw a pale gray horse out of the corner of my eye, brown hair that I suspected belonged to Emilia racing back to me, but I was afraid to fully turn and confirm it. I felt like I'd been running and was now trying to stop abruptly, tripping, stumbling forward as she and her uncle grew closer . . .

Leo smiled a little, but it was a sad expression. "I wonder if it worked."

"What do you mean?"

"They gave him a title and some fancy clothes, I wager. But I wonder if Minin was ever *really* a noble."

"Leo—"

He spun around to face me, and suddenly I wondered how I'd ever thought his face cold. It was anything but at the moment; it was hurt, disappointed, but not the slightest bit cold. Before I could stop him, he'd reached forward, grabbed my hand—at first tightly, like he planned to run with me, to yank me along behind him as we sprinted away. But then his grip loosened, and he looked down at his fingers around mine. The rest of my body was shaking, but my hand, small in his, was still. Leo lifted his eyes to mine for a moment, a small moment, before turning toward Emilia and her uncle.

Colonel Ivanovich was exactly how I remembered him: handsome, with dark eyes and a face that made it hard to pin down his age. He had a handgun in his lap, and his mouth was a hard line. Afraid Leo would run, I gripped his hand tighter; he responded by doing the same. Other than that, he didn't budge, hardly breathed.

"I suppose all's fair in war," Leo said under his breath.

"Just go with him," I said, unable to take my eyes off Colonel Ivanovich, like he was a dog about to attack. "Don't cause trouble." My words were severe, serious—because I knew if Leo so much as flinched, Emilia's uncle would kill him. There were two more soldiers now, approaching us from our left and right, moving slowly, silently so as not to cause a scene. I wanted to save Russia—but I didn't want Leo's blood on my hands.

I didn't want him dead at all.

"All right, comrade," Colonel Ivanovich said, not entirely unkindly. His voice was firm, his posture on the horse practiced and regal. "Let's be wise about this. See my friends here?" The Colonel nodded to the approaching soldiers, who were closing in. One brushed me out of the way unceremoniously, causing me to stumble into Emilia; Leo watched my hand slip from his like something precious was breaking.

"They're going to walk on either side of you, and you're going to move along quietly to my house. Are we clear?" Colonel Ivanovich said.

"Perfectly," Leo said, sounding defeated. He lowered his eyes to the ground, staying sandwiched between the men as they led him off without ever laying a hand on him. I expected him to run, expected that I would have to watch Colonel Ivanovich down him with a single, perfect shot. But no. Instead, I watched them move carefully through the crowd, across the square and around the various street vendors, until they vanished from sight. My knees were wobbly, my hands shaking. I couldn't find my voice to speak. How could this have happened so . . . quietly?

Colonel Ivanovich kicked down from his horse, pulled Emilia close, ignoring the stares of people who wondered why an officer was embracing a dirty maid. Emilia began to cry, clutched him till his uniform puckered around her fingers. The colonel looked shaken; he pushed Emilia back, looked at her, at the clothes, the smudges on her cheeks, the scrapes on her hands. He shook his head, like he found the entire thing impossible, and then pulled her close again. He extended a gloved hand to me over her shoulder, which I took more out of politeness than for comfort.

"What are they going to do with him?" I asked. "When they get to your house?"

Colonel Ivanovich frowned. "They'll watch him until I get there."

"And then?"

"And then I can assure you, I'll punish him as I see fit," he said, smiling kindly, now releasing Emilia. He bowed to me, drew my hand to his mouth and kissed it. It was a normal action, something dozens of other suitors had done a million times before, but I was unprepared and nearly jerked my hand away. He didn't seem to notice, instead adding, "You don't need to worry about such things, Lady Kutepova. You're safe now."

Colonel Ivanovich insisted I call him Misha, though, truth be told, I wasn't entirely comfortable with such a familiar moniker. Misha had an impressive house in the northern part of the city, back toward the train station. It wasn't in a particularly rich neighborhood, which I suspected was why he could afford it on an officer's salary. Emilia's title came from her father's side of the family; her mother's side—the side Misha was from—was of a lower rank. It became clear, as Misha showed us through his home, that he was doing everything he could to disguise that fact.

"I'll ask a dresser to come over this afternoon," he said, sounding hurried. He kept placing his hands behind us gently as we walked through doors, as if we might topple over. "I promise, by this evening, you'll look sparkling."

"Thank you, Misha," I said. When I found the Babushka, it would surely help persuade her that the egg was safe in my hands if I looked like my old self. "I don't suppose you know how to send a message to my father? I'm sure he's worried about me."

Misha nodded. "He was last stationed toward Siberia, on the eastern front of the war. I believe he's currently looking for the royal family—"

"You don't know where they are?" Emilia asked, sounding stunned.

"No," Misha said. "The Reds have managed to keep that information well-guarded—"

"Ekaterinberg," Emilia and I said in unison, eyes wide.

Misha raised an eyebrow at us. "Ekaterinberg? What makes you think that?"

"We *know* that, Uncle," Emilia said. "We heard the Reds."

"There's no doubt," I added. I couldn't help but feel pleased—I already planned to save the throne for Alexei, and now Emilia and I might shorten his suffering as well.

"Well," Misha said, like he wasn't sure how to handle two noble girls bearing such precious information. He cleared his throat, let his eyes glance around the room. "Well," he repeated. "I'll get word out soon, for them to give Ekaterinberg a once-over."

"Once-over?" I asked, offended. "That's where they *are*."

"Of course," Misha said, but I could tell he was still wary. I felt my face flushing in irritation, but clamped my mouth shut—he was convinced enough to pass along the information, and that was what mattered. Still, what did he think we were? Incapable ninnies?

"There are two guest bedrooms upstairs," Misha said, seemingly glad for the change of topic. "The maid is putting fresh linens in both as we speak." I looked up the dark wood staircase to the landing, where a portrait of a man I presumed to be Emilia's grandfather hung, keeping watch over the house. The furniture was clean and polished, the rugs freshly beaten, and there was already a tea service with sliver-rimmed teacups waiting in the sitting room. I suspected one of the colonel's men warned the help that company was arriving. Misha gestured toward it.

"I've prepared some tea, if you're hungry—did they serve a meal on the train?"

"Not really, Misha," Emilia said swiftly. She'd skipped the finer points of our trip—mainly riding in a freezing boxcar from Saint Petersburg to here. I couldn't tell if she'd done so for Leo's sake, or to keep a bit of our dignity.

"Well, tea, then. Please stay away from the dining room, though. Our prisoner is in the kitchen adjacent, and I wouldn't want you to be further traumatized should you hear his voice." I exhaled and almost commented on the absurdity of Misha's concern, but Emilia spoke first.

"Thank you," she said. "While we appreciate the tea, I think we'd both like a bath first and foremost."

"Of course," Misha said, and looked relieved she'd said it so he didn't have to suggest it. "I'm afraid there's only a single bathroom upstairs—"

"Natalya can go first," Emilia said. "She's more a guest than I am, after all. Perhaps the three of us can reconvene for supper after the dresser arrives?"

"Of course," Misha said kindly, nodding to the two of us before taking off his riding gloves and dropping them on the foyer table. He then made his way through the dining room—likely to the kitchen. The way Misha walked made my stomach turn; his fast, angry stride betrayed his plans for Leo.

"Take the tea with us upstairs?" Emilia suggested under her breath. Her eyes were locked on the tray, the biscuits and the slices of sugared grapefruit.

"Perfect," I said, and we grabbed the tray.

It was a relief to be out of Misha's sight. Emilia pulled the maid's clothes off without the slightest bit of restraint, tied a silk robe around herself, then fell onto the mattress in the guest room, clutching the grapefruit to her chest like it was a treasure. I poured myself a cup of tea, added far too much milk, and stirred it quickly. It wasn't until I lifted the cup and saucer, preparing to take it to the attached bathroom while I got in the tub, that it rattled and I realized how badly my hands were shaking.

"It's all right, Natalya," Emilia said gently. She was now leaning against a linen pillow, bare feet flexed so I could see the soot on them. "We're safe now." *Safe*. People kept using that word.

"The Constellation Egg isn't safe yet," I said. I stepped into the bathroom and set the cup down, then stooped to turn the faucets on. My body was stiff and achy; it took some effort to sit down on the white tile floor and pull my boots off. Emilia had to help me with the dress. It fell to the floor in a heap, so unlike the stiff dresses I typically wore that kept their shape on or off my body. Emilia slipped out of the bathroom, closing the door to a crack. I heard her tumble back onto the bed with an exhausted sigh.

The water wasn't that hot, but it still burned as I inched in. I took a sip of tea, leaned my head back, and looked up. There were exposed beams, bright white, against the pale yellow ceiling. There was a grand mirror on the wall, its frame painted gold. Glass vases awaited flowers, and a dozen fluffy, warm towels were stacked beside them.

I wanted to rest. I wanted to sleep. I wanted to *stop*. Go to Paris, be with Emilia, and wait for Alexei to arrive. Would life really be so terrible, if the Romanovs lost the Constellation Egg and their crown? Things would be like they were before, when he couldn't be a soldier, when I was a noble girl, when there were no white elk or blooming sunflowers . . . I reached up, touched the place where my lip healed after jumping from the train.

It would be easier.

And yet I felt sick at the thought of walking away. This was my country, and this power a *gift*. How could I just cross my fingers that the Babushka could keep it as safe as I could? How would I explain myself to Alexei, when we were together again?

Suddenly, a scream rose up through the house. A horrible sound, one that seemed to emanate from the floors and walls, muted but still intense. I jerked my knees to my chest, an action that caused the water to slosh everywhere and knock my teacup off the bathtub's edge. It shattered when it hit the floor.

Leo's voice. That was Leo's voice.

"I told my uncle not to kill him," Emilia said faintly from the other room, her voice wavering. "I told him Leo was confused, but not dangerous. Uncle said keeping him here was safer—that if he took him to the jail, it might cause a riot. But . . ."

I squeezed my eyes shut and dropped down under the water, listened to the sound of my heart pounding in my ears. Emilia was wrong—Leo wasn't confused. Not at all. Crazy, perhaps, but not confused. He knew exactly what he wanted, and he wasn't afraid, even though perhaps he should have been.

I was afraid for him.

# CHAPTER TWENTY-ONE

The dresser arrived at four o'clock: a tall, thin woman with quick fingers and sharp eyes. She clattered her way up the steps with a suitcase full of dresses and another of shoes, undergarments, even sanitary towels. I suspected the last was her own addition, as I couldn't imagine Misha thinking to request such a thing.

"I wish we'd had your measurements," the dresser said as she flung the suitcases open across the bed we'd just vacated. "Then we really could have done this right." Emilia and I glanced at each other as she opened the suitcases. *Right?* I thought. It seemed so strange, to hear a suitcase full of clothing described as "right." Nothing was right, nothing could be made right, nothing could undo what we'd gone through—it almost seemed insulting that anyone should think a dress would do the job.

The dresser grinned as she unpacked things into neat little piles, fabrics that looked like jewels on the white and blue blankets. "Your uncle said your arrival was unexpected?"

"I'm afraid so," Emilia said kindly, stepping forward and running a finger across the beaded trim of a dress, like it was something very precious.

"I understand," the dresser said, lowering her voice. "Nothing to be ashamed of. The trains are full of people hurrying here from Saint Petersburg. So many people coming disguised as workers—it's shameful. You'll be glad to know Moscow has managed to maintain its dignity—no need for hiding *here*," she said, a sniff of pride at her city as she motioned for us to choose our dresses.

*Just wait—it's amazing how quickly things can change*, I thought as I grabbed the nearest dress roughly, so much so that both Emilia and the dresser gave me a surprised look. I couldn't help it—not only was I keenly aware that every second I spent here was another second I wasn't finding the Babushka and the Constellation Egg, but the memory of Leo screaming was echoing around my mind.

"Apologies," I said swiftly. "It's been a long trip."

"Clearly," the dresser muttered as I hurried to change. It was a slightly more traditional dress than I usually wore—but all the options the dresser presented were, given that Moscow tended to be less Western than Saint Petersburg. The dress had long, wide sleeves and a straight form that didn't hug the curves of the corset enough to make the undergarment seem worthwhile. The thick brocade pattern that ran down the side and across the bottom was pretty, standing out against blue velvet. Emilia wore a matching one, red where mine was blue.

"I'd forgotten I looked like this, after so long in the maid's dress," she said under her breath, turning back and forth in the mirror outside the bathroom door. Was she not bothered by hearing Leo's cry earlier? By the fact that we were getting dressed up instead of rushing to save the country?

She wasn't. At least, I didn't think she was, and I couldn't help but wonder if something was wrong with *me* for feeling the opposite.

"What did you say, Emilia?" the dresser asked. She was bouncing toward us and back again—bounce forward, tug the fabric here, smooth there, bounce back, observe, repeat. It was a bit like watching a terrier spring in to bite.

"Just that travel is clearly easier on Natalya," Emilia answered, smiling. "Look at her! She looks brand new, and I'm covered in bruises."

"What train did you take?" the dresser said, frowning.

"A slow one," I answered. Emilia was right about the difference in our appearance. There were circles under her eyes, and earlier I'd seen bruises running along her spine, like a row of jewels under her skin.

I pinned my hair up tightly, turned my head to look at my profile. I looked like myself, and yet, not. Something was wrong, and I couldn't put my finger on what it was—perhaps I'd lost weight? I wasn't sure, but as I looked in the mirror, I couldn't help but feel like I was wearing a costume.

Shortly after the dresser left, a maid knocked to inform us dinner was ready; we walked downstairs together to where Misha had set up a meal in the parlor. The dining room table was moved in here, I suspected because of Leo's presence in the kitchen, and had been adorned with a dark green tablecloth and candlesticks with eagles on them, eagles that looked so much like the Romanov's double eagle crest that I had to smile. There was a bowl of pears at the end of the table, a basket of rolls, a soup tureen, a ham . . . the scent of food was overwhelming, nearly made me dizzy.

"Lady Kutepova. Emilia," Misha said, bowing a bit to us and

motioning toward the table. "I couldn't remember, Emilia, if you preferred ham or chicken. Did I guess correctly?"

"To be honest, Uncle, I'm just happy to see a warm meal," Emilia said, allowing the maid to slide her chair out for her. The maid came to me next—I felt my lip curl when I realized I'd been seated in front of a plate of biscuits with a dollop of caviar in the center. Emilia saw it as well, and looked as though she might be ill.

"Well, Lady Kutepova," Misha said, flipping a white napkin open and setting it in his lap. While he was looking away, I took the opportunity to shove the caviar plate a bit farther away from me. Misha continued, "You'll be happy to know I was able to reach your father by telephone, and tell him that you made it out of Saint Petersburg."

"What a relief," I said, smiling. "And the Romanovs? Is he en route to rescue them?"

"I believe so, but naturally, we couldn't discuss his plans in detail over the line," Misha said, looking a bit annoyed that I asked. I understood why at his next question. "You and the tsarevich—well, the tsar now, I suppose—are the two of you still . . . ?" There was no appropriate way for him to end the sentence; the tsarevich didn't just *court* in the traditional sense, nor were we engaged.

"Intended?" I offered, and he nodded. "Yes, Misha. I miss him immensely. You can understand my hurry to hear if he's out of the Reds' hands."

Misha was unable to avoid looking disappointed that I was still attached to another. "Well. I don't think you need to worry. The White Army is quick, and besides, the Reds certainly aren't bold enough to actually harm the royal family. All those girls! They wouldn't dare." Just as he finished, one of the maids swept in and began to pour wine for each of us, a dark red one that I could tell would be too dry for my taste. When I set down the glass and moved to take another buttered roll from the dish, my eyes accidentally fell on the door on the far side of the dining room, the one that led to the kitchen. Something in my stomach tightened.

"How is Mr. Uspensky, Misha?" I asked, pretending to sip my wine for appearance's sake.

"Mr. Uspensky? How kind of you," Misha said. "I can't say I call him anything so respectful, after seeing how battered the two of you looked when you arrived. I barely recognized you, Emilia—"

"How is he, Uncle?" Emilia asked softly. Hearing the note of concern in her voice was a much-needed relief. *So my worrying isn't insane.*

Misha shook his head, regarded us like we were crazy. "I was able to secure passage to Siberia for him on a train tomorrow evening. You won't have to see him again."

"Has he eaten?" I asked suddenly, looking down at the roll in my hand.

"Lady Kutepova," Misha said firmly, "I assure you, I can do my job." He paused, looked down. "My apologies. This happens a lot, you'll be relieved to know—people sympathizing with their captors. I suppose it's a survival mechanism. I promise, it will pass."

"Of course," I said shortly, then turned back to my food. I picked at the ham a bit more, the creamed corn, but found both had lost their appeal. I ladled myself a bowl of weak-looking borscht from the soup tureen instead, and sipped at it absently.

"In addition," Misha said, leaning forward and lifting his

eyebrows excitedly, "I was able to secure the two of you passage to Paris. Tomorrow afternoon!" He beamed, like he was showing us a particularly fine watch or a show pony.

"Tomorrow?" Emilia asked, grinning—it was a real grin, real happiness, unlike the one I was affecting. "How did you manage it so soon?"

"Well, for my dear niece and the tsar's intended, I pulled every string I had," he said warmly, looking pleased with himself.

"That's very kind of you, Misha, but I have a bit of business in Moscow before I go." I looked at Emilia, who sunk down in her chair. The circles under her eyes seemed suddenly more pronounced.

"Business?" Misha said, like that were a hilarious prospect.

"Indeed," I said. "Perhaps I can go out tonight—"

"Lady Kutepova," Misha said, like I was a very small girl. "Don't be foolish. Your father would have me shot if I took you back into that city for anything other than your departure."

I gave Misha a stiff look. "Colonel Ivanovich, while I appreciate your hospitality, I am not your wife, nor your daughter, nor your mistress. My business is no concern of yours."

Misha darkened; his face became hard lines, void of smiles or swagger. He took a long slug of wine, then spun the glass between his fingers. Emilia was staring at her hands. "Well. Perhaps your business is no concern of mine, but your safety is. So. You may tell me what your business is, and I'll have someone attend to it, or you may do it another day, once the Whites have secured the country again."

Emilia took a deep breath, unable to disguise the sorrow in her voice. "Or perhaps, Uncle, we can take a train the day after tomorrow instead? So Natalya can tend to her affairs?"

Misha released his fork, gave us an appalled look. "I don't think you two understand—the revolution is about to hit Moscow. Tomorrow's train is likely the last one out of the city. If you're not on board, you're not leaving the country."

Emilia turned to me, eyes pleading and panicked. "Natalya—please. I know your *business* is important to you, but please. We can't—I can't . . ."

"Of course, of course," I answered swiftly, putting a hand on her arm. "Of course." I took a deep breath. "We'll go to Paris and I'll work something else out. We've been through enough."

Emilia looked hurt, and I could tell she once again suspected I was lying—but that she wanted to believe the lie enough to keep quiet. It was clear: she would go with me, if I insisted. She would come along to find the Constellation Egg, knowing she was missing her last chance to leave the country.

Emilia Boldyreva was nothing if not loyal.

It was also clear that I couldn't let her come with me.

It felt like night fell on Moscow faster than it did on Saint Petersburg, though I suspected it was merely because Misha's street was too far from the main strip of town to warrant gaslights. The moon was bright overhead, the house asleep, so quiet, so still. The maids had gone home—they didn't live in residence, as my family's did back home—and Misha was asleep on the parlor couch, so he could keep a better ear open in case Leo tried to escape.

I was in a small bedroom with mauve walls and cherry furniture. After so long on the train, the bed seemed incredibly still, almost eerily so. I turned over, restless, and looked outside through the lace curtains—they did little to block the light, but combined with the moonlight created spiderweb-like shadows on the walls. The streets were bare, save the occasional vagrant wandering by.

I turned on my back, stared at the ceiling.

I wasn't going to fall asleep. I was tired, but it was never going to happen, not with the way my mind was racing. I was planning, scheming how I would sneak away from Misha, go after the egg on my own. Forgo Paris. Abandon Emilia. And then what?

Hide the egg from the Reds. Forever, if I had to.

I rose, grimacing as the floorboard squeaked at my weight, and pulled the dress from earlier back on. I stared at my reflection in the vanity for a moment, then pulled my hair up off my neck, pinned it perfectly with a sigh. I went to the door, pressed my ear against it. The house was silent, save the perfect ticking of the grandfather clock at the bottom of the stairs. I turned the porcelain knob, opened the door gently.

I moved along the hallway, breath held tight in my chest. I eased my way down to the first floor, trying to roll my feet in time with the clock to disguise my steps. I leaned over the staircase railing to make sure Misha was as asleep as his snoring indicated, and had to stifle a snicker when I saw him. His mouth was open, shirt askew, revealing his pale and unimpressive chest. There was a gun in his lap, and his legs had tumbled off the side of the couch, like he'd been thrown there.

I crept the rest of the way down, past Misha and to the kitchen door. I carefully opened it, slipped through, and shut it behind me, pausing to listen—yes, he was still snoring. Satisfied, I spun around, expecting to see Leo in front of me.

There was no one there.

It felt like something heavy was on my chest as I walked forward. But no—there were old wooden cabinets, cutting tables, bags of potatoes, all lit with ample moonlight. The scent of our dinner lingered in the room, now a sickening smell. I walked the length of the kitchen, peered out the back door into the house's garden, but it was too black to see far—

Something shifted behind me. I jumped, whirled around to see the source. Nothing.

There. The noise again. My eyes widened; I rushed to a door beside the behemoth of a stove, swung it open.

It was a pantry, well stocked with dry goods and jars and jars of canned food, globes of purple, beige, orange that caught the moonlight and bounced it back to me. And in the center, in a kitchen chair and darkened by my shadow, was Leo. His head was bowed down, his hair in his eyes, hands behind his back. He looked up at me, alarmed; I stepped back to see him better and grimaced when the light found his face.

His right eye was blackened, his left quickly becoming so. Half-dry blood clung to his lip, and I could see burn marks along his collarbone. He looked down, pulling his face into the shadows again.

"Miss Kutepova," he said, words garbled from his swollen face. "You're looking . . . clean."

"She . . . Emilia told him not to kill you," I whispered.

"He didn't, you'll notice," Leo answered. "Though he made a valiant effort."

"Be quiet," I said, shaking my head at him. I bit my lip, unsure if I should risk turning on the lights above a carving table. Instead, I walked across to the fireplace, then lit one of the oil lanterns sitting by the hearth. I walked back, set it at Leo's feet. He watched me cautiously, like he was afraid I might break the thing over his head at any moment. I wished I hadn't brought the light over, for a moment—perhaps I didn't want to see his injuries so clearly.

"It doesn't hurt," he said lowly, watching me.

"Don't lie," I said.

"I'm not," he answered. "It did, but it doesn't hurt now. Really."

I grabbed a rag from the counter, chanced to run a little water over it, then returned, pulling a rickety stool behind me. I looked back to the kitchen door for a moment, certain it was going to fling open, that Misha would see me.

"He's been asleep for hours," Leo said. "He's not coming. Besides, what could he do? Nag you?"

"He'll make me leave," I answered, annoyed. Confident Misha wasn't coming, I leaned forward, moved to run the cloth along Leo's lip.

Leo jerked away, found my eyes. "He can't make you do anything," he said. "You rode here in a freezing boxcar. With a dirty Red, no less."

"Believe me, I haven't forgotten," I answered, reaching for him again, but he still craned his face away from my hand.

"What are you doing?"

"You've got blood all—"

"No, *really*, Miss Kutepova. What are you doing? Why are you down here in a pantry with me instead of upstairs in what is almost certainly a disgustingly comfortable bed?" His eyes were steady, words even and careful.

I lowered my hand, my eyes. I opened my mouth, tried to find words that slipped from my grasp over and over. Finally, I sighed, looked up at him. The lantern made his eyes glow gray-black. "I'm going after the Constellation Egg tomorrow. On my own."

Leo grinned, though the act caused his split lip to bleed. "How?"

"On the way to the train station. I'll sneak away from Misha."

"The way he watches you? You'll need a distraction," Leo said thoughtfully. "Emilia could help."

"She could," I said, avoiding his eyes. "But . . . she'll miss the train to Paris if she does."

Leo was quiet for a moment, then nodded. "What about in the marketplace then? It's packed—you stand a much better chance of getting away there."

"That's what I was thinking. Perhaps I can ask Misha to buy me a necklace or something—he'd probably pay for anything I wanted—and then slip around toward the produce stands, where it's more crowded."

"That dress might draw attention. The Reds are spreading here—it'll be hard for you to make it through the city. Be careful."

"Right," I said, looking down at the shiny fabric. The nervousness, the racing thoughts slowed to a steady crawl. I lifted my hand again, and this time Leo didn't jerk away when the cloth touched his face. The blood wiped off easily—the cut was smaller than I expected, which gave me some comfort.

"Well, I, on the other hand, am headed for a Siberian labor camp tomorrow," Leo said as I wiped his hair back, squinted—there was another cut, one that might need stitches, but Misha would *certainly* notice someone had stitched up his prisoner during the night. "You're practically the tsarina now . . . I don't suppose you'd amend my sentence?"

"I can't . . ." I stumbled, shaking my head. "I'm not the tsarina."

"So you're just someone the tsar loves?" Leo asked. His voice was soft, delicate, like he was afraid the words would break me. I opened my mouth, tried to respond, but the words wouldn't come. I dropped the cloth, lowered my head to my hands, closed my eyes.

"I'm afraid."

"You don't have anything to be afraid of," Leo said quietly. "Wait—elk stampedes. Perhaps you should be afraid of elk stampedes, when they rush to see you." I looked up, saw he was smiling. I returned the expression without a second thought.

"The Constellation Egg works for me," I said, voice hushed. Saying it aloud was an unexpected release; I tilted my head back and exhaled, saw Leo looking very smug about having figured it out.

"So what will you do?" Leo asked gently. He leaned forward, as close to me as his restraints would allow.

"I have to do something," I answered. "I can't just . . . run away. Risk that sort of power falling to the Reds."

"But after that, Natalya? What will you do after that?"

I inhaled, tried not to notice the fact that I could feel Leo's breath on my collarbones. "Fix Russia," I finally said.

"We have the same goal, you know. I want to fix Russia too," he said. There was a certain defeat in his voice, like he was afraid I still wouldn't understand. And he was right—I still didn't understand what could make so many people turn against their leader, what could make so many think that riots and kidnappings and abdications were the only way.

Yet, I understood this much, at least—that Leo thought he was doing the right thing, every bit as strongly as I did. That the rioters in Saint Petersburg weren't Leo any more than the nobles who fled the country early on were me. Those people were afraid, they were cowards. Leo and I were . . .

Well. We were Russians.

I opened my mouth to say as much, but couldn't find the words; instead I lifted the cloth, touched it to a place on his neck. Leo pressed his lips together and tilted his head, till suddenly his cheek was in my palm, the cloth smooth between our skin. Everything told me to pull my hand away, that Leo was a Red and my kidnapper and *not Alexei*, and yet I brought my hand down slowly, ignoring the fact that the cloth was falling away. My fingers wandered down the length of Leo's jawbone, till suddenly the inside of my wrist was above his mouth. Leo tilted his head forward, till his lips were touching my skin, though he didn't kiss me, didn't move, barely breathed; he sat perfectly still, eyes shut, like he was trying to commit this moment to memory.

His eyes sprang open, though there was a heartbeat before he turned to look at me. I didn't pull my hand away. Leo grimaced, like it was painful, but turned his head out of my palm. The cloth fell to the floor, and I was left with my hand hanging in the air. I drew it back to my lap, the feeling of Leo's skin still shimmering across my fingertips.

"I'm sorry," he said swiftly, words choked. "I shouldn't have—"

"I should go," I said, rising fast. The chair scraped the floor behind me, the sound mean in my ears. "Besides, it's nearly dawn—"

"And you have a Fabergé egg to find in the morning," he

finished. He ran his tongue along his teeth, looked up, and tossed his hair from his face—he was flushed. "It was a pleasure working with you, Miss Kutepova. Mostly. Except for the part where you sent me to Siberia."

I looked down at the oil lamp. "Emilia was right. It'll all make a grand story for Paris." I inhaled, found his eyes one final, long time, then stepped back, went to shut the door.

"Miss Kutepova?" he said when the pantry door was only a sliver from being shut. I stopped, peered back around. "Good luck."

I smiled, shook my head at him, and shut the door. "Good night, Leo," I said as I stepped away, extinguished the lantern.

I almost missed it—the words hidden by walls and cans and space. His words, the last words I expected him to say to me. "Goodbye, Natalya."

Someone was screaming.

Someone was screaming, screaming, screaming, a long, drawn-out sound that pulled me to sitting, yanked my eyes open. It was Emilia—I ran for the door, crashed through it, nightgown flying behind me. She wasn't in her room, she was crying now, downstairs. I took the steps several at a time, sliding, eyes wild—there, in the parlor. She was in a robe, clutching her uncle, face contorted in sorrow. There were two other soldiers nearby; they saw me, then quickly turned away when they realized what I was wearing. I didn't care; I threw a hand against Emilia's shoulders, spun her to me.

"What's happened?" I asked. Emilia was choking, I could feel her tears against my neck. She pulled back, put her hands on my arms. There was a terrified look in her eyes, but it was one I hadn't seen before, not even when we were running for our lives in Saint Petersburg. That look was panic—this one, this one was *horror*.

"What's happened?" I repeated, prepared for a swelling of sympathy, to hug her tightly.

"Natalya," she said shaking her head. "They've killed Alexei."

# CHAPTER TWENTY-TWO

"Nicholas, Alexandra, all the girls too—they're all dead. They shot them." Words were falling from Emilia's mouth, and yet they weren't hers, they weren't right on her tongue, like she was speaking a foreign language. I stared, waited for the cogs in my mind to spin, to work and help me understand what she was trying to tell me.

"The White Army was approaching Ekaterinberg to investigate your claim that the family was hidden there," one of the nearby soldiers said gently, like I was a child who didn't understand something very simple. "They should have gone about it slower, but they drove forward in a frenzy. The Reds holding the family panicked."

I stepped backward. There were thoughts, hundreds of thoughts that slammed into my mind all at once, but one was louder than the rest, one kept circling like a lingering dream.

*This can't be real.*

I reached for the thought in my head, grabbed for it to make it real, make it true, but it slipped through my fingers like smoke.

*This can't be real.*

This couldn't be real because Alexei was the tsar, ordained b God and protected by a Fabergé egg that also protected *me*. And because he was alive in my head, talking, laughing, memories tha were too warm and comforting to be of a dead boy.

The soldiers were still talking in front of me, still saying words didn't understand.

"Natalya? Natalya, are you all right?" Emilia said, shaking me. couldn't answer her. My head was wrapped up, foggy.

"They didn't go down easy, you'll be glad to know," one of th soldiers said—to me? Perhaps not to me—he was talking to Misha "They had them all down in the basement, told them they wer taking a photo to prove they were in good health. When they starte shooting, the bullets bounced off the grand duchesses. Gave th Reds a good scare, but apparently they'd just sewn jewels into thei corsets."

Misha spoke—they were speaking so quietly, Emilia was yellin for my attention, but it was their words, their horrible words tha found my ears. "So in the end, they were able to—" he began.

"Finish the job," the soldier said somberly. "With bayonets an close-range shots. The heir was the last to go. Which is quite a thing really, given his condition. The revolution is spreading, though Colonel—the Reds in Moscow are starting to riot. We may becom another Saint Petersburg by sundown."

*This can't be real.*

He was the heir. He was a boy and they didn't care. He was min and they didn't care. And the others—his father, his mother, the girl Olga, she was a nurse; she cared for the sick. And Anastasia, she wa tiny, a wisp of a thing with a loud laugh and blue eyes. They weren just the royal family, they were *people*, children, parents, lovers.

They didn't care. And Alexei, my Alexei, with soft eyes and gentle hands and the playful way he called me Natashenka. With our future and our lives and our pasts, our stolen moments and our interlocked hands and the way he smiled at me, shamelessly leaning in too close during the waltz. My Alexei was dead, in a cold basement, in Ekaterinberg, with no one to hold him, no magic strong enough to heal him, no one to keep him warm. No one to tell him as he lay dying how much I loved him.

While I held Leo's cheek in the kitchen.

No. While I held a *Red's* cheek in the kitchen.

I stepped away from Emilia; as her hands left me, I began to feel again. Emotion bubbling up: sorrow, aching, raw, sorrow. Atop it, though, was guilt, hot and furious, rising like welts on my heart.

I spun around, ran into the kitchen. Emilia was fast behind me, shouting my name; perhaps her uncle and the others were there as well. I slammed through the door, to the pantry, flung it open so hard it upset some of the canned goods, which crashed to the floor and broke open. The maids were here, they were shouting, everyone was shouting, but my eyes found Leo's. He looked scared, began to speak fast, voice panicked and remorseful.

"I don't know what happened. They were never going to kill him. The Cheka who had him always said that. No one wanted to kill them." He seemed to be telling himself this as much as me, his words fast and needy.

"I sent them!" I was screaming, I thought I was screaming—but no, wait, I was sobbing. "They killed him because the Whites were closing in. Whites *I* sent."

"You couldn't have known—"

"And I . . . I was here, with you, when he was dying." My words sputtered, broke apart into syllables.

My knees shook, I began to crumble away. I don't know who caught me—Misha or one of the other soldiers?—but suddenly I was on the other side of the kitchen, fighting the black around the corners of my eyes, the black that was already in my lungs, stealing my breath. The whole time, Leo's eyes didn't leave mine, didn't blink, didn't do anything but apologize to me over, and over, and over.

But I was the one who was sorry. I was the one who needed to apologize to Alexei, though I'd never get the chance to do so. Just like I never got the chance to say I loved him.

The soldiers left quietly, assuring me that Alexei would be avenged, that Russia wouldn't fall, that I would love again. The promises were empty, almost comical in their ineffectiveness. They were going to meet with other Whites, my father included, to sort out a plan to put Nicholas's brother on the throne. Misha would drive us to the station so we could go to Paris as planned—we had to make it out before the revolution began. The Reds were gathering near the square, owned the south side of the city—they'd set up checkpoints, refused to allow any but their own through. The Whites patrolled the north and, for the time being, held the train station. If Saint Petersburg was any indication, however, that wouldn't last long.

I somehow forced my legs back up the stairs, to the guest room. Nothing seemed real, like the world was moving too slowly, like was a dream version of myself instead of the real me. I crashed onto the bed, longing to fall asleep, because I was certain, so certain that if I did, I'd wake up and find this had all been a nightmare. Emilia was sitting beside me, dabbing at my face with a cool cloth, as if this would do anything for my tear-stained cheeks.

"They said he was the last to die," I finally said. "I wonder if that means he suffered."

"Oh, don't think about that," Emilia said, voice breaking.

"I want to know," I said. "I want to know every detail. I want to know where they were shot, and how many shots it took, and what their last words were—"

"Why, Natalya?"

I ignored her, kept going. "And I want to know what they're doing with their . . . his . . ." I took a deep breath before managing the word. "Bodies."

"I'm sure the Whites will get them," Emilia said softly. "They'll be brought home."

"How long do you think they left them there? Bleeding together?"

"Natalya, please, stop," Emilia said, now crying again. "I can't—"

I stopped out of pity, but the questions kept coming. The soldiers said they brought in new guards, guards who didn't know the family as well as the ones who had traveled with them to Ekaterinberg. Each guard was assigned a specific family member. Which meant someone was told, "Shoot Anastasia. She'll be in the back, behind her mother, shaking. Shoot her." "Shoot Tatiana, shoot Olga—they'll be side by side, arms linked, best friends till the very end. Tatiana will have her little dog with her—kill it too." "Shoot Alexei. The boy with the bleeding disease, the boy who comforted the fathers of fallen soldiers. The boy who fell in love with a girl from Odessa. Kill him."

Did they flinch, when they heard their orders? Do the Reds have heart enough to care?

*I hate the Reds. I hate the Fabergé egg that made it so hard to kill the family, that bent bullets and bayonets to bounce off diamonds sewn into corsets, which kept Alexei alive through dozens and dozens of shots. I hate it for helping me believe what the Babushka told me.*

"She was wrong," I said aloud. "The Babushka. She said our lives were intertwined." I hesitated. "Or maybe I was. I thought she meant Alexei and I would be together. Maybe that was just what I wanted to believe. Because our lives *are* intertwined, even though his is . . ."

*Over.*

"You think you were foolish for believing you and Alexei would be together?" Emilia asked. I nodded; she reached up to wipe a tear off her face. "That wasn't foolish, Natalya. That was love. Love hopes for happy endings."

"I didn't think I *had* to hope. I thought it was fate."

Emilia had no reply for a few moments. Eventually, she rested her head against my shoulder and spoke in a whisper. "There's nothing left here. There's nothing anymore, nothing at all but memories and misery. We'll start new in Paris—"

"I don't want to start new," I answered, jaw trembling with the threat of fresh tears—how were there still more in me? "I want to know how a Russian could shoot his tsar. And I want to know what they'll do with Alexei."

"He's gone, Natalya. The body isn't really him."

"Those are the hands I held. Those are the eyes that watched me, the hair I ran my fingers through. I want to know what they're going to do to it."

Emilia couldn't answer. She was crying again, crying because she and I both knew that the bodies of war prisoners were not given burials and ceremonies and moving eulogies. They were thrown away like garbage. My Alexei, flung into a heap with his family, like they were nothing. I thought about Leo's brother, how they never got his body back, and suddenly realized how cruel that was.

My core was all sorrow, thick and heavy and powerful. But my mind, my heart, my body—these were all rage. The Reds took my future from me twice—the first time it was the future of crowns and courtiers, where Alexei and I would rule Russia together. This time, this second time, it was the last scraps of my happiness. They'd yanked it away, murdered it in Ekaterinberg.

*I never got to tell him that I love him.*

Did he know, wherever he was, that I spent his dying moments holding another boy's cheek?

I rose, walked to the bathroom. Emilia called after me, but I ignored her, let the door slam behind me. I dropped to the floor, lifted a scrap of porcelain from the teacup I had dropped the day before. I positioned the sharp end on the soft part of my hand and pushed in hard, till the porcelain broke my skin and bright red blood welled up. It hurt, it hurt horribly, but I pulled the scrap along until there was a thick line of red on my palm.

I dropped the piece of porcelain; it broke again as it hit the floor, but I didn't care. I stared at my hand, waiting, waiting.

A multitude of tiny stars rose through my skin, brilliant and bright, so bright that I had to squint. They filled the wound and suddenly the blood stopped rising. When the stars blinked out, I wiped the remaining blood on my palm away and stared.

My skin was clean. Unbroken. *Healed.* Which meant the Constellation Egg still belonged to the Romanovs through me. I was the last one, the last one the tsar loved. The tsarina. It was Alexei's last gift to me, Alexei's last hope. It was mine, inherited like a crown would be.

And I was going to make absolutely certain the Reds didn't get it.

# THE SANCTUARY

*It was over.*

*Maria stared at the egg, tears springing to her eyes. She hadn't really cried since her father died—it was hard to find anything worth weeping over, after the nightmare his death had been. She'd hoped, deep in her heart, to use the magic from the egg to avenge him; now she'd be happy to merely have the power to heat up a cup of tea without starting a fire.*

*She was so certain the Constellation Egg would surrender its magic to her once the Romanovs were dead—after all, once they were gone, who was it linked to?*

*She couldn't believe she'd acted so rashly, pushed for the death of the entire family without knowing for sure if it would be effective. But now they were, undeniably, dead—every last one of them shot and stabbed and, if Maria's vision was correct, their bodies dismembered and burned. Maria cursed herself for not realizing that their deaths wouldn't unbind the egg; after all, Grigori Rasputin was far too clever to create something so simple.*

Because Grigori Rasputin was a better leader than you.

*The people of Russia always underestimated him. They saw him as a drunk, a lunatic, a womanizer. They were so busy whispering about his hypnotic eyes and tangled beard that they overlooked how clever he was. It was so obvious, now, and Maria hated herself for not seeing it before: Rasputin didn't merely bind the mystics' magic to the Constellation Egg. He crafted it so its powers could only be obtained willingly. In order to claim the egg, someone from the Romanov family had to relinquish their claim.*

*And now there were no more Romanovs.*

*And soon, Maria thought, walking out of the sacristy, staring at the sky that looked infuriatingly similar to the diamond-studded egg, soon there would be no more mystics. She would be the priestess who let them die out. The girl who failed as a courtier, who failed as a mystic. Who failed as a daughter.*

*She'd never escape the stares.*

# CHAPTER TWENTY-THREE

My face was swollen and tender from tears as morning became afternoon, long rays of cold sunlight stretching across the mauve bedroom. Emilia was silent now, like she'd given up on speaking entirely, though she did help me tie a long silk scarf around my head to hide my sob-tousled hair a bit. Still, it was jarring when she finally did speak—like I'd been asleep, though I was certain that wasn't the case.

"Natalya," she whispered, "it's time. The train is leaving soon. Are you ready?"

I nodded. Nodded too many times, like my head was stuck doing so.

"I'm going to go gather a few things for the trip. Just . . . I'll be back. You'll be all right?"

I nodded too many times again. I was not ready. And I would not be all right.

But Emilia was correct about one thing—it was time.

She left the room, and I heard the water running in the sink, a sharp breath as she presumably splashed cold water against her face.

I swallowed, stood up, and crept to the door. I opened it, shut it gently behind me.

"Lady Kutepova." Misha's voice caused me to jump; I whirled around, saw him halfway up the stairs.

"Misha," I said cordially.

"How are you doing? All things considered, of course?"

"Not terribly well. I was hoping to go sit in the parlor for a bit before we leave—the bedroom is getting stuffy."

"Of course," Misha said, stepping aside on the staircase. He nodded toward the wide window above the front door. "The carriage is ready to go, so as soon as the maid's husband arrives to watch our prisoner, we'll be off."

"The maid's husband?" I asked, perplexed.

"My soldiers were needed in the city, I'm afraid. News of the royal family's demise has made tensions . . . Well, let's just say things grow less friendly every second—oh, but there's nothing to fear," he said, answering an expression I wasn't certain I was wearing. "I'll drive and escort you to the station myself. You're safer with me than anyone else in Moscow, I assure you."

"Thank you, Misha," I cut him off, and brushed past him. He reached out, put a hand on my shoulder—too familiar. I froze.

"Lady Kutepova," he said quietly. "We will win this war. Alexei will be avenged."

"Oh," I said, without looking at him. "I'm quite certain he will be, Misha. Thank you."

Misha seemed like he wanted to say more, but I didn't give him the chance. I floated down the rest of the steps, curved into the parlor, and took a seat in a stiff-backed chair with lemon upholstery.

Misha watched me for a heartbeat, then continued upstairs.

The Reds were spreading. Pride nagged me—I had the power of the Constellation Egg. I could undoubtedly survive a trek through Moscow alone. And yet . . .

I didn't need to be safe, right now—I needed to get the Constellation Egg. As soon as Misha vanished, I rose, rushed to the kitchen.

Leo was in the pantry, still tied to the chair. He looked up at me, and his lips parted in shock. I walked toward the basin and grabbed a knife from the adjacent countertop. I turned; Leo's eyes widened, but he didn't flinch, didn't speak. He swallowed, watched me approach him. He exhaled as I stepped behind him.

I sunk the knife into the ropes by his wrist, sawed at them until they broke away. Leo turned, looked at me in surprise. I slid in front, cut apart the ones around his ankles. He was frozen, watching me as I stood up. Leo pressed his lips together, let his eyes move from mine to my hand on the knife handle. Though it tore at me, made me feel like my heart was melting in my chest, there was only one person who could help me get around the Reds and to the mystics.

"The Reds have the southern half of the city," I said; my voice didn't shake the way my body did. "You're going to get me through."

Leo took a shallow breath. "All right."

"This doesn't mean . . ." I shook my head. "This doesn't mean I . . . *forgive* you."

"I didn't kill him, Natalya—"

"This doesn't mean I forgive you!" I repeated, voice shrill

now. I didn't mean *forgive*, I meant something else, though I was afraid to dwell too long on what the word I really wanted to use might be.

"The southern half?" he asked, rising and shaking his wrists out.

"That's what Misha said. I'm not sure how far—"

"Natalya," a new voice said. I turned toward the kitchen door.

It was Emilia, who looked frail and broken, like a doll whose joints weren't tight enough.

"What are you doing?" she asked, shaking her head almost pityingly. "Surely you're not still going after the egg? There's no point. The Romanovs are gone—"

"Emilia," I said. "Go to Paris. Go."

She opened her mouth, huffed as she tried to start several sentences. "Go . . . go to Paris? Go to Paris?" Her voice grew louder as she stepped through the kitchen door, arms flung out to her sides. "All I've wanted to do for ages is go to Paris! Alexei is gone, Natalya. There's no reason for us to find the Babushka, there's no crown to save—" She stopped short, and her jaw dropped. Her expression became one of horror, like she was witnessing a murder. "You're not trying to save the crown anymore, are you?"

I paused, unsure exactly what she meant.

Emilia's words were shaky. "Oh, Natalya. Natalya, no. Say I'm wrong. Tell me I'm wrong."

Leo looked between us and suddenly he reached forward and put an arm around my shoulders. The touch made me jump, and I wanted to protest, to argue, but I saw what Emilia was assuming and Leo was doing. Emilia would come with us, if she knew the truth. She'd forgo Paris, forgo her last chance to leave the country, a country that would turn on her soon enough—especially if I failed to get the Constellation Egg.

This is how it had to happen.

"You're not wrong, Emilia," Leo said lowly, and I was grateful—because I could never have said that aloud. I cleared my mind, forced myself to become numb in order to forgo seeing Alexei's face, hearing his voice in my head as Leo rubbed my arm with his thumb affectionately. My stomach churned with guilt and sorrow; I closed my eyes to get my bearings.

"God, I knew it! I knew something happened in the forest, and then the way you looked at each other . . ." Emilia said, crying again. "Natalya, he's a Red, he . . . he *kidnapped* us. And . . . you were Alexei's! He loved you!" I could practically see the questions bubbling from her mind, dark and terrible.

"Emilia," I repeated hoarsely. "Go to Paris." I reached up and placed a hand on top of Leo's. He turned his hand over, held mine tightly, and I hated how much the act steadied me.

Emilia looked like she might vomit, and her eyes grew colder by the second. It took her several beats to find the words, and when she did, they emerged from her throat like a curse. "You're a traitor, Natalya. To me. To Alexei. To your family. You didn't deserve to be tsarina. But I'm not letting you do something you'll regret," she whispered, shaking her head. She leaned her head backward. "Uncle! Uncle, he is escaping! Hurry! Come fast!"

"Natalya," Leo said fast, spinning me around to face him. "I need you to trust me."

I parted my lips, meant to speak, but stopped short. How could I say I trusted a Red, after what they'd done to Alexei?

A flicker of hurt raced through Leo's eyes at my hesitation, but it was gone in an instant. "Then I need you to believe I can get us both out of here. They're never going to willingly let you leave with me."

I was about to nod when suddenly the kitchen door slammed open; Emilia deftly leapt out of the way to avoid being hit. Misha stood in the entryway, hair askew, alarm in his eyes. Leo grabbed the knife from my hand, spun me around; before I realized what had happened, his left arm was around my throat, his right arm brandishing the knife by my neck.

"Stop," he shouted. "Not another step. I'll kill her."

"Don't be stupid, boy," Misha hissed. "You'll never make it out of here alive if you hurt a hair on her head."

"But she'll still be dead," Leo said, voice curling dangerously. His chest was pressed against my back; I could feel his heart pounding. He gripped me tighter, took a step forward, forcing me with him.

"He's bluffing!" Emilia shouted. "He's not going to hurt her, they're having a . . . they're in . . ."

Misha turned to her, lifted an eyebrow.

"They're in love! He's not going to hurt her!" she cried.

Leo and I bolted for the kitchen's garden door while Misha stood looking at his niece incredulously—it wasn't much of a head start, but it was enough. I slammed the door back behind me as we stumbled into the garden; I heard it crack against Misha's body, then the clacking of him struggling to reopen it. We stomped through a thick layer of mud encrusted with frost, toward the waiting carriage. The horse pranced warily as Leo leapt into the driver's seat, leaving me to haul myself up beside him. Misha was sprinting for us, his eyes and nostrils flared, his hands outstretched.

Leo cracked the reins and the horse launched itself forward. Wind whipped at us angrily as we charged away; I glanced over my shoulder to see Misha was already running toward the house, likely to telephone his men. Emilia, however, was standing in the road, arms at her sides, a portrait of defeat and betrayal.

I turned my back on her to blink away my tears.

# CHAPTER TWENTY-FOUR

Leo only glanced at me once, nervously, then trained his eyes on the road. The horse was fast, its feet light on the stones as it darted into town. The sky had taken on a bruised color as the last bits of sun faded. I could hear the hum of the crowd in the square ahead as we turned another corner and the Kremlin towers came into view.

"We have to get rid of this carriage," Leo said. "The colonel will be—"

"I know," I answered shortly. Leo wheeled onto a side street where rows of carriages were parked, drivers awaiting their masters' return. Our horse skidded to an uncomfortable stop and we leapt out, ran into the crowd as the other drivers watched us, confused. We hurried to the Iberian Gate, but I heard shouting behind us—it had to be Misha and his soldiers.

I grabbed the sleeve of Leo's coat and yanked him into the starry-roofed chapel between the gates. Gold statues of saints watched us slip through the plain brown doors and into a space hardly larger than a closet. Parishioners were already packed in, staring at an icon of the Virgin Mary by candlelight. I dropped to my knees, and Leo fell beside me as the shouting and hoofbeats outside grew closer, cutting through the mumbled prayers of our fellow visitors. The sound reached its peak as horses clattered through the gates beside us. Leo and I kept our heads bowed in prayer until the noise faded away; we rose together, ignored the annoyed eyes of the others, and slipped out of the chapel. We lingered by the chapel's pale green walls for a moment, then slipped through the brick gates, into the square.

In the strictest sense, it was the same square that it was yesterday—same buildings that had stood for hundreds of years, same towers, same carts, same statues. Yet, today it felt like a wildly different place: a place more sinister and less forgiving, like a cruel artist's copy. There were red banners on every building, horse, and cart on the south side and white banners all along the north walls. People's eyes were darker, colder, stones instead of pools in faces. They looked around at one another like every other person in the square was a potential enemy, not to be trusted.

"It looks like Saint Petersburg," Leo said under his breath. "Before—"

"The world ended," I finished for him. I expected him to shake his head, offer another conclusion to his sentence, but he merely nodded.

Shouting, movement toward the center of the square commanded my attention. It wasn't until a cart of potatoes moved out of the way that I saw the source: White soldiers, charging in from a side gate. Misha was with them, sitting tall and proud against a saddleless draft horse. The Reds instantly formed a line across the center, blocking Misha from venturing into the south side—their half of Moscow. Misha didn't seem to care about their presence, inching purposefully toward them, barking orders to his men. I lifted a hand to my mouth worriedly.

"Oh, Misha, no," I muttered. The square grew strangely quiet as Misha's eyes searched the crowd for me, for Leo—he looked panicked, desperate, painfully single-minded in his mission. He wasn't paying attention, had forgotten that every city in Russia was a single hair's width away from becoming Saint Petersburg.

"They're going to rush him," Leo said. His voice was full of horrified certainty as we crouched against the wall, watched the Reds advancing, closing in, fanning out to approach from all sides.

One of the Reds said something to Misha—I couldn't hear what. Misha replied, they went back and forth, both sets of eyes frequently flirting back to the uneasy crowd. Everyone was still, everyone staring at them. Would this be how Moscow's revolution began?

Misha inhaled. I could feel the stiffness of the action from here—he wasn't happy. The Red—a worker from a factory of some sort—began to back up carefully. Misha turned his horse and trotted away.

A collective sigh of relief rose into the air, mostly from the cart vendors, who didn't seem to care if their customers were White or Red so long as they were paying. Revolutions wouldn't be good for business. I stood up straight, exhaled, found I couldn't catch my breath for a minute. I pushed off the wall and started along the edge of the square, where I hoped I'd be better hidden.

"Natalya," Leo called after me as I snaked around a fruit cart's display of orange-filled baskets. I didn't turn. "*Miss Kutepova.* I don't know the Reds here. I don't know that I can convince them to let you through the southern half of the city. Especially on a night like this. We should wait till the morning."

I stopped, took a deep breath despite the fact that the air burned my lungs. Gaslights were flickering on now in the last of the afternoon light.

"I'm not staying on the streets," I told him, words acidic and angry. Even as I said this, I knew I might not have a choice—that Leo was right. Not only was it risky moving about when Misha was certainly out looking for me, but I looked like a noble again. The Reds would be suspicious.

"I daresay that of the two of us, you're far safer staying on the streets than me, given your recent . . . abilities. But fine. We can try to stay in the train station, if you'd rather," Leo said, sounding bothered. I ignored him, because I didn't want to tell him that staying in the train station would be too painful—a reminder that I'd broken Emilia's heart. That she was now on her way to Paris without me. That she very well might hate me. I let my eyes run around the square. Everyone was packing up, on their way home, save for the bakers, eager to get rid of their goods before they went bad.

"I have an idea," I said, and hurried away from Leo. "Stay away from me."

"Why did you *save me* if you want—"

"They'll think I'm robbing them if you're beside me," I hissed. Leo froze in his spot, held his hands up apologetically as I walked the last few yards to a scarf dealer. She was almost finished packing up, just a few boxes to go, and an array of girls I assumed to be her little sisters helped her. It choked me, for a moment, thinking of Alexei's many sisters, but I waved for her attention, smiled.

"Hello," I said. I swirled the silk scarf Emilia had put on me off my head as I spoke. "I'm sorry to bother you just as you're leaving, but I wondered—a . . . companion," I said, letting my lips curl so that she might make her own assumptions as to what I meant, "bought this for me, but it's so grand a gift, I worry my husband might see it and . . . well. It might cause too much trouble. I don't suppose you'd be interesting in buying it off me?"

It was an expensive scarf—the sort that was every bit as pricey as the entire dress I was wearing. Rooms in Moscow couldn't be terribly expensive, though; if she gave me a fraction of what it was worth, I might manage.

The girl took the scarf from my hands, ran her fingers over it. She held it up to the quickly fading light and frowned, lips a tiny arc. She picked at a thread in the corner that I knew was insignificant—I prepared for her to give me a ludicrously low offer in an attempt to make easy money on the resale.

The girl looked down, thrust the scarf back to me. "I'm afraid I can't afford to buy this off you, Mademoiselle."

I stared, surprised—did she have nothing at all? I tried again.

"Really, I can't use it. I'll take anything—"

"That scarf is worth more than I make here in a day," she said, gesturing to her cart. "These aren't silk. These are for women like me to feel like women like you." There was a note of scorn in her voice as she said this, though I didn't feel it as much as perhaps I should have—or would have, several days ago.

I dropped my voice again, stepping closer. One of the sisters, a tiny girl with thick black hair, clung to the girl's shins. "I just need enough to get out of this city before the revolution hits—my husband refuses to let me leave. Please. You know it's coming as well as I do."

The girl pressed her lips together, then nodded, began to fold the scarf haphazardly. "I really don't have much. Fifteen? I can't spare any more, I have to buy food for—" she began to gesture at the girls, but there was no need; I nodded enthusiastically.

The girl handed over the money from a purse she kept tucked against her chest.

"Well done," Leo said curtly as I met back up with him. Together, we turned in the direction of the Kremlin.

"Where should we go?" I asked, more of myself than Leo.

"I don't know," he said. "Your choice, Miss Kutepova. It's just for one night."

I spun around, chose the first hotel my eyes landed on—a fairly nice one on the eastern side of the square, the sort wealthy merchant families would stay in while visiting the city. The woman at the front desk gave Leo and me a suspicious look, but I wasn't willing to extend the illusion of us being a couple for her. Still, she handed Leo a key and led us to a room on the second floor, with windows that overlooked the Kremlin on one side and an alley of drunks on the other. I sat down on the edge of the bed; Leo sat in the chair on the far side.

We did not speak.

Not for a long time. Not until the sun had finally gone down and I was lying under the blankets, Leo still in the chair, arms folded and head down. I was staring outside, at the soldiers and Reds who lingered in the square, eyeing one another, waiting, watching. I was here, in a bed, warm, while Alexei was . . .

Dead.

"I shouldn't be here," I whispered, not exactly to Leo, not exactly to myself. I think my words were for Alexei; it was his face I saw when I closed my eyes after saying them. "Forgive me."

It was silent again.

"Where should you be, then?" Leo asked, muffled from where his chin was tucked into his coat collar.

"I should be with him." This didn't make sense, and I knew it, yet it was the only thing to say. I could feel a well in my chest opening, any strength I had left plummeting into it. Outside, somewhere, a clock chimed the hour—it was eleven, later than I thought. How long had I lain here, staring at nothing?

"You should be in a basement in Ekaterinberg?" Leo asked. I sat up straight, turned to glare at him. He looked like a giant, folded up to fit into a normal man's chair.

"I shouldn't be in a hotel room with another man in Moscow. I shouldn't be abandoning my best friend to Paris. I shouldn't be protected by the Constellation Egg—"

"Are you thinking of giving up?" Leo asked pointedly. I stopped.

"No." I took a long breath, ran my fingers along a seam of the bed's quilt. "But since I shouldn't be here, I don't know what I should do next."

"Well," Leo said unsteadily. "You're the tsarina. I suppose you could rule Russia."

"I'm not the tsarina," I answered, then, slowly, "and I don't *want* to rule Russia. But fate has nothing to do with what I want. If it did,

Alexei . . ." I stopped. I didn't want to cry anymore, didn't want to go on about it, and yet there was his face, haunting my mind.

Leo inhaled. "He asked me to help him with a joke once, a few years ago. Remember the state dinner, the one that French diplomat came to?" I shrugged—there'd been many state dinners. Leo continued, "It was my first waiter job—I'd been mostly doing errands for the cooks up till that point. Alexei asked me to distract the bartender while he was pouring vodka for the guests. I did, of course—he was the tsarevich, after all—so I dropped a bushel of potatoes and let them roll everywhere so everyone had to stop and help me pick them up."

Leo stopped for several breaths. "While we were doing that, I saw him switch the bottles: the bottle of vodka the bartender had just opened for a bottle he pulled out of his coat. I had no idea what was in it at the time—and to be honest, I forgot about it until hours later, when the bartender had drained the switched bottle and the dinner was ending."

"I *do* remember that dinner," I said slowly, sniffed. I wiped my nose in a remarkably unladylike way. "That was the one where Baron Orlovich flirted with Emilia all night! The man has no sense of boundaries as it is, but he got tremendously drunk. She said he kept touching her hands, but his palms were all sweaty."

"Right," Leo said, nodding. "The thing is, when we were clearing the tables afterward, I picked up one of the vodka glasses and took a drink—don't make that face, we did it all the time—and it was water."

"What?"

"It was water. Alexei switched the bottle with a bottle of water."

"What? Baron Orlovich and Prince Lvov were far too talkative with Emilia, given their age. And Prince Yusupov was sitting by me; he was clearly drunk too. I think. Though you never could tell with him . . ."

"They weren't," Leo said, laughing louder now. "Not one of them."

"How did they think water was *vodka?*" I said, daring to let a single snicker past my lips.

"I have no idea. Perhaps they thought they were just impressive drinkers. Do you know if Alexei got caught, afterward?"

"Not that I know of," I said, grinning—why was I grinning? How could I be grinning when Alexei was dead? Yet there I was, unable to stop. "That's just like him, though. The pranks—it used to make Nicholas so mad when he did it at formal occasions. He used to tell Alexei that the victim of his joke today would be his political ally tomorrow, but Alexei didn't care. He just got better about not getting caught." The words were dissolving into laughter now as I remembered the dinner. Alexei and I sat far from each other, but managed to be on the same side of the table, each of us leaning farther in than necessary to grab our drinks so we might catch a glimpse of the other.

I continued, my stomach aching from laughter, "I can't believe Baron Orlovich wasn't drunk! You should have seen him when we danced later—he tripped me. I don't mean he stepped on my foot, I mean he *tripped* me, tried to do some sort of leg move and cut me out at the knees."

"I remember," Leo said, snorting. "You were wearing that pink dress. You looked like a flower being flung across the dance floor."

"That's hardly my fault!"

"But it's still how it looked," Leo said, sliding down in his chair with laughter. I grabbed my waist and leaned back against the bed frame as the humor subsided, faded out slowly with abrupt chuckles and snickers here and there. I went to wipe tears of amusement from my eyes; doing so caused my heart to twist, and new tears, sorrowful ones began to fall silently. *Alexei, oh, Alexei* . . .

"He didn't deserve to die," Leo said now, voice turning serious again. He rose cautiously, walked to stand by the window. The orange glow of lamps silhouetted him; I pulled the blankets up around my chest protectively, used the corner of one to dry my tears. It was useless—more fell. They were endless, an impossible leak I felt could never be fixed, its source too deep, too full to be drained.

"I know," I finally said. "None of them did."

"True. Alexei's sisters were always very nice—"

"I don't just mean the Romanovs," I said quietly. "I mean Rasputin, and your brother, and the other soldiers and everyone in the riots and . . . None of them deserved to die. It isn't fair."

Leo considered this. "I suppose it's like you told me once, Miss Kutepova. Life isn't interested in fair."

I looked up at him, tried to blink away the tears glistening in my eyes. "Call me Natalya."

"All right," Leo answered, gaze steady.

I smiled weakly at him. "Help me get the egg. Keep it from the Reds."

Leo shifted uncomfortably, now dropped his eyes. "I still . . ."

My jaw dropped. "After this? You knew Alexei, you knew he was kind, and you still side with the men who killed him?" My voice was rising.

"No," Leo said firmly. "I don't side with the men who killed him. But I still want change, Natalya. I want the Russian people to choose their own path. I want you and me to be equals instead of people divided by money and a drunk mystic's blessing—"

"And if the Romanovs get shot in the process, so be it," I said.

"I didn't kill them!" Leo said sharply.

"But you were a piece," I said. "The smallest of cogs in the machine that did. Just like I'm a piece of the machine that failed to stop them. Failed to save the family."

"Even if you'd already gotten the egg, it wouldn't have helped," Leo reminded me.

"Trying on dresses and having dinner with Misha didn't help either. Sitting in the kitchen with you . . ."

We both fell silent again.

I could feel the heat in my chest fading, settling, trading itself out for more sorrow. Before it was gone completely, I spoke again.

"I'm not letting you take the egg for the Reds," I said.

"I'm not letting you keep it for the Whites," Leo answered.

I lay down and closed my eyes. "I'll see you in the morning, then."

# CHAPTER TWENTY-FIVE

At dawn, the streets were misty, gray, and full of movement: streetcars, carriages, and people rushing to work or home from a long night of revelry. Leo was asleep, limbs sprawled across the chair in a way that looked anything but comfortable. I could hear people shuffling around in the room beside us, the door to the hotel opening and closing. The windows were frosted a bit, the ice softening the square panes into round porthole-like shapes. I rolled out of the bed, keeping the blankets clutched around me, and pressed my lips together.

I reached forward, placed a finger in the center of the middle windowpane, and began to wipe away the frost. I exhaled as a bit beneath my finger melted, then expanded quickly, like ripples on a lake. The entire window defrosted, water dripping down the glass and puddling on the sill.

"That's a more useful trick than the elk," Leo said. I startled, turned to face him; he made a strange expression.

"What?"

"I've never seen you with your hair down," Leo said, shrugging and looking away quickly. He pulled his coat, which he'd been using as a blanket, down and twisted in his chair, cracking his back.

I pulled my hair tight, smoothed and straightened it into a bun. "Let's go."

"All right, all right," Leo said, rising. He handed me my coat from the rack by the door, yawning.

Downstairs, we returned the key to the lady at the counter. She lifted a bowl of rather beaten-looking oranges, a cheaper version of the pears the nicer hotels offered, and we each selected one.

"You know," she said, as she turned a few of the remaining fruits over so the bad spots didn't show, "there's a rumor. They say the Reds have killed the tsar."

She dropped it there, let it hang in front of us like she'd just revealed a great work of art we were meant to admire and fawn over. I felt my stomach lurch; Leo, luckily, was quick to recover.

"Really?" he asked, eyes wide in fake shock. I peeled my orange to busy my hands, so it wasn't obvious they were shaking.

"Indeed," the woman said. "They say Lenin just arrived at the Winter Palace in Saint Petersburg. Be careful out there, you," she said, looking at me specifically. "Where are you headed?"

"We're looking for a mystic camp," I answered. "Do you know where it is?"

"Somewhere toward the south, I think. Can't say I look for mystics often," the woman answered, confused. "But you're not gonna get there today anyhow. The Reds are taking over—they've started setting up blockades on the south side of the city." The woman pointed to the doors, at the blurry forms barely visible through the pattern of cut glass. "Whites have still got the north side, but I don't know if it'll last. Feels like any moment now, the whole place is going to blow. Just hoping they keep their fighting near the river. I don't care who you're with—come near my home with a torch, I'll shoot you." To emphasize this point, she reached down under the desk and pulled up an older-model rifle.

I could hear White commanders shouting orders just outside the door; I tried to ignore the noise and smiled at the woman as I ate an orange slice. "Is there a back door we can go through?"

She chuckled. "Not with the Whites anymore, huh? Guess I should've figured—Whites don't take kindly to their girls . . . well . . . *being* with someone like . . ." She motioned to Leo instead of choosing a word, and I felt my ears reddening. "But yeah, there's a back door. It's an extra two," she said, drumming her fingers on the desk. My mouth dropped open and I scowled at her, but Leo reached into his coat pocket and dropped the money on the counter without question. The woman grinned—her two front teeth overlapped a bit—and nodded for us to follow her. We went down the wood-paneled hall, into a kitchen with a dozen enormous soup pots and a sooty cast-iron stove. The woman pointed at a door on the other end, framed by mops and rattraps.

"It'll put you out in the alley," she said. "But if I were the two of you, I'd make for the train station and get on anything that's still running."

"Thanks for the advice," Leo said dully as the woman turned away. She cackled a bit as she left us, letting the kitchen door slam behind her. Outside, I heard the thud of soldiers' heavy boots on the ground, a drumbeat that made my heart race.

Leo and I turned to each other—he clanged his head against

a bunch of ladles hanging from a rack in the process. There was an unspoken question: *Ready?* We both nodded in response to it, and Leo reached forward, pressed the door open with his palm. We didn't have a plan, nothing remotely *close* to one, but standing in a kitchen that smelled like soap and potatoes wouldn't get us any closer to the Babushka.

The alley behind the hotel was thin, filled with puddles of standing dirty water and empty boxes from stores that bordered the hotel on either side—glove shops and hat shops, if the packaging was correct. At either end we could see White soldiers hurrying about, not exactly *marching* toward the square, but moving with purpose at the very least. There was a stretched feeling to the air out here, and I understood what the hotel woman meant about it being moments till everything blew apart—I felt like we were balancing on a taut cord as Leo and I stepped into the alley. I dropped the remains of my orange on the ground, cringing when I saw several mice scurry toward it.

"Which direction?" Leo asked just as a group of men on horseback galloped by the alley's eastern end.

"Misha's a cavalry officer. Let's go the other way."

We started toward the western end of the alley, where there were still plenty of White soldiers passing by. They looked proud, put together—I never thought I would be so unhappy to see them, yet couldn't help but wonder how differently things might have gone had Saint Petersburg been this well prepared.

I frowned, looked back at Leo. They'd spot him as a Red in a heartbeat, that was certain, and then they'd inevitably shush me off to some safe place, probably something involving Misha's unwelcome arms. I darted around Leo, began to gather boxes.

"Shouldn't we go?" he said. "There's a break in the soldiers coming after this group passes. We could run."

"Only if you're eager to get arrested," I said, searching the ground for the top of the somewhat crumpled hatbox I'd uncovered. I picked up a handful of tiny white glove boxes, yelping when I saw another mouse spring away from them. Leo walked over, likely to make sure I hadn't finally lost my mind; I shoved the boxes into his arms. They rose to his shoulders.

"I need another," I said. "Don't move."

He craned his neck around the armload as I found another pink-and-orange hatbox. I set it on top of the others. It covered Leo's face perfectly.

"Ready?" I asked him.

"What if I trip?"

"Then you're getting arrested," I answered, and walked out into the street. We were barely ahead of the second wave of White soldiers, several of whom chuckled at the sight of me with my head lifted, my dress swishing about my legs, and Leo, who stumbled and balanced his way over the cobblestones. They were quieted by their commanders, but I could tell their eyes were still on me as we made our way down the street.

I cringed as I heard a box drop to the ground—I couldn't turn around and fetch it for him; no noble woman would do that. I kept walking, listened for the sound of Leo picking it up, hurrying after me.

"Thank you, comrade," Leo's voice reached me. I couldn't take it. I paused, turned around, clasping my hands gently at my waist, like I was losing patience. One of the commanders was helping Leo set the box back on top of the others.

"Tell your mistress she'd best get home," I heard him say good-naturedly, his mustache quivering with amusement. "A revolution is coming, yet ladies still find time to go shopping."

"It's quite a thing, isn't it?" Leo muttered, and trotted to catch up with me. I waved politely to the commander, who tilted his head to me and returned to the front of his troops. They turned right at the next intersection, prompting Leo and me to go left.

"Now where?" I asked Leo after walking a block. I could see bridges leading across the river from here—but could also see that the Whites were pacing about in front of them, their guns trained on anyone who tried to cross up from the south side of the city. They certainly weren't going to let me and a shabbily dressed "butler" walk straight to the arms of the Reds.

We walked in silence till we were so close to the river that I could hear the water lapping along the cream-colored walls that contained it. Leo tossed his head, trying to keep the top box from brushing against his nose. He turned so he could survey the edge of the river better, then nodded. "There's a boat."

"We're going to take a boat across the Moskva in the middle of a revolution?"

"If you can make sunflowers grow and ice melt, you can probably move water. You can get us across in seconds," he said swiftly, walking toward a series of small docks tucked away behind a row of businesses. I finally saw the boat he was talking about—it was a small rowboat, the sort that held a few men at most.

"*Probably?*" I hissed, trying to walk fast and get ahead of him again just in case a soldier saw us. Aristocracy didn't trail behind their employees.

"All the egg's power used to be spread across the Romanovs—it used to be yours only because Alexei loved you. But now it belongs to you entirely. So yes, you *probably* can make the wind blow. You probably can do a lot more than that, I wager," he said as he walked down the tiny dock. He dropped the boxes—looking far too pleased about doing so—and they scattered about the dock, blowing into the water as Leo grabbed the rope and began to untie the boat from its mooring. I looked back at the bridges wishfully. I could see the Kremlin's walls, dark red brick with round towers at each corner. The Whites were surely in those towers, keeping watch.

"They'll see us," I said, nodding to the tower windows.

"I'm sure," Leo answered. "But if we can make it halfway before they do, their guns won't reach us. Besides, one shot and this whole city will go up like Saint Petersburg. The Whites don't want that."

"No," I muttered. "The Reds, however . . ."

Leo gave me an irritated look, extended a hand to help me into the boat. I took it, jumping in, nearly falling straight into the river when it rocked with my momentum. I dropped into a seat in the back, held onto it on either side.

"Let's go," I said when he didn't move.

"You're the one who can control the water," he reminded me. I scowled at him, looked at the water around me. The river was astonishingly still, tiny triangles of water lifting when the wind blew particularly hard, but otherwise the surface was calm and gentle. I tried to summon that feeling, the lightning in my veins I felt with the elk, but all I felt was mildly seasick. I turned back to Leo, who wore an irritatingly hopeful expression.

"I don't know how to do it—" I began, stopping when Leo's eyes left mine, flitted to the shore.

"You should work it out," he said. "Because they're going to see us." I whirled around—there were White soldiers farther up the bank, curiously pointing at the boxes Leo dropped in the water as they floated past. I watched their eyes gradually drift up the river.

"And that's Misha," I said, my heart sinking.

"What?" Leo snapped. He dove for the boat's oars, struggled to fit them into place. Misha began to run, rifle clutched to his chest. I reached over, shoved the boat away from the dock. Leo began to paddle furiously, but strong as he was, his arms would only do so much. We rolled away from the dock, into the river, but Misha was running down the grassy banks now, readying his rifle, waving to me. I leaned over—he wouldn't be able to shoot at Leo if there was a chance I would block the bullet.

"Go, go, go," I urged Leo, who was sweating now, grimacing with each stroke of the oars. Other Whites were joining Misha, confused but loyally training their guns on us. The wind was sharper out here, away from the shore, and we began to turn slightly, rotate around—they would have a shot. Not a good one, necessarily, but a shot, and there was no way I could position myself to stop them. Leo seemed to realize this as well, growled and tried to row faster, but we were still a good distance from the middle of the river. I looked back anxiously.

The wind picked up—but not to turn us. It felt like the wind was beneath us, rather, like we weren't on the water at all. It shoved us across the water, taking the time to rush around my arms, wrap round my face like it was embracing me. There it was, the feeling of lightning. It was faint underneath the cold air, but it was rushing around in my veins, ordering the air to push us forward like the magic was speaking on my behalf.

"Keep doing that," Leo shouted to be heard above the wind. I didn't bother to tell him that I wasn't entirely certain *how* I was doing this. A shot rang out, another, another, but the bullets were far from reaching Leo. The other side of the Moskva was coming into view now, the bank covered with peasants in browns, grays, blacks. I could see the Red sashes on their arms from here; looking at them, the lightning feeling seemed to increase, feed off my anger.

We began to slow; Leo stopped paddling altogether as we drifted toward a dock clearly meant for much larger boats. I could hear the Reds talking now, bright, young voices, as a group of them gathered at the mooring.

"How do I know they won't start shooting?" I asked warily.

"You don't," Leo said, gripping my shoulders. "I do."

"Well then, how do *you* know?" I asked. We were only a half-dozen yards out now. I could see their eyes, their unshaved faces and calloused hands.

"Because Reds are the people of Russia," he answered. "That means you and me, if we'll join them. Remember, they're not *defending* anything. They've got no reason to shoot someone coming at them."

I wasn't sure—especially when Leo tossed them the rope and they pulled us to the dock. Leo jumped out first, held up his hands to show he was unarmed, then he and a Red pulled me onto the shore. The Red had eyes like brown gemstones—hard, but sparkling.

"Who are you?" the gem-eyed Red asked, folding his arms and

blocking our route off the dock. I became keenly aware of the fact that if they were to charge forward, Leo and I would have nowhere to go but into the Moskva's icy water.

"Leo Uspensky," he said.

"And are you a traitor or spy?" the Red asked. The crowd around him shouted out their suspicions; my heart sank to see plenty of fingers pointed at me, attached to voices that cried, "Spy!"

"She's not a spy! She's with us," Leo shouted at them, stepping back to me. He grabbed my hand, pulled me toward him. "She's with us. She's with me." He clutched my hand so tightly it hurt. "I'm from the Palace Soviets in Saint Petersburg. I'm one of you."

"Palace Soviets? The tsar's own employees?" a different Red scoffed. "What would someone from Saint Petersburg be doing here?"

"Excellent question," the gem-eyed boy said. He was small compared to Leo, but looked fast, like a terrier. "You're not even wearing any red." I saw several of the boys behind him fidget with their guns. "Got any proof you're not a White in disguise?" the boy asked.

Leo nodded, shuffled his coat off. It slumped to the ground as he grabbed the sides of his shirt, hiked it up to his shoulders. The hair on his arms pricked up from the cold, and the Reds around us looked at him like he was crazy. They realized what he was doing at the same moment I did, and we inhaled in near unison. Two long, bumpy scars, the width of my arm, were raised angrily across his skin. They cut across his shoulders to halfway down his back, and looked horrible, more horrible still when I considered what the pain acquiring such scars must have been like.

"A plow," Leo said, rustling his shirt back down. He stared at the dock, like he was embarrassed. "You think I don't know hard work? That I'm not angry like you are?"

The gem-eyed boy looked down, firmed his lips. Everything about him changed, and he extended a hand toward Leo. "Forgive me, comrade. The Whites have sent more than one spy over here." Some of the Reds shuffled away, resumed their posts as Leo took his hand and shook it readily. "And you, miss?" the boy asked me, seemingly more out of curiosity than need. "Why are you with us?"

Leo was about to answer for me, but I broke in. "Because I want my country back," I said swiftly.

Leo exhaled. The gem-eyed boy grinned and gave me a look, one I wasn't prepared for—like he was proud of me, like he was eager to have me with him. "We've run out of guns," he said, "but there are some bayonet spears, should you want them. Miss, if you'd like to join the ladies toward the back—" he began.

Leo cut him off. "We came here—to Moscow, I mean—looking for a mystic. We need to find her before we can join you."

"You want a card reading in the middle of a revolution?"

"She's my grandmother," I lied. "I want to make sure she's safe."

The gem-eyed boy frowned, but seemed convinced. "If she wasn't at the square on the north side of town, she's probably at the monastery. They're protected there, I imagine—it's on an island in the river. But look." He motioned toward the other side of the water. The Whites were lining up, in formation; their guns were trained across the bridge. "It's starting now, miss."

"Which monastery?" I asked quickly.

"Down that way," he pointed. "Just south of the Saratovsky train station."

"Perfect," I said.

"But you'll come back to the front?" the boy asked. This question was aimed at Leo specifically. "You look like a man ready for a fight."

"I am," Leo said, nodding. "And I will be."

# CHAPTER TWENTY-SIX

As promised, the mystic camp was in a monastery, and yet it was not at all what I expected. This was not a place of neatly kept gardens and clean walls—or at least, not anymore. The monastery was falling apart, the outer wall reduced to a two- or three-foot-high pile of brick dust. The buildings inside the compound were no better. The roofs were patched with oilcloths, the walls had enormous holes missing, and vines were snaking along the entire thing, devouring whatever was left standing.

And yet, for as lifeless as the building itself was, the camp was vibrant. Tents in reds and purples, creams and golds, with wind chimes on the outsides and runes drawn on the fabric, were propped up against the monastery's walls. The edges of rooftops were used to hold the ends of laundry lines, and it looked like the granary had been converted into a chicken coop. As we crossed the bridge to the island, I turned to look back over Moscow and saw what I worried were traces of smoke blooming over buildings. I could feel the tension slicing toward me like an arrow. It was hard to believe the camp and Moscow's impending revolution could exist in the same country, much less the same city.

An arbor made of graying wood framed the camp's entrance on the far side of the bridge, gentle and sloping where the iron bridge railings ended, sharp and exact. Heads turned as Leo and I grew closer, mostly belonging to women with dark black eyes and heavy, wild hair. They wore long necklaces and cheap metal rings, eyeliner, and lipstick, like they were starring in a play rather than living on the outskirts of a city in turmoil. Their eyes skirted between me and Leo and the city's skyline, like they couldn't tell which was the more pressing danger.

When we were nearly at the halfway point on the bridge, a girl a few years older than me stepped through the arbor. Leo and I locked eyes briefly as she walked toward us.

"Lost?" she asked. She walked quickly, like she wanted to reach us before we got too much closer.

"Not exactly," I said. "I'm looking for a . . . mystic."

"No one here's working," she said curtly. "Perhaps you've noticed, the city is a bit preoccupied." She pointed behind us; I heard a rattling noise that I soon realized was gunfire. A rushing sound, a wave of cries, reached me on the breeze, though it fell away as soon as the wind stopped. Leo met my eyes—he heard it too.

So Moscow's revolution had begun while I had my back turned. Just like in Saint Petersburg.

I turned to the girl; behind her, other mystics were hurrying into their homes, sealing doors with ribbons like this could possibly keep a war out.

"This is about the revolution," I said quickly. "I can't explain—we just have to see her. We've always called her Babushka. Is she here?"

The girl folded her arms. She was gamine, with high cheekbones that suited her now, but I suspected would hollow when she got older. There were tattoos along her collarbone, runes that looked blurred, drawn on with a shaky hand. "If you don't know her given name, I'm afraid you don't know her well enough for me to hunt her down for you. Go. Go find shelter." The girl turned, began to walk back to the camp.

"Please!" I called out, chasing after her. Several older mystics were lining up around the outskirts of the camp, casting herbs about on the ground; they gave me cold looks, like I might ruin their charm with my presence.

"We've traveled a very long way," Leo called as he ran up behind me. "We think she may have something that can help us. That can help all of Russia, in fact."

"Can you just tell her that Lady Natalya Kutepova is here? She'll remember me. I'm sure of it," I added.

The girl stopped and sighed, rubbed the back of her head; a few of her fingers got caught in her hair, and it took her a moment to work them free. I heard a cannon fire, a sound that reminded me of the *Aurora* and made my heart stop. Leo looked back toward the city, and I heard him suck in a nervous breath. I kept my gaze on the girl. The revolution would happen if I was looking or not.

The girl scowled. "Fine. Wait here. *Don't* pass the arbor, clear?"

Leo and I nodded in unison. The older mystics continued to scatter dried leaves around the borders of the camp. Rasputin's Constellation Egg couldn't save the royal family, but they thought a handful of basil might save them? Still, I found myself hoping it would work. Perhaps the revolution wouldn't venture this far south . . .

Another cannon sounded. Leo closed his eyes.

"She said you can come in." The girl's voice rang out from farther inside the camp. "But I don't know that she'll do you much good."

We walked through the arbor and joined her in the camp. It was a maze of tents, of lean-tos, the scent of teas and incense heavy in the air. Now that we were inside, we could see the camp was set up like a sun, with all the tents circled around the monastery's crumbling main building. On the exposed interior walls, I could see the remains of murals, images of angels and saints whose faces were being chipped away by time.

"Here," the girl said, stopping at the edge of a sage-green tent. She swept a curtain back. "Go."

I hesitated, so Leo went first, dipping his head to go inside. As soon as I was through the door, the girl dropped the tent flap and, as best I could tell, walked away.

It was dark, so dark that it took a moment for my eyes to adjust. There were a few candles burning on the far side, giant things melted down to little more than lumps of wax. There were rugs on the ground, bells hanging from ropes on the ceilings, and tapestries on the wall with designs too vague to make out. Underneath the incense, the tea, and the candle smoke, was the smell of vodka, harsh and bright. I grimaced, continued to look around—I didn't see her here, and certainly didn't see the Constellation Egg. Was she going to meet us? I looked back at the door.

"Lady Kutepova!" a voice called out, slurred and sloppy. I whirled around, tried to find the source.

"Babushka?" I said. "Is that you?"

"Of course it is, *golubka*," she said. Movement drew my eyes to her—she was sitting near the back of the tent on a chair badly in need of new upholstery. She heaved herself up, toddled back and forth for a moment, then stumbled toward me.

"She's drunk," Leo said, annoyed.

"Very drunk," I agreed as she tripped, fell, and rolled a little. Leo and I hurried to her side, each took an arm, and pulled her back to the chair. The acrid smell of vomit was strong; I opted not to look around and find its source. Her hair was unbraided, her eyes watery, and I suspected her dress was on backward.

"Here," Leo said, vanishing from my side. He reappeared a moment later with a mug of water from a carafe on a table. I handed it to the Babushka, who stared at it for a moment, then gulped it down.

"Babushka," I said, kneeling in front of the chair so I was mostly eye level with her.

"Lady Kutepova," she said again, sounding the slightest bit better. "Cards? Runes?"

"No, Babushka," I said, snapping my fingers in front of her face. Leo returned with a second glass of water; I dipped my fingers into it and splashed her face. "I need to know about the Fabergé egg. The one I told you about the last time I saw you."

Her eyes widened; she looked to Leo accusingly, like he was intruding.

"Never mind him," I said swiftly, waving to draw her attention back. "Remember the egg, Babushka? Did you take it?"

"Of course," she said. She grinned, a wicked sort of expression. "I had to. Keep it safe."

"For the Romanovs," I said, relieved. I saw Leo shift uncomfortably, fought the urge to give him a smug look. The Babushka laughed loudly.

"Not that it did any good," she said. "They're dead. Every last one of them. Shot. Dead."

Something hollowed out in me, and a hand was suddenly on my shoulder—Leo's. I wanted to shake it off, but it felt like the only real thing in the room. Besides, I had to focus, had to get an answer out of her. The Babushka was breathing slower now, gaining her bearings.

"Where is the egg, Babushka?" I asked. "I need to get it. I'm Alexei's girl, remember? I need it, to get it out of the country so the Reds don't get it."

The hand on my shoulder tensed, then pulled away entirely. I didn't look back.

"The egg?" the Babushka said, sighing. "He was a fool, Lady Kutepova. Rasputin, I mean. Falling in love with a queen. He was great, he was powerful, he was a visionary. And in the end, he was no different from any other lovesick schoolboy."

"Where is it?" I asked, voice growing tense. I didn't get kidnapped, ride in a boxcar from Saint Petersburg, lie my way through Moscow just so she could dodge my question. I rose, looming above her.

"You don't understand," she said. "It doesn't matter. They're dead. Our powers are locked inside the egg forever."

"Your powers?" Leo asked. The Babushka blinked at him, confused, but answered anyhow.

"My powers. Their powers," she waved toward the door of the tent. "Rasputin didn't just put his own powers into that egg, he put *our* powers into it. And now the last people who could access it have been killed. It's useless. A charm. A demon."

"No," I said, shaking my head quickly. "Alexei was the tsar, and he loved me. The egg is mine now."

"So . . . even though the Romanovs are dead . . ." Her eyes were bleary.

"I'm not dead," I said hopefully, squeezing her arm. "Take me to the egg, Babushka. Help me keep it from the Reds."

The Babushka blinked hard, shook her head. She finally spoke, voice even, like she was fighting the alcohol in her blood. "You're the last one," she said. "The last one the egg can work for. You were his . . . I remember you were his . . ." She frowned, like she still wasn't sure she believed me.

"Yes," I said, nodding at her. Bits of my hair were coming loose, falling into my face, and I fought the urge not to flinch when the wind swept through the camp carrying another wave of battlecries. There wasn't much time—it would be hard to escape the city before too long, egg or no egg.

The Babushka stared at me, shook her head. "I'll take you to it. Come on." She hobbled forward, using the posts in the center of the tent to steady herself, and made for the door. We followed behind, toward the tent flap that she was holding open for us. Leo ducked through first, then me.

Mystics were starting to panic as the revolution fighting grew closer—I suppose the herbs weren't working as well as they hoped. Women were running over the bridge and away from the city, blankets filled with their belongings slung over their shoulders. The Babushka gave them a hard look, shook her head like she was disappointed as we hurried into a hallway.

Arched windows lined one wall of the monastery, most missing their glass and all framed with vines that had eaten their way up the exterior wall. Through the windows on the right, I could see the remains of a garden. To my left, however, was Moscow. Smoke billowing up, people forcing their way down the alleys and toward the monastery's bridge like a slow-moving flood. The compound's decrepit walls were almost comical in comparison to the shouting throngs of people who would surely be here in no time at all.

"Here we are," the Babushka said under her breath as we reached a large wooden door with fancy ironwork around the edges. She pressed the door open.

The room must have once been the church's sanctuary. The ceiling was high above us, holes in the roof revealing storm clouds in the sky and ravens perching amid the exposed beams. Pews were long gone, replaced with typical furniture: a dresser, a bed, a table Candles, candles everywhere, blurring upholstered chairs and rug and tapestries into a sea of jewel tones. One wall had crumbled away entirely and was replaced by a panel of fabric, a curtain that I supposed led to a tent.

"What are you doing?" a female voice snapped from somewhere toward the back of the room. "You brought strangers into my home?"

"This is the girl I told you about, Maria," the Babushka slurred a another cannon exploded somewhere outside. "Natalya Kutepova!"

I heard a faint sound of approval from the back of the room and the woman—no, Maria was a girl, barely older than me—stepped where we could see her. She was tall, as tall as Leo, who dwarfed me and was thin but sturdy-looking, like she wouldn't bend in a breeze Her hair was dark, like the other mystics', but her skin was pale and fine, well cared for, like a noble's. Something about her was familiar, like I'd seen her at court, but I couldn't place her exactly.

"Lady Natalya Kutepova," Maria said, nodding, walking ever closer. She moved so slowly, except when her tongue would dart out, lick her lips in an almost predatory way. Her eyes were bright blue, a color as striking as Alexei's, but wildly different. His were the sky, his were warmth, his were lakes and water. Maria's, however, were the aqua color of thick ice, and when she looked at me, I felt cold. She dropped into an overly dramatic but trained curtsey, then turned her gaze to Leo. "And he is?"

"I'm not sure," the Babushka said, shrugging. She frowned, patted her pockets until she found a flask, then took a long swig of whatever was inside it.

"Interesting," Maria said, tongue flicking out again. "And why are you here?"

"We're here for the Constellation Egg," I said swiftly. "I'd like to take it to Paris, where it'll be safe."

Maria frowned, turned toward a table in the center of the room. It was covered in loose tarot cards, goblets and feathers, herbs and crystals. Indeed, covered in so much that I didn't see what Maria was looking at right away.

But then—there. There it was.

Such a small thing, but such a perfect thing. It gleamed in the bits of daylight that filtered in through broken stained-glass windows high above us, sitting plainly on the table as if it were nothing more than another trinket. It was exactly as I remembered. Dark, almost black-blue, with a base like clouds. Diamonds for stars, a gold band around the edge. It was precious, priceless, and yet that's not what struck me—after all, there were many priceless things in the world, many pretty things.

What struck me was it felt like I was looking at Alexei. I would never see his eyes again, but this—this was him, this was all that was left of him. This was mine in the same way he was.

Maria walked toward it, her steps slow and deliberate, protective of the egg. Leo and I ignored her, turning instead to face each other.

There was nothing to be said, nothing that hadn't already been said. We were here. This was the end.

Still, Leo's lips parted. He looked like words were there, words were ready, but they refused to come out of hiding. In the end, he clamped his lips together. One of us had to run, to move, to dash for it first, and yet neither of us wanted to be the one to cut the delicate thread of this moment.

Footsteps, loud and masculine, getting closer, the sound of the mystics screaming. The sound severed the moment for us—we turned to see as they approached the sanctuary door.

"How dare they come to *my* temple—" Maria began, muttering under her breath. She was cut off when the doors burst open.

A gunshot. Bright and clear, a sound that bounced off the church walls and forced me to pull my hands to my ears. Everything was ringing, I saw Maria's eyes widen, something struck me in the back and I stumbled forward—Leo, Leo was knocking me over. Was he trying to grab for the egg, beat me to it in the chaos? I caught myself before crashing onto the broken stone tiles that covered the floor, stumbled along a few steps, extended a hand toward the egg on the table.

"Lady Kutepova! Lady Kutepova, I've found you!"

The voice was not one I knew. Standing in the doorway was a soldier, a White, so young that he didn't even have the idea of a beard on his face.

"Lady Kutepova, you're safe now. Colonel Ivanovich sent me. Come with me," he said, extending a hand. "I can't believe I found you in this—"

I blinked, spun around—where was Leo? The egg was still in the center of the table, but Leo, I had felt him, I had felt him hit me, he was behind me, and now I didn't see him. The soldier continued to shout, his voice echoed around the room.

Leo was on the ground.

On his side, one leg and arm crumpled under him, his chest rising and falling unevenly. His eyes were closed, but he turned, flopped onto his back, and his hand wandered to his stomach, grasping at his shirt like he was trying to pull it away. I took a step toward him, another, and suddenly I was on my knees at his side, pushing his hand away, trying to see what was wrong.

"You're fine," I demanded, voice rattling. "It's nothing, Leo." My voice was a whisper and yet louder than the chaos happening outside. The soldier was now beside me, pulling at my arm, but I didn't rise. There was no blood, no mark, what was wrong? Water seeped into my clothing where my knees pressed against the tile floor—

It wasn't water. It was blood. I shoved the soldier away, tried to breathe, pushed Leo up to make certain I was correct. Blood, blood everywhere, pouring from a place on his back, a place I couldn't even see for all the red. I pressed against his back, tried to find the bullet hole, but it was no use, I couldn't find it.

"I'll go get Colonel Ivanovich," the soldier said, giving up on my cooperation. He thought I was crazy; he didn't understand as he ran from the sanctuary, shouting for his brethren to come quick. I pulled Leo back over, wrapped my fingers against the side of his face, cringing at the bloody prints they left. His eyes drifted shut.

"Leo," I said, though my voice didn't sound like my own. "Open your eyes." I left one hand on his cheek, let the other fall beside his head to brace myself. Grass began to force its way up under my palm, forcing its way through the broken stone floor. He opened his eyes, his lips parted, but he didn't speak. I shook my head.

"I can fix this. I was a nurse, remember? It'll be fine," I said, nodding at him, trying to smile. The grass was spreading, overpowering the stones, moving them apart as more and more shoots sprung up. A tiny white flower opened beside me, its petals stained crimson, drops of blood rolling down them to pool in its center. Leo breathed, the sound torn, and his eyes shut again. I grabbed his shoulders, shook him as grass raced around me, grew taller, grew greener, the most useless magic I could imagine. I turned around to the egg, glared at it, useless, stupid thing. It didn't save Alexei, it didn't save his family, it couldn't save—

I released him, dropped my head into my arms, and muffled a scream. There was no point. No point in any of this. I reached down, grabbed a handful of the grass and ripped it from the ground. Another shoot sprung up in its place.

Leo was shaking violently. I closed my eyes. I didn't want to see the moment when he stopped, when he gave in. When he became a body instead of a person. I couldn't stop myself from listening, though, listening to the sound of his breathing growing shallower and shallower.

I wondered if Alexei would be kind to him, in heaven.

The blood on my knees was growing cold, the grass underneath me so thick I could no longer feel the tiles. Leo's breathing fell in time with my heart, slowing, slowing, slowing . . . Maria was behind me; I heard the door to the sanctuary swung shut, muting the sound of the riot, forcing me to focus on the ragged sound of Leo's breathing . . . until he was silent.

It was the loudest silence I had ever known.

Leo took a deep breath.

A breath too large for someone whose lungs were filling with blood. I didn't look, didn't dare, until he took another, then another. Deep, full breaths. I finally lifted just my eyes, peered over my arm, through the hair strewn into my face.

His chest was rising, falling evenly. His eyes were open, he was staring at the ceiling, blinking. Leo's hand wandered across his stomach, not in the distracted, dream way, but like he was really feeling for something, something he could not find.

And then there were stars.

A million tiny stars, rising through the blood staining his clothing, glowing so bright that I flinched and held a hand to my head. They glowed white and flashed at me, stirred up memories of the first time I saw stars heal a boy. Then, quickly as they arose, the stars were gone. I blinked, rubbed my eyes.

Leo sat up. The ground beneath him was still tiled floor, a void in the grass the shape of his body. Leo tried to grab at his lower back, but couldn't reach. The motion, however, caused something to fall off his back and clink to the floor. He spun around, groped at the floor until he picked it up, held it in front of his eyes. A single bullet. Leo's eyes moved from it to me, searching me, asking me questions I didn't know the answers to.

"Well," Maria said quietly. "Look at that."

Leo took a shaky breath, started a few sentences—but before he could finish a complete thought, we heard shouting from the hallway outside. The soldier, back with Misha, as he promised. Maria, whose eyes were now sparking, almost crazed, looked at us in panic.

"Hide," she said, pointing to the table in the sanctuary's center, the one where the Constellation Egg rested. "Hide now."

Still shaking, I wrapped an arm under Leo and pulled him up. We hurried across the sanctuary—Leo seemed weak on his knees—then ducked down behind the table. Leo was barely able to curl himself small enough to be hidden. His back was still wet with blood; I stared until he noticed and curved so I couldn't see.

The door to the sanctuary burst open, a square of light appearing on the far wall, filled with the shadows of men wearing military epaulettes and hats. The Babushka was near but stepped forward, beside the table and just out of our line of sight.

"Lady Kutepova!" a voice—Misha's—shouted. I closed my eyes, tried to make myself even smaller.

"Colonel Ivanovich!" Maria said, though I hardly recognized her tone—it was light now, flirtatious and familiar. "How can I help you?"

"Hello, madame. My man says he shot a hardened criminal in here," Misha said swiftly, walking so far into the room that his shadow disappeared from the wall. Leo hunched in till we were nearly pressed together. I could hear the confusion in Misha's voice when he didn't see me. "And my niece's companion was with him . . ."

"I saw her! I shot the boy right here, but there wasn't . . . there wasn't all this grass," the young soldier protested, sounding like a child trying to convince his mother of fairies.

"I assure you, we harbor no criminals here," Maria said. Her voice was strange, different than it sounded before. It was her voice, and yet, something entirely different, in the way that wind is just moving air or waves are just drops of water. Something about it was strong, was a force instead of a sound. She continued. "The revolution is happening. You're needed in the city, I suspect."

"Perhaps we are . . ." Misha said, voice distant, like a boy's instead of a colonel's.

"Certainly," Maria said. "Go on now. Take your search elsewhere."

The shadows in the door shifted for a moment, looking at one another, flinching as gunfire sounded out from the city. Slowly, slowly they backed up. The other shadows vanished just as Misha's reappeared in the door.

"My apologies," he said in the faraway voice.

"Of course," Maria said. "Go on."

"Farewell," Misha said, reaching forward to shut the door. "Stay safe amid this danger, Lady Rasputin."

# CHAPTER TWENTY-SEVEN

Leo and I sat side by side at the table, on rickety wooden chairs. There were cups of tea in front of us, something mint-scented and dark yellow, but neither of us touched them. The egg was on the center of the table, amid the haphazard tarot cards. The Babushka stood behind us, while Maria paced back and forth in front. Leo looked like he wanted to grab the egg and run, but was too unsettled by being magically healed and watching Maria Rasputin hypnotize a soldier to do anything other than stare.

I now remembered Maria, though only slightly. She came to court occasionally with Grigori Rasputin, her father, though he acted less like a parent and more like a drunk chaperone, waving her toward crowds like her presence annoyed him. She always wore the sorts of dresses Emilia did; the peak of fashion, so stylish they were nearly gauche, but while they worked on Emilia, they never quite looked right on Maria. She was always too bright, too expensive, too vulgar, the girl who never quite fit in. Perhaps it wasn't her clothes—perhaps it was that strange look in her eyes, like her mind was haunted.

This Maria, however, was different from the one I remembered. At court, she was something to point at, to mumble about. Here, she was the ruler, every bit as regal in her movements as Alexandra ever was. She paced around like the sanctuary was a throne room.

"It makes sense. Alexei Romanov *was* the tsar, if only for a few days," Maria said, stroking her chin with a hand covered in so many rings that it looked dipped in silver. "I never considered that the egg wouldn't care about marriage—you're the one he loved, so the power is yours. I suppose it makes sense, really—my father didn't think much of marriage, seeing as he couldn't marry his Alexandra." Maria walked forward; the Babushka scurried out of her way so that Maria could run her knuckles along the edge of the Constellation Egg, like she wanted to punch it. It prickled at me—it was all I could do not to reach forward and swipe her hand away.

There seemed to be a lull in the riots outside as the sun set. The cannons had been stopped for an hour or so, and gunfire was sporadic instead of regular. The roar of people was now a seamless hum, and according to a young mystic girl who came to report to Maria, most of the mystics who remained at the camp were fine, if shaken. It wasn't clear if the Reds or Whites were claiming victory, or if this was just a pause in the chaos.

Maria rapped her fingers across the egg; the rings clinked against it, like a strange instrument. "And now all that power, all yours," she said, looking from the egg to me wondrously. "What a thing that is. Strange how my father loving a queen could lead to a noble girl possessing the power of all Russia's mystics."

I inhaled. "I came all the way from Saint Petersburg," I said, starting slow. "On a train, in the cold. I was nearly killed a half-dozen times, and now Alexei is dead . . . I'm all that's left. I thank you, Babushka"—I looked to the old woman, tried to smile but found my lips incapable of the expression right now—"and the other mystics for keeping the Constellation Egg safe. But please, you have to give it to me. The Reds mean to claim it for Lenin. If it were to fall to them now, the monarchy would be lost for good."

Maria and the Babushka looked at each other, and something like a smile played at Maria's lips. "Ah yes," she finally said. "The monarchy *would* be lost, I suppose. Though I daresay, perhaps the monarchy has outlived its usefulness, Miss Kutepova. After all, they were failing before my father empowered the Constellation Egg. The egg was a life raft, holding the tsar afloat, but without a tsar, I suspect even my father's tricks aren't enough to stop the Reds."

I took a shaky breath, felt Leo shift beside me. "You mean to give it to the Reds, then?" Maria didn't answer, so I continued, my voice rising, panicked—I hadn't come all this way to learn the mystics were traitors. "But Rasputin—your father. He loved Alexandra. He loved the family. He would never have supported them falling, them being shot in a basement in Siberia. They invited him into the palace, they made him a noble—"

"Made him a noble? What a laugh, Miss Kutepova. He was never one of you, not really. Your people betrayed him," Maria said icily. "They poisoned him. Stabbed him. Shot him. Drowned him. I was home when they fetched him from our apartment for 'dinner.' I knew something was strange. I knew something was *wrong,* but I didn't say anything. Why would I? These were his friends. And besides, no one would ever hurt the man who healed the tsarevich."

"Those people didn't represent *all* the Whites, Maria, any more than the rioters represent all the Reds. They were wrong. They shouldn't have hurt him. But still, Rasputin gave his magic to the Romanovs—"

"*Our* magic. He stole *ours*. My father had no right to steal our magic for his precious *Sunny*." She spit the tsarina's nickname out like a curse. "And she had no right to accept it. She was a monster. I went to Saint Petersburg with a father, and suddenly all he cared about was the tsarina, her children. Like he forgot he had any of his own. She broke him."

My instinct was to speak out for Alexandra, but I managed to muffle my protests. Maria seemed to be crumbling—were she a softer woman, I suspected tears would be falling. Instead, she went to lean against a crooked dresser, resting her thumb and forefinger on her temples. She pulled on her thick black hair with her other hand, like she might yank the more sorrowful thoughts from her head. She glanced up, realized that Leo, the Babushka, and I were all looking at her.

"Stop. Staring at me!" she screeched, then turned around and dropped her head. The Babushka immediately turned away, and even I found it impossible not to avert my eyes.

Leo, however, rose cautiously, gave me a mournful look before taking a step toward Maria. "You mean to give it to the Reds then?" he asked gently.

Maria snorted, looked up. "That's the problem with people like the both of you. Reds. Whites. You're all under the impression that there are only two sides in a war."

"I don't understand," I said slowly.

"Of course not," Maria answered. "You know, the mystics were never interested in politics, in society. I grew up wearing pants, riding horses with a leg on each side, never learned a single dance. And then suddenly I was in Saint Petersburg and my father was famous and I had parties and dresses and purchased friends and then . . . then I realized it was all fake. Everything the Whites are is fake." She walked to the table with crystals, where she'd hidden the Constellation Egg earlier, and ran her fingers across the cloth draped across it. "But now the Reds are burning cities and stomping around like children, bitter that rich people won't hand them money. Both sides are lined with fools, and it's all very exhausting."

"It's not that simple," Leo muttered.

"It never is," Maria said. "Which is why it's time we brought peace to Russia. Miss Kutepova, you've seen what the magic can do for you. Imagine that power in the hands of someone who knows how to use it."

Thunder rolled outside; a wave of even darker clouds crept over the holes in the roof above. I heard the splatter of a few raindrops on the stone floor. "So you mean to claim the egg for yourself?" I asked, baffled. I glanced at the Babushka, who looked as astounded as I felt.

"Maria, you mean to return the power to the mystics," she said swiftly. "Tell her. The power is rightfully ours."

"And I will," Maria said. Her words were stilted, like she was trying to sound kind but failing. "As soon as the nobles pay for what they did to my father. As soon as the Reds pay for what they've done to Russia. As soon as I set things right, set a course for Russia that won't fall to peasants or yield to gold."

"With *you* at the helm?" Leo scoffed. Maria took a hard breath, flicked her tongue out again.

"I am the only one in Russia who has seen both sides of this country," she said confidently. "I am the only one strong enough."

"No," the Babushka said slowly. "No, Maria. This is our power. I brought the egg here for *us*."

Maria whirled around, stared hard at the Babushka. "You brought the egg here for your priestess," she snapped. She walked forward until she was in front of the Babushka, towering over her. "Me."

The Babushka shook her head again, stomped forward to the table, reached out for the Constellation Egg. I meant to rise, meant to grab for it first, but a whistling noise streaked by me, followed by a loud slap. I startled, tried to understand what had just happened—to my left was Maria, hair in front of her wild, ice-blue eyes, face contorted with anger and hand extended. And to my right—

"Oh God," I said, words falling from my mouth before I could stop them. The Babushka. She was on the ground, a kitchen knife sticking out of her chest. I dove to her side, dropped down as her fingers twitched, her eyes already shut. I felt my mouth twist into something ugly and horrible as I grabbed for the knife, yanked it out. Blood bubbled up; I grimaced and put my hands on top of the wound, tried to think of grass, of flowers, of stars—I had to heal her.

"That won't work," Maria said, laughing like she were watching some sort of skit. "The egg doesn't mean you can heal anyone you please." Leo's arms were on me, pulling me away from the Babushka's body. I tried to fight him for a moment, then gave in, turned into his chest with my hands clasped together at my throat, stained with the old woman's blood. Leo held me tightly for a moment, till he was convinced I wouldn't fall back to the Babushka's body. I turned to Maria, my face distorted with horror.

"She was one of you!" I snarled. "She's one of your subjects! How could you betray her?"

Maria scowled at me like I was something particularly repulsive. "I'm the traitor? The tsarevich loved you, Miss Kutepova. Loved you so much that the Constellation Egg guarded you with the same ferocity it guarded him, his parents, the grand duchesses. And how do you repay him?" She looked at Leo, surveyed him and seemed to find him unimpressive. "You love another. Enough that the magic extends to him."

I opened my mouth to protest, but there were tears in my eyes, rocks in my throat. Leo exhaled, a deep, shaking breath, but I was grateful he didn't say anything aloud. I didn't want it to be true, I couldn't *admit* that it was true, but the egg saved him. The egg saved him, which meant . . .

I couldn't even think it. I glanced at Leo, who avoided my eyes.

Maria scoffed at us, which turned Leo's avoidance into red-faced anger. He looked down at the Babushka's body, then at me.

"Enough," he growled at Maria, and bolted for her. He'd only made it three or four steps when Maria whipped a hand up, palm facing him.

"Stop." Her voice was the hypnotic, creeping one she'd used on Misha. Leo instantly froze in place. His eyes widened, he turned his head just enough to look at me, like he wanted me to help him, like he thought I had any idea *how* to help him. Maria smiled wickedly, picked up another knife, and spun it around between her fingers.

"You're strong," she said, eyeing him up and down. "You're fighting me much harder than Colonel Ivanovich did. You should be proud."

"Go ahead," Leo muttered, as if it were hard to speak. "Cut me. I survived a shot to the stomach. I can survive a crazy lady with a chef's knife."

Maria snarled, rushed in, let the knife drift along his collarbone, gently enough that it didn't break his skin. "Just because you can heal doesn't mean it won't hurt, darling. And you'll recall—a blessed egg couldn't save Alexei Romanov from a hail of bullets. If they can kill him, I can kill you." The words made my stomach feel heavy, made my heart beat faster; Leo didn't look afraid, but I was afraid for him. Maria was right. She could kill him. He could die, just as Alexei died.

I couldn't bear another drop of blood on my hands.

"Leave him alone," I said, jaw tight. Maria's eyes flickered from Leo; this seemed to break the spell, as he fell backward, clutching his chest like it ached. I walked forward, placed myself between the two of them. "What do you want, Maria?"

Maria smiled. "It's rather complicated. You see, we retrieved the egg from the Winter Palace, and our powers didn't return. The Romanovs died and our powers didn't return. This leads me to believe, dear Miss Kutepova, that we are approaching this incorrectly. Perhaps rather than breaking my father's curse, we should endeavor to untie it."

"How do you plan to do that?" I asked, voice steelier now.

"Tonight," she said. "We'll complete the claiming ceremony. Give me claim to the egg, Miss Kutepova, and you both can go.

Give me trouble, and . . . well . . . perhaps we'll use your companion to test the limits of the egg's healing powers . . ." She ran her fingers along the edge of the knife lovingly, staring at Leo the whole while. He didn't flinch, but I did.

"If I help you, how do I know you'll let us go?" I asked.

Maria smiled. "I suppose you don't." She turned around, dropped the knife on the table by the Constellation Egg, and walked to the curtain in the back of the room. She swept it open, revealing, as expected, a tent room with an open side that revealed the monastery's garden. The sun had fully set now, and the tiny ribbon of sky I could see above the tree line was starless and black.

"Come along, dear Leo," Maria said. She waited, then sighed. "You can come willingly, or I can make you come."

"Where are you taking me?" he asked, voice soft for my benefit.

"You're my prisoner. Obviously, I'm locking you up," she said simply. "Where I can know you won't run off and return with an army of boys wearing red ribbons."

Leo inhaled. I could tell he was looking at me, trying to make eye contact, but I couldn't drag my eyes off the ground. Finally, he walked away, vanished with Maria into the camp. I let out a shuddering sob, gasping at the weight on my chest. I lifted my eyes, looked at the Constellation Egg.

I couldn't give it to Maria.

But I couldn't lose Leo too.

# CHAPTER TWENTY-EIGHT

The ceremony was like a play. I had lines to memorize. A script to follow. Maria watched me carefully as she sat at a vanity in the sanctuary, raking a comb through her hair and admiring herself. She looked annoyed when another cannon sounded.

The revolution in Moscow reignited, fire and gunshots and crashes in a largely blackened city. Most of the streetlamps were out, and any building that still had power had long turned its lights off for fear of attack. I wondered how either side could see who they were shooting, but suspected they didn't care anymore. The world was dissolving around them, and they had no plans to go out quietly. Occasional thunder promised rain, which I supposed would at least wash the sharp smell of spent powder and burned homes from the air.

Maria snapped her fingers at me in the mirror. "Keep studying," she said shortly.

I lowered my eyes back to the page where Maria had hastily scrawled out my lines.

It was simple. Maria, in fact, would do most of the work. She would cut her hand, put it on the egg, say a few words. Then I had to cut mine, put it on the egg, and say several lines. *My name is Natalya Kutepova. I relinquish my claim to this power. Let it flow from me to you.* At which point, I was to take Maria's hand, a thought that gave me chills on its own. *I renounce the Romanov dynasty. I renounce myself as tsarina. I renounce their claim to power.*

I struggled to say the final lines even in my head—I certainly wouldn't be able to say them aloud. But I still had no plan, no escape. Maria wouldn't kill me, I was certain; she couldn't risk losing the Constellation Egg's powers forever. But Leo . . .

I remembered Maria's words. *Just because you can heal doesn't mean it won't hurt, darling.*

She would cut him. Slice him, make him beg. Kill him, if she had to. And I would break, eventually. I would break, I'd complete the ceremony, and Maria would have it all. Perhaps not tonight, maybe not even tomorrow, but eventually . . .

There had to be another way, but I surely couldn't think of it. *How could so much magic be so useless?* I wondered about the egg. If only melting ice and growing sunflowers could stop this.

I smoothed my hair, adjusted one of the pins so I could see the page better, as if I were really having trouble memorizing the words. Mystics were moving around outside, arranging hundreds and hundreds of candles in the garden outside Maria's door. They moved obediently, easily, questioning nothing—they even hauled the Babushka's body out on Maria's word that the old woman had betrayed them. They trusted her implicitly, though I wondered how much of that trust she'd earned, and how much of it was merely her powers.

"Maria?" a young mystic, hardly my age, asked from the tent

door. Maria turned to her. "It's stopped raining," the girl said. "At least for a bit. The candles will light. Should we?"

Maria smiled. "Yes, yes. Is the moon out?"

The girl nodded.

"Well," Maria said. She rose, looked across the room to me at the table. "Are you ready?"

"I don't have much choice," I said, rising, letting the paper fall to the floor.

"Don't be foolish," Maria said, gathering up the Constellation Egg. She cradled it against her like a baby. "There's always a choice. Sometimes there's merely a clear winner."

I rolled my eyes at her and followed her out of the sanctuary into the garden where the other mystics were now striking matches, lowering them to the candlewicks. The air was damp and cold, and the wicks fought to take the flames. I turned to look back at the church, crumbling and dying against a night full of bright stars. I searched among them for Alexei's constellation, the one on the egg—the lion, *Leo*, I thought bitterly at the coincidence. As if I needed one to remind me of the other. I was never terribly good with stars, though; there were so many—it felt impossible to see only a few and turn them into a shape. Thunder clapped above me; I continued to stare, continued to watch.

A single snowflake. It drifted down gently on the breeze. I held out my hand, let it perch and melt on my fingertips. Then another, another. The mystics were smiling, looking up as clouds rolled in and covered the stars. Flurries began to flutter down as the thunder continued to roll overhead. Maria ignored all of this, lighting the closest candle herself then walking toward me, forcing my eyes from the sky.

Something clattered—something closer than the rioters, on the far side of the garden. I looked toward the noise.

Leo was leaning against the cage doors of the mausoleum. Watching. Staring, face half in shadow in the moonlight. The tombs behind him were broken, probably robbed long ago, and the cage doors rusty. His head nearly brushed the ceiling, his fingers curled easily around the thin bars. I inhaled, didn't look away, couldn't look away.

I ran.

I ran across the garden, knocking over candles, sliding in the wet grass and tripping over mounds of long forgotten flowerbeds. There were shouts behind me, voices, Maria was screeching, but I didn't stop. Leo watched me run toward him, and as I neared the cage doors, he pushed his arms through. I stumbled up to the mausoleum; Leo took my hands and pulled me against him easily. I could feel his chest rising and falling against mine, warm despite the cold bars between us. Tears ran down my face, but there were no words, there was nothing I could say, nothing I could allow myself to admit.

"Don't do it," Leo said lowly, trying to put his lips by my ear—the bars prevented it. "Don't do it. Don't let her have that power."

"I have to," I choked, leaning back to see his face. I blinked away the snowflakes that clung to my eyelashes. The other mystics were arriving now, slowing down once they realized I had no tricks up my sleeve—I wasn't *really* running away. I was just a girl standing at a cage, wondering where things went so very wrong.

"You don't," he whispered, letting one hand run along the back of my neck, like I was something wondrous.

"I want it to be over." My voice was squeaky now, and I gripped Leo's arms ever tighter. "If I do this, at least it will be over."

Leo shook his head; his hair fell across his forehead, casting linear shadows across his face. "Revolutions can't end this easily, Natalya."

"This wasn't easy," I answered, stifling something between laughter and weeping. Leo smiled, suddenly, and the expression warmed me, warmed me in a way that I couldn't feel guilty about even as a darkened part of my heart drew up Alexei's face.

"That's because it isn't over," he whispered. He paused—his eyes flickered behind me, and I saw his shoulders tense. Maria was surely walking up, but I didn't want to turn around, didn't want to see her right now. Leo ducked his head, pulled me back to him. I pressed my face against his chest, closed my eyes—

"Enough," Maria said. Her voice was serrated, carved between me and Leo. I whirled around to face her just as her tongue darted out. Snowflakes dotted her black hair; the ground was starting to be more white than brown. "It's time." She walked away; the nearest mystics swooped in, all skirts and hair and the smell of incense.

Leo was wrong—it was over. I wrested one hand away from the girls guiding me and yanked the pins from my hair, threw them down. My hair caught in the wind, swirled around me. I looked like the mystics, I suspected, like the peasants, like a girl without a reputation to protect. Without years of cotillion training, without a wardrobe that cost more than most make in the year. Without the clothes, the hair, the crown, the powers, I was no different from the corpses behind Leo, no different from Leo himself. No different from Alexei. It was strangely warming, the thought that there would be no need for revolution or jealousy one day: we'd all be equal in the grave.

The candles were all lit, flickering in the wind. The mystics stood in a circle behind them, looking anxious. They became a sea of dark eyes, dark hair, hands clasped and skirts rustling. Maria positioned me on one side of the pedestal that held the Constellation Egg; she stood on the other. I could see Leo from the corner of my eye, though I didn't dare actually *look* at him. Maria seemed to notice this and rotated us around again so he was behind me. I tried to ignore the smug look on her face but failed.

"Calm down," she said. "In a quarter hour, the two of you will be free."

She reached toward the pedestal with the egg, pausing to admire it lovingly. A knife, an elaborate dagger with onyx in the handle, was sitting beside the egg. She lifted it, held it up in the light of the moon, and muttered something in a language I didn't know. Maria then brought the dagger down to her palm. She licked her lips, closed her hand around the blade, then yanked the knife through. Several of the mystics sucked a breath in through their teeth as blood dripped through her closed fingers to the ground, staining the ever-increasing layer of snow. I swallowed a curse as she opened her palm, placing it over the egg. Her blood looked almost black in the moonlight as it trickled down around the diamonds, ran a course around the quartz base, finally pooling around the bottom.

"I am Matryona Rasputin," she cried out to the sky. Her voice was the loudest thing, louder than gunfire, louder than the wind, louder than my heart. "Daughter of Grigori Rasputin. I claim this magic for myself. Let it be mine. I renounce those who have possessed it before me. I renounce all who would keep it from me." She gripped the egg tight, so tight her fingers slipped on her own blood, and for a moment, I thought the entire pedestal might flip over. I looked up to the sky, the snow clouds and the stars that hung between them.

"Here," Maria said, and spun the knife around, offering me the hilt. "Do you remember—"

"Yes," I answered, taking it quickly. I stared down at the blade, wet with Maria's blood.

"Do it and put it on the egg fast," Maria said. "Before it heals."

I nodded. Looked over at the Constellation Egg, which now had a little heap of snow balanced atop it. The egg was the color of Alexei's eyes. Eyes I would never see again, eyes that would never see me again. Despite Leo, despite what healing him meant, I still loved Alexei. I loved him in a way that I knew would never stop, in a way that would hurt forever. It felt like something was unfurling in my chest, rising around my heart, my lungs, my arms.

*"Natalya," he said, voice gentle. "You and I . . . we're . . . it's us, isn't it?"*

*"It's us," I whispered. "It's always us."*

Because our futures were intertwined. Even if he wasn't in mine.

I took the blade in my hand. I didn't close my eyes, though I couldn't help but flinch as I ripped it through the skin, cut so deep I felt the knife rake across bone. Maria's mouth spread into a grin just as a clap of thunder echoed across the sky, followed by a collective gasp from the circle around us.

I opened my eyes and followed their line of sight to the sky. Stars, shooting stars raining toward us. They streaked across the sky, leaving trails of pale gold that flickered away so quickly that it was impossible to tell when the light began and ended. The mystics gasped, pointed at the stars as Maria smiled harder, face devilish and wild. I dropped the knife on the ground, stared at my palm for a moment, then placed it over the Constellation Egg. The snow was intensifying; when I looked up again, it was tricky to tell the falling stars from the flakes.

"Hurry," Maria hissed at me, unable to take her eyes off the world around us. Under my hand, the Constellation Egg felt warm, then hot. It hummed to me, the liquid lightning pouring from it into my hand, up my arm, filling my body like it was replacing the blood in my veins. The snow increased again, now pouring down on us almost like rain, and I felt the temperature drop. It was getting more and more difficult to see the mystics that surrounded us amid the snowfall.

"My name is Natalya Kutepova," I called out, though my voice was a hoarse whisper. "I . . ."

"Relinquish my claim . . ." Maria whispered. The snow continued to pour down, the temperature to drop, drop, lower and lower.

"I relinquish my claim . . ." I repeated. I stalled again. Maria growled like an animal, so I continued, "Let it . . . let it move from me to—"

Someone grabbed me, grabbed the arm I had extended over the Constellation Egg and pulled me around, so fast I had no time to understand what was happening. Leo's hands held tight to my shoulders, his eyes found mine easily, like they were well practiced at doing so. A shadow behind him, Maria—

I grabbed hold of Leo's shirt, pulled him to me, and pressed my lips to his. Leo's arm slipped from my shoulders, wrapped around me, lifted me up easily against him. His lips were soft, softer than I expected, and when he finally pulled away, he kept his face beside mine so I could feel his breath, could feel his lips curl into a gentle smile that I couldn't help but match even though doing so frightened me.

"Natalya—" he began, setting me down as he reached up to grab his chest. He frowned, then his eyes widened. I gasped as we both turned to look at the Constellation Egg.

Maria grabbed my bloodied hand, yanked me so hard I fell from Leo's arms.

"Stop!" she demanded him, and he froze, hypnotized. She couldn't look at me—it would break the hypnosis—so she merely growled from the corner of her mouth, "Natalya. Finish it! I'll kill you both."

I turned to her—how did she not realize it was already finished? Maria gave a snarl-like smile, and I saw the cold rush into her mouth, turn the water there to a thin layer of ice. The snow was clumping in her hair, in her lashes, on her shoulders, like it was trying to bury her alive—the other mystics, I realized, were already buried, lumps of odd shapes in the snow. But the flakes barely touched me, a fact that Maria suddenly realized. She broke the spell on Leo to stare at me, then at the sky. Maria lifted her fingertips, ran them across her lips delicately; they split as the cold—*my* cold—caused the skin to crack and bleed. When she found my eyes again, she looked horrified.

"I renounce nothing," I said. "I renounce nothing and no one."

Russia listened to me—and only me—now. I could thaw ice, I could grow flowers, I could tame animals, I could heal.

Leo was right—I could do a lot more than make the wind blow. I could make it very, very cold.

Maria grimaced, causing her lips to crack further; the blood that spilled to her chin quickly froze in a dark purple line. She reached for me, but her motions were slow, deadened; I easily dodged her bony fingers and grabbed the Constellation Egg from the pedestal. I lifted the egg high above my head, then brought it down on the edge of the pedestal, hard. It shattered easily, a million flecks of light, each the color of Alexei's eyes, splashing out into the snow. Maria tried to scream—her face made an expression like she was being killed, like someone she loved was being killed. But no sound came out, her voice devoured by the cold.

Maria lowered herself to her knees—or fell, I wasn't sure which—her eyes black and angry as her fingertips turned blue, her nails pale purple. She made a motion with her mouth, like she was trying to dart her tongue out, but her muscles were too stiff to do so.

I glanced behind me; Leo was fine, standing straight as me despite the freezing temperature. He smiled at me wryly as we both turned to look at Maria. She was on the ground now, limbs blue, eyes dark and furious and wild.

*You should have learned from Napoleon. From the Poles. You can't survive a Russian winter*, I thought, *unless you're a true Russian.*

I looked to the sky as I urged the temperature to drop again.

Snowflakes filtered around us, avoiding our eyes, and stars continued to streak down like a rainstorm of light. Finally, the blizzard I'd created turned to flurries, and the moon broke through the clouds to light the monastery in a silvery glow. It was quiet, so quiet now, as the snow absorbed every sound except our steady breathing. The world was blanketed with perfect white snow, uneven in places where it covered stones or garden beds.

"Remind me," Leo finally said, voice low, "to thank Emilia for teaching me the hairpin trick."

"I'm just glad you figured it out," I said, wiping my nose with the back of my wrist. I glanced at the nearest lump in the snow, the shape that was Maria. I wondered if I should feel guilty. I didn't.

"I'm not sure I *have* figured all of it out just yet," Leo said, touching the center of his chest. "It feels like I swallowed the sky."

"I'm sorry," I said. "I didn't know—I didn't mean to."

Leo smiled. "Oh, I know you didn't, Natalya. Because now you're really stuck with me."

# EPILOGUE

## (FOUR MONTHS LATER)

I was writing Emilia a letter. Again. I'd started it a half-dozen times, at least, and each incarnation felt more ludicrous than the previous. I owed her an apology. I owed her an explanation. The first was easy, but the second, I worried, was impossible. I tried to conquer it immediately in the letter.

*Dear Emilia,*
*I'm alive. I never told you, but I possessed the Constellation Egg's powers.*

The train rumbled in a way that made my handwriting shaky, but I held back my scowl—after all, Leo and I had our own sleeping compartment with wool blankets and tea service in the afternoon. If we arrived in Ekaterinberg according to schedule, the trip would take even less time than the ride from Saint Petersburg to Moscow. After eating stolen caviar in a freezing cargo hold, I wouldn't dream of complaining about this trip. I sighed, looked outside.

"We're cutting through Samara," Leo said, nodding toward the window when he noticed my gaze.

"By your house?"

"No." He was in the seat across from me, back against the compartment's sliding door so he could easily watch the world rolling by. He barely fit on the seat at all this direction; one arm and one leg hung off awkwardly, like he'd been poorly packed for the trip. He continued, "We lived north of the tracks. Lenin lived in this area, though, when he was young."

"How marvelous," I said drily, and tried the letter again.

*Dear Emilia,*
*I'm alive. Leo and I weren't together, not in the way you thought. We're going to Ekaterinberg.*

I refused to go back to Saint Petersburg, unwilling to see my city occupied by the people who killed Alexei. Leo refused to stay in Moscow, as the Whites were slowly but surely holding on to the city. We settled on Ekaterinberg. Leo seemed surprised when I suggested it, and questioned me until I said it aloud: Alexei was, in my mind, still trapped in Ekaterinberg. I had to visit him, if only his ghost.

Leo didn't question me after that.

"Are those sunflower fields?" I asked, nodding out the window. The sky was bold, unapologetically blue, a color that reminded me of the ceiling of that chapel we hid in back in Moscow. The fields were freshly planted, full of rich, chocolate-colored earth.

"Yes. But they planted too early," Leo said, frowning, though I could tell seeing it tweaked something in him anyhow. He shifted, slid across the seat until he was so close to the window that it fogged where his breath hit. "I suppose there aren't any sunflowers in Ekaterinberg."

"No," I said. "Only snow, I think."

This seemed to crush something in Leo; he sank back a little in the chair, and while his face didn't change, his gray eyes wavered. He focused on the fields rushing by, like he was determined to see at least one bloom before we left Samara and headed to colder land. I pushed my pen aside and lifted a hand to the window. Leo didn't notice, but suddenly looked down, grabbed his chest. I supposed he was still getting used to it.

*Dear Emilia,*
*I'm alive. The Constellation Egg's magic is too, but it's different now.*

Leo looked up at me, shook his head as an amused sort of smirk played at his lips. Outside, the fields began to change. We were moving so fast that it was mostly a blur; brown fields twisted, turned, were suddenly green, plants growing taller, taller, till there was a wall of green outside our window. Dots of yellow thickened like paintbrush heads held against a canvas too long, and then in one moment, they exploded into a thousand plate-sized suns, curling their heads up toward the real sun above. Leo laughed under his breath as we reached the edge of the sunflower fields. He turned his head to watch them vanish, then sat back in his seat, exhaled.

"That was a lot," he said, rubbing the center of his chest with his palm.

"You could have stopped me," I reminded him. He didn't answer, instead casting me a grateful look, a small smile. I nodded, turned back to my paper, but it was useless. This, *this* was the thing I could not find a way to explain to Emilia. Not only that the Constellation Egg's power worked for me, but that it was no longer in the Constellation Egg.

It was in Leo.

When I kissed Leo at the moment I was supposed to take Maria's hand, the power went to him instead of her. The magic was still mine in every way, but Leo felt it too—deep in his chest, where it now lived. It healed him and worked for him in the slightest of ways, but he couldn't draw it up of his own accord. At the very most, he could stop *me* from accessing it to make flowers bloom or candles spark and light, and even that took considerable effort on his part.

I didn't know the details—in fact, I suspected only Rasputin did.

Was it because Leo and I kissed, or because I loved him?

This was something I could not wonder aloud, could barely entertain the thought of, and something Leo and I spoke of only with awkward glances. Something I likely would not have admitted to myself, were it not for the egg revealing the secret to the world. Perhaps the Constellation Egg knew how I hated myself for not telling Alexei I loved him and was making it impossible for me to make the same mistake with Leo.

It wasn't a curiosity I allowed myself to dwell on often—after all, I would always love Alexei. Even though I knew he was gone, I still heard his voice in my dreams. There, he called me Natashenka, laughed with me, guided me through waltzes, and held my hand as we ran through the Winter Palace gardens in the moonlight. There, he always leaned in, whispered in my ear about Russia, about his plans, about his hopes for our country. Plans that now I was the only one left to see through.

*Dear Emilia,*
*I'm alive, but I am not finished.*

# AUTHOR'S NOTE

The Russian Revolution, truth be told, needs little to no fictionalization to be a fascinating time period, full of beauty and horror and wonder. However, *Tsarina* isn't meant to be a textbook—it's meant to be a novel. I did an immense amount of research for this story and I'm proud to say that anything in this story that *could* be historically accurate *is* historically accurate. But . . . don't write your history term papers based on this story, as there are more than a few historical indiscretions, which I'll confess to here.

First and foremost, I'm sad to report that Natalya Kutepova, Leo Uspensky, and Emilia Boldyreva are not real people. Many of the other characters are, however, very real—namely Grigori Rasputin and the Romanov family. It gave me great joy to write Alexei Romanov as a boy healed by the Constellation Egg, since in reality his hemophilia plagued him for his entire short life. I suspect he would have indeed been an excellent boyfriend, as he was every bit as empathetic, noble, and compassionate as described in this book, though he unfortunately died before he could undergo any romantic pursuits.

Nicholas and Alexandra Romanov were, as described, very much in love. Olga and Tatiana really did train as Red Cross nurses during World War I. Rasputin's love for Alexandra is fictional—I was excited to tell a story where he wasn't merely a somewhat mentally unstable monk, though I'll confess that's the conclusion much of the historical record points to. The murder of the Romanov family is real, as are all the details about what happened in that Ekaterinburg basement—despite persistent rumors to the contrary, there were no survivors. All seven members of Russia's last royal family are accounted for and rest in the Peter and Paul Fortress in St. Petersburg, Russia. I confess I cried more than once while writing about their deaths.

Maria Rasputin is real; she was indeed brought to court by her father, where she was doted on by noble ladies despite being a rather dirty, strange child. Her role as leader of the mystics, however, is entirely false—she actually left Russia after the revolution to become a tiger trainer in Paris, all the while fighting to salvage her father's reputation and punish his murderers. She succeeded at neither.

On a smaller scale: clothing is described based on images I found in period fashion catalogs. Street names, city details, and house descriptions are accurate as per 1916 maps of St. Petersburg and Moscow. The Winter Palace, the Iberian Chapel, and the statue of Minin and Pozharsky are real places you can visit. The battle of Tannenberg is real, as is the detail of Russian soldiers being sent into battle without weapons, instructed to take guns off their dead comrades. Russia's tendency to burn down its cities and let the country's brutal winter destroy invaders is real.

While the Constellation Egg is real, its powers are, needless to say, not. I also did a bit of reorganizing with the Russian Revolution itself. In order to not have my characters milling around for the entire summer, I combined the February Revolution and October Revolution into a single event. Combining those revolutions means that the Provisional Government, which ran Russia in-between Tsar Nicholas's fall and Lenin's formal rise, is also omitted from the story.

I would love to break down each and every historical accuracy (or inaccuracy) in this book, but obviously that would take another hundred pages or so. My hope is that, factual or fabricated, every line in *Tsarina* leads to a single truth: that when you forget that those you disagree with are *people*, not just your faceless opposition, you don't end up proving who is right and who is wrong. You end up with a body count.

In that way, perhaps, I suppose I do hope this story serves as a textbook.

4-9-14

11-4-19 -1-4-22

17 18 (LNO)

1 1